LOVE THY ENEMY

"Moira gave me a long lecture this morning on how you've bewitched me. Is it true, Breyandra?"

"That's for you to say, my lord," she answered breathlessly.

"Then I would have to say, she may be right. So bewitch me, my lady. It would be a simple task. No potions. No amulets. Just a soft taste of those tempting lips . . . a gentle touch of those silken fingertips," he whispered huskily.

"It's a temptation, Sir Knave. It would almost be worth the dishonor to bring you to your knees." She brushed aside some strands of hair that had fallen across his forehead and smiled up into his eyes. "Indeed, Sir Knave, it would be a moment to savor," she said with a throaty sigh.

"I think a shared moment, my lady." For a breathless instant their gazes remained locked. "So let us savor it."

Other Leisure books by Ana Leigh

THESE HALLOWED HILLS
A QUESTION OF HONOR
OH, PROMISED DESTINY
A KINDLED FLAME
PARADISE REDEEMED

ANA LEIGH

Sweet Enemy Mine

LEISURE BOOKS ◧ NEW YORK CITY

A LEISURE BOOK ®

May 1991

Published by

Dorchester Publishing Co., Inc.
276 Fifth Avenue
New York, NY 10001

Printed in the United States of America.

Sweet Enemy Mine

This book is dedicated to the little ladies who hold a special spot in my heart, whose lovely names formed the *Breyandra* of my heroine—my granddaughters,

Aubrey and Andrea.

And, of course, to the little Whawhosits—

Melanie.

And in loving memory of *the Buffer*. *You were with me at the beginning; would that you were here at the end.*

PART ONE

Saltoun

Chapter One

Fall 1655

Sweeping across the Grampian peaks, the autumn wind drove a chilling mist before it, glazing the dank towers and parapets of the castle that towered defiantly in its path.

The lone woman standing on the corbeled battlement shivered and drew her cloak tighter about her slim body. The simple motion caused her to wince with pain.

Elysia Gordon was no stranger to pain. Twenty years of marriage to Duncan Gordon had taught her to live with the physical and mental consequences of the beatings, the humiliation.

Steeped in thought, she was unaware of the tall man who had moved to her side. "I heard he struck you again."

Startled, Elysia turned, and then relaxed with a smile of relief at the sight of her son. His

9

handsome face hardened into a grim line and his dark eyes flared with anger when he saw the bruise that marred his mother's face. David Gordon reached out, tenderly stroking the injured cheek.

"Why do you continue to suffer his abuse?"

Quickly her slender hand reached up to cover the blemish on a delicate face regal with blond loveliness. "Your father wasn't himself, David."

The young man turned away angrily. "If he was drunk, he was himself. Don't try to defend him, Mother. He was drunk, wasn't he? What other state does he know? I am told he even knocked you down the stairs this time. As a child, I was helpless to prevent his abuse of you. Now, I return to find it still continues. I'll not bode it any longer, Mother." In his frustration David's hands had balled into fists. "I swear, if he doesn't stop abusing you, one day I shall kill him."

Elysia's eyes widened with panic as she clutched her son's arm. "Don't voice such thoughts, David. Don't even think them. Were he to hear them, he would banish you, or, worse, turn you over to Cromwell. I could never bear that. You alone give my life a purpose."

"Then leave him, Mother. Moira tells me his drunken rages are increasing and grow more dangerous daily. Leave him before he kills you."

Elysia sighed deeply. "Where would I go? My family is long dead. You are away serving the King's cause." She stretched up to place a kiss

10

on his cheek. "You are home for such a short while, do not trouble your thoughts with these matters. Come, we mustn't tarry too long. It will only anger your father more."

The image of the huge, burly figure of his father evoked a note of contempt in David's voice. "He's passed out. The hard labor of thrashing his wife has taxed his strength. The servants have carried him to bed." A sudden thought crossed his mind and David grinned. "What say you to a ride, Mother? I know how much you enjoy riding. Soon it will be winter and the opportunity will have passed."

"A ride?" Elysia Gordon's smile was radiant as she slipped her arm through his. "I would love a ride, David."

A short while later the sound of hoofbeats struck a hollow clatter as the riders crossed the courtyard and passed under the iron portcullis.

The bright sun overhead belied the cool breeze that whipped Elysia's skirt about her legs. She seemed oblivious to the chill as they rode through a glen of pine and rowan.

David Gordon was once again amazed and proud of the skill with which his mother sat her saddle and handled the mount beneath her. Elysia was a true daughter of the Gordon clan, a clan renowned for superb horsemanship. Their cavalry was considered to be the finest, the most disciplined, in all of Scotland. In the past, the Stuart kings had courted the contingent with doting respect. Even Cromwell's contempt for the Scots had not blinded him to the folly of incurring the wrath of the mighty cavalry.

Stopping beside a stream to rest the horses, the two riders sat on the ground engrossed in thought as the mountain rill before them danced across scattered rocks and pebbles in a rush to frolic in the loch below. Finally, David broke the silence to express a thought that had been weighing heavily on his mind.

"Mother, why don't you take your plight to Lord Huntley? Father could not ignore a demand from the Laird of the Gordon Clan."

Elysia smiled sadly and put a hand on his arm. "I've thought of it often, David, but I know it would be useless. What help would I get from George Gordon? You know, as well as I, your father has always been one of his favorite cousins. The Marquis would merely chastise him lightly over a tankard of usquebaugh and that would be the end of it."

Resolutely, Elysia rose to her feet and began to brush fallen leaves off her skirt. "Must we ruin our time together with these glum thoughts? Enough of them, for there is a more pressing matter." She smiled sheepishly. "I am famished. It was foolhardy for us to venture this distance without a lunch. By the time we return, we will have missed the evening fare as well."

"If you are that hungry, Mother, I know of a way to appease your appetite. There are some apple trees just a short distance from here."

Elysia's eyes sparkled with warmth. "At this moment, an apple sounds as inviting as a roast grouse."

"Then wait here. I will return shortly." David

swung lithely into his saddle, but Elysia detained him.

"Why can't I accompany you?"

"The trees are quite close to the boundary that separates us from the Frasers."

The woman's eyes widened with sudden apprehension. "I know those trees. They are on Fraser land." She shook her head. "No, David, I think we best forget it. I will satisfy my hunger with a draught of this mountain stream."

The young man scoffed at her misgivings. "Mother, there is no danger. I have gone there often as a child and never encountered a single Fraser." He rode away before Elysia could voice any further protest.

Elysia Gordon quickly untied her mount and followed.

They reached the site only to discover that the trees had already been harvested of their fruit except for a scattered few that had been missed in the high branches.

Anxious to depart the dangerous territory, Elysia glanced warily around. "The cause is a lost one, David, so let's return."

"You yield too easily, Mother. No cause is a lost one until you wage the battle," David insisted with a purposeful grin. "Steady, Whirlwind." At the crisp command, the huge black charger immediately dropped his head and stood motionless. From his frozen stance, it was safe to assume the horse would not render even a gentle flick of his tail until commanded.

Elysia gasped when her son slipped his feet out of the stirrups and stood upright on the saddle. "Good Lord, David, will you get down before you fall and break your neck? That horse just has to move a step for you to lose your balance."

"I can assure you, Mother, Whirlwind will not move a muscle until I tell him to," David announced from the lofty perch.

"You are as stubborn as your father," Elysia groaned. Her apprehension proved well founded when two men suddenly rushed out from the concealment of nearby bushes. One grabbed the reins of David's horse, while the other seized those of Elysia's mount.

"Wha' hae we 'ere? W'eve cough' us a Gordon up a trae," one snickered. Elysia cried out in alarm when the man gave Whirlwind a vicious swat on the flank with a heavy cudgel.

The battle-trained horse, used to obeying his master's commands, stood his ground. The man rendered another blow, which caused Whirlwind to whinny with pain. David dropped to the ground and quickly drew his sword, but he lowered his arm and released his weapon at the sight of the dirk being held to his mother's throat.

The man swung his cudgel, striking David on the side of the head. Dazed, he fell to the ground. His arms were quickly tied behind him. Elysia was also bound. After removing the jeweled dirk at her waist, the man tethered the other end of the rope to the pommel of her horse's saddle.

Although David was bleeding from the blow on the head, he was dragged to his feet and similarly tied to Whirlwind. The two men climbed on the horses while David and Elysia were forced to stumble along beside them.

The lone figure sitting cross-legged on the floor before the fire had neither spoken nor moved for some time. No more than a maiden of twelve, she rested her chin on her hand as she leaned over a chess board and studied the situation intently. The shaggy head of a sleeping dog lay on her lap.

She looked up casually when two crofters entered the hall towing a pair of bound prisoners, each on the end of a long rope. The dog sprang to a stance at his mistress's feet. The hound looked more wolf than dog as he bared his fangs, a low, bloodcurdling growl rumbling from his throat.

"We be saekin' the Laird, m'lady," one of the men said.

Before Breyandra could reply, a tall, imposing woman strode into the room. "Lord Lovet is away at this time. What is your wont?" The woman spoke with a thick Spanish accent.

The man quickly doffed his hat. "We faund these Gordons snitchin' apples frae 'r tree, m'lady," he offered in explanation.

Contemptuously the woman's eyes swept over David and Elysia. "Gordons! Stealing apples? Then put them in the dungeon where they belong."

David exploded with anger. "You have no right to put my mother in a dungeon."

The woman's face was laced with scorn. "*Right?* Who are you to dare question my right?"

Her eyes gleamed with malevolence. "A good flogging will teach you to question *my* right. Perhaps, a taste of the cat will show you the wisdom of curbing your loose tongue."

"But, Lucretia," the young girl interjected, "Father would not—"

"Silence, you little snipe!" the woman demanded. "Must I remind you that *I* am mistress here?" She gestured to the men. "Ten lashes at dawn."

"Oh, my God, that is insanity," Elysia cried out in horror.

The woman's cruel eyes pierced Elysia like a lance. "You'll rue this day, whore." Her obsidian eyes gleamed in evil trance. "Apply the same to this Gordon bitch as well. Now take them away. Let them spend their night thinking about the fate that awaits them on the morn."

"You'll pay for this," David shouted as he struggled in vain to free himself. "I swear by all that's holy, I'll make you pay for this."

The woman's laughter echoed through the castle as the two prisoners were dragged away.

At dawn the following morning, David and Elysia Gordon were brought to the courtyard. For years the long-standing feud between the Gordons and Frasers had consisted of an occasional raid on livestock or a kidnapping for the sake of ransom. Now, word of the beatings had spread rapidly to the neighboring clachan. Those lacking faint hearts had gathered to watch.

The young man's doublet was stripped off, his

arms were stretched above his head, and his wrists were tied to ringbolts on the castle wall. The woman was bound next to him in similar fashion. As their eyes met, David Gordon could see the fright in his mother's eyes.

"Have courage, Mother. I swear on my honor, for every lash they render to you, I will seek revenge a hundredfold."

Breyandra Fraser watched the scene with trepidation. Last night she had sent a message to her father, hoping he would return in time to stop the beatings. Even though she hated Gordons, the thought of beating a woman was horrifying to her, and she was uncertain whether she would remain to watch the floggings.

Majestically, Lucretia Fraser stepped out onto the courtyard. The people began to whisper among themselves, a reaction fueled by their fear of this woman. As the anointed Caesar, Lucretia raised her hand and the whip whistled through the air, cutting a bloody stripe on the back of the young man.

Elysia Gordon closed her eyes, tears streaking her cheeks. Her body trembled at the sound of the whip striking her son. Each lash was a knife being driven into her heart. Although his back was soon crisscrossed with welts, the young Gordon did not cry out.

After the final lash had been dealt, the unfortunate blacksmith who had been given the thankless task looked to Lucretia in the hope she had changed her mind about the woman.

Lucretia Fraser appeared undaunted, and nodded for him to continue. Elysia braced herself when she felt the man's hand at her nape. He grasped the neck of her gown in his huge hand and was about to rend it apart when several horsemen galloped into the courtyard.

Simon Fraser, the Laird of Saltoun, leaped from his horse and grabbed the whip from the blacksmith's hand. He threw it to the ground in disgust. "Cut these prisoners down and take them inside," he ordered. His eyes were black with fury as he stormed over to Lucretia. "This time you have gone too far with your madness, madam. I'll not bode another moment of it. You may have started a bloody war!" He turned to the serving woman standing at Lucretia's side. "Take her to her room. She is not to leave it."

Lucretia Fraser glared in contempt at her husband, then shrugged off the woman's hand and haughtily walked away.

The relieved blacksmith assisted the beaten prisoner into the castle and seated him at a long tester table in the Great Hall. Simon Fraser sent him to the scullery to get unguent for the young man's back.

Fraser turned his attention to the bewildered pair. He regarded the male first. Blood from an earlier head wound had caked on the prisoner's face; yet, despite the beating he had just suffered, the young man held his head proudly, his eyes glaring defiance as Fraser studied him. Simon admired courage and felt a momentary respect for the young prisoner. "Your name, sir?"

"Lord Wilkes, Viscount of Strehlow." Fraser's brow immediately rose in surprise. *Lord Wilkes!*

So this is the son of Duncan Gordon! Simon mused with contempt at the thought of his lifelong enemy. He marveled at his good fortune in capturing such a prize; the Gordon heir was a bounty worthy of high ransom, and despite his youth had already achieved a reputation in the Highlands for being a skilled warrior.

Fraser then turned his attention to the woman. He halted in amazement at the vision of loveliness he beheld. Her hair was as fair as corn silk and her eyes were as blue as a Highland sky. Despite her small stature, he recognized that the woman was no maiden.

His eyes flashed in displeasure when he spied an ugly bruise on her delicate cheek. "Did my men do that to you, my lady?" There was controlled anger in his voice, and the glare he bestowed upon the blacksmith was withering.

"Twasna us, m'lord. I swear we nae pu' a hand to her face," the blacksmith quickly protested.

Fraser was confused by the guilty downward shift of the woman's eyes. "My apology, my lady. Simon Fraser at your service," he declared with a polite bow. "I regret this unfortunate situation. Had I been here, it would not have happened."

Elysia's eyes flashed with indignation as she rubbed her chafed wrists. "I advise you to apologize to my son, my lord. He was the one who suffered the dastardly blows."

"Your son?" For a brief moment Fraser's glance swung in surprise to the young man before returning to Elysia. "You are the Countess of Strehlow?" His astonishment was evident.

Not only had they flogged the Gordon heir, they had almost beaten Gordon's wife as well. He knew that if the Marquis of Huntley, or even the King, were to hear of this, it could lead to open war.

"That is correct, Lord Lovet," Elysia responded, acknowledging his lineage. "I would appreciate your informing the Earl at once, so he can arrange for our release."

As Fraser and the woman talked, the blacksmith applied the ointment to David Gordon's burning back. To distract his mind from the excruciating pain, the prisoner surveyed his surroundings. With mild curiosity his gaze stopped to rest on the young girl standing in front of the fireplace. An unruly mass of dark hair hung to her shoulders, framing an exquisite face which already evinced the promise of the beauty that womanhood would bring to it. Her round, expressive brown eyes, usually sparkling with vivacity, were now veiled by thick dark lashes as she listened, idly stroking the head of the dog that stood by her side. She must be Fraser's illegitimate daughter, David reasoned, remembering the cruel, disdainful manner in which Fraser's wife spoke to the girl.

Breyandra Fraser regarded David with equal curiosity. She was at the age when a young girl would naturally begin to place a lingering eye on the vassals and squires who frequented Saltoun. She found his tanned face with its stubborn chin, and the dark rumpled head held proudly above wide shoulders, to be quite handsome. Nearly as handsome as her father's, were that possible. His legs, sheathed in black breeks and knee-high boots, were long and muscular. His chest was well-proportioned, and his broad shoulders sloped down into muscular arms. Breyandra realized grudgingly that it was quite possible his shoulders might even be broader than her father's.

The arrogance she saw in the man's stare caused her to make an instant reassessment. Her dark eyes deepened with contempt. He was one of those accursed, horse-thieving Gordons.

"I am afraid it will be necessary to chain you, Lord Wilkes," Simon Fraser said contritely.

"Chain him?" Elysia protested. "After one of your craven clansmen dealt him a cowardly blow to the head, and another has applied a whip to his back? Surely he can't be a threat to you. If you fear for your safety, my lord, yon clansman can again hold a dirk to my throat."

David Gordon glanced with irritation at Breyandra as the dog began to growl at him. "Can't you quiet that flea-bitten hound?"

The dog sensed the hostility in the young man's tone. The growl intensified. Breyandra patted the dog's head defiantly. "The scent of vermin always raises his hackles."

"Quiet, Wolf," Simon Fraser snapped.

The dog gave a final portentous growl, then lay down at Breyandra's feet. His feral yellow eyes remained fixed on David Gordon.

Fraser turned to the blacksmith. "I'll need some shackles for his legs. Breyandra, you get some water and cloth for his head."

The young girl shook her head defiantly, her

dark hair flying wildly about her shoulders. "I'll not tend the wound of any Gordon."

"Do as you are told, Breyandra. This day has already been enough drain on my patience." He modified the harsh tone in his voice as he addressed Elysia. "If you will be seated, my lady, we will soon see to your son's head wound."

Elysia crossed her arms across her chest. "I'll not sit until he is treated," she declared resolutely.

Exasperation swirled furiously in Simon Fraser's dark eyes. He had attempted to be as gracious as possible under the circumstances, but his patience was beginning to wear thin.

"And *I* will be happy to tend to my son's wound," Elysia added haughtily.

"And *I* would be happy if you would just sit down." Fraser's voice had risen with every word until it was a roar. Breyandra needed no further encouragement to hasten from the room, with the blacksmith scuttling closely at her heels. Elysia wasted not a moment in seating herself beside David at the table.

They sat silently waiting for Breyandra's return. Trying to determine how he should proceed, Simon Fraser nervously drummed his fingers on the table. He found himself in an awkward situation. He could hardly return the Countess and her son to the dungeon, yet he could not release the young Gordon to roam freely. The man was a warrior and would soon find a weapon.

"I hope you understand why it is necessary to keep your son in shackles, my lady. I have to consider the safety of my own people."

"My son is no cutthroat, Lord Lovet. He is hardly going to slay you in your sleep."

Fraser turned to David. "Do I have your word, sir, you will not attempt to harm any of my people?"

"I can't make such a promise," David replied honestly. "If the opportunity presents itself, I will do whatever is necessary to free my mother and myself."

Resigned, Simon got to his feet. "Then you leave me no other choice but to keep you shackled." His dark eyes flashed to Elysia, stifling any further protest on her part. "I have spoken."

"Then shackle me as well, next to my son."

"You must realize that is an arrangement which I will not consider," Simon declared. "Your son will be kept here; your quarters are above."

"If my son's pallet is to be a hard floor, I prefer the same," Elysia insisted.

Simon turned to the waiting servants. "Take the Countess to the east chamber. Lock her in for the night and bring me the key."

Having no other recourse, Elysia rose to follow the servants. As she neared the door, she heard Simon call behind her, "My lady." She stopped and glanced back at Fraser, hoping he had reconsidered.

"Your chamber has a most comfortable bed and a very hard floor. Whichever you prefer is at your disposal." For the first time that evening, Simon Fraser was able to grin at the scathing glare bestowed upon him by Elysia as she stormed out of the room.

By nightfall, Elysia was still too angry to sleep. She paced the floor of her chamber. At the sound of a key turning in the lock, she braced herself defiantly to confront Simon Fraser, and was surprised to see his daughter enter the room.

"My father thought you would like a gown and rayle to sleep in." She laid down the garments and turned to depart.

"Lady Breyandra, may I prevail upon your compassion to see that my son has a quilt for warmth during the night?"

"There is plenty of wood for the fire. If he tends it, he can stay warm enough," the young girl replied.

"Yes, I suppose you are right." Elysia walked to the fireplace and stood gazing down into the fire. Breyandra watched her with curiosity. There was still something bothering the woman. She looked so desolate that Breyandra lingered at the door. She couldn't help but feel compassion for the woman, Gordon though she may be.

"Father won't harm your son if he behaves himself. Father could have returned him to the dungeon below, but he didn't."

"I hadn't thought of that. I suppose you are right." She smiled warmly at Breyandra. "I must sound unappreciative. You have been most kind. Please thank your father for his thoughtfulness."

"Goodnight, my lady."

In her twelve years Breyandra had known

little contact with women of noble birth. With her father away most of the time, her life was lonely. Lucretia, his wife, was mentally deranged, and were the truth known, Breyandra was afraid of the woman. Lacking the guidance of a tender woman, Breyandra was taken aback by Elysia's natural warmth.

Simon Fraser sat before the fireplace engrossed in reading when Breyandra tapped on his chamber door. He looked up as she entered.

"I've done what you asked, Father." She put the key on a nearby toilet chest.

"Thank you, Breyandra. May your night be comfortable." When she lingered, Simon put aside the book. "Is something troubling you, Sweetling?"

"Father, what was my mother like?"

Fraser patted the floor beside him. "Come over here, dear." Breyandra hurried over and sat down. "Your mother was a very beautiful woman."

"Was she as beautiful as the Countess of Strehlow?"

"Well . . . they are very different in coloring. Your mother was tall with dark hair."

"Do you mean like Lucretia?" Simon nodded. "Is that why you married Lucretia, because she reminded you of Mother?"

"I saw a resemblance." His face twisted grimly. "But I was mistaken."

"But what was Mother like, Father? The Countess is so genteel, yet she is not lacking in spirit or courage."

"Well, your mother was a happy person, quick

25

to laughter. Her face was seldom without a smile. As for spirit and courage, perhaps she had too much. She might be alive today had it not been so."

Breyandra knew that her mother had been killed during a raid on Saltoun by Cromwell's army. She waited silently while Simon gazed pensively into the fire. He finally shrugged aside his brooding thoughts and smiled at her.

"You resemble your mother very much, Sweetling."

"Do I really, Father?" Breyandra exclaimed with a pleased smile. "I thought I bore a resemblance to you."

"Aye, that you do. But the way you walk and the special way you hold your head when you are concentrating are so like her." He rose to his feet, and Breyandra followed suit. "Now off to bed with you."

"Goodnight, Father." Breyandra rose up and placed a kiss on his cheek.

Breyandra decided to honor the Countess's request and take David Gordon a blanket. Wolf followed her into her chamber and stretched out on the rug in front of the fireplace. He was asleep before she could pull a quilt off the bed.

The hall was lit only by the glow from the fire. Breyandra's tread was light as she approached the figure lying on the floor beside the hearth, his legs in shackles attached to the wall by short chains. He appeared to be asleep, so she bent down to spread the blanket over him. She gasped when a hand reached up and pulled her to the floor. She called out for help, but her cries went unheeded as she fought hopelessly to free herself from his viselike grip.

"Damnation!" David Gordon snarled when she bit him. He raised his head and discovered it was Breyandra he was fighting. He rolled over with another muttered oath, grimacing with pain when his back touched the floor. "What in hell are you trying to do?"

Breyandra jumped to her feet, rubbing her bruised elbows. Her eyes were blazing with anger and contempt. "You brute! If I tell my father, he will have you flogged again."

"Is flogging helpless prisoners all you people think about? I didn't know it was you. You should have better sense than to sneak up on a man while he is asleep. What are you doing down here?"

"I was only bringing you a blanket, but as far as I'm concerned, you can freeze to death." Breyandra snatched up the quilt which was lying in a heap on the floor, and stormed away.

The following morning when Breyandra descended the stairway with Wolf at her heels, the hall was empty except for David Gordon sitting by the fireplace looking anxiously at the stairway.

"What has happened to my mother?" he snapped accusingly.

"Why do you ask, Lord Vermin?"

David rose to his feet. "I swear, if your father has harmed one hair on my mother's head, I'm going to cut out his heart before your eyes."

Wolf recognized a threat to his mistress in

David's tone and began to growl. The animal stood stiffly with raised hackles, ready to spring.

Breyandra laughed aloud. "Ha! Do you think my father fears any Gordon? They all stink like swine, have the hearts of rabbits, the livers of chickens and the braying mouths of asses. Stay, Wolf," she ordered the dog, and flounced away, leaving David to face the growling animal.

He was afraid to move as Wolf snarled at him with his upper lip pulled back, exposing long fangs. Perspiration began to dot David's brow, and he said a silent prayer of gratitude when Simon Fraser appeared in the hall.

"Down, Wolf," Simon ordered. "What have you done to rile this dog?"

David ignored his question. "Where is my mother? Have you harmed her in any way?"

"When I ask a question, I expect a reply. What did you do to rile this dog?" Simon Fraser demanded.

"I didn't do anything to the damn dog. It should be obvious that, being chained to this wall, I am incapable of harming anyone."

"I hope you keep that thought foremost in your head," the Laird of Saltoun declared, eying David suspiciously.

A short while later David's anxiety was relieved when his mother appeared in the hall. Elysia spent the day applying to her son's back a healing salve which the cook had brought her. By evening, under Elysia's prudent nursing, his pain had subsided.

In the days that followed, Elysia lost her tension and found herself able to relax in the presence of Simon Fraser and his daughter. Were it not for the beating David had endured, and the fact he was forced to remain chained except for meals, she would have found the imprisonment a welcome relief from the brutal treatment she had endured under the roof of Duncan Gordon. Having noticed a garden in the courtyard, she finally gained enough courage to ask Simon Fraser for permission to tend the flowers.

"I can't spare anyone to keep an eye on you, Lady Gordon."

"I give you my word, sir, I will not attempt to escape."

Simon had no objection to her request, but there was a consideration he had to keep in mind. Her son was a dangerous prisoner. "If I give you free rein of the castle and courtyard, I must extract your promise that you will not attempt to give your son a weapon."

"You have my word, my lord."

That night before retiring, Elysia took advantage of the freedom Fraser had allowed her and climbed the narrow stairway leading to the battlement.

On the crisp, moonlit night, the valley below was streaked with silver rays that seemed to shimmer like ice. Elysia was unaware that the moonlight also produced a dazzling effect on her own face.

Suddenly Simon Fraser spoke beside her. "Moonlight becomes you, my lady."

Elysia disguised her surprise with a gracious smile. "You are most kind, my Lord Lovet."

"I was concerned about you up here alone."

Elysia turned back to the enjoyment of the view. "I have a confession to make, my lord. I love the solitude of the battlements. It isolates me from all the evils of the world."

"I would think you would seek a more corporeal protector, my lady," he said softly.

She turned to him amused. "My lord?"

"A man, madam."

His tone matched her own, and Elysia realized he was drawing as much pleasure from the conversation as she. Her eyes danced with merriment. "It has been my experience, my Lord Lovet, that men *are* the evils of the world."

The smile on his face was barely perceptible as he dipped his head in a polite bow. "Then inasmuch as I appear to be one such evil, I apologize for invading your privacy. May you pass a peaceful night." He departed as quietly as he had appeared.

Breyandra, as well as her father, enjoyed Elysia's presence at Saltoun. The poor girl, starved for companionship, found herself drawn to Elysia, as if she were the mother she could not remember. Elysia showed her how to do needlepoint, they worked together in the garden, and on occasion Simon permitted them short rides under his watchful eye.

David seemed to be the only one unaware of the closeness developing between his mother and Simon Fraser and his daughter. He himself avoided speaking to either Fraser, even during the meals when Simon released him from bondage to join them.

Elysia found contentment in watching Simon and Breyandra together; the relationship was so close. She had often wished her son could have known such a father. Never was she more conscious of that thought than one evening while watching the Frasers at their chess game before the fire. The two figures had been concentrating for a lengthy time. Breyandra finally reached out and moved an ivory piece onto a black square. "Checkmate." She sat back with a grin of satisfaction on her youthful face.

Simon leaned over to study the board intently. His brows knit into a frown. Without moving his head, his eyes shifted to the young girl seated across from him.

"It is disrespectful to best your sire. Have I not taught you better manners?"

Breyandra giggled in delight. "You have also taught me the game too well, Father."

Simon Fraser could no longer maintain a guise of disapproval. He got to his feet and opened his arms. "Come here, Sweetling."

Breyandra was in his arms at once, wrapping her own around his waist as he hugged her. "I'm proud of you. You've learned the game wisely and well, as you've done all else I have taught you." He kissed her cheek affectionately, then drew back and studied her with pride and love as the fire cast golden flecks in her round brown eyes which were brimming with laughter. He shook his head sadly. "You're ugly enough to be a lad. Now if you could wield a claymore, you would be the perfect son."

Breyandra was neither hurt nor deceived by the teasing remark. It was an oft-played joke enacted between them. She knew how much her father loved her.

Elysia chose the moment to make a suggestion she had long wanted to propose. "Breyandra dear, perhaps you will allow me to brush your hair." The young girl blushed, but sat down at Elysia's feet.

"Your cheekbones are too lovely to be kept hidden beneath this hair, my dear," Elysia exclaimed as she pulled the brush through Breyandra's tousled hair.

David Gordon had deliberately avoided watching the whole affair. He now glanced over the top of the book he was reading. "Good God, Mother, do be cautious," he scoffed. "Lord knows what might crawl out from amid that grubby entanglement."

Simon Fraser exploded into laughter, but Elysia frowned in disapproval. "That is unkind of you, David."

David Gordon grinned as Breyandra stuck her tongue out at him, and returned to his reading. When Elysia finished the difficult task of freeing the snarled mass, she wove it into a long, thick plait. The change in the girl's appearance was amazing, and Simon Fraser's proud smile was evidence of his pleasure.

When Elysia returned to the battlements that night, she was soon joined by Simon. "I know you prefer solitude, my lady. I tried to stay away, but I couldn't," he offered in apology.

Elysia blushed with guilt, for she had been hoping he would join her. All through the day she had felt his dark gaze upon her, and their eyes had met frequently in stolen glances, before modesty compelled her to turn away.

Realizing the danger in this growing affection, Elysia panicked and attempted to leave, but Simon grabbed her arm to detain her. "Please don't leave, Elysia. Stay for just a few more moments. I want to thank you for the care you show Breyandra. She has very little opportunity to enjoy a woman's gentle hand."

"But what of your wife, Lord Lovet?"

"Lucretia? You must have guessed by now she is a wife to me in name only, and certainly no mother to my daughter. The poor woman is hopelessly deranged and has been from the time I married her. Breyandra's real mother died when my daughter was just a child."

"I'm sorry, Sim."

Simon's head shot up in surprise. "My wife Kathleen was the only other person who ever called me Sim."

Elysia's blush only enhanced her beauty. "It just slipped out. I'm sorry if I have—"

"No. I want you to."

Her eyes filled with compassion, sensing the grief he bore so silently. "I can tell you loved your wife very much, just by the way you say her name."

Simon nodded. "I was devastated when she died ten years ago."

Elysia could see he was beginning to withdraw and regretted she was responsible for reminding him of his grief. "Lady Fraser is quite lovely. Was that a Spanish accent I detected?"

He nodded, and his face hardened in a grim line. "Shortly after Kathleen's death, I journeyed to Spain. While there I caught a glimpse of Lucretia. She looked so much like Kathleen, I thought I was seeing a ghost. In my state of grief, I saw her as the reincarnation of my wife, so I petitioned her parents for her hand in marriage without ever having met her. They never told me of her mental condition. On our wedding night as soon as she found herself alone in my company, she drove a dirk into me."

"Oh, dear God, Sim," Elysia said and touched his sleeve.

"There are times Lucretia appears to be quite lucid, but as you saw, she is very dangerous. I have been able to avoid any serious problems until now, but it becomes more difficult with every passing day. Juanita is the only person she trusts. The woman has been her duenna from the day Lucretia was born."

"Surely you could have the marriage annulled if it was never consummated. Then you would be free to wed again."

Simon shook his head. "I have had no desire to wed again. I learned, too late, the folly of marrying hastily in an attempt to replace a lost love. Poor Breyandra is the one who has suffered because of it. She is in need of a mother."

"Can't you, at least, have your wife confined to a nunnery?"

"The good Sisters are willing to take her, but

it would mean separating her from Juanita. I don't have the heart to do it. It would be like severing a child from its mother.''

"You're a charitable man, Simon Fraser," Elysia said kindly.

He gazed down at her intensely. "Not to my enemies, Elysia."

"And we *are* enemies, are we not?"

"Are we, Elysia?" For a moment their gazes remained locked. Then he broached the subject of Duncan Gordon. "I see the bruise on your cheek has finally disappeared."

"It was unsightly, wasn't it?" she said sheepishly.

Simon's expression hardened into a scowl. "Does he hit you often?"

Elysia flushed under his intense stare. "What do you mean?"

"Don't try to defend him, Elysia. I knew Duncan Gordon as a young man when we both served under Montrose. Gordon was a drunken bully. I can't believe he has changed his habits."

"I never realized you knew my husband," Elysia said, flustered.

"Yes, I know him. But serving together in a common cause did not make us friends. It only added to the ill feeling that already existed between our clans."

"Whatever your opinion of him, Sim, I must remind you, he is my husband."

Simon grasped her shoulders in a firm grip, glaring down at her in frustration. "Do you believe you have to remind me, Elysia? The thought is forever foremost in my mind. It haunts me. How is it you are married to that brute?"

"I don't owe you an explanation, so please don't demand it of me. You have reminded me of one thing; you and I are enemies. I have permitted myself to forget that fact, but the scars on my son's back will help me to remember."

"Scars caused by a madwoman. Insane she is, just like everything else about this accursed feud. God's truth, I've had my fill of it. When does it end? When do we cease to live our lives governed by the dictates of the past? There will always be Lucretia Frasers and Duncan Gordons. Do we let them vent their madness under the guise of clan honor? Nay, Elysia, it must end before more blood is spilled."

He stormed away angrily.

There was no sign of Simon the following day until they sat down to the evening meal, at which time he made an astonishing announcement to his prisoners. "You will be returning to Strehlow in the morning."

David Gordon's expression was one of sheer relief, while Elysia's eyes swung to Simon in question. "Then you have heard from my husband?"

"No, there has been no word from him as yet. I doubt if he even knows your predicament. I am told he departed for Perth the very day you were taken prisoners."

"Then I don't understand," David declared, confused. "Why would you release us without first receiving our ransom?"

"I have my reasons, Lord Wilkes, all of which

I'm sure would appear quite strange to you. Just be prepared to depart in the morning. I will send an escort with you to assure your safe passage to the boundary." He shoved back his chair and left the room.

For several moments they were all speechless, struggling to understand the unexpected development. Finally Elysia broke the silence. "I'll miss you, Breyandra. Were it not for the trouble between our clans, you would be a welcome guest at Strehlow."

"Not as long as I'm living there," David put in. "I never again want to see the little hellion or her mangy dog."

Breyandra jumped to her feet. "The feeling is mutual, Sir Knave." She raced from the room.

Exasperated, he turned to Elysia. "What is going on here, Mother? Why is Fraser releasing us without ransom? He even forgot to chain me."

"What would be the purpose of chaining you now? He has told you he is releasing us. Surely you wouldn't attempt to harm him?" she asked worriedly.

"I have reason to seek revenge, but this is not the time. I will decide what is the best tack when I return to Strehlow."

"I want no blood spilled, David. I thank God there has been none as yet."

"That, too, is my decision, Mother," David said firmly.

Later, as Elysia stood gazing out sadly for the last time at the valley below, her mind was full of jumbled thoughts. The past two weeks had been contented days for her, and now she would again have to cope with her life at Strehlow.

Another thought plagued her, one she was ashamed to admit to herself: the depth of her feeling for Simon Fraser. She knew she had fallen in love with him. How could she return to Duncan and his brutal ways, after the peaceful moments she had shared with Simon? It would be impossible. Elysia sighed deeply, resigned to the only course left to her. Upon her return, she would leave Duncan and enter a convent. There could be no other solution to the hopeless situation.

Elysia could not bear to turn and look at Simon when he spoke behind her. "I planned to watch you leave without saying goodbye, but I am unable to do so. I'll miss you, Elysia. You've brought a joy to my life that has been absent for a long time."

"Yet you appear most anxious to hasten my departure, my Lord Lovet."

"I think you know the reason. I no longer can trust myself." His voice was a husky caress at her ear. "I shall never be able to walk these battlements again without thinking of you."

Simon turned her to him, cupping her face in his hands, and gazed down into her brimming eyes. "For you see, dear woman, I am hopelessly in love with you."

He slowly lowered his head and covered her mouth in a gentle kiss.

His touch was exquisitely tender as his fingers explored the delicate lines of her upturned face.

"I know it was dishonorable of me, but I do not regret kissing you."

Elysia raised her hand and gently covered his mouth to silence him. "Then we must share the guilt, for I am as much at fault. I wanted you to kiss me, Sim."

Her words shattered his remaining control. His mouth once again covered hers, his arms embraced her, pulling her against him. Elysia slid her arms around his neck, returning his kiss. Breathlessness forced them apart, and Simon buried his face in her hair, his voice a tortured cry at her ear.

"How can I let you go, my love? How can I send you back to him?"

"I don't want to go. I love you, Sim. I love you," she sobbed.

With a strangled groan, he swept her into his arms and carried her to his chamber.

The following morning, David Gordon paced the floor nervously as he anxiously awaited his mother. He watched her descending the stairway and knew by the look on her face that all was not well. His fears were confirmed when she asked him to sit down.

"I prefer standing, I have had enough of sitting to last me for a lifetime. What is it, Mother?"

"David, I know that what I am about to say will hurt you deeply. I wish I knew a way to make it easier." Her chin quivered with emotion as she faced him. "I will not be returning to

Strehlow with you. I am leaving for France with Simon Fraser."

"With Fraser? Good Lord, Mother, why?"

"I'm in love with Simon Fraser, David. We are going to France for an extended visit."

The full implication of his mother's words hit him with startling clarity. David turned away, shaking his head. "Don't say any more. I don't want to hear this. I can't believe you intend to become his mistress."

"I have already become his mistress, David."

He spun around, anger blazing from his injured eyes. "My mother an adulteress! I'll kill the bastard before I'll let him make a whore of you."

"Then kill me as well, David, because Simon and you are the only two people I love. If one of you were destroyed by the hand of the other, I could never bear it." Elysia put a hand on his arm, but David shrugged it off. The ache in her heart was almost more than she could endure. "David, I was a fourteen-year-old maiden when your father came to visit my home. He raped me and I found myself with child. My father demanded he wed me, and for whatever his reasons, your father agreed. Had you been a girl, he would have cast me aside because your birth was a complicated one and I have not borne a child since. But I gave him a legal heir, so I was permitted to remain." She sighed at the sight of his unrelenting back still turned to her. "I have never known a tender moment with Duncan Gordon. He is a cruel, insensitive animal who has abused me physically for the past twenty years."

David swung back to her in a rage. "Then why didn't you leave him long ago?"

Elysia wanted to weep at the pain and bitterness in his eyes. "Had I left, I would have had to leave you behind. I could never do that. Your father knew that as well. It only incited his cruelty."

David Gordon had always suspected that his mother remained at Strehlow because of him. But as a son, he could not now justify the immorality of his mother's plans. Heretofore she had been above reproach in his eyes. Now he was struggling with disillusionment. His idol had fallen.

"I am telling you this not to seek your sympathy, David, to try and ease the pain of your suffering. I know I can no longer win your respect, but I pray you will not deny me your love."

"I could never stop loving you, Mother. Were that possible, it would ease the sting of your words."

"Perhaps some day you will find it in your heart to forgive me."

He smiled sadly. "Forgiveness can only come with time, Mother. Now I am in need of understanding. I don't deny you are deserving of happiness, but you are worthy of much more than the role you will be playing. What will happen when Fraser tires of you and tosses you aside?"

"Sim wouldn't do that to me, David. We love one another."

"I hope that love is worth the price you must pay when Father seeks revenge."

"Your father will not care. He doesn't love me, he never has. He will probably rejoice to be rid of me."

"You are being naive, Mother. What if he chooses to defend his honor and comes after you? It will mean a battle."

David saw her sudden panic. "And if he does come to wage battle, would you be joining him?" She held her breath, fearful of the answer.

"Of course." At her gasp of despair, he added, "But only to guarantee your safety. I don't doubt he would attempt to destroy you as well as Fraser." David shook his head, still unable to accept his mother's decision. "Simon Fraser! I can't believe it! The man is our enemy."

"You are wrong, David. You do not know him. You are allowing your prejudice to blind you. Simon has no heart for this feud. How I wish you would talk to him and get to know the side of him that I know." Her face softened with the intensity of her feelings. "Sim is a strong man, yet he is not ashamed to show tenderness and compassion. He is a powerful man, yet he sees no weakness in being gentle."

"I fear it is you who has become blinded by prejudice," David scoffed.

Before she could deny it, Simon Fraser entered the room. "It is time, Lord Wilkes."

Resentment blazed through David Gordon at

the sound of Fraser's voice. Elysia watched her son's inner struggle to control himself. He bent over abruptly and kissed her cheek. "God be with you, Mother." Then he stormed out of the room without a glance in Simon's direction.

Long after his departure, Elysia stood on the battlements watching the figures fade in the distance. Simon Fraser approached her and put his arm around her shoulders.

"I've hurt him so much, Sim. Will he ever forgive me?"

"He is a strong man, my love. He will deal with his pain. When he does, he will want your happiness."

Elysia smiled at him through her tears. "And you have brought me that happiness. More than I have ever known."

Simon took her in his arms and kissed her, unaware of the brokenhearted young girl watching them from below.

Chapter Two

After cresting the hill overlooking the glen, David turned around for a backward glance. Bathed in sunlight, the granite walls of Saltoun shimmered in brilliant blazonry with the Fraser banner fluttering from the highest turret. His face hardened for a moment into a grim line. Then, turning his mount westward, he goaded the horse to a gallop. The two men Simon had sent to accompany David to the border trailed behind.

David rode hard throughout the day without making any effort to remain with the escort. He stopped only to rest and water his horse. The poor men assigned to his safety tried, unsuccessfully, to remain with him, and turned around in relief when the young man reached the Gordon boundary. Tired and hungry, David reached the gates of Strehlow past midnight.

He waited impatiently while a drowsy sentinel cranked the wheel that raised the postern gate. When the opening was high enough to duck beneath, David entered the keep. He paused as the sentry lowered the creaking gate. "Has my father returned from Perth?"

"Aye, m'lord, this same night," the man replied, stifling a yawn behind a raised hand. He returned to his snoozing.

After stabling Whirlwind, David entered the castle. Dying embers on the hearth offered the only light in the darkened room. The housekeeper, Moira MacPherson, scuttled into the room to light a few tapers, and David ordered her to bring him some food.

Sound asleep, Duncan Gordon sat in a chair in front of the fireplace. The letter from Simon Fraser lay on the floor amid the remains of a spilled tankard of ale. David picked up the spattered ransom note and proceeded to read it. The young man's shoulders slumped in dejection. He walked to the fireplace and wearily leaned his forehead against the marble mantel.

The silence of the room was broken by the loud snores of Duncan Gordon as David stared broodingly into the fire, the letter hanging limply in his hand.

Finally, in frustration he crumpled the letter and tossed it into the fireplace. For several seconds the piece of white parchment lay unscathed on the embers. The heat began to lick at the letter until, gradually, the edges of the paper began to curl. Then in a brief eruption, the fire flared into a blaze and consumed the document until all that remained was black residue.

David's reflections ended when Moira returned with a tray bearing half of a rabbit, a round of cheese, and a loaf of dark bread. He sat down at the table and hungrily began to devour the food.

Duncan Gordon awoke with a loud snort and peered at David through an alcoholic stupor until he was certain the figure he saw through the blur was his son. "So, it's you!" His mouth twisted into a derisive sneer. "Only a careless fool let's himself get caught by those accursed Frasers."

The big man rose and lumbered over to the table. He filled a tankard with ale, quaffed down the liquid without stopping, and emitted a hideous belch. "How did you escape?" he asked as he refilled the tankard.

David paused to glance up at him. "I didn't escape; Fraser released me." He continued with his repast.

Surprised, Duncan spun around. His eyes, filled with suspicion, narrowed to two slits in his bloated face. "Release you? Why would Fraser release you and your mother?"

The dreaded moment had come. During the long ride home, David had weighed various responses to his father's inevitable question. No truthful answer, carefully worded though it be, could avoid the fact of Elysia's desertion. Now, confronted by his drunken father, tired and burdened with his own heartache, David simply replied, "Father, I am weary. We will discuss the matter in the morning."

Duncan exploded into a rage. Tyrannically bellowing, he swept the tray off the table. "We will discuss it *now*. I am master here, and when I speak, I'm to be obeyed." His eyes bulged with fury. "Why did Fraser release you and your mother without ransom?"

The scene was inescapable. Resigned, David rose to his feet and returned to the fireplace. He leaned on outstretched arms against the mantel, his head bowed. Finally he replied to his father's question. "Fraser released me. Mother has chosen to remain."

To a mind dulled by alcohol, David's announcement was too vague for Duncan to comprehend. "Remained? He kept a worthless woman and released my heir?" Duncan threw back his head in a loud burst of laughter. "The fool has bested himself out of most of the ransom."

At David's next statement, Duncan's laughter died as quickly as it had begun. "He's not asking for any ransom. Mother has freely chosen to remain." The man's brows knit together in confusion. "Fraser and his daughter are leaving for the Continent. Mother is accompanying them."

The look on the older man's face gradually changed from perplexity to incredulity as the truth began to penetrate his befuddled mind.

"You see, Mother has grown quite attached to Fraser's young daughter."

"Daughter, hell!" Duncan roared. "The whore

has grown attached to Fraser's loins."

Before his father could utter another word, David grasped him by the shirt front and, despite Duncan's huge size, slammed him against the wall. The young man's eyes blazed with fury as he glared into the face of his father. "Hear me, and hear me well, Father. Your brutality drove her to desperation. You are never again to call my mother a whore. I'll kill you if you do." The contempt he felt for his father was blazoned on his face and in his eyes. He shoved him away in disgust and stormed from the room.

Once behind the closed door of his chamber, David cast aside his weapons and clothing. Frustrated and angry, he snatched a bottle of brandy from a toilet chest and began to drink as he paced the floor.

Shortly before dawn, overcome by weariness and the effect of the brandy, he passed out on the bed.

David awoke naked and shivering. The room was in semidarkness, and there was no fire on the hearth. Disgruntled, he rose to his feet, then clutched his throbbing head and slumped down on the edge of the bed. He could not remember when he had gone to bed, but the sight of the empty brandy bottle lying on the floor told him all he needed to know. Disgusted with himself, David rose to his feet and snatched up a quilt. He wrapped the cover around himself for warmth, then padded barefoot to the fireplace and hunched down to build a fire.

In a short time the room was heated and David cast aside the quilt to begin dressing.

Moira tapped on the door, interrupting the painful effort.

"M'lord, are ye awake?" she called softly through the closed portal.

"Hush your shouting, Moira, and come in," he groaned.

The woman opened the door a crack and peeked cautiously through the opening. Seeing David awake and partially clothed, she stepped into the room.

Moira MacPherson had been a servant at Strehlow for thirty-five of her fifty years. A Gordon by birth, she had been born and raised in the nearby clachan of Streyside. Her husband, Donald, had been the blacksmith at Strehlow until five years earlier, when a horse kicked him in the head. The blow had rendered the man a cripple and confined him to bed. Elysia Gordon had insisted the couple abandon their tiny cottage and move under the roof of Strehlow so Moira could be with Donald during the day in the course of her duties at the castle.

"Will ye be wantin' yer high tea now, m'lord?" she asked.

David had returned to his former pose on the bed. He raised his dark head and regarded her skeptically. "Dinner? Why would I want dinner when I haven't broke the fast?"

"The low tea hae lang cum an' gane, m'lord."

David couldn't believe his ears. He rose to his feet, crossed to the window, and pushed the heavy drape aside. To his astonishment, what he had taken for granted as light coming from a

rising sun was actually coming from the west—
it was sundown.

"My God, woman, I've slept the day away."
The first thing that crossed his mind was the
previous night's scene with his father. He somehow had to convince the intolerant man to put
the matter behind him.

David turned worriedly to the woman. "Is my
father sober enough to join me for dinner?"

Moira's eyes filled with fervor and her voice
trembled with pride. "The Laird hae gaed to
Saltoun wi' a army."

David's eyes widened in shock. "Oh, my God!"
His headache was forgotten as he began to
scurry about the room to complete his dressing.
"How long ago did he leave?"

"Wheen the mist wae sti' on the brea,
m'lord."

The knowledge that his father had a full day's
start on him was horrifying to David. "Damnit,
woman, why didn't you wake me?"

Defiantly, Moira put her hands on her hips. "I
peeked in yer room an' ye wae as niked as a wee
bairn. 'Tis nae fer the likes o' me eye," she
carped in disgust.

"You fool! If that sodden brute harms my
mother, the guilt will rest on your shoulders."

"An' I'm thinkin' she be weel deservin' o'it if
he wad," Moira declared righteously.

David raised his hand to strike her, but
stopped himself in time. He lowered his arm.
"Were it not for the debt we owe your husband, I
would order you out of this house." He grabbed

his sword and bolted from the room.

Moira followed him to the stairway. "An' a woman wha' gied harsif to the likes o' a Fraser be nae bu' a whore," she mumbled for her own ears alone as David sped down the stairway.

Simon Fraser was on the battlements talking to Breyandra when one of the guards shouted an alarm. "What the devil?" Simon uttered in surprise, leaning over the parapet for a better view. At least fifty mounted and armed men were approaching under the blue and yellow banner of Duncan Gordon.

"Hurry and close the gate," he shouted to those in the courtyard below. "Prepare for an attack."

The pitifully small garrison of soldiers scurried to take positions on the walls and battlements as the cogs of the huge gear began lowering the heavy portcullis to the ground.

Simon grabbed Breyandra's hand and hurried inside. "I want you to remain off the battlements," he ordered. He shoved her into her room and hurried down the hallway to his chamber.

When he burst through the door, Elysia spun around in surprise. The look on his face was all she needed to know that something serious was amiss. "What is it, Sim?" she asked with alarm.

Simon Fraser strapped on his scabbard. "Duncan Gordon is approaching the gate with an army."

"Oh, dear God," Elysia groaned. She slumped down in despair onto a nearby chair. "I prayed this wouldn't happen. It must end now, before anyone is hurt."

Simon grasped her shoulders and drew her to her feet. "Elysia, I haven't time to talk. I want you to remain inside no matter what happens."

Elysia forced the next words out of her mouth as if wrought from the depth of her soul. "Is David with them?" Tears were streaking her cheeks.

"I don't know." Simon kissed her quickly. "I'm sorry, I must leave you and join my men." He grabbed his shield and hurried from the room before she could utter further protest.

Duncan Gordon had halted his force outside the gate and was standing in the middle of a ring of shields. A plumed helmet covered his head. Now sober, with claymore in hand, the man looked like the formidable Highland warrior he once had been.

"Simon Fraser, you spawn-of-a-whore, show yourself," Duncan shouted in a booming voice.

"Why have you come here?" Simon called down to him from his position on the battlements.

Duncan snorted derisively. "You dare ask? No man can cuckold Duncan Gordon. You'll pay with your head for the act."

"You would be wise to leave now while you still can, you braying ass," Simon shouted. "When word of your attack spreads to my clansmen, you will have lost the chance."

Gordon preened, undaunted by the threat. "I'll leave when your bowels are at the end of my sword and your head is sitting on a pike."

He raised his sword as a signal to his archers concealed behind nearby bushes. The air was rent with a shrill whine as a cluster of arrows soared toward the battlements.

The Fraser bowmen retaliated; their shafts rained down at the men below, only to harmlessly bounce off the wall of metal shields. Two of Simon's men fell wounded, one with an arrow in his shoulder and the other sustaining a hit in his leg.

"Get the wounded inside," Simon ordered when the supply of arrows of both armies became exhausted. Returning his attention to the battle, he saw several groups of Gordons, carrying scaling ladders, begin to rush the walls. Simon's small force struggled to repel the latest assault. Despite their small number, the defenders put up a gallant defense and succeeded in shoving the ladders away from the walls before any of the attackers could scale them. Finally, after numerous unsuccessful attempts, the invaders returned to the safety of the bushes.

Within the castle walls the women were busily tending to the wounded or rolling strips of linen into bandages. Several times, Elysia looked up from her work to find Breyandra's accusing eyes on her.

The lull in the battle allowed the harried women to slow their actions. Fatigued, Elysia slumped down on the floor to rest. Breyandra took the opportunity to sit in front of the fireplace and give her attention to Wolf. During the siege, the dog had been restrained inside for his own protection.

"You!" a voice cried out in a harrowing scream that brought a chill to the spine. All heads in the room turned to the source.

Lucretia Fraser stood on the stairway pointing an accusing finger at the dejected figure in the corner. Draped in a flowing nightgown of white lawn, she personified a ghostly specter. Her raven-black hair hung unrestrained to her hips, and her piercing black eyes gleamed demonically against the pallor of her face. "*You* are to blame!" she shrieked.

The eyes of all swung to the object of her impugnment—Elysia Gordon, who sat petrified in the corner staring at the frightening apparition.

"You Gordon whore. Your sins have wrought havoc on this house."

Lucretia raised her other arm in the air revealing the long knife clutched in her hand. Screeching maniacally, she streaked across the room toward Elysia.

One of the wounded men lying on the floor was able to reach out and grab the skirt of her gown. He pulled her to the floor as others hurried to aid him. The deranged woman fought wildly, but she was finally overpowered and the knife wrested from her hand. "She is evil. She must be destroyed," Lucretia sobbed, now subdued and submissive.

Juanita came hurrying down the stairway. A nasty bruise marred her forehead where Lucretia, in escaping the servant, had struck her.

The duenna gathered Lucretia in her arms and rocked her as if she were a baby. "There,

there, *pequeña*. Juanita is here." The older woman helped Lucretia to her feet and, with an arm around her shoulders, led the sobbing woman up the stairway.

Elysia had sat transfixed throughout the whole spectacle. Finally, unable to bear the covert glances of the curious any longer, she rushed up the stairway to seek privacy. Then, ignoring Simon's orders to remain inside, she continued up the stairway and stepped out onto the battlements.

Below, a brutish scene involving her husband caused a quick shudder to her spine. In full view of those behind the castle walls, Duncan Gordon had led out three Fraser croftsmen he had captured on the road. The hands of the hostages were bound behind their backs.

"You can watch me hang them one at a time, Fraser," Duncan snarled.

"My God, let them go, Gordon. What purpose is served by slaying innocent farmers?" Simon shouted down to him.

One of the men stepped boldly forward. "Dinna fret, m'lord, fae wer willin' to dee, than sae ye baw to the likes o' a Gordon."

The man's bravery produced an outburst of laughter from Duncan. "Hear that, Fraser? I'll give this fool the privilege of being the first one I hang."

Simon would not see his innocent clansmen murdered. "You're not hanging anyone," he said calmly. "This is our fight, Gordon. Let it remain between you and me." He removed his gauntlet and flung it to the ground.

The code of honor governing his noble rank required Duncan Gordon to accept Fraser's challenge. A low murmur swept through the Gordon soldiers at this unexpected turn, for all knew that Fraser could have chosen to remain within the safety of the castle walls. It would have been just a matter of time before reinforcements arrived to aid the beleaguered defenders. "Your weapon?" Simon inquired, with cool composure.

Duncan sneered with confidence. "The claymore." Because of his power, Duncan knew that the size and weight of the weapon would give him a distinct advantage over Fraser. Appraising the situation, the witnesses speculated that Simon was doomed.

Simon turned to leave the battlement and stopped at the sight of Elysia's stricken face. "You heard?" Dazed, she nodded. She felt numb. He reached for her hand, which was icy with fear, and led her down the stairways to the Great Hall.

Word of the duel had already spread to the room below. Breyandra ran to her father the moment he appeared. Simon embraced her and for a long moment held her silently in his arms, then smiled down into her youthful face. "I'll be back, Sweetling," he said gently before he kissed her.

Simon handed his heavy sword and shield to one of the wounded men and removed his scabbard. Then he took Elysia by the hand and stepped outside in the courtyard. Those inside followed behind.

His grim-faced soldiers stood silently. The Captain of the Guard approached Simon. "If it pleases you, my lord, we all would rather fight to the last man."

Moved by the valiant offer, Simon clasped the man's shoulder in comradeship. "It's a stout offer, captain, but speaks little for any confidence in my sword arm."

"Good luck, my lord," the officer said soberly and moved away.

Simon turned to Elysia and they smiled into one another's eyes. Elysia spoke first. "Our dream was doomed from the start, wasn't it, Sim?" She was unable to contain her tears.

"Regrets, my lady?" he gently teased.

She smiled at him through her tears. "No regrets. And you, my lord?"

"None, my love."

Simon quickly kissed her and turned away. "Raise the gate," he ordered crisply. He took his sword and targe in hand as the portcullis began to rise slowly with every creaking turn of the wheel.

The burly figure of Duncan Gordon waited on the opposite side.

Before Simon could step out, Elysia rushed past him and ran up to her husband. "Please, my lord, I beg of you to leave before any more blood is shed. I will come with you."

"You adulterous bitch, get out of my sight," Duncan snarled. He knocked her aside with a vicious swipe of his backhand and Elysia fell to the ground. Instantly, Simon stepped forward to assist her to her feet.

"You bastard! Damn your black-hearted soul," Simon cursed. His eyes blazed with hatred and loathing. "Try fighting a man for a change." He raised his sword and shield.

With a triumphant roar, Duncan tossed aside his helmet and snatched his targe from his clansman. All stepped back to give wide berth to the adversaries.

The two men circled each other warily. Duncan made the first move by lunging forward with a slicing blow, but Simon met the assault with his targe. They parried, meeting one another's thrusts.

Duncan took the initiative, slashing out with powerful swipes. The clash of steel upon steel echoed through the glen like a steeple bell tolling a dirge. Simon continued to evade and repel the man's powerful, relentless sallies.

If Duncan had the superior strength, Simon had an advantage just as propitious: agility. He was playing a waiting game, letting Duncan exhaust his strength. However, in doing so, his own danger increased, for if one of the brute's blows found its mark, he knew he would be dismembered or decapitated.

Elysia cried out when Simon raised his shield to ward off a powerful downward hack of Duncan's sword. Simon fell to his knee under the force of the blow, but managed to roll away from the strike and spring to his feet before Duncan could land a fatal thrust.

Again they faced each other with poised weapons. The duel had lasted longer than Duncan had anticipated. He was breathing heavily, and his doublet was wet with perspiration as the strain of the combat began to take its toll.

A force of horsemen rapidly approached the castle. From the trees and hillside around Saltoun there appeared several hundred Frasers, who had rallied to the aid of their laird. Some carried swords, others bows, but most carried hoes, shovels, picks—any implement that could be used as a weapon.

The Gordons were now hopelessly outnumbered, assuring that the tide of victory had now swung toward the Frasers. The horsemen drew up at the sight of the open gates of Saltoun, but no one raised a weapon, for all eyes were riveted on the two men in mortal combat, where the outcome of the battle would be decided.

Simon saw that Duncan was tiring and he intensified the attack. Lunging at the man, he succeeded in inflicting a wound. The sleeve of the big man's doublet was stained with blood; the sight of it threw Duncan into a blind fury. With a cry of outrage he raised his weapon above his head to cleave Simon's skull.

Simon stepped aside, avoiding the charge, and drove his sword into Duncan's side. Wounded, Duncan let his sword fall through his fingers and slide across the ground as he tripped and lost his balance. He lay helpless. Simon raised his weapon to render the *coup de grace*; the fight had been fair and the moment had come when Gordon's brutality could be destroyed forever.

At that moment David Gordon galloped up to the two figures and leaped from his horse. He had ridden furiously throughout the night, hoping to overtake his father before any blood would be spilled. "Stop!" he shouted. He drew his weapon and faced Simon. "If you deal that blow, you will have to account to me."

"This is a duel of honor, Sir Wilkes," Simon declared.

"If you kill my father, Fraser, the debt of honor becomes mine to consummate."

The young warrior's reputation was well heralded. However, Simon was twice the age of David Gordon and his prowess carried the advantage of skill and experience. He had borne his baptism of combat before the young man had been in swaddling.

His glance sought Elysia's. Her face was ashen. Simon knew that if he fought her son, whoever the victor the sword would be driven into her heart. He stepped back and lowered his weapon.

David looked at his mother. He saw the gratitude and love in her eyes as she smiled at Simon Fraser. He knew then that the older man had backed down not from cowardice, but rather for the sake of the woman he loved.

David sheathed his sword and the two men faced each other in a grudging compromise. "Take your father and leave us in peace," Simon declared. He turned away and reached for Elysia's hand.

PART TWO

Strehlow

Chapter Three

Spring 1661

David Gordon dismounted slowly, his right leg stiff and sore from an English lance he had suffered at Dunkirk. He sat down in the shadows of a mammoth oak, his gaze fixed on a clump of apple trees. The trees were in full bloom, and the air was permeated by the sweet fragrance of their blossoms.

As he sat brooding, one image kept returning to haunt him. *Apple trees . . . these same trees . . . five years ago . . .*

David's face hardened. Why had fate led him to this spot five years ago? Five years of yearning for the sight of his mother. Had she died, his heart and mind could have accepted the loss by now, but knowing she was alive and inaccessible only intensified the ache of her absence.

There had been no happiness or comfort in

returning to Strehlow. Without her gentle presence to soften its bleakness, the castle ceased to be a home to him. The shame of the disastrous defeat at the hand of Simon Fraser had driven his father deeper into a bottle. Duncan Gordon's drinking had increased to the point that he rarely left his room.

With Duncan continually besotted, and without Elysia's guiding hand, the servants had become slovenly in their duties. Strehlow had deteriorated rapidly.

So why had he returned? What was the invisible magnet that had led him back in spring? He realized he would have been wiser to remain in London, where there were diversions for his mind and body.

At Strehlow, there were only memories—memories best forgotten.

David got to his feet, rubbing his aching leg. The wound had been slow to heal. *Wars and wounds. Cause and effect. Would it never end?* he thought bitterly. He was tired of fighting Charles's wars on the Continent.

First the English and then the French. The latter campaign had been long, and he was glad when the King had finally made his peace with the French. Cromwell was dead, and at last Charles sat on the throne of England and Scotland.

David wanted to come home to stay. But Strehlow was no longer a home.

He had just mounted Whirlwind when the sound of an approaching rider caused him to pull back into the concealment of a copse of trees. Peering through the thick foliage, he saw a young woman on a roan mare stop under one of the apple trees.

David drew back in surprise at the sight of the dog trotting at her side.

Breyandra Fraser had ridden through a resplendent countryside that spring had bejeweled in hues of emerald and purple. The bright sun sparkled with brilliance on the snow-capped Grampian peaks rising above the glen. Wherever she rode, the hills were covered with purple heather and white wild flowers. Birch and ash trees were thick with leaves, and the streams ran swift and clear through the mountains or tumbled gloriously down granite walls.

After a five-year absence, Breyandra couldn't remember anything that matched the magnificence of the Highlands. She reveled in the sight of it, her Scot heart swelling with pride at the beauty of her beloved homeland. She would never leave Scotland again, she vowed to herself. She had come home to remain no matter what her father and Elysia chose to do.

Breyandra gasped with pleasure at the sight of pink blossoms on nearby apple trees. She galloped over to them with Wolf scampering at her side.

Eagerly she broke off a sprig and brought it to her nose to inhale the fragrance. When a rabbit burst from the brush, the dog bolted after it in fast pursuit.

Breyandra dismounted to rest her mare and began to stroll idly through the trees, teasing her nostrils with the perfumed spray in her hand.

"Can it really be the troublesome twit, or are my eyes betraying me?"

Startled, she spun around and gasped in shock at the man who sat mounted on the huge black stallion. She recognized David Gordon at once. Five years had matured his face and body, but the disturbing eyes and dark hair were still the same. He was as handsome as ever, she conceded grudgingly as he grinned down at her from his height in the saddle.

David Gordon was finding it hard to believe that this woman was the same ill-kept urchin he remembered. Her hair was long and straight, hanging to her waist like a mantle of smooth black satin. The reed-thin body of the young girl was now rounded into enticing curves. And she was tall, he thought approvingly; the top of her head would easily reach his chin.

His glance lingered momentarily on the full lower lip of her mouth, now curved into a defiant pout. But it was her brown eyes that were incredible. Round and provocative, the mahogany depths were blazing with hostility from under thick, dark lashes.

Breyandra attempted to move to her mare, but David maneuvered his stallion to force the girl against a tree. As he sat arrogantly atop the charger, she glared her defiance at him. Cornered she might be, but she would not cower before the likes of any Gordon.

"What is your wont, Lord Wilkes?"

" 'What is your wont, Lord Wilkes?' " he mocked. "I'm impressed, Lady Breyandra. But have you misspoke my name? When last we met, I was Lord Vermin. Or was it Sir Knave?" The sight of his smirk was maddening as he continued, "And lest I am mistaken, I would guess the gown you are wearing is freshly laundered, your hair appears neatly brushed, and your face, my lady, I would swear your face actually shows recent signs of soap and water! Dare I guess all this is due to my mother's influence?"

Breyandra saw a chance to wipe the insulting grin off his face. "Your mother? Oh, you mean my father's whore?" Her defiant pout had quickly changed to a contemptuous smirk.

All humor left David's eyes, replaced by a cold fury that set him into action. He reached down and snatched her off her feet.

"What are you doing? Take your hands off me," she cried as he plopped her down before him on his saddle.

"You're my prisoner, Mistress Fraser. Your father will have to pay dearly for your venomous tongue." David lost no time in retrieving the reins of her mare, then prodded his horse into a gallop.

Breyandra was held so tightly against him that she was unable even to squirm. Once deep within the Gordon boundary, he halted the horses beside a mountain stream. David dismounted to tend to the mare, which had been forced to keep up with the strong stride of the stallion. Breyandra grabbed Whirlwind's reins and gave the horse a hard prod with her heels. The stallion responded and began to run.

"Steady, Whirlwind!" David barked sharply.

The horse came to a sudden stop, dropped his head, and Breyandra went tumbling into the stream. Sputtering, she sat up with water dripping from her face and hair, her gown sodden and muddy.

The sight of her caused David to throw back his head with laughter. His teeth flashed white against his tanned face as he reached out a hand to assist her.

"I can say now, my lady, you bear a great resemblance to that disgusting twit I remember so well."

Breyandra slapped aside the proffered hand and rose from the stream. Water rolled off her.

"My, my, such ingratitude, when I'm trying to be charitable to a prisoner. Wouldst that your father were here to see you now."

"Oh, spare me your sarcasm," she snarled, her shoes sloshing with water as she walked over to a tree and plopped down under it.

Breyandra removed what had once been a pair of fetching pumps and emptied the water out of them. "Oh, what is the use, they're ruined," she moaned, throwing them down in frustration. Her scathing glare swung to the man responsible for her plight. *Oh, why did this have to happen to me with this scurrilous knave as a witness?*

David Gordon was more amused than intimidated by her displeasure. "You have no one to blame but yourself, Mistress Fraser." Reaching into his saddlebags, David retrieved the plaid, which no Highlander was ever without, and offered it to her. "I suggest you remove that sodden clothing and put this around you. Then we had best be on our way."

Breyandra snatched the colorful tartan out of his hands and disappeared into the bushes. Moments later she reappeared, the bright plaid wrapped securely about her.

David Gordon paid her no heed. He was standing by his horse listening intently to a steady barking in the distance. Breyandra recognized the familiar sound and her heart leapt with renewed hope.

"Wolf! It's Wolf!" she cried joyously. "He's trailed us."

David drew his pistol just as the huge animal bounded into the clearing. Wolf stopped and slouched low at the sight of the man. In a lethal warning, his lips curled back to expose huge fangs. The dog's feral eyes gleamed ferociously as a growl rumbled from his throat.

David cocked his pistol and took careful aim. If he missed the shot, he would have no other. Breyandra cried out frantically, "No, don't kill him! Please don't kill him!"

"I'm afraid it's too late not to."

Tears were streaming down her cheeks. "I'll send him away. I swear to you. I'll send him home," she pleaded.

David was unable to withstand her pitiful pleas. Against his better judgment, he did not pull the trigger, but kept the weapon aimed. "Then I suggest you do it quickly, mistress, or it will give me a great deal of pleasure to blow his head off."

Breyandra's relief was an unrestrained mixture of laughter and tears. She slumped down on her knees and opened her arms. "Come, Wolf, come," she cried. The dog trotted to her with his tail wagging uncontrollably. "Good boy. Good boy," she crooned affectionately as she hugged him. The dog's big tongue came out and began to lick the salty tears off her cheeks.

David watched warily as Breyandra rose to her feet. "Home, Wolf. Go home," she ordered.

Clearly confused by the unexpected command, Wolf cocked his head with ears erect. The animal regarded his mistress with alert and inquisitive eyes. Breyandra pointed her finger. "Go home, Wolf. Now," she ordered sharply.

Reluctantly the huge dog turned and trotted off. He stopped a short distance away and looked back woefully. Another emphatic gesture with her finger convinced the animal of her sincerity, and Wolf continued on his way.

Breyandra brushed aside her remaining tears and stole a timid glance at David. "Thank you," she said softly.

David suddenly was uncomfortable in the position he now found himself in. Silently he gathered her wet clothing and rolled it into a bundle. He quickly tied it to his saddle. "You can ride your mare." Effortlessly he lifted Breyandra onto the mare, and she waited as he mounted Whirlwind.

David's leg was aching painfully. His face etched into a grim line from the effort of swinging himself into the saddle. They rode in silence the rest of the distance to Strehlow.

Chapter Four

The hour was late when they reached the massive castle. As they passed through the postern gate and into the courtyard, Breyandra eyed the huge structure resentfully. Overhead on one of the high turrets the blue and yellow Gordon banner fluttered in the night breeze.

Their arrival created a stir of interest. Breyandra could feel a dozen pair of eyes on her as David swung her off the mare. She was relieved when the big door slammed shut behind them, closing out the curious stares.

The Great Hall of Strehlow was in darkness, lit only by a single sconce on the wall. David went over to a long tester table and soon had two candelabra burning.

The additional light gave Breyandra an opportunity to look about. The room was enormous, easily twice the size of the Great Hall at Saltoun, but in pitifully neglected condition. An imposing fireplace dominated the far wall. Breyandra was surprised not to see a fire burning in anticipation of the young Lord's return. She knew of no occasion at Saltoun when a cheerful fire was not blazing in the hearth for her father's return.

"Moira!" David shouted at the top of his voice.

The woman hurried into the room and stopped abruptly at the sight of Breyandra wrapped in David's plaid.

"Moira, tell the cook to bring the evening meal. The day has been a long one, and I am hungry."

The woman appeared indignant at the request. "Och! Ye gaed aff wi' nae a word o' yer return. Sae Enid dinna see fi' tu mok aught, m'lord."

"What?" he roared in a show of temper fueled, due to Breyandra's presence, more by embarrassment than by anger. "A man goes for a ride and it is assumed he is not returning? Since when are decisions made in the scullery?" He slammed his fist so hard on the table that one of the candelabra fell to the floor. "God's truth, Moira, I have had enough of this. I want to see hot fare on this table within the hour."

The woman stood firm. "Dinna be faultin' the cook, m'lord. 'Twas the Laird wha saed he dinna wist aught."

David shook his head in disgust. It was useless to argue with her. Since his mother's absence and his father's indifference, the woman's actions had daily grown bolder and more slovenly. "Very well, Moira. Just bring us cheese and bread. The Lady Fraser is in need of dry clothing. See if you can find some."

Moira's eyes rounded in shock as her glance swung to Breyandra. "The Lady Fraser!"

"Lady Fraser is my prisoner, Moira. Unfortunately, she fell into the stream. You will find her wet clothing on my saddle. See that it is laundered. By morning, Moira," he accentuated. "In the meantime, bring whatever you can find that will fit her."

"Yes, m'lord." She scurried away, anxious to pass on this latest bit of gossip to those in the scullery.

Feeling awkward and embarrassed, David turned to Breyandra. Her dark eyes were regarding him with curiosity. "Sit down while I build a fire."

Breyandra had listened with interest to the exchange between him and the woman. "Do you always shout at your servants?"

"Mistress Fraser, look about you. This castle is going to ruin because of their indolent habits. Ever since my mother has been . . ." He stopped what he was saying and turned away.

Breyandra took his advice and sat down in a nearby chair. She noticed he winced with pain when he knelt down at the fireplace.

Barefoot as she was, Breyandra was beginning to feel chilled to the bone and welcomed the fire that soon was blazing on the hearth. She shifted to the floor in front of the fire to be nearer the warmth and tucked her knees under her chin, gazing pensively into the flames. Her mind began to dwell on the full measure of the plight in which she found herself, confined within the gloomy walls of Strehlow.

What lay ahead for her? How long must she remain here? What would her father do when he heard of her abduction?

Breyandra had no idea how appealing she appeared to David Gordon, who was watching her closely. He regretted the hasty act of bringing her with him. He had merely intended to tease the lass, but when she had made the unkind remark about his mother, he had lost his temper.

He sat down in a chair and stared glumly into the fire, as if to find a solution in its fiery depths. Moira appeared with a tray holding a makeshift meal consisting of some cold venison and a loaf of bread. After depositing the tray on the table, she returned with a robe, hose and a pair of slippers for Breyandra.

"Here be ol' the claes I cae fand." Tossing the clothing on a chair, she departed, grumbling under her breath about having to serve Frasers.

Breyandra sought the privacy of a darkened corner to slip into the clothing, then returned to the table to sample the fare awaiting her. Having eaten only a dish of oatmeal early that morning, she began to devour the food ravenously.

Angry with himself as much as with Moira, David lashed out at Breyandra. "Your face may have been cleansed and your hair brushed, Mistress Fraser, but I see your table manners sadly lacking."

Not one to bear anyone's tongue-lashing, Breyandra parried with her own riposte. "For one accustomed to lolling in this squalor, I doubt my manners could be an affront, Lord Vermin."

"You have a nasty tongue, Mistress Fraser. You would be wise to curb it before you try the limit of my patience."

Breyandra was not afraid of his threats. Her eyes flared scornfully. "What will you do to me? Throw me in a dungeon? Chain me to a wall? Oh, please show mercy, Sir Knave," she whimpered in a mocking trill.

David's temper, already taxed by an insolent servant, could bear no more ridicule. He jumped to his feet and grasped Breyandra's arm. He had intended to give her the use of an upstairs chamber, but her taunting goaded him to more drastic action. Yanking her away from the table, he pulled her to a wall.

Breyandra struggled wildly to free herself. She struck several blows to his face and head, but David succeeded in attaching a chain, normally meant for a dog, to one of her arms. Breyandra found herself shackled to the wall.

"Turnabout is fair play, my lady."

Seething with rage, Breyandra kicked out at him and landed a blow to his wounded thigh. His face whitened from the shock of the pain. "You vicious bitch," he cursed, grabbing his throbbing leg. He turned and limped up the stairway.

In her fury, Breyandra yanked and pulled at the chain, but it held fast and she could not release it. She finally gave up in frustration and slumped, exhausted, to the floor. The day had been long and tiring. The warmth of the fire added to her weariness, and before she knew it, she was fast asleep.

Breyandra opened her eyes, and wondered what had awakened her. She sat up startled, confused by the strange environment. The tug of the chain on her wrist reminded her of her imprisonment. She tried to stretch her cramped body and cursed the name of David Gordon as her aching muscles protested the strain.

Her head turned sharply toward a shuffling sound near the stairway. She realized it was the sound that had awakened her. The fire had long burned out and the Great Hall was in darkness. She peered fretfully through the blackness to discern the identity of the intruder.

As her eyes focused toward the sound, the huge figure of a man took shape. Breyandra huddled in fear against the wall, but the figure was upon her before she could maneuver to avoid him, and the man tripped over her foot.

"What is this?" a loud voice roared.

The man staggered to the table and fumbled for a candle. After lighting it, he raised it in the air and stared down at Breyandra. She found herself lying at the feet of the large, burly man, a frightening specter from the past—Duncan Gordon.

Standing in the flickering light, Duncan appeared more fearsome than ever. Powerfully built, he now had the girth of a bear. Long, unkempt hair and a shaggy beard drooping from his face added to the apparition.

"Who are you?" he snarled. His face was bloated from alcohol and he reeked of stale ale.

At the sight of the robe she was wearing, he grumbled irascibly, "Are you my son's whore?"

Breyandra rallied enough courage to take exception to the remark. The man frightened her like no other she had ever known, but she would not bear his insults.

"I am the Lady Breyandra Fraser."

"Fraser? Did you say Fraser?" The drunken man looked confused. "What is a Fraser wench doing here? It will be a cold day in hell when a Fraser walks the halls of Strehlow. How did you get here?" he demanded.

"I was brought here by Lord Wilkes."

"My son brought you here? For what reason would he bring a Fraser to Strehlow?"

The man was loathsome to behold. Breyandra was revolted by the nearness of him. How could Elysia ever have borne the barbarian's touch? For the first time, Breyandra understood the desperation that had driven Elysia to adultery.

"I am your son's prisoner, Lord Gordon."

The man threw back his head and laughed. "Let me get a closer look at you." He grabbed her arm and tried to jerk her to her feet. Breyandra cried out with pain as the chain around her wrist held firm.

Duncan's eyes swept her in a lecherous perusal and she cringed under the lustful look in the bloodshot eyes. "From what I can see, you're a comely wench. Let's see if what's beneath is just as bonny."

With an arm shackled to the wall, Breyandra was helpless to ward off the huge paws forcing apart the front of her robe. "Worth a tumble, I would say."

Horrified, she struggled to draw the robe around her. "Keep your animal paws off me," she railed. The huge man growled his displeasure and ripped the gown off her body.

Breyandra shrieked and pelted his face with her unshackled hand. He pressed her back to the wall and pulled her into his arms as he attempted to kiss her.

Breyandra shook her head from side to side, struggling to avoid his mouth. She reached up and grasped a handful of his hair and pulled until he released her with an angry growl. He picked her up and slammed her down. Her head struck the floor from the force of the impact, and she lay momentarily dazed and helpless. Duncan straddled her clumsily and began an assault with his hands and mouth, pawing at her naked breasts.

The instinct for self-preservation rallied her strength, and she fought to repel this newest offense, clawing at his face to force him away.

Breyandra began sobbing with indignation and fear. She knew she was waging a helpless struggle against his overwhelming power, but she was determined to fight him until her strength was exhausted.

She wanted to gag when his foul-smelling

mouth closed over hers, and she clenched her lips together. He brutally squeezed the nipple of her breast. The pain forced her to part her lips, and Gordon drove his tongue into her mouth. She tried to bite down on the fat organ strangling her. Duncan raised his head and she thrashed out, kicking wildly when his huge hand attempted to pry apart her legs. Her foot made contact with his loin, and Duncan doubled over, grunting with pain.

Enraged, he raised his hand to strike her face. She instinctively closed her eyes, turning her head aside in anticipation of the coming blow.

Suddenly Duncan was seized from behind by strong hands that yanked him away and threw him to the floor. Breyandra opened her eyes when she felt her body freed of his ponderous weight. Painfully, she pulled herself up into a sitting position and snatched up the discarded robe, wrapping it around herself in an effort to cover her nakedness.

Dressed only in breeks, David Gordon glared at his father. His hands were clenched at his sides as the older man lumbered to his feet.

"Don't ever touch this woman again," David ordered. "She is my prisoner, and as such, I am also responsible for her protection."

Duncan Gordon was incensed at having his sport interrupted. "This is my house, you ungrateful bastard. I'll skewer any wench in it I choose. So step aside."

"I have no intention of stepping aside," David said grimly.

Duncan was past wisdom or reasoning. "I can

break you with one hand," he warned savagely.

David remained unintimidated and stoutly held his ground. "Don't underestimate my strength, Father. I haven't spent the last twenty-five years trying to preserve it in alcohol."

Duncan roared thunderously, lowered his head, and set upon his son like a charging bull. David adroitly stepped aside, and the drunken man crashed into the stone wall, slamming his head.

Duncan fell to the floor, and David knelt over his father to examine him. The man began to snore loudly.

"Moira!" David called at the top of his voice.

The woman scurried into the room, wrapping a shawl about her. "Father has fallen asleep on the floor. See that he is taken to his room."

He walked over to Breyandra, who was sitting stunned in a desolate heap against the wall. David released her shackle, and she shrugged aside his hand as he attempted to help her to her feet. "You are safe now, my lady."

Her eyes blazed with contempt as she looked up at him. "Safe? How can I be safe from that beast as long as I am under this roof?"

She was startled when he lifted her into his arms. "Because henceforth you will remain in my chamber." Against her protests and ranting, he carried her up the stairway.

David Gordon entered a chamber on the floor above. He paused to kick the door shut, then strode across the room and dumped her unceremoniously on a huge bed.

Sprawled wantonly before him, Breyandra

glared up at him, determined not to show any less courage than she had shown his father. "Is it your intent to finish the debauchery begun by the beast that sired you?"

David's mouth curved in amusement as his eyes traveled down the long length of her. "You are a bonny sight to behold, Breyandra Fraser, but you exaggerate the temptation. Let me assure you I have never had to force myself on a woman. They've been as willing as they were abundant."

He turned away and walked to the fireplace. Breyandra sat up quickly and smoothed the torn robe about her as best she could. "A fanciful boast, Sir Knave. I have no intention of remaining in this chamber with you."

She bolted off the bed and had not taken more than two steps before he seized her from behind. She was spun around to meet the full measure of David Gordon's dark eyes, now blackened in fury. "You will do as I say or I'll have you confined to a dungeon."

A muscle jumped in his cheek as he fought to restrain his anger. "Or perhaps you would prefer a flogging, mistress. If my memory serves me correctly, such manner of chastisement is to the liking of you Frasers."

The strength in the hand crushing her shoulder convinced Breyandra that her struggle was pointless. Yet, relenting was not an easy decision for her. "Just how long do you intend to keep me a prisoner in this chamber?" Her tone remained haughty, but she eased her body's resistance.

David relaxed his grip, and she shrugged aside

his hand. "I have not yet decided. It was foolhardy indeed to allow you to goad me into bringing you to Strehlow. But it is too late to ponder the folly of the act."

He sat down in a chair in front of the fireplace, stretched out his long legs, and closed his eyes.

Reluctantly, Breyandra returned to the bed. She was relieved to see he wasn't going to claim any part of the bedstead. She pulled up the quilt and lay back on the pillow. However, sleep appeared as elusive as the freedom she was seeking.

She lay watching David Gordon. The chair he was sitting on was inadequate to accommodate his long frame. Breyandra garnered a great deal of satisfaction from watching him shift restlessly in the chair.

She boldly forced conversation. "Why do you accuse me of goading you into bringing me here?"

The moment lengthened as she waited for his reply. When it seemed that he was ignoring her, Breyandra was about to repeat the question when he finally answered, without opening his eyes.

"I did not take kindly to your insult to my mother, Mistress Fraser. Were you a man, you would have paid the price for your vindictive tongue . . . as others have done," he added ominously.

Breyandra shot up in surprise. "As others have done? You, too? And how many duels have *you* had to fight? My father has already parried twice in the past two years defending your mother's honor." She was unaware of the soft sigh that slipped past her lips. "I live with the fear that one day he will die in the attempt."

David opened his eyes and glared at her in disgust. "Do forgive my lack of compassion, my lady. Your father's self-indulgence is what created the situation. Perhaps if his brain were somewhere other than between his legs, none of us would have this problem."

Modesty was forsaken as Breyandra sprang out of the bed to come to the defense of her beloved hero. "How dare you say that about him!" She attacked David with flying fists, raining one blow after another upon his face and head.

Staggering to his feet, David fought to ward off the attack. In the tussle, her robe opened and slipped off her shoulders before David succeeded in pulling her into his embrace and pinning her arms behind her back.

As Breyandra struggled against the solid wall of his bare chest, she was suddenly aware of a feeling that she had never known before. The more she strained to resist him, the greater the response within. This new sensation was becoming more disconcerting to her than the struggle. She finally capitulated against the muscular brawn of his bare chest as her face was pressed against a mat of dark curly hair that tapered seductively down across a flat, lean stomach.

She looked up, and for an infinite moment their startled gazes locked before David's glance swung down to her exposed breasts. Raw and primitive lust surged through him at the sight of the firm and thrusting peaks of the luscious mounds.

Breyandra gasped with shock at the feel of him swelling against her as David was helpless to maintain his control. Angry with himself as well as with her, he grasped her shoulders and began to shake her. Her long black hair flew about her face and head in wild dishevelment until at last he shoved her away and she fell backward across the bed.

Breyandra's body was now fully exposed to his perusal, and, angry as he was, he allowed his eyes to sweep the full measure of the alluring hollows and curves.

His gaze stopped on her round, brown eyes; David was intrigued that their expression seemed to blend fright with excitement. *Lord, the twit is as beautiful as she is troublesome*, he thought helplessly.

"For one who cries *rape* so loudly, mistress, you do much to invite it."

He turned and strode out of the room, loudly slamming the door behind him. Breyandra sat up, confused and shaken. Stifling a sob, she pulled the robe around her, crawled under the quilt, and curled up with her cheek on the pillow.

Immersed in despair, she mused on her plight. How would she escape from this horrid place and David Gordon? His actions had convinced her that he would do her no harm, but now she had a new cause to fear him.

As she lay pondering her latest dilemma, the memory of the contempt in his dark eyes was as tormenting as his subtle scent lingering on the pillow.

Chapter Five

When Wolf trotted into the Great Hall, Simon Fraser was concentrating on his ledgers. He paid no attention to the animal until Wolf slipped his snout under Simon's hand. Preoccupied, Simon patted the dog's head, but whenever he attempted to stop the fondling, Wolf would again force his snout under the man's hand. After several repetitions of the gesture, Simon finally closed the ledger and leaned back in his chair.

"So, Wolf, you and your mistress have finally returned. And none too soon, I must say. It will soon be time to dine."

Simon rose to his feet and left in search of Elysia, leaving Wolf alone to curl up before the fireplace.

When there was no sign of Elysia in his

chamber, Simon knew where to find her. He climbed the stairway to the battlements.

Elysia was gazing pensively across the sweeping slopes of the glen. Simon slipped his arms around her waist and drew her back against him. She sighed contentedly and relaxed in his embrace. "You miss your home, don't you, my love?"

Elysia's smile was elusive. "The Highlands are my home, Sim. I miss my son. Five years is a long time without the sight of him."

Simon turned her in his arms and tenderly cupped her face in his hands. His eyes mirrored the pain in Elysia's. "Regrets, my love?"

Elysia's smile carried to her eyes, as they gazed up lovingly at him. "What do you think?" She pressed a kiss to his palm and laid her cheek against his chest. "This is only a mother's yearning for the presence of her son. Part of me is always with him, Sim."

His arms secured her in the circle of his embrace. Simon pressed his cheek to her head, and they stood watching the sun slide behind the distant peak of Ben Nevis.

Deep in their musings, Simon and Elysia were unaware of the two figures observing from the shadows. Lucretia Fraser's eyes filled with malevolence when her husband embraced Elysia Gordon.

"So, he has returned," the man beside her remarked with scorn.

"And his whore with him," Lucretia snarled venomously. "Now I will be locked in my room again like a crazed animal." She uttered a string of vituperative curses.

Before more could be said between the secreted pair, Juanita hastened to their side. "Come. Quickly, before you are seen," she cautioned in a whisper of panic.

Lucretia allowed the older woman to take her arm and lead her away. For a few seconds the man lingered, glaring in contempt at the two lovers. Then he turned away and slipped into the deepening shadows as stealthily as a cat.

Nightfall had descended by the time Simon discovered that Breyandra was missing. He questioned several of the castle's staff, but none remembered seeing the girl from the time she rode away that morning. At first he feared foul play, with Lucretia as his prime suspect. Then he learned that the mare Breyandra often rode was missing as well.

He immediately summoned the captain of the guard. "Who rode with my daughter this morning when she left the keep?"

The man had been dreading the question since word of Breyandra's disappearance had spread around the keep. He knew the distress his answer would provoke. "No one, my lord."

Simon was a tolerant man by nature, but the safety of his daughter was paramount to him. His orders had been explicit, and now his temper exploded. "What! You allowed my daughter to ride away without escort?"

"My lord, when the Lady Breyandra left with

her dog, she insisted she was only going a short distance to exercise the animal. She refused an escort."

Simon knew his daughter was headstrong, but his concern for her overshadowed his sense of fairness. "Refused an escort!" Simon shouted. "That was not her decision to make. My orders have always been that she never leave the keep without one. Lord knows what might have happened to her. She could be lying injured, or could have encountered a wild animal or cutthroat."

"Or a witchie," the cook mumbled, who was standing nearby.

The comment carried to Simon's ears. "What's that about witches?" he asked.

The captain of the guard cast a disgruntled look toward the woman for broaching the subject. "There have been some strange happenings lately, my lord. Dead animals with certain parts removed, and a fortnight ago we found a crofter with the heart cut out of his chest."

The cook made a quick sign of the cross. "'Tis a witchie fer shur, m'lord."

Simon was aghast. "Enough! I'll hear no talk of witches. Good Lord, what has been happening here in my absence? Ready patrols to leave at once."

When the room cleared, Elysia walked over and slipped her hand into Simon's. "I'm sure she is safe, Sim."

He squeezed her hand and brought it to his lips. "The girl is so headstrong. She never thinks about danger."

Elysia eyed him hesitantly, wondering if she should voice the thought that had entered her head. "I know this sounds unlikely, but perhaps she is with . . . a lover."

Simon was skeptical. "Unlikely indeed, madam. Why, the girl is just a—"

"She is no longer a girl, Sim. Breyandra is a woman. I had a two-year-old son by the time I was her age."

The father in him struggled to reject the theory. He shook his head in refusal. "No, it couldn't be. Besides, we have just returned after a five-year absence. She hasn't had an opportunity to meet a young man."

"Unless one followed her from France," Elysia said wisely. "Or perhaps she met him this very day." Elysia tried to ease his mental anguish. "Forgive me, Sim, but my instinct tells me that Breyandra is in safe hands."

Elysia's calmness had a soothing effect on him. Simon smiled in gratitude. "Thank you, my love. Your confidence has eased some of my worry."

His glance swung down to Wolf, stretched out and sleeping peacefully before the fireplace. Simon was struck with an obvious fact that had escaped his reasoning. "Wolf!" he cried out excitedly. His outcry took Elysia by surprise and she looked at him baffled. "Look, Elysia. Look at Wolf. Does he appear to you like a dog who has lost his mistress? He knows where he can find her."

Simon's eyes were aglow, showing no sign of the anxiety that had haunted them. "Wolf would never come home without Breyandra. He would never leave her if she was hurt or in danger. He'd attack anything or anyone that threatened her and would die trying to save her."

Simon hunched down and began to examine the dog carefully. The sleepy animal bore the disruption with drowsy patience, then closed his eyes and returned to his slumber when Simon rose to his feet. "There's not a mark or wound on him."

New hope glimmered in his eyes. "You may be right, my love. In the morning we'll have Wolf take us to where we can find my prodigal daughter."

Elysia departed, leaving Simon to formulate his plans for the next day. The Laird of Saltoun was still dumbfounded by the turn of events. Despite his concern for his daughter, Simon's handsome face curved with amusement. *Why, it seems like just yesterday my little girl declared she would never love anyone but me*. Then his mood shifted to poignancy as he remembered her heartache that day.

Breyandra had been terribly jealous of his relationship with Elysia at first. That jealousy had caused her to lash out at both of them, then run away to hide.

Simon had found her huddled against the parapet of the battlements with her chin propped on her knees. Breyandra didn't look up when his black boots appeared before her.

"Sweetling, I want to talk to you."

Breyandra pouted childishly at him. "Don't call

me Sweetling. My name's Breyandra. Call your precious Lady Elysia Sweetling."

Simon Fraser hunched down and tipped her chin up to look into her face. Breyandra's round brown eyes glared in resentment. *"I'm afraid that would be very hard to do, my dear, because I've called you by that name since the very first time I held you in my arms."*

The endearment only seemed to intensify his daughter's misery. When her chin began to quiver, Simon sat down and put an arm around her shoulders. He hugged her to his side.

"I know you are hurt and confused by what is happening, and I'm to blame for not taking the time to speak to you sooner."

"That's for certain. You never have time for me any more. All your time is spent with that woman."

"Sweetling, Lady Elysia's presence here doesn't change anything between you and me. You hold a place in my heart that no other one could ever take."

Breyandra shook her head in denial. *"You're just saying that, Father, to try and cheer me."*

Simon smiled gently at her childish suspicion. *"Have I ever given you cause to doubt my word?"*

"No," she sniffled.

"If a man is fortunate, he will know the love of three women in his lifetime—a mother, a wife, and a daughter. And he will reciprocate their love, but each in a unique manner.

"The love a son feels for his mother is an intrinsic love—a bonding at birth that he can only feel for that woman alone. His wife or daughter

will never know that love from him, for they are not part of that bonding. I knew such a love with your grandmother." Simon smiled down at her. *"Do you remember your grandmother, Sweetling?"*

Breyandra nodded. *"She was very nice to me."*

With the patience intrinsic to his nature, Simon continued, *"Now, when a man finds the woman he chooses to be his mate, he discovers a different love—an instinctive love. A total commitment of his body and soul. This love is an emotional . . . physical . . . and spiritual need and dependency. The love becomes so integral to his being that he no longer is whole without it. It transcends any love he will ever feel for any other woman."*

Simon glanced down at Breyandra. She had ceased her sniffling and was watching him intently. He reached out and brushed aside a tear lingering on her cheek. *"I knew such a love with your mother,"* he said softly.

He hugged her to his side again and was relieved to feel the tension ease from her as she relaxed in his arms.

"Then to this man is born a daughter. And with her birth is born the third love he will know. That love is an inherent love experienced from the moment of her birth when he picks her up and holds her in his arms for the first time. An overwhelming sense of pride and protectiveness are associated with that love . . . and a realization of his own immortality. And no woman, Sweetling, no woman, neither mother nor mate, can transgress on the love a man feels for his daughter. It is inviolable, because this woman is the seed of his

loins. And this is the love I have for you."

He stopped to press a kiss on the top of her head. *"No one love is lessened by either of the other two; each remains unique within him, for each is built on a different need, and each draws strength from a distinct source within him."* He paused momentarily. *"And a woman too will know three loves: her father, her son, and the man she takes for her mate."*

Breyandra shook her head emphatically. *"I will never love any man but you, for I shall never take a mate, Father."*

Simon smiled tolerantly, and with a glint in his eyes said, *"I will hope you have reason to change your mind, Sweetling."*

David Gordon opened the door and entered the room. He put down the tray he was carrying and crossed to the bed. Breyandra was sound asleep, and for several moments he studied the sleeping girl. Her face and jaw were exquisite, patrician in their delicacy. His eyes lingered on the wide mouth. In sleep it was even more inviting then when she was awake, and her coffee-colored eyes would flash a challenge that dared him to sample the lusciousness of those lips.

The quilt was tucked beneath her chin, but David remembered all too well the seductive curves that lay beneath the counterpane. Perfect breasts. Long, lithesome legs. A flat, smooth stomach that dipped into rounded hips.

He tried to force his mind away from the temptation that lay just a few feet away. All he would have to do is snatch the quilt off her and it would all be there for him to touch . . . or taste . . . or take. Last night her eyes had told him as much. His hand trembled as he reached out, and then he curled his fingers around the edge of the blanket.

Breyandra opened her eyes, which widened in alarm at seeing him loom above her. For the breath of a second, they stared at one another. Then he yanked off the quilt. "Get up, mistress. It's time we're on our way," he ordered. David turned away sharply as she attempted to pull together the tattered robe to conceal her nakedness.

Breyandra, not fully awake, was as drowsy as she was startled. The man disturbed her, no doubt about that. The sooner she saw the last of him, the better she would like it. "What . . . what am I supposed to wear?" she stammered.

His face wore a sullen scowl. "Your clothes are on the table. Put them on and let's be on our way. As it is, you've slept away most of the morning." He quickly departed the room expecting his command to be obeyed.

Breyandra rose to her feet with a slothful stretch and cast a dreamy glance at the bed. She had felt snug and cozy cuddled in the middle of the huge bed. In a flight of whimsy, the speculation of what it would have been like if David Gordon had lain there beside her danced in her thoughts. With a guilty start, she shrugged aside the traitorous thought and hastened to the table.

Thankfully, Breyandra threw aside the tattered robe and donned her clothing. Moira had tiot pressed her gown, but at least the dress was freshly laundered. She regretted her hasty act of tossing her shoes away. She now had to make do with the soft slippers Moira had brought her the previous evening.

Breyandra spied a basin and ewer on the toilet chest. She picked up the pewter pitcher and poured water into the shallow pan. After rinsing her face and mouth, she observed her disheveled image in the mirror, and looked about for something with which to groom her tangled hair.

Her glance fell on a silver brush. She reached for it, knowing the bristled implement belonged to *him*. As she drew the brush through her long, straight strands, the action called to her mind how the thick hair of David Gordon dropped to his shoulders in soft waves. Hurriedly she cast aside the brush, as if the mirror could read her thoughts.

Breyandra looked around for a tie to bind her hair. She crossed the room to an oak armoire against the wall. She opened the doors and began to rifle through the drawers. Overcome by an emotion she did not understand, she leisurely began to examine the contents. Her fingers barely brushed the folded garments, yet the intimacy of the moment excited her, and she was helpless to stop her exploration.

In the corner of one of the drawers she discovered a small portrait of Elysia in a pewter frame. Breyandra picked up the picture and studied it. Elysia's face jolted her back to the present. She had foolishly allowed her thoughts to stray from reality—David Gordon was her enemy.

Breyandra quickly ripped a satin ribbon off a pair of trousers and slammed the drawer. She bound her hair and with a resolute expression sat down at the table.

The tray David had brought her held a pot of tea and several scones. Breyandra spread the biscuits with butter and quince jelly. Knowing how distasteful David would find it, she gobbled them down with quick bites. The tea had cooled, but was still warm to the taste. Breyandra gulped the tepid liquid quickly, grabbed her cloak, opened the chamber door and rushed from the room.

She nearly bumped into David Gordon, who was pacing nervously outside the room. He peered at her with a foreboding look. "Well finally, Mistress Fraser. Are you always this laggardly in the morning? The day is practically half gone." He spun on his heel and stormed down the stairway.

Mouthing the oath she wanted to fling at him, Breyandra gritted her teeth and followed behind.

Her saddled mare stood next to the black stallion Whirlwind as the two horses snorted and pranced. Feeling their morning oats, they were anxious for the exercise and impatient with the delay.

David brushed aside a sullen-faced livery boy, who was reluctant to help Breyandra to mount, and lifted her into the saddle himself. She hooked her right leg over the pommel and reached for the reins.

As they rode away, Breyandra turned her head and looked back. Moira was standing in a circle of Gordons with her hands on her hips and shaking her head in disgust.

Breyandra's mouth curved in amusement. "Good riddance to you as well," she retaliated in a soft mumble.

Chapter Six

Under any other circumstances the realization that she was returning to Saltoun would have been a source of exhilaration to Breyandra Fraser. But not this time.

Granted, she was glad to be going home, she told herself. Granted, she was relieved to no longer be under the same roof as Duncan Gordon. Granted, the same sights that had thrilled her so much the previous day still abounded about her. The blossoms smelled as sweet, the trees rose just as leafy and majestic, the streams and rills knew no Fraser boundary as they channeled a passage to the lochs below. So what was spoiling her appreciation of these sights?

The pair of very wide shoulders riding on the trail ahead of her.

His shoulders were just another provocative

irritation about David Gordon, along with long muscular legs, strong arms, brawny chest, rippling muscles, dark eyes, thick eyelashes, sensuous mouth, devastating grin, and a damned dimple right in the center of a very stubborn jaw.

Breyandra had thought of nothing but David Gordon from the time they had left Strehlow that morning. She had had ample opportunity to dwell on her disturbing feelings for him, because he had been silent throughout the journey. In truth, she reasoned irascibly, what else could he be? Breyandra Fraser and David Gordon certainly had nothing to say to one another.

Although curious, Breyandra voiced no question when David swung off the regular route through the forest to follow a path that struck out along the coastline.

A misty spray from the ocean glazed the granite rock of the road that wove through the huge precipices of the sea wall. The faces and clothing of the riders were soon coated with the chilly moisture. Footing became treacherous, so David dismounted and took her horse by the bridle to lead the mare along the narrow trail. Whirlwind followed obediently behind.

Flushed from their nests among the crevices, white gulls and sea swallows fluttered away, flapping and skimming above the heads of the gray seals sunbathing below on the islets that marked the rocky coastline.

David climbed back on Whirlwind when the path finally broadened and opened onto a moor.

Purple heather and yellow grass covered a rolling marshland spotted with patches of brown peaty bogs and tiny lochans of water blackened with moss.

For the next hour, the sun played hide and seek with low clouds that threatened to release their torrent at any time. One moment the travelers were in a beam of warm sunlight, and the next a patch of fog came rolling in from the sea to envelop them in a chilly, damp haze. Eventually a steady drizzle began to fall and the boggy ground beneath them became wet and spongy.

The moor was gloomy in the fog and drizzle. Breyandra shivered and tightened her cloak about her. She groused silently to herself as to why David had chosen this route. Under the best of circumstances, a moor was difficult and often treacherous to cross, she reflected with disgust. In the rain, the difficulty was increased tenfold. Breyandra was fatigued, and horrible doubts crossed her mind; perhaps he had brought her to this bleak spot to murder her and dispose of her remains!

Engrossed in her thoughts, Breyandra failed to notice that David had stopped on the trail. She rode right into him.

"Damn it, woman, you are awkward."

Her retort died in her throat when she saw what had caused him to halt. The body of a man lay grotesquely sprawled across the path. The man's throat had been cut from ear to ear.

David dismounted and knelt down to examine the corpse. The garb the victim wore was that of a Highland farmer—a belted plaid and a plain, homespun wiz; the white shirt now stained with blood.

David grimaced in outrage. "Why would anyone murder a simple croftsman harvesting some peat for fuel?" Suddenly his expression hardened at the sight of the man's hands. All the fingers had been cut off. "Good Lord!" David exclaimed. He turned to Breyandra in fury. "Is this nefarious deed some more Fraser villainy?"

Breyandra was revolted by the savagery, and she deeply resented the accusation against her kinsmen. She climbed down from her mare, rising in defense of her clan. "This is not the act of a Fraser. My people are not murderers."

Her protest produced a contemptuous shrug of his shoulders. "Well, no Gordon would do this." He checked the corpse further and glanced up at her in surprise. "The body is still warm. The blood has not congealed. The blackguards that did this must still be nearby."

As soon as he spoke, David sensed danger and bolted to his feet. Moving with a speed so swift it appeared to be a single motion, David grabbed Breyandra, shoved her behind him, and unsheathed his sword.

Before she realized what was happening, three men brandishing weapons rushed at them through the fog. David faced the attackers and slowly inched backwards until Breyandra's back was pressed protectively against Whirlwind's side. "Steady, Whirlwind," he ordered.

Now with Breyandra safely shielded, David drew a dirk from his waist. The assassins, all attired in black, fanned out as they cautiously approached, held in abeyance by the sweeping arc of David's sword.

Breyandra trembled with fright as she tried to peer over David's shoulder. The cutthroats pressed their attack, and David fought off their thrusts, but he had to remain immobile to shield her. Breyandra realized that her position was a handicap to him, and she glanced about, frantically seeking a way to help him. Spying a pistol sheathed on his saddle, she grabbed it.

No stranger to firearms because of her father's careful tutelage as a child, Breyandra cocked the pistol, took careful aim at the nearest assailant, and pulled the trigger. The blast went off in his face, and the man fell to the ground. Spooked by the loud noise, her mare bolted and galloped away.

The unexpected blast startled David, and he momentarily dropped his guard long enough for one of the attackers to inflict a grazing wound to his leg. As he continued to parry and fend with the other two men, his doublet became bloody from a shoulder wound. A lethal thrust to the heart killed one of the attackers, but before David could extract his sword, the other man was upon him and succeeded in piercing David's side. David knocked aside the man's arm with his knife and drove the dirk into his attacker's stomach.

The startled man's mouth gaped open and for several seconds he stood as if suspended. Then his weapon slipped through his fingers and he fell to the ground.

Weakened by the loss of blood, David slumped to a knee. Breyandra stared in horror at the carnage around her. Four dead men lay on the ground. Sometime during the fight, the rain had begun falling heavily, and the water now blended with the blood of the corpses to form several red, watery pools.

Sickened, she turned away from the sight. Her face was ashen with shock; she couldn't believe she had shot and killed a man.

"Well, mistress, are you going to stand there until I bleed to death?" David grumbled.

Breyandra, jolted to action, turned back to aid him. His doublet and trousers bore bloody evidence of his wounds, and the pouring rain had saturated his clothing.

Weakly rising to his feet, David stumbled against Whirlwind. "We must get out of this downpour where we can tend your wounds," Breyandra said worriedly. Her own hair was hanging in sodden strands and rain was running off her face.

"My plaid. Give me my plaid." Any movement was a painful effort for him. Reaching for his plaid from the saddle, Breyandra spread it around him. "I know of a hut nearby," David mumbled. His condition was worsening steadily, and he barely had enough strength to mount his horse. Breyandra climbed on behind him.

Turning Whirlwind around, David retraced the route over the trail until he turned off from the narrow path. The falling rain helped him to remain conscious as he led them to a small shack in the middle of the bog. He slid off

Whirlwind and stumbled into the deserted hut, where he collapsed on a straw pallet.

Breyandra found some matches and tow by the fireplace and quickly ignited the fiber. She held the burning hemp aloft and, peering around the room, spied a candle on the table. After lighting the taper, she tossed the burning tow in the fireplace, then added some kindling, and soon a fire burned on the hearth.

Finding a tattered blanket, she spread the heavy plaid before the fire to dry while she tended to David's wounds.

Besides being wet with rain, his clothes were soaked with blood, and she had to remove them. Feeling timid at first, she took a deep breath and proceeded with determination. After all, this was no time for modesty, and, she told herself objectively, he already had seen *her* naked.

Breyandra struggled to pull off his wet, knee-high boots and then slipped the hose off each long muscular leg. The task of removing the doublet and shirt was more difficult. She had to hold up his head and shoulders while sliding the garments over his head. The wound to his shoulder had been seeping blood, and the movement increased the flow.

The final job remaining was to remove his trousers. With a shuddering sigh, she pulled them down and slipped them off his legs.

Breyandra gasped at the sight of the long, jagged scar that ran from above his knee to the inside of his groin. Obviously an old injury, the puckered, reddish gash was still in the stage of healing and was more unsightly than the

109

wounds he had just received. She felt a twinge of guilt as she recalled the vicious kick she had rendered to the area during their struggle the previous evening. Tenderly she covered his naked body with the tattered blanket.

Water was a prime consideration in tending to his wounds, so she put out several kettles to catch the rain, then searched the small hut for something to cleanse and bind the wounds with. Finding nothing, she ripped strips from the underskirt of her gown.

Breyandra went out into the driving rain, removed the saddle from Whirlwind, and toted the heavy burden into the hut. Then she went out again to bring in the rainwater that had collected. She put a kettle of water over the fire to boil.

Her cloak was now sodden, so she stretched the garment out before the fire in the hope it would soon dry. Also soaked, her slippers were almost falling apart. Breyandra removed them and set them on the hearth.

When the water finally came to a boil, Breyandra was able to tend to David. Dismayed that he was still unconscious, she set about her task. The wound on his leg was a surface graze that had caused a great deal of bleeding without inflicting serious damage. Within minutes, Breyandra had cleansed and bound the leg.

The injuries to his side and shoulder were more severe. The point of a sword had deeply penetrated the flesh. She slowly and carefully cleansed the wounds, and then pressed compresses against them to stop the bleeding.

Unable to think of anything else she could do to help David for the time being, she covered him with the blanket.

Moving to the table, Breyandra sat down on a chair and began to study the hut in detail. The small room felt strange, and, even more disconcerting, it harbored an unusual collection of bottles. Bottles in all sizes and shapes littered the floor and shelves. She had no idea what they contained, but the sight of them caused her to shudder. In addition, neither food provisions nor clothing were to be found anywhere. Yet, the fireplace was stacked with wood, and the hut appeared to be lived-in.

She leaned back in the rickety chair and sighed disconsolately. What was she doing in this strange place? She should flee while the opportunity presented itself.

Her gaze shifted to the helpless man on the corner pallet. She couldn't leave him alone. But then, what did she owe David Gordon—or any Gordon for that matter? She vowed to herself that when he regained consciousness, she would leave and go back to where she belonged.

To keep busy in the wretched hut, Breyandra took another kettle of rainwater and, as best she could, rinsed out his bloody garments, then strung them up to dry. Her own damp clothing had dried on her back, except for her hose. She slipped off her stockings and added them to the many garments now hanging about the room.

When her stomach began to growl, Breyandra realized she hadn't eaten anything since the two scones that morning. A search of the saddlebags produced oats, obviously for Whirlwind, several hard-boiled eggs, a piece of cheese, and two apples. She was well pleased with her scavenging, and after eating an egg and one of the apples, she put the rest aside for the morning.

The rain had slackened to a drizzle, and Breyandra took the opportunity to feed and water Whirlwind. The plaid had dried, so she covered David with it and put the tattered blanket over Whirlwind to ward off the night's damp chill.

Now nothing remained to be done except to build up the fire. The heat from the blaze was a welcome comfort to her chilled bones. Breyandra stretched out before the fire. Her mind quickly drifted to thoughts of Saltoun, and she wondered what her father was thinking about her absence. If, somehow, he had learned of her capture, what might he be doing to secure her release?

Simon Fraser and his retinue clattered across the Outer Bailey, and the heavy portcullis clanged down behind them as the weary and sodden group returned to Saltoun.

Elysia anxiously jumped to her feet as Simon entered the Great Hall. His spurs beat an angry staccato on the stone floor as he strode across the room to the fireplace. He leaned his head against the mantel and stared into the flames. His very bearing and posture told her what she had been dreading to hear.

Elysia waited in silence for him to speak. Finally he turned, and she saw that the anger in his eyes had been replaced by bleakness. "The Gordons have her."

Elysia's despair was released in a mournful sigh. "Dear God."

Simon drew a pair of sodden pumps out of the pocket of his doublet. "These are Breyandra's, aren't they? They were on Gordon land. Wolf led us to them and then the damned dog disappeared."

Elysia covered her mouth to force back a strangled sob. She recognized the slippers at once and remembered a happier day in France when the young girl had selected them. "What are you going to do, Sim?"

He looked up wearily. "Wait for a ransom note, I suppose." His shoulders slumped in despair. She had never seen Simon so dejected. Her heart cried out to this man she loved. Elysia went over to Simon and put her arms around him.

Simon's arms encircled Elysia and he clung to her, needing the comfort of her steadying strength. "Oh, God, love, if Duncan Gordon harms one hair on her head, so help me, I'll call up my clan and arm it for war."

Elysia's eyes brimmed with unshed tears as she drew him tighter into her embrace. The two remained standing alone, clinging to one another in mutual despair.

Chapter Seven

Breyandra awoke to the sound of David crying out from the pallet in the corner. Startled, she hurried over to him. His eyes were closed, and he seemed to be tossing in the torment of a nightmare. She placed a hand on his forehead and found he was hot to the touch. Breyandra snatched aside the plaid that covered him to find his body trembling and sweating, obviously burning with fever.

She ripped another strip off her underskirt. The rapidly diminishing garment now hung only to a pair of fetching, seldom-seen, dimpled knees. Wetting the torn cloth, Breyandra began to cleanse David's feverish body with the cool rag. The muscles of his wide shoulders and powerful biceps were taut as he lay in the throes of delirium. *You're a braw man, David Gordon,* she thought with admiration. Her hands moved smoothly and gently as she sponged the muscular brawn of his chest in her effort to cool him.

Breyandra stopped at the sight of the ragged gash on the inside of his thigh, and wondered how he had received the dreadful injury. Avoiding the area surrounding the scar, she finished the task as swiftly as she could.

Fretting with concern, she changed the dressings on his side and shoulder wounds. The supply of strips she had boiled was becoming scarce, and the water cask was low. Resigned, she had to make do with what she had. Seeing that the blood had congealed in his leg wound, Breyandra decided the laceration must be healing, and she removed the bandage.

To her surprise, David's eyes opened, but the usual alertness in their depths was obscured by a lusterless sheen wrought by his high temperature. He appeared startled at the sight of Breyandra, then, despite the fever, a cautiousness returned to his expression.

David tried to raise his head but Breyandra pressed him back to the pallet with a firm hand to his chest. "Don't move. You might start the bleeding again."

David groaned and relented willingly. "I feel as if my body's on fire. How bad are my wounds?"

Breyandra answered hesitantly, "The leg wound doesn't look serious, but I can't say about the side and shoulder wounds. They've stopped bleeding, and I've done the best I can for them."

He closed his eyes, and for a moment she thought he had slipped back into unconsciousness. "Thank you," he murmured so softly she barely heard him.

Breyandra sighed. Even though he was helpless, she was relieved to see that he was conscious. The strange hut along with the eerie moor outside the tiny hovel's bleak walls had caused her unaccustomed anxiety. David's delirium had added to her desolation. After putting a cool cloth to his brow, she regarded him quizzically. "Why are you thanking me?"

He grinned weakly. "For tending to me. I am certain I would have bled to death had you not aided me."

As weak as he was, Breyandra was astonished by the appeal of his smile, which she was helpless not to return. Her face softened into a tentative smile. "I am certain I would have met a similar fate without your intervention, Lord Wilkes."

Her remark amused him, and he managed a light chuckle. "Indeed, Mistress Fraser, you are something of a troublesome twit."

Breyandra sat down on the floor beside the pallet. "I should remind you, Sir Knave, you chose the route that put us on the same path as those blackguards."

He closed his eyes again. Breyandra knew he was exhausted and needed rest, but, vivacious by nature, she welcomed the opportunity to talk. The past days had put an unusual restraint upon her liveliness. "Would you like some water?" she asked.

Once again David Gordon opened his eyes and rested his warm gaze on her. "If it's not too much trouble, Twit."

David appeared to be sleeping when she returned to his side. Although Breyandra knew he needed the water, she was uncertain whether it would be wise to disturb him again.

"I'm awake," David murmured as if reading her thoughts. "It's an effort to keep my eyes open."

Breyandra helped him to raise his head and shoulders high enough to swallow the water. After a few sips, the exertion was so taxing that David fell back in disgust. "God's truth, this is a sorry state to find oneself in."

"At least you managed to drink some water," Breyandra said in an effort to bolster his spirits. She started to turn away and he grabbed her hand. "Please don't leave, Twit."

Breyandra was as pleased as she was surprised by this plaintive request. When he did not release his grasp on her hand, she sat down on the floor. "Would you like to try to eat something?"

He shook his head. "Perhaps later." He slipped back into sleep, still holding her hand.

Breyandra studied him with mixed emotions. This Gordon was an enemy of her clan; he had seized her against her will; he had manhandled her outrageously; he was solely responsible for her being in this desolate spot. Yet, physically, the man fascinated her. He was so beautiful to behold that she felt she could gaze upon him forever and not weary of the sight. His very presence provoked an excitement within her she had never known with any other man. *Foolhardy, forbidden temptations!* Breyandra shuddered at her disturbing fixation. He was wounded and hurt, and her feeling for him was merely pity, she told herself with a decisive toss of her head.

In slumber his face appeared almost boyish to her, except for a dark moustache that lined the top of a wide, sensuous mouth. Thick eyelashes, closed now, rested above high Celtic cheekbones, and she realized the long lashes were the reason his eyes appeared so dark.

None of his mother's rounded, delicate features were present in David's rugged face except for the deep dimple in the chin. *Of course you would prefer to think of your dimple as a cleft, wouldn't you, Sir Knave?* she thought capriciously.

No, the dark eyes, the breadth of the shoulders, and the length of the muscular legs all marked him as his father's son. Her face shifted to a girlish pout. *Yes, you're a true son of a . . . Gordon*, she sighed in remorse.

Soon David's sleep became troubled, and his grip tightened as he thrashed about in torment, muttering incoherently. Several times he cried out to his mother in anguish.

Throughout the night, Breyandra remained at his side, changing the cool cloth on his head and making sure he did not dislodge the bandages on his wounds.

As she listened to his indistinct ravings and tortured outcries, Breyandra came to know a measure of the misery and heartache he had suffered over his mother's defection. For the first time, she realized that not once in the past five years had she given one thought to the effect the turn of events had had on Elysia's son.

Finally, when David lapsed into a calm sleep, Breyandra slipped away from his side to check on Whirlwind. The moor was shrouded in morning fog, and after confirming the well-being of the animal, Breyandra hurried back into the hut, shivering from the chilly air. She wasted no time in adding more wood to build up the fire.

To her dismay, the woodpile was almost depleted. After gulping down a few bites of cheese, Breyandra grabbed her cloak and ventured outside to gather firewood.

The pickings were meager until she came upon an unusually hardy patch of rowan and pine trees struggling to survive amidst the boggy bracken. Breyandra soon had a full armload of the precious fuel and was about to return when she heard hoofbeats. Her spirits soaring, she peered into the fog, hoping the rider could assist her with David Gordon.

Just as she was about to call out, four riders came into view through the thickness of the fog. The words froze in her throat. The men were garbed in long, black-hooded cloaks identical to those worn by the men who had attacked them the previous night. Breyandra quickly stepped back into the concealment of the trees. Her heart pounded in her chest as she waited for them to pass. The sight of three bodies slung over the backs of two horses confirmed her suspicions. Then she bit down on her lip to keep from crying out in anger when she saw that one of the pack horses was her own mare.

When the mysterious riders were safely out of sight and sound, she bolted from her hiding place and sped back to the hut, still toting the heavy firewood in her arms.

David was awake, and his face brightened when Breyandra came in the door. She dumped the wood by the fireplace and hurried to the pallet.

"I was afraid you had left," he said hoarsely.

Breyandra got a cup of water and allowed him to slowly sip the liquid. "I wouldn't desert even a . . . Gordon at a time of need," she chided reassuringly.

He lay back exhausted. "I couldn't blame you if you had gone."

Breyandra set aside the cup and leaned over him excitedly. "My lord, I just saw four more of the same band of cutthroats who attacked us last night. And more's the pity, the blackguards have my mare as well."

David grimaced in alarm at the implication, but kept his voice calm. "Did you recognize any of them?"

"Of course not. I told you the attackers were not Frasers," she replied emphatically.

He pressed his hand to his throbbing head. "Then I wonder who they could be."

Breyandra did not take kindly to his continual aspersions on her clan. Furthermore, she reasoned, if the band were Frasers, why would they head deeper into Gordon country? There was no doubt in her mind to which plaid the loyalty of these cutthroats belonged. "Gordons most likely," she answered with assurance.

David was too weak to argue. *Somehow . . . they had to get back to Strehlow. Somehow . . . he would have to . . .* He fell asleep before he could finish the thought.

He slipped in and out of sleep throughout the day. To pass time, Breyandra tried to analyze the contents of the unappealing powdery substances in the many bottles and jars that lined the floor, wondering where the occupant who lived in the hut had gone. She finally abandoned the effort with a shiver of distaste.

The supply of water was dwindling rapidly, and food was so scarce she barely sampled any more in order to save the remainder for David.

In the evening she checked David's wounds. They appeared not to be showing signs of infection, but he was still feverish. Amid his sporadic mumbling, he repeatedly insisted they would return to Strehlow in the morning.

Before settling down that night, Breyandra loaded David's pistol and slipped the weapon into the pocket of her cloak in order to have protection close at hand.

When she awoke the following morning, she saw David sitting on the chair with his head slumped over on the table. He seemed to have exhausted his strength pulling on his trousers and hose.

"Why didn't you wait for me to help you?"

Breyandra admonished. She cast a fretful glance at the blood-stained dressing on his side. "You've opened your wound. I insist you lie down."

Although David was weary of his invalid condition, the vulnerability of the hut caused him intolerable restlessness. Perspiration dotted his forehead, but his chin jutted forward with obstinacy. "We are returning to Strehlow now, Mistress Fraser."

He rose to his feet and immediately pitched forward into her arms, toppling both of them to the floor. Breyandra had the wind knocked out of her. For several seconds she lay crushed under his weight until she gained enough breath to squirm out from beneath him and sit up.

She rolled David onto his back and leaned over to check his injuries. She was horrified to discover that the shoulder wound had reopened. "I hope your Gordon hide is as thick as your head," she carped angrily.

"I'm sorry, my lady." The faint apology was all he was able to voice in his weakened state.

At the moment, *sorry* was a sorry word indeed to Breyandra Fraser. She was furious with him. She saw two days of diligent nursing gone for naught because of his pigheadedness. Well, she would bode no more. Beautiful or not, the man was a Gordon. In a fanciful moment, because of his injuries, she had permitted herself to overlook that fact, but a Gordon was a Gordon. *A leopard could not change its spots*, she reiterated to herself. They were a murdering, father-stealing, horse-thieving, wretched species which had already degenerated beyond redemption.

Breyandra bolted to her feet. With arms akimbo and flashing eyes, she glared down at him. "Do you have the strength to return to the pallet, or do you need my assistance to drag you there?"

David Gordon lay on his back and stared up at her, appalled. Beautiful or not, the woman was a Fraser. In a feverish state, due to his injuries, he had permitted himself to forget that fact. But a Fraser was a Fraser, and *birds of a feather flocked together*, he remembered bitterly. They were a murdering, mother-stealing, horse-thieving, lawless lot of miscreants, who had not advanced beyond the Stone Age.

"You, Mistress Fraser, have a disposition as vituperative as your tongue."

"Well then, since I am so abusive, Lord Simpleton, you can just lie there and bleed to death." Grabbing her cloak, Breyandra stormed out of the hut. A nicker from Whirlwind tempted her to mount the horse, but she knew that, in his condition, David Gordon could not make it back to Strehlow on foot. Besides, she told herself, to ride the horse she would have to go back inside to get the saddle. She would *walk* to Saltoun. She made up her mind. Once she reached the border, she was certain to encounter someone who would offer her aid.

Breyandra seethed with fury as she strode along, mumbling. "Why should I remain and take his verbal assault? What debt do I owe

David Gordon? It's time I remember that I'm the daughter of Simon Fraser. Just because we're fair and merciful by nature, our enemies think us weak. Well, many have learned too late the folly of that belief," she chafed, kicking angrily at the purple heather in her path.

"For two days I've tended the wounds of that Gordon ingrate, gone without food, and suffered his taunts. But no longer. Nay, Mistress Fraser, the self-appointed despot is never going to take advantage of your charitable nature again."

With that resolve, the charitable Breyandra drew the pistol from her cloak, took careful aim, and blew the head off a grouse in the bracken.

For several minutes after Breyandra's stormy departure, David Gordon lay still, attempting to restore his waning strength. "Good riddance to the harridan," he grumbled in disgust. "I've suffered wounds before and borne them with much less fuss and ado than her cloying ministrations. Good Lord, every time I fall asleep the troublesome twit wakes me with her fidgeting and twattle. Her libertine father may be willing to tolerate her shrewish tongue, but not me, not David Gordon. I'm a Highland warrior. I've walked with giants, cast my shadow with kings."

With that resolve, the Highland warrior crawled across the floor to the corner pallet on his hands and knees.

The succulent aroma of roasting fowl teased David to wakefulness. When he opened his eyes, Breyandra was sitting before the fireplace holding a grouse on a spit. For several moments he lay quietly, watching her carefully turn the long stick to keep the bird from charring.

Finally he attempted to speak in a feigned gruff growl. "So you're back." Somehow the remark contained more pleasure than reproach in its delivery.

"What does it look like?" Breyandra grumbled. "Or is shortsightedness another Gordon infirmity?"

David lay back on the pallet. He was too pleased to be riled. "Why did you come back?"

He had asked the very question Breyandra had been pondering for the past few hours. Why *had* she come back? Conscience, of course; the thought of a human being lying wounded and helpless would instinctively impel her to respond. But conscience alone had not caused her to return. Her feeling for *him* had brought her back. *Him! David Gordon!*

No! Her mind refused to accept the reckless emotion. Somehow, common sense must prevail. But how does one use mere reason to smother the heart's desire?

Breyandra decided to try disdain.

"I decided the walk to Saltoun was too long. I could suffer your presence easier than blistered feet."

He did not believe her explanation for a moment. "You could have taken Whirlwind and *ridden* home."

"I had no more inclination to struggle with an obstinate horse than with its equally mulish master," she retorted.

"I'm glad you're back, Twit."

Breyandra turned her head and found his gaze resting on her. The warmth in his dark eyes stirred a response in her heart. Disdain withered, and she grinned sheepishly. "The grouse is roasted. I'll check your dressings, then we can eat."

Self-consciously, Breyandra set to the task. David's gaze did not waver from her face. Under his fixed stare, every movement and touch as she examined the wounds took on intimacy. The hot blush that swept her rose to nearly the degree of the fever that had ravaged his body. She turned away in relief when the task was completed.

Rain had begun to fall at sundown, and Breyandra had been able to catch more water. She placed the candle on the floor near his pallet, and they ate the roasted fowl and drank the fresh rainwater. To the weary pair, the meal tasted scrumptious, comparable to a royal feast.

David's fever had broken, but he was still very weak. Traces of his illness were evident in the pallor and drawn hollows of his face. Still, he was confident he would be well enough to ride in the morning. This time, Breyandra had no quarrel with his judgment, and agreed to return to Strehlow the next day.

When David finished the grouse, she handed him an apple. "Here, you eat this. I've had enough."

His fingers closed over hers when he reached for the piece of fruit and for a moment their eyes locked until David grinned crookedly. "Shall I check it for worm holes? I remember the last time you offered me an apple."

Breyandra remembered the occasion and smiled sheepishly. She began to busy herself by cleaning up the few dishes. David chomped on the apple, his eyes following her movements, grinning to himself as he recalled that bygone day.

With each passing day of his incarceration, David was becoming more irritable. His nerves were so raw he was no longer able to tolerate the childish teasing of Breyandra. At every opportunity the young girl plagued him with taunts, ranging from the serious threat of having Wolf attack him to her silly pleasure in calling him Lord Vermin. Despite Simon Fraser's leniency toward the Gordons, Breyandra did not let David forget for a moment that he was their prisoner.

Consequently, he was quite surprised one after-noon when Breyandra entered the hall with a contrite smile, carrying a basket of apples as a peace offering. He grabbed a piece of the succulent fruit and bit into it. Only to find a worm! David rummaged through the other pieces of fruit and discovered they all contained worm holes. At the sight of Breyandra laughing as she peered around the door, he realized he had been duped. Angry with himself for allowing her to hoodwink him so easily, David threw the basket at her just as Simon Fraser entered the hall.

Sighing sorrowfully, Breyandra got down on her hands and knees to pick up the apples while her father glared his disapproval at the young man. "He is so ungrateful, Father," Breyandra purred. "I don't understand why you continue to be so charitable to him." She departed the hall, shaking her head sadly.

Now grinning from the memory of that day, David lay back on his pallet. "My compliments to the chef. Tell me, my lady, how did you learn to roast a fowl so skillfully?"

"Frankly, Sir Knave, I think you were overly hungry, but I'll accept the compliment because I'm sure it doesn't come easily from you." She grinned to lighten the sting of the words and hugged her knees to her chin.

"When I was younger, my father often took me hunting," she said. "He taught me the ways of the wild, and how to prepare our meals. We spent many nights in the forest by a campfire." She rested her head on her knees with a soft smile, recalling the happier bygone days. "They were wonderful times. Usually there were just the two of us." Her face sobered. "But we don't do that any more since . . . because . . ."

". . . of my mother," David finished sagely.

She lifted her head and met the wary glance in his eyes. Breyandra didn't want the pleasant mood between them to change, but realized that the mention of Elysia had affected him. "I want to apologize to you, David."

She saw his expression alter in surprise, but did not know whether the change was due to her words or the use of his name. Breyandra had no choice but to sail the course she had set. "I didn't mean the unkind remark I made about your mother."

She saw a muscle begin to twitch nervously in his jaw as he tried to hold his feelings in check. "In the time Elysia's been with us, I've grown most fond of her."

"Yet you were quick to malign her name," he challenged defensively.

"Only to strike out at you. I am truly sorry for spitefully using her name."

David allowed himself to relax. He had waited a long time to hear word of his mother. "Is she well?" Breyandra nodded. "And content?" he asked, fearful of the answer.

Breyandra smiled in understanding. "I think she's very content, except for missing you. A day never passes that Elysia does not think of you."

"And he treats her kindly?" David asked.

Breyandra was aghast to think David could believe anything to the contrary. "Father? Why, he adores her. He'd lay down his life for her."

David thought of the brutality his mother had suffered at the hands of his own father. "Then I am glad for her."

Breyandra knew David was struggling with his own loss and understood the heartache, for she had suffered similar pain. "I know how you feel, David. At first I was jealous of the relationship and irritated by your mother's presence. I soon saw the error of my resentment. Elysia has brought so much happiness into my father's life. I couldn't hate the one who has brought him such love. I'm grateful to her. And I know she is happy too, because Father loves her just as much."

Breyandra glanced sheepishly at David. He

appeared lost in his own thoughts. She saw the bittersweet mixture of sorrow and relief on his face, and her heart cried out to him. How would she have endured the pain of being denied her father for five years?

"But what of your father's wife? It must be awkward for my mother at Saltoun," David said.

"We have not been in Scotland these past years. Father purchased a villa in France, and Lucretia remained at Saltoun."

The news came as a shock to David. "But your father is laird of his clan. What of his duties?"

"Of course, my father returned to Saltoun several times, but my uncle, who was my father's heir, took over the duties of Saltoun in his absence. My uncle had a fatal accident, and we had to return."

"So now all of you will be remaining in Scotland," David mused pensively.

Breyandra suspected the reason for his reflection. "When you heal, come to Saltoun and visit your mother, David. I know my father will open the gate to you. He desires Elysia's happiness as much as you do."

David knew a reunion would be out of the question. His mother had betrayed the honor of the Gordon clan. As the next Laird of Strehlow, duty compelled him to put the interests of his clan ahead of his own.

David closed his eyes. "More important matters than my mother's happiness must be considered, my lady. Tomorrow we return to Strehlow."

* * *

"Please, my lord, 'tis my place to go," the Captain of the Guard pleaded. "The Lady Breyandra's safety was my responsibility, and I failed my duty."

Simon Fraser shook his head. "Breyandra is my daughter, captain. I will dress in the garb of a simple crofter and rescue her myself."

"My lord, a peasant's garb will not disguise your noble bearing," the soldier contended. "Allow me, my lord. My face is not known at Strehlow, so I will be able to move in and out of the gate without difficulty. I will take one of my men with me to bring back word to you as soon as we are able to learn the circumstances of Lady Breyandra."

Elysia Gordon saw the wisdom in the captain's reasoning. She had been listening to the argument between the two men. Several days had passed since Breyandra's disappearance with neither word nor ransom note, and Simon was too concerned about her welfare to wait longer. He had devised a plan to travel to Strehlow incognito.

"Captain Trevor is right, Sim. Many at Strehlow would know you on sight. Particularly Duncan, were he to spy you. The captain's suggestion is prudent. You could be of no help to Breyandra in a dungeon cell of Strehlow."

Simon balled his fists in frustration. He knew their arguments were valid. Breyandra's interests would best be served by cautious wisdom rather than blundering emotion. As difficult as waiting would be, he would have to be patient.

Chapter Eight

Approaching the main entrance in daylight, Breyandra marveled at the massive splendor of Strehlow. She had not seen the magnificence of the castle the night they had slipped through the smaller postern gate.

Norman arches curved over large Tudor windows and the broad doors were carved with armorial patterns. A pepper-box turret topped each of the four, square-cut corners, and several more of these turrets perched along the crenellated battlements.

Breyandra looked up at the tall structure and was forced to shield her eyes from the glare of the bright sunlight reflecting off the immense glass windows of the gabled bays.

The clachan of Streyside had sprung up outside the palisades of the Outer Bailey, and small thatched cottages were spread out on the hillside below the high walls.

As they waited for the gateman to raise the heavy portcullis that separated the castle from this outer ward, Breyandra glanced with interest at the Gordon crest carved into the arch of the gatehouse.

The passages of the Outer Bailey were narrow, but they bustled with the sights, sounds, and odors of artisan shops, cattle pens, horse stables, and the garrison of soldiers retained within the walls. Crofters from the clachan wandered about, freely hawking their wares or seeking services.

As she and David rode into the secure interior of the keep, Breyandra was unaware of the two men dressed in peasants' garb who had been watching her with keen interest.

The return journey had taken a toll on David Gordon. He could barely remain in the saddle and was on the brink of toppling to the ground. Breyandra called for help, and two guards rushed over to catch him just as he slipped from the saddle.

Disheveled and dressed in a gown torn to her knees, Breyandra presented a wild image to the curious crowd that quickly gathered around the young lord. The assemblage was even more startled when she drew a pistol and recklessly brandished the weapon before her.

"Take him straightaway to his room and don't stop for anyone," she ordered.

Breyandra had made up her mind she would

bode no interference from David's drunken father or the slovenly housekeeper. If the staggering beast who sired David took one step toward her, she was prepared to shoot him right between the eyes.

Breyandra succeeded in conveying her message. No one attempted to block her entrance when she stormed across the inner ward and entered the Great Hall.

With another menacing wave of the weapon, Breyandra motioned to the two soldiers carrying David to mount the stairway. Once at the top, the bewildered men followed behind as she led them down the long gallery to David's chamber and threw open the door.

"Put him on the bed," she ordered curtly. Looking about, she saw with disgust that the room had not been tidied since the morning they had departed.

At that moment, Moira came bustling into the room. "Jus' wha' be ye doin' hee?" The housekeeper drew up in surprise, knitting her brow into a frown at the sight of Breyandra standing at the bedside.

"I want some clean linen strips and hot water at once," Breyandra ordered.

Both men looked at Moira in confusion, anticipating that with the arrival of the housekeeper they could be gone from the room and the intimidating pistol.

"An' I'll be lang cauld in me grave befer I take auders frae a Fraser hizzy." Moira, not one to be easily coerced; stood her ground.

"You do what I say, old woman, or you soon

135

will be cold in that grave," Breyandra snapped feistily, brandishing the weapon.

Breyandra had expected resistance from either Duncan Gordon or this wretched woman; she herself was not about to back down.

"Do what she tells you, Moira," David weakly intervened. He had regained consciousness and had heard the hostile exchange between the two women.

Breyandra cut off any further objection from Moira with a sharp command. "Bring a tub with hot water for bathing as well. And be quick about it."

"'Tis a piteous day fer 'r clan wheen a Fraser cay speek sic a wa' 'n a hall or hame o' a Gordon." With a disgruntled glare in Breyandra's direction, the woman turned on her heel and flounced from the room. The two soldiers followed behind, gratified to get away.

"You're a bold wench, I'll say that for you, Twit." Admiration shone in David's eyes as he grinned at her.

Smiling culpably, Breyandra slipped the pistol into the pocket of her cloak. "What was I to do? With you unconscious, the situation called for a bold action, or I'd have found myself chained to the wall again."

She slipped off her cloak and sat down on the bed. David could feel himself slipping away in drowsiness and reached for her hand. "Don't leave me, Twit," he murmured just before closing his eyes.

Breyandra felt his brow and discovered his fever had flared up again. She waited anxiously for the water and linen with which to cleanse him. It seemed an eternity before Moira entered the room carrying a tray. Swaggering haughtily, the servant was accompanied by an older man who was so stooped over he appeared to be humpbacked. Gray hair fringed the bald pate of his head.

"Ay brae th' a'chemest an' hea wea be tendin' tu th' yang laird. Ye cain be aff ta th' raam ney daar," Moira declared smugly.

Breyandra cast a hesitant glance toward the bed. David seemed awake, but looked pallid. The old man began to examine the wounds. *He looks competent enough*, Breyandra thought grudgingly, *and obviously an alchemist is more medically qualified than I*. Against her better judgment, and with a fretful backward look toward the silent figure on the bed, Breyandra departed.

She entered the chamber next to David's and found the small room sparsely furnished; a bed, a table, and a single lighted candle were its only contents. Oddly, there was no fireplace. *At least the bed hasn't been slept in*, Breyandra thought with relief after a brief inspection of the room. She shivered from the cold, and then remembering her discarded cloak in David's room, turned about to retrieve it.

Breyandra opened the door to his chamber and stepped inside. For a moment, she froze in horror at the sight; the old man was applying leeches to David! He had removed the dressings on the wounds, and already one of the parasites was gorged on David's shoulder.

"What are you doing?" Breyandra cried, rushing to the bed. "Get that horrid thing off him at once!" She shoved the old man aside and pulled the suckling worm from the wound. At least three inches in length, the leech squirmed, hideously swollen with David's blood. She flung it down on the tray.

David's eyes were closed and he appeared to be unconscious. "What have you done to him," Breyandra cried, wide-eyed and distraught.

Shocked, the old man regained his footing and looked at her as if she were demented. "I gie him a pawder fer the fever. Bu' air ye daft, lass, the yang mon mus' be bled."

Breyandra drove him away from the bedside. "He's lost too much blood already. Both of you get out of here at once. And take those bloody things with you. I'll take care of him myself," she cried frantically.

Suddenly aware that she must appear hysterical to the startled pair, Breyandra took several deep breaths to regain control of herself. When her composure was restored, Breyandra turned to Moira. "I gave you instructions earlier to bring hot water and linen. Why haven't you obeyed them?"

The icy calm in her voice was more menacing to the housekeeper than Breyandra's earlier threats. Moira picked up the tray. "Cum alang, Ian Fletcher, we're nae nided hey."

Breyandra closed the door firmly, slipped the bolt in place, and returned to the bed. Tears misted her eyes as she gazed down at David's face. "I'll take care of you," she sniffed. Her hand reached out and tenderly brushed the hair off his forehead. "I won't leave you again, Sir Knave."

Soon a servant arrived with the supplies she had requested. While she sponged David and bandaged the wounds, the man returned with a tub and began to fill it with buckets of hot water.

"What is your name?" she asked kindly as the man busied himself building a fire on the hearth.

"Angus Gordon, m'lady." From the look of his suspicious sideward glance, Breyandra knew that Moira's tongue had been busy wagging in the scullery.

"Well, Angus Gordon, we will need a tray of food in about two hours," she instructed, hoping David would be awake by that time. The man nodded and shuffled out of the room without uttering another word.

Breyandra bolted the door behind him and returned to David's bedside. She sat down on the bed, comforted by the even rise and fall of his chest as he slept. The powder the old man had given him appeared to have helped, because his forehead no longer felt feverish.

"You needed at least one more day of rest before attempting such an arduous journey," she chided tenderly. "But no, you stubborn coof, you wouldn't listen to reason." She turned away with an indulgent shake of her head.

Satisfied that David's needs had been served for the moment, Breyandra stripped off her clothing and climbed into the tub. As the warm water enveloped her weary body, the fatigue gradually dispelled, and she relaxed, savoring the sheer luxury of being in a bath. Nothing, she reflected, had ever felt so sublime. She allowed herself the pleasure of lolling in the soothing water until it became tepid. Then, in a flurry of activity, she vigorously scrubbed herself and washed her hair.

Her skin glowed with a rosy hue when she reluctantly stepped out of the tub and toweled herself. After a disgruntled glance at her soiled clothing, she rummaged through the armoire and found a white shirt that belonged to David. The garment hung to her knees and the sleeves to her fingertips, but being clean, it satisfied her present need.

Snatching the brush from the clothespress, Breyandra sat down on the floor before the fireplace. She basked in the warmth of the fire as she ran the silver-handled brush through her long hair in slow, sensuous strokes. She had no idea of what a provocative picture she made to the young man who had awakened and lay watching her.

Still oblivious to his attention, Breyandra stopped brushing as her eyes became arrested by the dance of the flames, and for a while she sat motionless, mesmerized by the fire. Suddenly, whether by capricious chance or by Fate's design, she sensed his eyes on her. Slowly obeying the compelling command, she turned her head and their gazes locked in an undisguised message of desire. The quickening of her breath matched the rhythm of his, and for an interminable moment their hearts beat as one. As she rose to her feet and was drawn to the bed, neither gaze wavered from the depths of the other's eyes.

Breyandra groped for the bedside and sat down gingerly. "How are you feeling?" The hushed breathlessness of the query made them acutely aware of the intimacy of their seclusion.

David raised his hand and curved it around the nape of her neck, then slowly drew her head down to meet his own. She closed her eyes and with a sigh of surrender parted her lips.

The kiss was warm and persuasive, his mouth taking possession of her lips. Long-suppressed emotions and desires surged into passion, and his mouth hungrily began to devour hers. An erotic shudder swept her spine when his tongue slipped into the intimate chamber of her mouth.

David sat up and pulled her down to his lap. With no evidence of weakness in the arms that held her, he leaned across to trail moist kisses down the slim column of her neck.

Her arm slipped to his neck, drawing his head back to her own. His mouth crushed down in an overpowering demand that drained the breath from her, leaving her struggling for air. He shoved up the shirt to bare her breasts, dipping his head to brush the sensitive tips of her breasts with his tongue. Then with a tantalizing stroke that reduced her to involuntary moans, he trailed his hand along the sensitive plane of her stomach and cupped the throbbing core of her being in his heated palm.

Her moans turned to breathless gasps when his mouth closed moistly around an extended nipple. He shifted his mouth to her other breast.

Her body became sensitized with rapture, and the brush of his bristled chin on the swollen tips was an erotic torture. She groaned from the ecstatic sensation.

A loud rapping on the door wrenched her back to an awareness of the world, which only seconds before had existed solely within the sensuous bounds of their bodies. Her startled stare met the astonishment in his eyes, now heavily laden with passion, and the blush that crept to her cheeks made her even more desirable to him. Breyandra pushed herself from his arms and bolted from the bed. Her composure shaken, she immediately responded to the summons at the door.

Moira was waiting impatiently with a tray. Her censuring glance swept the young woman's disheveled appearance, and Breyandra regretted that she hadn't taken the extra moment to pull on her cloak to conceal her scanty garb.

The housekeeper brushed past her and slammed down the tray on the bed stand. "Hir be yer vittals, m'lord. Wey ye be wantin' annathen' mare?" Her pinched face registered her disapproval.

"Address that question to the Lady Breyandra, Moira," David replied calmly.

"Weel?" she asked disgustedly, slanting an insolent glance at Breyandra.

"Our clothing needs to be laundered and my underskirt replaced. It is beyond repair." Then, as if testing her might, Breyandra added firmly, "Furthermore, I want this room thoroughly cleaned tomorrow, and the linen changed on the bed. When those tasks are completed, you will begin a thorough cleaning of the whole castle, which your slovenliness has allowed to be turned into a sty. Do you understand?"

Moira was enraged and turned to David in supplication. "De' ye hee wha' she saed, m'lord?"

David's brow raised in amusement. "I did indeed, Moira. I would advise you to carry out her wishes, or she's likely to set you to mucking out the stalls."

Moira turned to Breyandra, malevolence glaring in her eyes. "'Tis a Fraser witch ye be, an' yev cast a spell on 'im. Moy yer black hourt bern 'n hell befer ye bring thees walls duwn upun us." She kissed a cross hanging from a chain around her neck and rushed from the room.

Breyandra slipped the bolt in place. Turning around with a giggle, she leaned back against the door. "I swear the woman would like to take a claymore to me."

David's passion may have been thwarted, but it had not waned. He patted the bed beside him. "Come back here, Breyandra."

Sobering, Breyandra walked to the tray with a purposeful stride. She did not want to be reminded of the few exquisite moments in his arms. Divine moments during which she had foolishly forsaken all common sense! She knew she had allowed her emotions to control her actions. How often in the past had her father warned her of that dangerous folly, especially when dealing with an enemy. Victory is gained by the coolest head, not the hottest, he had cautioned. Heat slows the brain as well as the body. Well, she would never permit herself to make that mistake again.

"You must eat," she advised stiffly, unable to look at him. She knew that if she did her resolve would weaken.

"I don't want anything to eat, Breyandra. I want you," David declared haplessly. He needed her. His body ached for her.

Breyandra ignored his plea and picked up the tray. "This soup will do you good," she said gruffly and sat down to spoon the broth into his mouth.

David grabbed her hand. "Breyandra, please listen to me."

The spoon flipped and the soup flew in all directions as she slammed the bowl down on the tray. Instantly she sprang to her feet, but his grasp held firm on her wrist, and she turned her face away from him. "No, David, I won't listen to you. What happened earlier between us was a mistake—a dreadful mistake that could have had irrevocable consequences. It must never happen again."

Tears misted her eyes as she turned back to him. "A Fraser and a Gordon—we are enemies, David. We dare not forget that ever again."

David did not intend to accept her argument as the final word, but at the moment he was subdued by her tears. His fingers slipped off her arm and he leaned back.

Accepting the move as capitulation, Breyandra returned to her seat and ladled soup from a tureen into the bowl. "Are you ready to eat now?"

Moving forward, he sniffed the brew, wrinkled his nose in distaste and shook his head. "Smells like muslin-kail. Moira knows how much I hate it." David sat back and, like a pouting child, crossed his arms. "The old harridan probably brought the concoction intentionally."

Breyandra sampled a spoonful of the barley and greens broth. "Well, at least it's hot."

She scooped a second spoonful and was about to sip it when he leaned forward. "Very well, I'll have a taste."

Breyandra raised the spoon to his mouth. "You see, it's quite good, isn't it?" He shrugged negligently without answering.

Several times in the course of finishing the soup, David interrupted her to sip a spoonful himself. Each time, Breyandra suggested filling a bowl for him, but he consistently rejected the offer.

When Breyandra poured herself a cup of tea, David reached for the cup and sampled the brew. Exasperated by his game, her patience dwindled. "Do you want me to pour a cup for you?" He shook his head.

He continued to be a nuisance throughout the meal; whatever she chose to eat, David sampled a portion. Even though his boyish smile revealed his intent to annoy her, Breyandra verbally ignored his teasing. She decided to play her own game by nibbling from all of the food on the tray to make certain that *he* had a proper meal.

Her strategy was successful, and when every bite of food and every drop of tea had been consumed, David glanced at the barren tray and shook his head in mock condemnation. "It's a blessing I wasn't hungry. For such a scrawny lass, you have an enormous appetite, Twit."

Breyandra gritted her teeth at the remark, then grinned at her undetected ploy. "And I trust, Sir Knave, in the morn you will be well enough to eat your own food, so I can enjoy mine."

He chuckled warmly, and she rose to her feet with a smile. "Now I suggest you rest."

David lay back. Deviltry danced in his dark eyes. "Where are you sleeping?"

"There's a bed for me in the next room."

"There's a bed for you right here." Then all mockery left his eyes. "Please, Breyandra, spend the night with me. The chamber next door has no bolt on the door, and I would fear for your safety. I will sleep before the fireplace, and I promise you I will not touch you."

By his sincere demeanor, Breyandra realized she could trust him. Besides, he was right. She was an enemy to all in this household and a captive in the portentous fortress where Duncan Gordon roamed the long gallery at night.

"Thank you, David. But you do need the comfort of your bed. I will fetch the quilt from the other room and sleep by the fireplace myself."

Breyandra hurriedly procured a quilt and

pillow from the other room and arranged the bedding before the fire. After the nights spent in the spartan hut, her new pallet seemed as inviting as a feather bed.

Although she had made her bed in the very center of the Gordon stronghold, Breyandra lay down with a smile of contentment and within minutes was sound asleep.

Later, David climbed out of bed and moved to her side. For a long moment he stood staring down at her, marveling at her exquisite beauty, marred only by faint purple circles under her eyes. With a twinge of guilt, David realized he was the cause of the minor flaw. He wanted to reach out and run his fingertips along the delicate lines of her face, but knew he didn't dare.

This woman would be his. No senseless feud would keep them apart. The Fate that decreed them enemies had drawn them back to the Highlands to find one another.

Despite his wounds, David knelt and lifted her into his arms, then carried her to the bed and gently laid her down. Breyandra sighed softly in her sleep, and a faint smile of contentment curved her sensuous lips.

Her formidable words echoed through his mind. *A Fraser and a Gordon—we are enemies, David.*

His face softened and he pulled up the quilt to cover her. Somehow the walls that stood between them would be scaled, feuds forgotten.

"So sleep content, my sweet, sweet enemy. Sleep content, sweet enemy mine."

Chapter Nine

Breyandra stirred from slumber with a sense of tranquillity, at peace with her surroundings. She realized instinctively that she was not in her own bed. And yet, a subliminal impression that she had been here before gently drifted through her mind. She burrowed deeper into the feather mattress and, in the final moments before wakefulness, basked in a warm and secure languor.

Sunlight streamed into the room and began to filter through her eyelids as the feeling of déjà vu continued to tease her memory. . . . Had she awakened in this bed at some earlier time?

Her eyelids quivered in the morning light, and Breyandra opened her eyes.

Any morning lethargy that might have lingered dissolved in one flick of her astonished eyes; the head of David Gordon lay on the pillow beside her! For an instant she stared in disbelief at the sleeping man, and then shot up to a sitting position. Perplexed, she looked about the room. She saw the crumpled quilt and pillow on the floor and clearly remembered having gone to sleep on them in front of the fireplace.

But that was all she remembered.

How had she gotten into the bed? Surely she hadn't walked in her sleep! Someone must have carried her here. Casting a furtive glance toward the door, she saw that the bolt was still firmly in place.

Breyandra returned her attention to David Gordon. Relaxed in sleep, his face had a boyish innocence. He couldn't have carried her to the bed. He was much too weak.

At a loss, she shook her head. The only logical explanation was that she had crawled in beside him during the night. A mortifying thought struck her; suppose he awoke and found her there. Visualizing his mischievous grin, she recoiled from the thought of trying to give him an explanation.

Slowly and carefully, Breyandra inched her way out of the bed.

She padded barefoot across the cold floor and knelt beside the tub. Brushing aside the film of soap scum, she rinsed her face and hands in the discarded bathwater. Her feet felt as if they must be turning blue. A hasty search produced her slippers, and she pulled them on her frigid feet.

Shivering, she rubbed her arms to ward off the chill and looked about the room in dismay. She had given all her soiled clothes to Moira and had nothing to wear except David's shirt and her cloak. The situation called for another foray of the armoire.

She selected a pair of David's pants. The knee-high breeches hung off her hips and almost down to her ankles. In another drawer she found a neatly rolled baldric. By the elegance of the belt, she knew that David must use the silk sash for formal occasions at the court. Breyandra hiked up the breeches and wrapped the sword sash around her waist several times to hold up the trousers.

Once again making use of his brush, she swept her hair to the top of her head and tucked the long strands under the wide, cocked brim of his cavalier's hat. Then wrapping her cloak snugly about her, Breyandra stepped back to view the results in the mirror.

She grinned in satisfaction and, with a snappy flick of her finger to the bright green plume adorning the brim, she strode to the door. She poked out her head cautiously. There was no one in the gallery. Her hand closed firmly around the pistol in her pocket and she descended the stairway to the Great Hall.

The sun streamed brightly through an open door at the far end of the large room. Breyandra was drawn to the open door. She stepped outside onto a narrow cobblestone walk tucked between high masonry walls.

Taking the path, she passed beneath a curved arch that supported one of several overhead galleries linking the labyrinth of the battlements and soon found herself in a secluded garden.

A white marble fountain stood amidst a brilliant array of roses in bloom. Set on a dais in the center of the fountain was a carved lion with a crown perched on its marble head. Water sprouted from jets that encircled the rim of the pedestal.

With Breyandra's gasp of pleasure at the beauty of the garden, an old woman who had been rooting among the plants rose up with a guilty start. Her withered face was crisscrossed with wrinkles, and strands of gray hair straggled out from beneath a ragged plaid draped around her head and shoulders.

She brought a bony, gnarled finger to her mouth, cautioning Breyandra to silence, then stuffed the rose petals she held into a shabby poke and heaved the bag over her stooped shoulders.

The old woman's eyes were bright blue. Round and alert, they twinkled with mischief when she paused at Breyandra's side.

Breyandra dipped her head to hear as the old woman whispered, "The past stands betwixt ye, an' it wilt nae dee. 'Til a lion wi'a crown, wilt moik it cum to be." The old crone flashed a toothless grin, then with a parting conspiratorial wink scurried down the walk. To Breyandra's further astonishment, the old woman slipped through a door in the wall.

Breyandra couldn't believe her eyes. She had just come down the same passage and was certain there was no door in that wall. Had she imagined the old woman? And just what did the cryptic message mean?

She bolted to action and hurried to the spot where the old woman had disappeared. Her fingers skimmed the brick in exploration. Sure enough, after close scrutiny she detected the faint outline of a door. However, there was no knob with which to open it.

She was about to abandon her efforts when her probing fingers touched one brick which made the door swing open to reveal a stairway.

Castles were customarily built with an escape passage in the event of a prolonged siege, and, to Breyandra's delight, she realized she had discovered the concealed exit for Strehlow. As soon as she stepped through the narrow gap, the door shut behind her, leaving her in darkness.

She groped along the wall until her fingers encountered a wall sconce containing candles and matches. She lit a taper and held it aloft. The stairway led down into a narrow passage. Breyandra could hear the old woman scuttling somewhere ahead and followed her.

The passage seemed to go on for a very long distance. When she could no longer hear the old woman's footsteps, Breyandra realized she must be nearing the end of the tunnel. She sighed with relief as a stairway appeared, promising an exit. But the stairs led up to a brick wall, and there seemed to be no way out. But since the wall was identical to the one she had passed through getting into the tunnel, Breyandra pressed the brick that was located in the same position as the one on the castle wall. A door swung open.

Before she could extinguish the candle, the

door closed. Breyandra had to repeat the action, this time slipping through before the door closed behind her.

Breyandra discovered she was in a remote section outside the castle walls. She saw the old woman just passing through the portcullis. Driven by curiosity, Breyandra followed.

The Outer Bailey was the usual hub of activity. Spying the woman in the crowd, Breyandra hurried to her side and grabbed her arm. The old woman did not appear to be surprised as Breyandra demanded, "Who are you? Is your message meant for me?"

Before the woman could answer, a man approached them. "Lady Breyandra," he whispered.

At the sight of her father's Captain of the Guard at Strehlow and dressed in the garb of a peasant, Breyandra was so surprised that she relaxed her hold on the woman's arm. The old crone took advantage of the opportunity and hastened away.

"Captain Trevor! What are you doing here?" Breyandra exclaimed.

The soldier took her arm and drew her into the shadows. "I've come seeking you, my lady. Your father is frantic about your safety. Come with me now and we will return to Saltoun."

Breyandra complied instinctively when he took her arm, and they moved toward the gate. She stopped suddenly, remembering David asleep in his chamber. She couldn't leave without saying goodbye. "Tell my father I am fine. I will return to Saltoun as soon as Lord Wilkes is well enough to travel."

The captain was astounded by her sudden refusal. "But, my lady, you will not have a better opportunity to escape."

"I don't have to escape, Captain Trevor. I am not a prisoner here. Lord Wilkes was escorting me to Saltoun when he was wounded. As soon as he is well, I will return." At the dubious frown on the man's face, Breyandra flashed a dimpled smile. "Tell my father not to worry. All is well with me."

The captain was skeptical at her assurance and uncertain of what action he should take. He could hardly drag her to his mount without attracting attention. "Lord Lovet will not tolerate my returning without you, my lady."

"For the time, my remaining here is the wisest course. Now please go, before your identity is discovered."

Against his better judgment, the man departed. Breyandra watched him leave the bailey and climb on his horse. Relieved, she turned back to the business at hand. But there was no sign of the old woman.

There was nothing to be done except complete the task she had set out to do. She asked a passing woman where she could find the shoemaker but received only a glare for an answer. "Gordons are just naturally an unfriendly lot," she reasoned aloud to herself. Searching the various shops, she finally spied a sign bearing the word *Souter*.

The shoemaker looked up curiously when she entered. Priding himself on the ability to discern the peerage at a glance, he realized immediately this must be the Fraser woman who had caused so much gossip about the castle. Truly her dress was strange for a woman of noble birth. But one look at the round eyes flashing beneath the wide brim of the hat brought a wily grin to the cobbler's face. *Witchie or nae, the yang laird hae a discernin' e'e*, he thought appreciatively.

The run-down shop reeked with the stench of tanning hides and glue. Breyandra was relieved when the cobbler finished measuring her foot and she could leave with his assurance that she would have a pair of boots by morning.

She hurried back to the wall, but could not find the hidden entrance. Fearing she might accidentally be detected, Breyandra abandoned the attempt and entered the castle through the front portal.

A young girl was sweeping the floor of the Great Hall. Breyandra offered a friendly smile —which went unreturned—and climbed the stairway. When she opened the door to David's chamber, she found him sitting in the tub.

"What are you doing out of bed?" she exclaimed.

"I might ask you the same question," he replied drolly, and returned to scrubbing his long legs hanging over the edge of the tub.

"And you're getting your wounds wet. How do you expect them to heal?" she scolded. She turned away quickly with a blush when he stood up to climb out of the tub. Hurrying to the window, she kept her attention trained on the court below.

"Where have you been? When Moira told me you were not below, I thought you had left." His voice was at her ear, and she spun around in surprise to find David right behind her. He had wrapped a linen around his waist, but his bare chest and dark hair glistened with moisture.

"I . . . I wouldn't leave without saying goodbye," she mumbled nervously. His nearness disturbed her. He smelled clean and masculine. "You're going to catch a chill if you don't dry yourself and put some clothes on," she cautioned, unable to meet his eyes.

David turned and walked away. Breyandra realized the girlishness of her actions and how foolish she must appear to him. After all, she had seen him naked when she had dressed his wounds. She raised her head. "Should I check your wounds?"

He swung back with an amused grin and spread his arms open. Breyandra approached him, studied the shoulder injury, and found that it was healing. She could feel his tension as he waited for her to check the side wound. Despite her resolve, Breyandra could not bring herself to release the towel.

She looked up into his dark eyes, which were beaming with mischief. "Your wounds appear to be healing rapidly."

"You haven't checked them all, my lady," he challenged with a warm chuckle.

She swallowed nervously. "The shoulder was the worst. I'm sure the others are fine."

David's arms closed, confining her in the circle of his arms. His head dipped and a shiver shook her spine when his mouth slid in a moist trail to her ear. She closed her eyes and enjoyed the exquisite sensation when he began to nibble at the tiny lobe.

He raised his head and smiled down at her. Her thick hair spilled down and dropped to her shoulders as he pulled the large hat off her head and tossed it aside. "Now that we've disposed of that obstacle, let's rid you of this one."

Before Breyandra could respond, David had released the tie on her cloak and brushed it off her shoulders. "What the devil?" He stepped back a step to study her garb. "My baldric? Breeches, too?" he chuckled. He deftly released the knot she had tied in the sash, and Breyandra stood helpless as he slowly unwound the belt from around her waist. The breeches dropped to the floor, leaving her bare except for his shirt.

She finally found her voice. "Stop this at once!" she ordered, and attempted to move out of the arms that had closed around her again.

He lowered his head and kissed the tip of her nose. "I'm only assisting you in your grooming, my lady. Moira brought you some fresh clothes."

Breyandra squealed with pleasure and slipped out of his arms. Several underskirts were lying on the end of the bed beside her own gown, now freshly laundered and pressed.

She hurried over to examine them. "Well, I see the old harridan can obey an order after all." She smiled with delight. "It will be a pleasure to dress like a woman again."

"I like the way you're dressed now," he murmured. Before she knew it, he shoved her on the bed and was upon her.

She tried to maintain a stern expression, frowning under the full force of the devilishness gleaming in his eyes. It was an impossible task. "You're a devil, David Gordon," she chided.

David tenderly cupped her face in his hands and Breyandra's brown eyes became wide with apprehension. She knew her weakness and feared he did as well. Resolve. Honor. They were noble sentiments which rapidly burned beneath the heat of his touch.

"While she filled my bath, Moira gave me a long lecture this morning on how you've bewitched me. Is it true, Breyandra?"

"That's for you to say, my lord," she answered breathlessly.

"Then I would have to say, she may be right. So bewitch me, my lady. It would be a simple task. No potions. No amulets. Just a soft taste of those tempting lips . . . a gentle touch of those silken fingertips," he whispered huskily.

"It's a temptation, Sir Knave. It would almost be worth the dishonor to bring you to your knees." She brushed aside some strands of hair that had fallen across his forehead and smiled up into his eyes. "Indeed, Sir Knave, it would be a moment to savor," she said with a throaty sigh.

"I think a shared moment, my lady." For a breathless instant their gazes remained locked. "So let us savor it."

When he lowered his head, she closed her

eyes and parted her lips in anticipation of the firm pressure of his mouth. Instead, she felt only the warm draft of his breath.

Her eyelids fluttered open and she discovered his head poised above her own, so close their breaths mingled intimately. David's mouth was curved in a vague smile, which did not go undetected by Breyandra. She blushed, and her glance shifted downward. "So now you're mocking me," she accused.

He lifted her chin to force her to meet his gaze, dark eyes gleaming with tenderness. "I'm not mocking you, Breyandra. I'm smiling because it pleases me to hold you in my arms." He threaded his fingers through her hair and his thumbs toyed with the corners of her mouth.

She wanted to believe him, but how could she when she couldn't even trust herself? He began to nibble at her lips and she tried to turn away, but he stopped her and forced her to face him again.

"You know as well as I that naught can be gained by this," she protested breathlessly as he continued his tantalizing play at her lips.

Breyandra glimpsed a flash of anger in his eyes. "Naught? You call this nothing?" he rasped. His mouth crushed down on hers. The drugging kiss turned reservation to provocation, replaced doubt with certainty; the only reality was their awareness of each other.

When breathlessness parted them, he covered her face with tender kisses, then returned to draw the sweetness from her lips. He slid his hand to her breast, eliciting a soft moan when his tongue followed suit.

His play was leisurely. Breyandra still had a grasp on her sanity; she knew she should attempt to resist him. Instead, as if by their own volition, her hands cupped his neck and pressed his head to her breasts in an effort to prolong the pleasure.

Breyandra made no effort to stop him when he slipped the shirt over her head, stopping to place a light kiss on the tip of each breast. When he rose to remove the towel wrapped around him, she reveled under his hungry gaze devouring her nakedness. The desire in his intense perusal lifted her excitement higher, with clan feuds and virginal modesty forsaken as she waited in expectation for the return of his touch.

Pulsating with newly discovered passion, she realized the banality of her earlier protests. Her mouth curved into a smile of the tempting Circe. "You are a determined knave indeed, my Lord Wilkes," she whispered throatily.

He chuckled warmly and lowered himself, gathering her into his arms so that her back rested not on the bed, but on his arms beneath her. His firm thigh anchored between her legs inflamed her. She wrapped her legs around the long, muscular limb as her heated blood surged to the throbbing core of her being and spread throughout her body.

The curves and hollows of her body conformed to the solid length of him in mute testimony to God's divine wisdom in fashioning male and female in matching symmetry. She coiled her arms around his neck, molding their bodies even closer.

The light brush of his moustache was an erotic tickle when his mouth slid to the base of her neck and closed moistly around the pounding pulse. Drawn to the temptation of her parted lips, he resumed the sensual persuasion. The darted forays of his tongue drove her to a mindless fervor and she clutched at the solid flesh of his shoulders, thrilling to the feel of the rippling muscles beneath her fingertips.

Their mouths remained joined and they breathed as one. He rolled over onto his back and his hands shifted down to cup her buttocks. The nerve ends of her spine leapt in response under his fingers when he traced a tantalizing trail up her back. He reached her shoulders and slipped his hands beneath her arms, raising her slightly above him. Suspending her by his powerful arms, David closed his mouth around her breast and began to suckle the tip of first one and then the other. Breyandra threw back her head and gave herself up to the libidinous glory of her feelings.

Her hips and legs still rested on him and the bulge of his manhood pressed against her. Seeking an unknown culmination, her body was building toward eruption. She spread her legs instinctively and his throbbing phallus slipped between them.

David groaned with pleasure and began to move in and out of her. The tempo of his movements increased and she sensed his passion was nearing the explosive stage as was her own. Each breath was wrenched from her lungs as her pounding heart threatened to bludgeon the wall of her chest.

Stifling a groan, David rolled over and drove into her. She sucked in her breath to keep from fainting as her body was wracked with the intermingling of pain and rapture. Then the pain faded, and only ecstasy remained. The exquisite sensation mounting within her was seized and tossed into the swirling force of their combined passion until their bodies erupted simultaneously in cataclysmic tremors.

David collapsed on her with his head buried in the pillow. He remained motionless, his beating heart against her chest. When her own breathing stabilized and he still hadn't moved a muscle, she became concerned. For the first time since he began to make love to her, Breyandra remembered his wounds, and fearing he had harmed himself, she tried to sit up. The weight of his body made the effort impossible. "What are you trying to do?" The words were muffled in the pillow.

"Are you ailing, David?"

He raised his head. His dark eyes were heavy-lidded as he stared down at her with a distracting grin. "What a question at a time like this. You don't attempt to inflate a man's vanity, do you, Twit?"

He hooked an arm around her waist and rolled over. Then he bent down and pulled up the quilt to protect their naked bodies from the chill of the room.

Her head rested on his chest with an arm flung across him. She raised her head and stared down at a pair of audaciously devilish eyes. "I was referring to your wounds. Have they re-opened?"

"Damn the wounds," he mumbled. "If it's a concern to you, check them yourself."

It took little effort to lean across him to see that the shoulder injury appeared unmolested. She slipped her hand down his body in search of the side wound. "Where is it?" she questioned impatiently.

"You're too high," he prompted. Her fingers continued to grope for the injury. "Lower," he cued.

Her hand encountered his swollen phallus and the organ hardened and extended at her touch. "You knave!" she chided, realizing how he had duped her. She started to remove her hand, but his fingers clamped around hers and began to move her hand up and down the extended shaft. "That's where my ache is now," he rasped through gritted teeth, his eyes slotted with passion.

"David, I can't believe you have the strength to—"

"Then do it for me, my lady," he groaned hoarsely and closed his eyes.

Instinct replaced naiveté. With a perceptive smile, Breyandra brushed aside the quilt.

Chapter Ten

"She did what!" Simon Fraser jumped to his feet, uncertain whether he had understood Captain Trevor correctly. Two days earlier, when the rider had returned with the news that his daughter was unharmed, Simon had been jubilant. Now Trevor's arrival had changed his relief to outrage. His exasperation with his incorrigible daughter was unbounded, and the hapless officer tried not to cringe under Simon's anger.

"Lady Breyandra refused to come with me, my lord. She said to tell you she is not a prisoner. The decision to remain is her own, she said, and she will return to Saltoun as soon as Lord Wilkes recovers from his wounds."

"David! Wounded!" Elysia had been listening quietly and sympathetically. Now her eyes widened with alarm and her face paled. "How serious are his wounds?"

Trevor turned contritely to Elysia. Despite the demeaning position she had chosen for herself, the soldier admired the woman's graciousness and dignity. "I don't know, my lady. I only had a brief glance of Lord Wilkes at Strehlow." Trevor couldn't bring himself to tell the distraught woman of her son's pallor and the fact that David was so weak he had fallen from the saddle. "Lady Breyandra said Lord Wilkes was wounded while returning her to Saltoun."

This news added to Simon's agitation. "Good Lord, you mean he was wounded by a Fraser?"

"I can't say, my lord."

Elysia sped from the room to avoid breaking down in front of the two men. As Simon's gaze followed her hasty departure, his eyes filled with apprehension. In the force of the premonition that swept him, all the anger and frustration drained from him. "That will be all for now, Captain Trevor. Thank you for the report." Disheartened, Simon turned and stared pensively into the fire.

For a moment Trevor stood quietly regarding Simon's dejected stance. The only time the captain could recall seeing his beloved laird so forlorn was the night Lady Kathleen had died. Saddened, Trevor pivoted to leave and had reached the door when Simon called out to him. "Captain Trevor, I apologize if I appear ungrateful. I am most appreciative of the risk you took."

"Thank you, my lord," Trevor said simply, overwhelmed with empathy for Simon without understanding the cause for his laird's misery. Trevor decided to go to the scullery. Perhaps a hot meal would lighten his spirits. Somehow he doubted it.

Simon found Elysia on the battlements. His arms encircled her waist and drew her back against him.

"I have to go to him, Sim." She spoke the words he had dreaded hearing.

"Why? Why must you go, Elysia? If the worst has passed, what service can you be to your son?" The desperation in the plea wrenched at her heart.

"As his mother, I have to see for myself. I must know that my son is out of danger."

"And what of the danger to you?" He blurted his foremost fear. "He won't let you return." Without mentioning the name, Elysia knew that Simon was referring to Duncan Gordon, not David. "Oh, Elysia . . . Elysia." He hugged her in desperation. "How can I let you go? Bear the daily torture of not knowing if you are suffering his abuse?"

Elysia's eyes moistened with tears as she turned in the circle of his arms. "David will be there, Sim. He won't let Duncan harm me. And when I can, I will return to you." They both knew the unlikeliness of Duncan Gordon allowing her to return to Saltoun.

Simon cupped her cheeks in his hands and gazed down into her upturned face. "And until then, my love, how am I to bear a life without you? To awake and not find you beside me? To prevail without the warmth of your smile, or the sweet, sweet comfort of your touch?"

Tears streaked Elysia's cheeks. "Beloved, we both knew that one day we would have to face this moment." A sob escaped her and she closed her eyes. "But, dear God, it's so unbearably painful."

Elysia buried her head against him and Simon swooped her up into his arms.

David found Breyandra sitting on a stone bench in the sequestered garden. For a long moment he could only stare, mesmerized. Her long hair, brushed to a sheen, hung like a black silk shawl about her shoulders, and her flawless profile was silhouetted in the reddish glow of the rising sun. Deep in thought, she was staring pensively into space with a suggestion of a smile tugging at the corners of her mouth.

He knew he was in love with her. These past days had intertwined their lives forever. But there were still so many obstacles ahead for them to overcome, so many wrongs to make right, so many wounds of the past that could scar the future.

"Good morning, Twit."

Lost in her thoughts of David Gordon, Breyandra had been unaware of his presence. She turned her head at the sound of the warm, husky timbre of the greeting. At the sight of him, a heated flush surged through her and the breath caught in her throat.

He lounged lazily against the brick wall of the garden, clad only in a pair of breeks that hugged his slim hips and long legs. Thick spiky lashes seemed to hang suspended above his cheeks as he studied her with a slumberous stare. His wide shoulders sloped to powerful biceps, and dark curly hair tapered in a seductive trail down from the muscular brawn of his chest to his lean, flat stomach.

His body is magnificent, she thought. *He is magnificent. I am in love with him.*

They regarded one another with a penetrating stare. For the moment, their eyes conveyed all their unspoken words.

"When I awoke and you were gone, I knew I would find you here."

The rising sun glistened on the moist petals of the flowers. The only sound stirring the air was the light drip of the water fountain and the hushed murmur of their voices. "This is such a beautiful spot," she sighed with a soft smile.

He thought regretfully of the past glory of the stately castle. How easily her presence here could again restore its former magnificence. If he were to succeed in convincing her to remain, she would have to come to see that for herself. "Strehlow holds many attractions."

"Yes, it is all extraordinary. But this garden is my favorite."

Compelled to touch her, he walked over to the bench and leaned down. Breyandra closed her eyes and turned her face up to him. David's mouth was firm and she parted her lips beneath the sweet pressure as the kiss deepened and their passion became aroused.

Now he needed to feel her in his arms. To love her. Breyandra felt the same urgency. He

reached out and clasped her hands. She offered
no resistance when he pulled her to her feet.
Slipping an arm around her shoulders, they
followed the narrow path into the castle and
climbed the stairway to his room.

Later when Moira glanced toward the stairway, her sullen face deepened in disgust at the
spectacle of the young lovers descending the
stairs. David's arm was around Breyandra's
shoulders and the young woman was laughing
up at him, in response to whatever he had just
whispered in her ear.

"I ken 'twas about me," the woman grumbled
suspiciously. She resumed polishing a table with
greater intensity.

The sight of Breyandra Fraser was blasphe-
mous to Moira MacPherson. Yesterday the
young woman had disrupted the whole scullery.
She had forced the castle's servants to sweep the
chimney and hearth, clean out the larder, scrub
the floor, and she didn't leave until the pots and
kettles glistened as brightly as the window
panes. *Weel, the hie faut'ng hizzy dinna moke
mony frinds tha' dey*, Moira thought viciously.

And this morning Breyandra had demanded
that all the slop pots in the upper chambers be
scrubbed spotless, with orders to do so daily.
Even now the interfering young woman had all
the servants polishing the paneling and furniture in the whole castle. "The Laird hisself be
grumblin' a' 'em to stoy ou' of hie chomber. An'
a' the yang laird daes is smile a' her wi' luve sick

e'es. Bewitched, he be," she mumbled, disgruntled.

Spying the housekeeper, David called out to her. "Moira, we are going for a short ride. We'll be returning for dinner. Lady Breyandra has told you what to prepare."

"Aye, m'lord. Bu' wi' a' the ridin' ye've been duin' in ye bed, I'd be kenning ye hae ha'ed eniff to las' ye fer a munth o' Sundays," Moira snorted insolently. Breyandra blushed at the servant woman's outspoken allusion to the intimacy between David and herself.

David was incensed. The old woman's vicious tongue had become intolerable. "Mistress MacPherson, on the day I become the Laird of Strehlow, you are forbidden to step foot in the keep." He took Breyandra's arm and led her to the door.

Moira's eyes gleamed with malevolence as she watched them depart. She flung down the polishing rag. "Wha' e'er ye do, dinna fa' aff yer harses an' briik yer bluidy necks."

The two riders received interested glances from the villagers as they rode past the tiny clachan and followed a narrow forest trail lined with birch and pine.

Within the hour David dismounted gingerly. The old wound in his thigh was still too stiff for a prolonged ride. From the height of her saddle, Breyandra looked down on a hidden valley. Rolling hills of purple heather surrounded the azure waters of a mountain loch. Several tiny tree-shrouded islands studded the lake, and in the hazy sunshine the islets seemed like leafy oases in a desert of rippling blue sand.

She gasped with pleasure at the beauty of the scene as David lifted her out of the saddle. As soon as her feet touched the ground, Breyandra started to race down the hillside. Grinning at her exuberance, David followed slowly behind. Laughing gaily, Breyandra ran back to him, then hand in hand they strolled through a purple floral carpet.

David tired quickly on the steep descent. Halting, he sat down and stretched out his aching leg. Breyandra pivoted slowly around in a circle for a final panoramic view, then dropped down on her knees and placed a light kiss on his cheek.

Clasping her shoulders, he pulled her against him and claimed a deep, satisfying kiss. With a sigh of contentment, Breyandra shifted and lay back with her head in his lap. She smiled up at him. "I think the sky is even bluer in Scotland."

David began to toy idly with the long strands of hair that framed her face. "You would never be content anywhere else, would you, Twit?"

If Breyandra had not been so enraptured, she would have realized that David's question was not a casual one. "How could I be? The Highlands are my home." Breyandra glowed with happiness. For the first time, she was sharing this sight of her adored Highlands with a man she loved. A man who was as much a part of that milieu as the heather beneath her feet.

David nodded in understanding. He had

thought that, if necessary, they could go to England or France, even the American colonies. He now realized the foolishness of such hopes. They would not be able to escape their problem by running away. *Breyandra's love for her native land was so deep she would not be happy anywhere but in Scotland.*

Sensing that his thoughts had drifted, Breyandra smiled slyly. "David, I have a secret to tell you."

A smile of pleasure came into play at the corners of his mouth. He leaned down and kissed the tip of her nose. "And just what is that?"

Seeing she now had his full attention, Breyandra drew out the suspense by nonchalantly breaking off a tiny spray of heather and twiddling with the sprig. "I met the strangest old woman in the rose garden."

"Ancient and stooped over?"

Breyandra nodded. "She was gathering rose petals and putting them into a poke."

David chuckled warmly. "That would be Gwendys. As a matter of fact, you enjoyed her hospitality when I was wounded on the moor."

Her face curled derisively. "You mean she's the one who lives in that wretched hut?"

David nodded, enjoying her displeasure. "Many claim she's a witch. And she spends her time out on the moor concocting evil brews or conjuring up black spells."

"Well, I wouldn't doubt that she is a witch, especially with all those bottles filled with who knows what sitting about her hut." Breyandra frowned. "But the woman said the strangest thing to me."

"You mean the old crone actually talked to you?"

Breyandra nodded. "She mumbled something about the past not dying."

"What exactly did she say?"

Breyandra laughed lightly. "Well, if you mean *exactly* . . . what she said was, 'The pas' stands betwixt ye, it wilt nae dee.'" Breyandra smiled in satisfaction and tweaked his nose with the sprig of heather.

David didn't view her linguistic accomplishment quite as appreciatively. "That was all of it?" He frowned skeptically. "The past stands between you, it will not die?"

"'Til a lion wi' a crown wilt moik it cum to be,'" Breyandra added.

David was deep in thought as he reflected on her words. "Hum . . . mmm," he droned with a sage frown. "Amazing. Truly amazing."

Breyandra sprung up, tossing aside the heather in her haste to sit up. Her eyes were alight with excitement. "Do you mean you've solved her riddle?"

"No. I'm just surprised she even spoke to you. I don't think I've ever heard the old witch say a word to anyone. I thought she was probably mute."

"Oh, you coof!" She shoved him down and David grabbed her, pulling her with him. Laughing like children, they rolled over and she ended up slumped across him as he stretched out on the ground. She found herself eye to eye with the darkest, most roguish eyes she had ever seen.

Breyandra raised her head and regarded him with mock sternness. "Can't you ever be serious?" Laughter came easily to David, the infectious warmth carrying to his eyes. The sight was too irresistible for Breyandra to ignore. She smiled down tenderly at him and began to trace the outline of his mouth with her fingertip. "Truthfully, David, what do you think the message means?"

He tried to force himself to concentrate, but it was difficult with her disturbing nearness. "Well, let's think about it. 'The past comes between you, it will not die, until a lion with a crown will make it come to be.'" He shrugged his shoulders. "It could be referring to Scotland's past. To your past. To my past. Even to her own past."

Breyandra was beginning to have her own theory on the matter. "A lion's mane is a crown, isn't it? Or what about that lion wearing a crown on the fountain in the garden? Maybe that has something to do with the prophecy."

"A water fountain?" he asked, amused.

Breyandra's eyes rounded with speculation. "Well, maybe something about the past is buried beneath the fountain. Or maybe if you pull one of the points on the crown, it will open a secret passage, or something mysterious like that."

David rolled over and she now lay beneath him. "Breyandra! Secret passage!"

He began to nibble at her neck and she felt her body respond to the evocative summons. "Don't scoff, David. I know about Strehlow's underground passage."

He raised his head and studied her with a dubious frown, trying to decide if she was teasing or serious. Breyandra arched her brow. "The brick in the wall," she replied smugly in response to the doubt she saw in his eyes.

"How did you ever discover that passage? That secret is known only to the Laird of Strehlow and his family. It's been passed from one generation to another. Even the servants don't know the passage exists."

"Well, I can tell you for sure that not only are Strehlow's Laird and his family aware it exists, but old Gwendys does too, and . . . forsooth, my lord, a Fraser as well! You see, I followed Gwendys into the passageway." Breyandra chuckled lightly, pleased to know she had uncovered such a guarded Gordon secret.

"Oh, Twit," David sighed, hopelessly shaking his head, "just what am I to do with you now?"

Smiling seductively, Breyandra slipped her arms around his neck. "Let me remind you, Sir Knave."

Chapter Eleven

David opened the door of the Grand Chamber
and cautiously peered into his father's room.
Duncan Gordon was asleep on the mammoth
bed that dominated the far wall. Loud guttural
snores rumbled from his open mouth.

The room reeked of the combined odors of
the sleeping man, stale ale, and the chamber pot
in the corner. David felt a tinge of sympathy for
the pathetic figure on the bed—a now degener-
ate man lying oblivious to the foul stench of his
own vomit and defecation.

Had this animality always existed in his father? Was his mother's presence at Strehlow the
only influence that had elevated Duncan
Gordon's existence to humanity?

He looked about with curiosity at the massive

chamber. The Grand Chamber of Strehlow had been inaccessible to the young boy growing up within the walls of the castle, and David could remember being in the room on only two occasions.

Heavy damask drapes reaching from floor to ceiling shrouded the room in darkness. The only light came from the dying embers in the fireplace. Once-beautiful baroque chairs were overturned, lying where Duncan had fallen against them in his drunken tottering. The doors of an elegantly carved armoire stood ajar, with clothes hanging in disarray from open drawers.

David shook his head in disgust and was about to leave when his attention was drawn to a framed picture on an ivory-inlaid toilet chest. The portrait seemed to be the only object in the room that was standing neatly in place. Curious, he crossed the room to examine it.

The likeness was of himself, painted when he was about ten years old. Stunned to discover a painted portrait of himself in his father's room, he shifted his glance to the figure on the bed. Was it possible that Duncan Gordon actually harbored some feeling for his son?

Unwilling to analyze the unexpected revelation of sentiment, David hurriedly put the picture down. In his haste to depart, his boot made contact with a discarded tankard and the large cup went spinning across the floor and slammed into a wall.

The noise awoke Duncan. He raised his bleary head. "Didn't I tell you to get out of here?" Then seeing David, he frowned in confusion. "Oh! It's you, is it? What are you doing here?"

"Becoming nauseated," David replied with disgust. "Good God, Father, even an animal doesn't root in its own filth." He yanked aside the drapes and opened the shutters. Sunlight streamed into the room, but the fresh air did little to alleviate the odor.

The chamber was even more appalling in the light. An exquisite woven carpet of red and gold had been stained with spilled whiskey.

Duncan sat up, his bloodshot eyes seeming to glow with anger. "Get out! I didn't summon you. Or have you come skulking about my chamber to spy on me like that dimwitted housekeeper?"

David regretted his hastiness in approaching the man and decided to simply state his message. "I came to tell you I intend to wed, Father."

"Wed, you say?" Duncan shifted to the side of the bed and poured whiskey into a tankard. He quaffed the potent drink thirstily, then wiped his mouth with the back of his hand. "You're a fool if you do. All women are whores."

Seeing the uselessness of the conversation, David turned to leave. "Wait up," Duncan ordered.

Exasperated, David turned back. "What do you want, Father?"

Duncan's eyes already had begun to droop. "Who is the wench you're wedding?"

"I intend to wed the Lady Breyandra."

Duncan belched loudly and scratched his

beard. "Lady Breyandra. Have I met her?"

"As a matter of fact, you are acquainted," David said grimly. "Just last week you attempted to rape her."

Duncan took David's sarcasm for ribaldry. He burst into booming laughter. "I don't remember the wench, but bring her to me and I'll finish the task."

As he fought to control his anger, a telltale muscle began to jump in David's jaw. "I told you at the time, Father, if you ever touch her again, I'll kill you."

At his son's threat, Duncan's eyes narrowed to slits. "Who is this wench?" he repeated.

"The Lady Breyandra Fraser."

His father's mouth curled in contempt. "A Fraser! Well, I suppose once you fill her belly with enough Gordons, she'll forget where she came from."

David had hoped that somehow the news of his intention to wed would spark a redeeming response from his father. He realized now that such a hope had been a foolish one. "I doubt that very much, Father. You see, Breyandra is the daughter of Simon Fraser."

"Simon Fraser!" Duncan roared. He appeared apoplectic as he shot to his feet in anger, then fell back when he lost his balance. "No son of mine is going to wed the daughter of Simon Fraser. You wed that whore and you'll be banned from Strehlow. I'll disown you as my heir."

"I've made my decision. I didn't come here to

ask for your blessing, Father," David replied contemptuously.

Duncan's huge fist banged down on the table beside the bed. "You wed the whore brat of Simon Fraser and I'll curse both of you with my dying breath," he shouted at the top of his voice. But he was talking to an empty room, for David had spun on his heels and slammed the door behind him.

Duncan staggered across the room and out into the hallway. "And when you breed that whore, I'll cut the heart out of any bastards with the blood of Simon Fraser in their veins."

His angry glare met the horrified eyes of Breyandra, who had just returned from the Solar. She stared, mesmerized, at the enraged man until David put his arm around her and led her back into his chamber.

Once inside the sanctuary of David's room, Breyandra crossed to the window. Woodenly she stared down at the activity below in the courtyard. David walked over and enveloped her in his arms. He pressed a light kiss to the top of her head. "How about a ride before we lose the afternoon sun?"

Breyandra realized that for the past several days she had permitted herself to float in a sublime state, thinking that she and David would be wed, and had pushed aside the memory of the horrid man's existence. But the malevolence that throbbed in Duncan Gordon's shocking words just now was beyond Breyandra's comprehension. His sudden, startling appearance was a shattering reminder of how much Duncan Gordon was a part of Strehlow—and of David.

"How can one man have so much hate in him?" she asked, dazed.

David reached for her hand. Her fingers felt icy. "I suppose his hatred for others is what gives his life a purpose. Forget about him, Twit," he cajoled softly.

She turned in his arms, her eyes wide with disbelief. "Forget about him? How can I? He's your father. He has just cursed us—and our children!"

"Breyandra, the man has never been a father to me. I was not conceived in love. My father hates my mother and tolerates me only because I'm his heir. He has never loved anyone. Mother, myself, and others have tried to reach him. He seeks nothing but a bottle."

His firm fingers tipped her chin up to meet his gaze. David smiled tenderly into her troubled eyes. "For the sake of both of us, put him out of your mind. What say you now to that ride?"

Under the warmth of his grin, Breyandra cast aside her gloom and a dimpled smile came into play. "I think I would like that, David."

As soon as they rode out of the Outer Bailey, a shaggy beast bolted out of the trees and raced toward them. One look at the loping animal and Breyandra's heart leaped to her throat. "Wolf!" she cried out joyously at the sight of her beloved pet.

A hapless archer on the tower turret, seeing

the huge beast sprinting toward Breyandra, assumed the woman was crying for help. He raised his bow and released an arrow. The shaft found its mark, and the animal fell to the ground.

Breyandra screamed in horror. She leapt from her horse and rushed to the fallen dog. Sobbing, she squatted down, tenderly lifted his head into her lap, and laid her cheek against his lifeless head.

David approached her slowly, knowing he was helpless to be of comfort to her in this tragic moment. He put a hand on her shoulder and she looked up. The pain in her eyes wrenched at his very soul.

"No," she cried. "Don't touch me. Don't any of you touch me."

Breyandra was hysterical. In the past weeks she had endured the trauma of near-rape by Duncan Gordon, and the grizzly murder on the moor. She had suffered through the torment of nursing David. She had borne Moira's hatred, the taunts and slurs inflicted upon her by the Gordons, and Duncan's curse. Throughout all of these wretched experiences, her courage and fortitude had not faltered.

But now all the ordeals she had bravely withstood began to swirl within and against her. Sobbing hysterically, she leapt on her horse and rode heedlessly into the forest.

David climbed onto Whirlwind and followed her. A few mangy dogs trotted over, sniffed at Wolf's body, then moved away. Soon the incident was forgotten, and no one paid attention to the old crone who heaved the heavy body of the animal onto a rickety cart.

Unmindful of the rugged terrain or her own safety, Breyandra goaded her horse to a faster gait, her vision clouded by a steady stream of tears. As the horse splashed across a mountain rill, her skirt was dampened by the cold water. Pebbles skittered underfoot, and branches whipped at her head as the plucky mare, already at a full gallop, strained to respond to her command.

The horse finally began to tire, and David's stout stallion thundered up beside them. David reached over, snatching Breyandra from the mare. He reined up Whirlwind and lowered her to the ground. Sobbing, Breyandra sank to her knees and buried her head in her hands. David knelt beside her, gathering her into his arms.

The unrestrained mare ambled back to the side of Whirlwind, and the two horses stood with bowed heads as if commiserating with the grieving young woman.

Long after her tears subsided, David continued to hold her until her body no longer trembled with intermittent sobs. He wanted to say something to console her, but David Gordon was not a man of words. Wolf's death had not been an act of malice. The tragic scene might have been enacted anywhere—but, regrettably, the accident had happened here. Yet, he knew that in the twisted abyss of her sorrow

Breyandra was attaching the guilt to Strehlow.

"I want to go home, David." The first words she had spoken since leaving the keep were a mournful declaration that came as no surprise to him.

David released his hold on her and Breyandra rose to her feet. Distraught, he followed. "Breyandra, will you please listen to me?" He grasped her shoulders and forced her to face him, but she wouldn't raise her head to look at him. "I regret what happened to Wolf, but it was an accident . . . an unfortunate accident that could have happened anywhere."

His statement generated an instant response, proving that, at least, she was listening to what he was saying. Her head shot up and a spark of her former spunkiness flashed accusingly in the depths of her eyes. "It wouldn't have happened at Saltoun. That is where I belong."

"You're upset now, Breyandra. Can't we discuss this later, after you've rested?"

She shook her head. "There's nothing to discuss." She had already reached the conclusion that their situation was without hope.

When Breyandra tried to shrug out of his arms, David's grasp tightened. "I love you, Breyandra. You love me. Damnit, isn't our love strong enough to withstand a tragic accident?"

Her glance swung up to him. "You don't understand, David. Do you believe that it's just Wolf's death?" Her eyes moistened with unshed tears. "We can never have a life together. I'm not wanted here. Your people hate me. Our love is hopeless . . . doomed from the start. We've been living a dream, David. We can never wed. It was just a foolish dream."

He tried to pull her into his arms, but she resisted. "I won't accept that," he stated firmly. "You and I are all that matter. Do you think I care what others have to say about us? If you remain, my people will grow to love you as I have."

"Remain? Remain with your father's curse still ringing in my ears?" The sad smile on her face made it clear that she was not speaking out of hysteria. "We're Highlanders, David. Raised in traditions . . . clan loyalties . . . noblesse oblige. These are your people. One day you will be their laird. Your duty lies at Strehlow." She drew a shuddering breath. "Please take me home, David. Please take me home." She repeated the words as if reciting a sorrowful litany.

David saw the uselessness of further argument. At the moment she was too wrought with grief to try to change her mind. But change it he would. He would not give her up. This was the woman he wanted to fill his life, share his bed, and bear his children. He would not let the maniacal ravings of a crazed man, long ago consigned to madness by hatred and alcohol, force her from his arms. Nor would he permit the woman he loved to be driven from the halls of his home because of the spiteful muttering of a malicious housekeeper.

"Very well, Breyandra. If you feel the same way in the morning, we will leave for Saltoun."

But there's still tonight. Tonight, to hold you in my arms . . . to make love to you . . . to arouse, again and again, that wanton, sensuous passion in you until you are writhing mindlessly beneath me. The smile on his face was barely perceptible. *And then . . . and then, my love, that's when I'll get your promise to remain.*

His hands slipped off her shoulders. With tears streaking her cheeks, Breyandra turned from him and moved to the mare.

They rode back in silence.

As the pair entered the gates of Strehlow, the stares that followed them were more curious than ever. After assisting her in dismounting, David handed the reins of the horses to a silent groom.

Absorbed in individual thoughts, the troubled lovers were unprepared for the shock that greeted them when they entered the Great Hall.

Elysia Gordon, smiling anxiously, rose from a chair.

Chapter Twelve

From the moment she heard that David had been wounded, Elysia lived with a mother's anxiety for the welfare of her son. Not knowing what his condition would be when she reached Strehlow, she had made the journey from Saltoun in a blur of apprehension and fear.

But her torment quickly dissolved when David entered the room.

She glowed with happiness at the sight of her tall, handsome son who appeared to be strong and healthy. Her heart swelled with joy, and, whatever consequence might follow due to Duncan's ire, her mind was at peace for the first time in five years. After the long separation, she could only gaze intently at her son, and, scarcely aware of the woman at his side, she waited with a tremulous smile, uncertain of what David's reaction would be to her homecoming.

Crossing the floor to Elysia, David momentarily forgot his problem with Breyandra. "Mother." The single word conveyed the depth of his emotions as he gathered her into his arms.

He stepped back, and Elysia smiled up into his eyes. "It's good to see you, David. I've missed you so much." Elysia's ability to express the sentiment without bursting into tears was a testimony to the woman's inner strength.

"What are you doing here, Mother? When Father hears of your arrival, there's no telling what he'll do."

Her eyes were misty as she gazed lovingly at him. "I had to come. I heard you were wounded, and I feared for your safety."

Her gaze moved past him to Breyandra, who had remained motionless in the entrance. The young woman was as surprised as David to see Elysia. "Breyandra, dear." Elysia opened her arms, and Breyandra hurried over. Elysia hugged and kissed her. "Your father is very worried about you."

The unexpected appearance of Elysia did not alter Breyandra's earlier decision. "I will be returning to Saltoun in the morning." She cast a sideward glance at David, who was listening to the exchange between the women as a wave of nostalgia brought a frown to his brow.

Memories of the past flashed through his mind—deep-rooted memories that had haunted him for five years: his mother sitting through the night at his bedside when he was ill, his mother stitching needlepoint and glancing up with a smile of pride as she listened to his beginning attempts to read, his mother laughing with him as they rode side by side through the Highland countryside.

One memory melded into another: her cool hand on his brow when he was feverish, her soft smile when he was sad, her compassionate eyes when he suffered the painful lessons of a boy growing to manhood.

How he would like to be with her again, recapturing shared moments and anticipating the future. But the pleasure of seeing his mother now would be short-lived, for he knew that every moment she spent at Strehlow was a danger for her. His father would not hesitate to kill her if the opportunity presented itself, and as long as she remained at Strehlow, his mother's safety was his responsibility. To protect her from his father's wrath, he would have to return her to Saltoun, which offered the only safe refuge for her.

David's glance swung to Breyandra, and he realized with sadness that his mother's arrival would set back his plans to keep Breyandra with him. He was certain he could have convinced her to remain at Strehlow, but now he would have to find another way to achieve that goal. *Damnit!* he cursed silently. *Is Breyandra right? Is it Fate's design to keep us apart?*

"Mother, you must return to Saltoun. Do you have an escort?" he asked worriedly.

Elysia shook her head. "I sent them back. There was no place they could safely remain in Streyside."

The scene with his father that morning was still vivid in David's mind. Another confrontation with the enraged man might prove disastrous. "Has Moira told Father of your arrival?"

To his relief, she shook her head. "I just arrived within the hour. Moira said your father was asleep."

"Well, that's fortunate anyway. I must get you away as soon as possible."

Elysia sank down in a chair, her face the picture of dejection. "I'm sorry to be such a problem. I suppose I should have listened to Simon. He told me not to come."

The sight of the disheartened woman was more than Breyandra could bear. She raised her voice in vexation. "David, how thoughtless of you. Your mother came here out of concern for you." At his mother's stricken look and Breyandra's remark, David realized how annoyed he must appear to the two women.

David's leg ached painfully as he knelt down on a bended knee. Reaching out, he gently cupped Elysia's cheek in his palm. "Mother, if I appeared disturbed by your presence, I beg you to forgive me. I've missed you very much." He clasped Elysia's hands in the warmth of his own. "But the danger to you is so great. Father has become crazed. There's no reasoning with him."

He rose stiffly to his feet, drawing her up with him. "Your well-being is foremost in my mind." Automatically reacting to the pain, David unconsciously began to rub his aching thigh.

Elysia glanced anxiously at his leg. "How

serious is your wound, David?"

He relaxed his intense expression, smiling to ease his mother's fear. "This is an old war injury, Mother. It will just take time to heal. We must all rest tonight, and we'll leave at first light in the morning." David put an arm around each of them and pulled them against him. "It's not often I'm fortunate enough to have dinner with two beautiful women. So let's have our high tea."

As they ate their meal, Breyandra was reminded of a long-ago time at Saltoun when David and Elysia were captives. The atmosphere then had been reserved, as it was now, with forced conversation. David's eyes strayed continually to the stairway, as if he were expecting Duncan Gordon to come thundering down the steps at any moment.

When they finished their meal, David insisted that both women accompany him to the stable while he made arrangements for the following morning.

After they returned to the Great Hall, Elysia excused herself and went outside to spend a few moments in the rose garden. Breyandra watched her leave and turned to David. "Go to her, David. Let her have some time alone with you."

He took her in his arms and tenderly smiled down at her. "I intended to, Twit." For a long moment David gazed lovingly into her eyes, then dipped his head and kissed her gently. "I'll be up shortly."

He watched Breyandra climb the stairway and listened to her footsteps until the chamber door closed behind her. Then turning away, he followed the cobblestone path.

The garden was lit only by pale moonlight, and, though she could not see the delicate blossoms, Elysia sat down, enjoying the sweet fragrance of the roses. She turned to David with a sad smile when he joined her.

"You know, David, this castle was home to me for over twenty years. Yet, I feel like a stranger here. I have no remorse about leaving Strehlow. This visit has purged any lingering doubt from my mind." Sorrowfully, she looked about at the granite walls.

"Whatever lies ahead, Mother, the gates of Strehlow will always be open to you."

Elysia's smile was wistful as she recalled an earlier time. "When I was a child, I remember what a grand castle Strehlow was. It was the pride of the clan. Perhaps one day you will return all of this to the eminence of a far-gone day."

David sat down beside her. "Have you been happy, Mother?" he asked softly.

Elysia reached for his hand. "Happier than I've ever been, except that I miss you . . . always. Simon is a wonderful man, David."

"I'm glad to hear he was worth the sacrifice you made for him."

Elysia smiled wisely. "My beloved son, the day will come when you will understand that sacrifice is often the price one pays for love. That is why it is the most precious of all sentiments. I wish you could come to know Simon. Then you would understand."

"Perhaps some day I will, Mother. You see, I intend to wed Breyandra."

Elysia's face curved into a smile of radiance. The sadness that had enveloped her during the meal diminished instantly. "So often in the past five years countless questions have plagued my mind. What was happening in your life? Were you in love? Had you married? And now, to hear that you are going to wed Breyandra . . ." She could no longer contain her tears and was forced to stop to compose herself. "If ever a mother dreamed of the daughter of her heart, that lass would be Breyandra. And were a mother to hope for a loving maiden to bring love and joy to her son, Breyandra would be that woman."

David chuckled warmly and squeezed her hand. "Then I can assume my selection meets with your approval, Mother?"

"Oh, David! There are no words to express how happy you've made me."

"Mother, your face alone expresses your happiness."

Elysia sobered. "Have you told your father of your intentions?"

"This morn. Naturally, he threatened to disown me." At Elysia's shocked gasp, David shrugged negligently. "Fear not, Mother, it's a worthless threat. On returning to Strehlow from London, I spent the night at Gight where Lord Huntly was in residence. He said that Father's demented condition is common talk throughout the whole clan. Huntly feels that Father has neglected his duties and obligations, and that he is no longer capable of governing Strehlow. As head of the Gordon clan, Huntly has ordered me to accept my responsibilities to the clan. He wants to declare Father the Lord Emeritus, and proclaim me the Seventh Lord of Strehlow."

Elysia remained silent, staring into space. Finally she spoke. "So Duncan has lost everything. Strange, I feel sorry for him."

"I've not told him as yet. I must have time to determine how to proceed. But he does pose a threat to Breyandra."

David rose to his feet, and Elysia could tell by his stance that there was more troubling him. "What haven't you told me, David?"

His glance was wary. "What of the feud between the clans? I am certain that Breyandra will not wed me without her father's blessing. Do you think Lord Lovet will permit his daughter to wed a Gordon?"

Elysia wanted to laugh aloud at his baseless worry. David had much to learn about Simon Fraser; the dear man would never stand in the way of his daughter's happiness. "From what I observed, my beloved son, I would suspect that Lord Lovet's daughter may be the one with the objection." Her eyes were alight with merriment as she pictured her handsome son charming all of Breyandra's objections away.

Elysia had touched on a subject that was still unresolved—Breyandra's declaration that they could not wed. He must yet change her mind. "It's of no matter, Mother. A minor misunderstanding yet to be resolved. Come, I will escort you to your room. You must be tired after such a long journey, and tomorrow begins yet another."

David waited outside Elysia's chamber door until he heard the bolt slide into place, then with a determined stride he continued down the gallery to his room.

The fire on the hearth offered the only light in the room. Breyandra had undressed and was sitting on the floor wearing David's shirt. She turned her head when he entered, a smile disguising the heartache she felt at the thought of parting with him.

He sat down on the bed and removed his boots. "How is your mother?" she asked, to break the long silence.

"Mother is fine now."

Since Breyandra made no effort to rise, he walked over to her and stood towering above her. She lifted her head and their gazes locked, their eyes conveying the dreaded question that neither dared to voice. *Was this to be their last night together?*

Wordlessly David reached out to her, and she slipped her hands into his. He pulled her to her feet. To prolong the moment, he allowed his eyes to caress her face. In the glow of the fire, streaks of carmine glimmered throughout the silky gloss of her long black hair, and he gathered a handful of the ebony strands, bringing them to his lips.

He lowered his head, and his mouth and tongue began to savor the slender column of her neck as he inched the shirt off her shoulders. When she stood naked before him, the satin sheen of her body shimmered translucently in the flames. He stroked her shoulders, his warm touch sliding down the length of her arms until he filled his hands with her breasts. "Your body is so beautiful," he said hoarsely.

Breyandra's eyes were wide and luminous as she began to unbutton his doublet. She undressed him slowly, first his doublet, then his shirt. Like David, she wanted the moment to linger.

In a loving caress, her hands followed the slope of his shoulders across the muscular pectorals of his chest. She dipped her head and placed a light kiss in the midst of the dark hair that trailed into his trousers.

Breyandra slid to her knees and pulled the hose off his muscular legs, then released the buttons of his trousers and pulled them off his hips.

Her eyes fell on the gash running from knee to groin, and she pressed a kiss to the ugly wound.

David felt his control slipping, and with a ragged gasp he buried his hands in her hair and drew her head away. Kneeling down, he lowered her to the floor. Overpowered by passion and love, his mouth plummeted down to claim hers.

And when the moment came, despite his earlier resolve to wring a promise from her, he did not try to turn the moment to serve his own purpose. He only wanted to love her.

Later, as they lay before the fireplace, David

leaned on his elbow, cradling his head in his hand, and gazed down into her face. He brushed aside some errant strands of hair clinging to her cheeks. "God, I love you, Breyandra," he murmured huskily.

She reached up, her finger toying with the cleft in his chin. "I wish this moment would never end, David."

"I was going to make certain it wouldn't. My intention when we made love was to force you to agree to remain at Strehlow."

Her face curved into a soft smile as she continued to trace the firm line of his jaw with her fingertip. "You would have succeeded, my Lord Wilkes."

David lay back and pulled her across him. "I couldn't, Twit. No matter how much I want you to stay, I love you too much to use our lovemaking as a weapon for barter. When I make love to you, I want to give you the pleasure you are giving me."

Breyandra's eyes began to well with tears. "Will we ever know this moment again?"

"Oh God, we must. We must," he pleaded hoarsely, and gathered her into his arms.

This time, the tempo of their loving was tender, each of them haunted by the knowledge that they would have to part until neither the opposition of Duncan Gordon nor the feud between the clans had the sway to prevent their union.

With David's name on her lips, Breyandra finally fell asleep in his arms.

Chapter Thirteen

Early the following morning, the small party set off on the journey to Saltoun. As the walls of Strehlow disappeared behind them, Elysia, who was looking forward to her reunion with Simon, was the only one of the three in good spirits.

They rode in silence. Elysia occasionally turned her head to glance to Breyandra, but the young girl appeared deep in desolation, and the older woman knew there was nothing she could say to comfort her. She understood the misery Breyandra was feeling. The heartache of parting from Simon was still a painful memory to her, and the knowledge she would soon see him was now becoming overshadowed by the unhappiness of David and Breyandra. Her attempts at conversation were met by the couple with scant replies or half-hearted smiles. Finally, in defeat, she abandoned the attempt.

David called a halt at midday. While he watered the horses, the two women spread a blanket on the ground to eat the lunch the cook had prepared for them at Strehlow. Throughout the meal, David's gaze lingered on Breyandra. Each time the young girl looked up to meet his solemn stare, she quickly shifted her eyes downward.

Elysia could only shake her head sorrowfully over the exchanges of the unhappy pair. Last night David had been confident that the obstacles standing between Breyandra and himself were minor. Whatever had transpired during the night appeared to have dampened his assurance.

Unbeknown to them, the actions of the travelers were being watched intently by four men who huddled covertly amid the trees. The dark eyes of the leader gleamed with malevolence as they fell upon Elysia. Stealthily, the secreted four stalked the small party.

"Damn you, woman!" Duncan Gordon roared, throwing his tankard at the portal. Moira MacPherson scurried out of the chamber with her hands clamped over her ears.

Duncan was incensed at the housekeeper for not informing him immediately when Elysia had returned to Strehlow. Now, once again his whoring wife had slipped through his grasp. But this time, with luck, he would catch her, and he vowed to himself that if the effort took his last breath, he would run his sword through her treacherous heart.

Duncan staggered across the floor, snatched up his claymore, and went to the stable to saddle his horse.

He rode hard without stopping. The weary animal carrying the man's massive bulk was soon near collapse. Disgruntled, Duncan was forced to dismount, and man and horse continued, walking on the trail.

Years had passed since Duncan had been outside the walls of Strehlow and longer yet since he had walked any distance. The natural act did not come easily to him. He lumbered from side to side as clumsily as a bear. But the fresh air and exercise felt good to him. Good to be out, he thought, and when he overtook Elysia, he would feel even better. His face curled into a cruel smile as his hand tightened instinctively on the scabbard at his hip.

I will ravish her before I kill her, he thought salaciously. *I'll be the last man between her whoring legs before she dies.*

Leading his horse along the trail, Duncan continued to formulate his plan. He knew he would have to overpower his misguided son. He ought to kill all of them, he reasoned. His traitorous son, his whore of a wife, and the Fraser slut. *Yes, that's what I'll do. I'll be rid of all the scum at one time, and then I will never have to fear that any bastards with the blood of Simon Fraser will bear the name of Gordon.*

The big man stumbled and almost lost his balance. He needed a drink. The stream of fresh water running adjacent to the path held no attraction for him. Duncan needed a drink of whiskey or ale. He cursed his son and wife because it was their fault he had left Strehlow without his liquor.

But what did either of them care about his needs? The bitch who always cringed beneath his touch, or the ungrateful son! She had turned his son against him from the day the boy was born. *"An animal,"* his son had called him. *I am a Gordon! We Gordons stood with The Bruce at Bannockburn, and spilled our blood with a Stuart king on Flodden Field. When Montrose tried to regain the crown for the Stuarts, I was with him, freezing in the snows at Inverlochy and sweltering in the heat at Kilsyth. Do not these heroic deeds speak of a man's worth?*

Duncan's ire increased. *Animal! I'm no animal. No common bogtrotter. I am the Laird of Strehlow! I'm not accountable to the bitch or the bitch's son.*

The big man was unaware he had begun to sniffle. *It's all her fault. Elysia's. Beautiful Elysia. Cringing beneath my touch. Blue eyes the color of a Highland sky. Always filled with loathing for me.* He wiped his eyes and nose on the sleeve of a fleshy forearm. *I made her my Countess and how did she reward me? Turned my son against me and ran off to whore with Simon Fraser! She is the one at fault.*

The sound of snorting horses disrupted his self-pitying reverie, and his ruddy face brightened. He had found his prey.

Duncan stepped off the path into the trees to

stalk his quarry. His eyes gleamed with malice when he sighted the three near the river. But he stopped abruptly when he spied four men huddled together observing the three people eating their meal.

Despite the past years of deterioration, Duncan Gordon was too seasoned a campaigner not to guess that these men, dressed in long black cloaks, were up to skulduggery. His suspicions were confirmed when he saw them draw their weapons and begin to creep closer to the three unsuspecting victims.

Duncan saw David rise to his feet and stretch. Then his son said something to the women that Duncan could not hear. Elysia and Breyandra nodded, stood up, and each picked up a corner of the blanket to refold it.

Stitched in the center of the white quilt, Duncan saw the bright blue crest with three yellow boar heads. The Gordon crest. The same crest that flew over the turrets at Strehlow . . . at Gight . . . at Strathbogie.

Duncan's quick glance sought his son—his son who had worn the Gordon crest into battle. Now Duncan saw that David, greatly outnumbered, would surely fall under the swords of these culprits.

And, as often happens during remorseful reckoning when one becomes cognizant of an obvious truth he had previously refused to perceive, Duncan saw how much of himself was in his son.

Elysia's light laughter floated to his ears, and his glance shifted to her. Whatever the woman had become, she still bore his name.

Duncan Gordon was suddenly engulfed with outrage that harm might come to his own flesh and blood.

Breyandra screamed when the four men rushed out from cover, their long black cloaks a vivid reminder of the grim night on the moor.

David spun around, instinctively drawing his sword. "Quick, get out of here," he shouted to the two women as he braced to fight off the attackers. Elysia and Breyandra responded immediately, dropping the blanket and running toward a copse of trees with two of the ambushers in pursuit.

In her haste, Elysia stumbled over a twisted root of a tree and fell to the ground. Breyandra stopped and ran back to help her, but before Elysia could regain her footing, the two men were upon them.

One of the assailants seized Breyandra and they began to struggle. She clawed furiously at his face and eyes, preventing him from running her through with his weapon. The other man grabbed Elysia by the hair. Yanking back her head, he was about to slit the fallen woman's throat when the air was rent by a hair-raising battle cry that froze the two miscreants into immobility.

Brandishing his claymore in the air, Duncan Gordon charged at the cloaked figures from atop his steed. He leapt from the saddle and threw his ponderous body into the two men. All went sprawling to the ground. The two scoundrels clambered to their feet, retrieved their weapons, and turned on Duncan. Momentarily forgotten, Elysia and Breyandra crawled to one another. Horrified, they clung together watching the struggle before their eyes.

Duncan slashed at his opponents with powerful swipes of his claymore. Years of inactivity had slowed his movements but had not diminished his strength. He was still a potent force in combat.

A short distance away, David had disposed of one of the attackers and was engaged in a death duel with the leader of the scurrilous band.

By sheer power and aggressiveness, Duncan succeeded in rendering a lethal wound to one of his adversaries, but the dying man managed to thrust his weapon into Duncan.

With the culprit's sword embedded in his chest, Duncan let his claymore slip from his hand as he dropped to his knee. His shirt became crimson with blood when his big hands grasped the blade in his body and pulled it out.

Just as David finished off his opponent, he whirled around and saw the other assailant leap at his father. David lunged forward but was too late to prevent the assassin from driving his sword through Duncan's throat. No match for the young Gordon, the henchman quickly fell to the ground from a mortal thrust to his heart.

Stunned, Elysia crawled on hands and knees to where Duncan was lying. The man's breath was coming in short, painful gasps as he lay choking on the blood curdling in his throat.

Elysia lifted his head into her lap. Her eyes were fraught with desperation. As she witnessed

Duncan's suffering in the final moments of his life, past grievances were forgotten, and with tears of compassion she uttered a supplication for the dying man. "Oh, Lord, be merciful."

David knelt beside her and saw Duncan's hand grope urgently toward the fallen sword just out of his reach.

The doomed man's eyes pleaded with his son for understanding, and in one brief moment a covenant passed between the two men. David nodded, picked up Duncan's heavy weapon, and slipped the claymore into his father's hand. As soon as Duncan's hand closed around the hilt of the sword, an aura of peace transfigured the dying man.

With gratitude, the older man's gaze lifted to his son. Then Duncan Gordon closed his eyes.

"He's gone, Mother," David said softly. Elysia laid Duncan's head on the ground. As she struggled to compose herself, David helped Elysia to her feet.

Breyandra gazed sadly at the body of Duncan. Until a few moments ago, he had been the most heinous man she could imagine, and now she no longer felt hatred toward the man who had just saved her life. She turned to David, who was grimly staring down at the still figure on the ground, and reached out, gingerly placing a hand on his arm. "Why did he save us, David? He hated your mother and me."

Deep in introspection, David raised his head. "Who can say? Impulse . . . anger . . . loyalty? Or perhaps for a moment he remembered who he was . . . Duncan Gordon, Laird of Strehlow."

Breyandra pondered his words, and then, remembering Duncan's desperate countenance, she timidly asked, "Do you think he was afraid of dying?"

"Afraid?" David decisively shook his head. "No, Duncan Gordon did not fear death. He feared only the manner in which he would die." At her questioning look, pride gleamed in David's eyes. "My father was a Highland warrior. He had to die with his claymore in his hand."

Chapter Fourteen

David began to search the bodies of the assailants for some clue to their identity. As he knelt over one of the men, Breyandra's attention was drawn to the face of the corpse. Staring lifelessly, the dead man's dark eyes were open and there was a familiarity about them, but she could not place the man. Had she seen him at Strehlow or Saltoun?

David showed no sign of recognition. He rose to his feet after failing to establish identification. Breyandra kept her suspicions to herself, but the impression continued to trouble her thoughts.

Suddenly alerted by the sound of approaching riders, David drew his sword and prepared to fight off a further assault. When two Gordon cavalrymen came into view, he relaxed and sheathed his weapon.

The appearance of the soldiers was not by accident. After Duncan's hasty departure, the Captain of the Guard had wisely dispatched searching parties. The two soldiers dismounted and knelt down to examine the body of their fallen leader. Then, rising solemnly, they bowed their heads to David and cupped their fists to their hearts in a salute. "My Laird," one declared succinctly.

Both Breyandra and Elysia gasped in surprise. The terror of the attack was still so fresh in their minds that neither of the women had stopped to consider the significance of Duncan's death. David was now the Laird of Strehlow. The stunned look on his face made it evident that David had just been struck by the same realization.

Tears of pride glistened in Elysia's eyes at the innate stateliness of her son as he composed himself, then raised his head. "Let us take my father home."

After a great effort, the three men succeeded in getting Duncan's lifeless body slung over the back of a horse. The hour was late when the glum party returned to Strehlow, bearing the remains of Duncan Gordon.

Breyandra awoke to the streaks of lightning and the crash of thunder rumbling across the glen. David was not beside her. She sat up, and a quick glance disclosed the room was empty. How long had she been sleeping? Her hand brushed her swollen lips, and she realized that only a short time must have passed since David had made love to her.

Unlike the tenderness and poignancy of the previous night, his lovemaking had been fierce, almost wild in its urgency, as David reached out in a desperation that had never been a part of their previous occasions.

Breyandra knew that the man she loved was hurting, but did not fully understand the reason. David had not loved his father, yet it was obvious that the death of Duncan Gordon had affected his son deeply.

Breyandra slipped out of bed and pulled on David's heavy robe, then padded barefoot to the door. She was about to descend the stairway when her attention was drawn to a light shining beneath the door at the opposite end of the gallery. The Grand Chamber. Duncan Gordon's room. Instinct told her where she would find David.

She opened the door cautiously. David was standing by the open window deep in thought. Dressed only in breeks, he was oblivious to the cold rain pelting his chest. His right arm hung limply at his side, with a framed picture clasped in his hand.

Breyandra walked up behind him and slipped her arms around his waist, snuggling her cheek against his broad back. "Damn him, Breyandra! Damn him to hell!" David cursed. He turned and in frustration flung the picture across the room. The pewter frame bounced against the wall and fell to the floor, shattering into several pieces.

In his fury David grabbed Breyandra's shoulders, his long fingers digging painfully into her flesh. "Why did he do this to me?"

His anger drained at the sight of Breyandra's stricken look as she winced beneath his grasp. At once his dark eyes filled with remorse. "Oh, dear God! Forgive me, love." He pulled her into his arms.

Breyandra slipped her arms around him and for several seconds held him, feeling the tension begin to ease from his body. Finally she smiled up into his troubled eyes. "Come back from the window, David, before you catch a chill."

She stepped away from him, moving over to close the shutters, then took his hand and led him down the long gallery to his room. Sitting down before the burning hearth, she drew him down beside her.

David had slipped back into his dark mood, and for several moments Breyandra sat silently, savoring his nearness and the warmth of the fire. She knew she had to get him to release the anguish pent up within him.

She clasped his hand and brought it to her lips, pressing a light kiss to the palm. "David, tell me what is troubling you. Perhaps speaking about it will help to ease the pain."

Her steady gaze saw his chiseled jaw shift sternly and a steely glint cloud his eyes. Breyandra feared he was angry with her prying, until he began to speak. "When I was a child, my father projected the image of an insensitive brute. I feared him. My skills with weaponry were learned, not to please him . . . but to avoid his wrath." He smiled grimly. "So I grew up with two certainties—my mother's love . . . and my father's enmity."

When her eyes filled with compassion, David shook his head. "I'm not seeking your sympathy, Breyandra. You see, I never regretted not having his love. It made my loathing of him simple . . . and uncomplicated. And through the years, that loathing increased in proportion to his cruelty."

David stretched out his long legs and laid his head on her lap. When he didn't continue, she asked softly, "So now are you regretting the past, David?"

For a few seconds he ignored the question as he stared pensively into the fire. "No, I don't regret the past; I'm confused by it. My whole life, I believed I was a scourge to my father, and now . . . now I discover he kept a portrait of me as a ten-year-old. Why? And why . . . when he could have just ridden away, did he try to save us?"

The pain in his heart was reflected in his eyes as he looked up to her beseechingly. He spoke in hesitation, trying to formulate an answer to his disquieting thoughts. "Could it be, in truth, that my . . . unloving father was actually . . . seeking love?"

Breyandra threaded her fingers through the thickness of his hair as she gazed down into the torment swirling in the depths of his dark eyes. "If, in truth, David, your father had sought his son's love, I am sure he would have found it. For by nature you are a loving man, David Gordon."

Her fingertips lovingly stroked his cheek. "I

215

am grateful to him for saving my life," she said. "Yet, had he continued to live, he could easily have destroyed it. Instead, Duncan Gordon died nobly . . . heroically . . . and as you said yourself . . . in the manner he wished to die, with his claymore in his hand. But why do you make his death a burden of guilt for the living? The act of dying does not exonerate the misdeeds of a man's life. So often, we human beings tend to believe so. David, let God make the final judgment."

A silence rose between them when Breyandra turned away and gazed into the fire, until she voiced questions that had entered her mind on the mournful ride back to Strehlow. "Have you asked yourself why your father followed us? What would have happened had he encountered us before those blackguards did?"

David's voice trailed off as he mumbled drowsily, "I hadn't thought about that."

She glanced down and discovered David had drifted into merciful slumber. Breyandra smiled tenderly and dipped her head to kiss his cheek.

The following morning the mournful skirl of a lone piper floated across the glen from the ramparts of Strehlow as Duncan Gordon was laid to rest.

In honor of the solemn occasion, David had shed his usual attire of trousers and doublet for kilts and a fitted jacket. His long legs were encased in tartan hose, and Highland brogues had replaced his knee-high boots. A bright red tam was perched on his dark head. Throughout the ceremony, David's face was impassive. Whatever he was thinking remained obscured by a stern frown.

Elysia Gordon stood stoically at his side, her head and shoulders covered by a shawl of matching tartan. Although she had never loved her husband, he was the father of her son. She glanced with pride at David and mourned Duncan Gordon for denying himself the son he could have known.

An all-night rain followed by a steady drizzle had turned the dirt to mud. Water ran off the heads and faces of the villagers and crofters of Streyside assembled at the graveside.

Breyandra shifted restively, unaware of how her every movement was being observed by Moira MacPherson. The woman stood apart from the crowd with an unwavering, venomous glare fixed on Breyandra.

When the last scoop of dirt had been heaped on the grave, the villagers scuttled for the gates of the keep. As was the custom in the death of a laird, the Great Hall of Strehlow was opened to the clan. Several lambs had been slaughtered and casks of ale had been tapped for the villagers to pay homage to their dead leader and toast the health of the new one.

All had been invited except Moira MacPherson. That morning, over Elysia's compassionate protests, David had permanently dismissed the servant woman from the gates of Strehlow. A small cottage on the outskirts of the clachan had been provided for Donald MacPherson and his wife, along with an annual stipend.

As the day progressed, the villagers did not disguise the fact that they resented the presence of Elysia as much as they did that of Breyandra. Each scathing glare or *sotto voce* slur, in either woman's direction, became a mounting irritant to David. His rank required him to fulfill this obligation to his clansmen, so he held rein on his annoyance. To avoid an outburst on David's part, both women soon wisely retired to their chambers and left David to his guests.

Breyandra was asleep when David came into the room later that night. He stood above the bed as he undressed, his eyes hungrily devouring her loveliness.

When he climbed in beside her, he pulled her into his arms. She was naked, her skin smooth and sleek beneath his hands. He lowered his head and his mouth closed around the tempting nub of a breast. Breyandra stirred in his arms, a faint smile curling her lips.

"So, you have returned, my Lord Gordon," she said drowsily.

She opened her eyes, her brown orbs dark and slumberous, heavy with sleep and aroused passion. She parted her lips in invitation and he kissed her. A long, drugging kiss that seemed to draw the very soul from her.

"All I could think of, from the moment you left the hall, was that you were up here waiting for me," he murmured hoarsely.

Overcome with love for him, Breyandra

slipped her arms around his neck, molding her body to the hard plane of his.

"I must leave you in the morning, Twit," David sighed later as she began to slip back into slumber.

"Leave me?" Sleep was forgotten.

"I have been summoned by Lord Huntley, the Laird of our clan. Now that I am Laird of Strehlow, there are several matters to be resolved."

At Breyandra's look of distress, David hugged her tighter. "But when I return, I will take you and my mother back to Saltoun and speak to your father." His eyes flashed with mischief. "If your dowry is inviting enough, I might even offer to wed you."

She smiled lazily and began to toy with the cleft in his chin. "After I tell Father how I've spent these past few nights—"

"And most of the days," he added with a lustful grin.

". . . and most of the days," she continued throatily, "I don't think he'll give you much say in the matter, Sir Knave."

The nerve ends of her stomach leaped beneath his touch as David slid his hand across the silky hollow to the throbbing core of her. "Perhaps I should give him further cause for concern," he whispered wickedly. His lips trailed moist kisses down the slender column of her neck, stopping to suckle the pounding pulse.

"Perhaps you should, my Lord Gordon," she gasped in a ragged plea.

Chapter Fifteen

Time passed slowly for Breyandra while she waited for David's return. Elysia's presence helped somewhat, but the Gordon clan's animosity toward both women made venturing beyond the inner ward unadvisable.

Elysia spent her days supervising the refurbishing of the Grand Chamber in preparation for David's return. She had all of Duncan Gordon's clothing burned and David's personal belongings moved into the chamber.

Three days after David's departure, an incident at Streyside caused further distress for Breyandra; Donald MacPherson died in his sleep. Moira, thinking her husband's stipend would slip through her fingers, quickly declared Breyandra's witchcraft responsible for the poor man's death. The Gordons, already hostile to the

Fraser woman, were easily convinced by Moira that Breyandra had also cast a spell upon David, prompting their new laird to eject the faithful servant from the castle.

Furthermore, in her bitterness Moira played upon the superstitions of the villagers and claimed that Breyandra's evil powers had caused the recent raft of mysterious deaths and mutilated bodies. The situation became so tense that Breyandra found herself as much a prisoner as when David had chained her to the wall.

She was lamenting on that very thought one day as she stood in the inner ward, tolerating the glares and verbal curses of the hostile crowd outside the gate. Sadly she turned away from the unwarranted rancor. Immediately her back and head were pelted by a barrage of hurled rocks. Despite the sharp pain, Breyandra refused to cower under the attack, and with dignity she continued to stroll back to the safety of the castle.

Later, as she sat alone in the tranquillity of the rose garden, Breyandra couldn't contain the tears that slid down her cheeks. It was clear that Duncan Gordon's death had not changed a thing. The dead man's hatred had been replaced a hundredfold by that of the villagers. She sighed hopelessly and dabbed at her red eyes.

"Psssst."

Startled, Breyandra raised her head. *Good Lord, has one of those vicious villagers somehow put a snake in the garden?* She was petrified of snakes.

"Psssst." The hissing sound was repeated.

Breyandra's eyes became wide with terror. Her frightened glance swept the area, and to her surprise she spied the head of Gwendys peeking around the opening of the underground passageway. The old crone crooked a finger, motioning for Breyandra to come, and then stepped back. The door closed behind her.

Breyandra had no reason to believe the old woman would be more friendly than the other villagers, but she hurried to the wall and found the brick that opened the door.

The passage was lit by several candles. Gwendys scurried away, and Breyandra was swept with a moment of panic when the door closed behind her. Dare she proceed further or should she return to the safety of her room? After a few seconds of hesitation, her instinct told her to trust the old crone.

With each step she took, her courage waned. What if the old woman was leading her into a trap? Breyandra slowed her step when she spied Gwendys waiting at the end of the passage, her face wreathed in a toothless smile. *Surely the old woman doesn't think I'll follow her outside!*

Breyandra halted abruptly when she sighted a heap at the woman's feet. The mound began to wiggle. Breyandra was about to turn around and bolt when the head of a dog popped up. The animal began to whimper at the sight of her.

Breyandra's eyes widened incredulously. She rushed over to the dog and sank to her knees. "Wolf! Oh, Wolf." Laughing and sobbing joyously, she hugged the animal.

Whimpering, Wolf squirmed to his feet and

began to lick Breyandra's face. Tears streaked down her cheeks as Breyandra looked up at Gwendys. "I thought he was dead."

The old woman's bright eyes lit up merrily. "Aye, I ken he wae gane fer shur. Fuil'd auld Gwand's, hie ded," she cackled. Then the old woman's face sobered. "Bu' ye canna lea hie rin. The dag's nae braw, a' ye'," she cautioned.

Breyandra hugged Wolf and laid her cheek against his furry head. "I won't, Gwendys. I promise you. I'll make certain he's fully recovered before I run him."

When she looked up, the woman was disappearing through the door. "Wait, Gwendys. Stay with us," Breyandra called out. But the plea was ignored. The old woman was gone, and Breyandra knew it would be too dangerous to follow her outside. Laughing through her tears, she returned to the castle with Wolf trotting slowly at her side.

Elysia was astonished when the dog padded across the floor of the Great Hall, stopping to lick her hand. "I thought you said Wolf was dead," she exclaimed to Breyandra.

The young girl was flushed with happiness, and her voice came out in a lilt. "I swear he was, or so I thought, but Gwendys nursed him back to health."

Elysia's eyes glowed with warmth. "Gwendys? The old woman who lives alone on the moor?" At Breyandra's nod, Elysia smiled reflectively. "She always had wondrous methods of healing. When I was a child, I often took a wounded rabbit or bird to her hut and laid the crippled little creature at her door. She would mend the helpless little critter and return it to me. I never understood how she knew that I was the one who had left it, but somehow she did. People always called her a witch, but I believe she was as gentle as the little creatures she healed."

Breyandra sat down on the floor and gathered Wolf into her lap. "Well, I for one am eternally grateful to her. Whenever David returns and I'm free from this prison, I intend to repay her for saving Wolf's life."

The next day Breyandra's appearance in the courtyard, with Wolf at her side, convinced the villagers, and a few of the guards, that Moira's accusation against the girl was correct.

Wolf's physical characteristics made him easily recognizable, and most of the villagers had seen the animal killed. Furthermore, no other dog resembling Wolf had entered through the gates of Strehlow. Consequently, the few skeptics in the village who had scoffed at the accusation conceded that Wolf had been resurrected by witchcraft. Breyandra Fraser's witchcraft.

The rage against her increased to a degree that made it no longer safe for her to walk in the inner ward, for even the sentiments of a few guards had turned against her. Artisans in the outer ward remained behind locked doors, to avoid being drawn into the mounting fervor.

Most of Strehlow's garrison had accompanied David. The small remaining contingent was loyal to the new laird and would not be swayed by the few among them who believed in turning Breyandra over to the mob. Nevertheless, the soldiers began arguing among themselves.

Another day passed without a sign or word from David. That night Breyandra found sleep impossible. Restless, she climbed out of bed and glanced fondly at Wolf. The beloved dog was stretched out, snoring before the fireplace. Although this was not Breyandra's home, the familiar sight conjured up pleasant memories of Saltoun.

Donning her robe, she tiptoed out of the room so as not to disturb the dozing animal.

The fire in the Great Hall had turned to ashes, but Breyandra paid no heed, for her destination was the rose garden. She followed the dark cobblestone path to the secluded garden and sank down on a bench. David's long delay and the tension at Strehlow were more than a strain on her reasoning. A foolish doubt entered her mind. *What was detaining David? Had another woman caught his fancy?*

Shaking off the wretched notion, she was about to rise to her feet when suddenly she was grabbed from behind. A hand clamped over her mouth before she could cry for help.

Breyandra struggled, but was quickly thrown to the ground. Her assailant removed his hand and instantly shoved a gag into her mouth before she could cry out for help. An accomplice blindfolded her, then bound her hands and legs. He lifted her up and tossed her over his shoulder.

Cautiously the two men moved back to the Great Hall and carried her out of the castle. Once in the inner ward, they remained in the shadows to avoid being observed by the few sentries on the battlements. The pair stole stealthily through the shadows until they reached the postern gate, and, after raising it slightly, shoved Breyandra beneath the portcullis. She was immediately snatched up by a man waiting outside who threw her over his shoulder.

Smiling in satisfaction to one another, the two soldiers returned to their posts.

At a considerable distance from the castle, Breyandra was thrown to the ground. She heard a great commotion of vicious shouts as she was being untied. When the blindfold was removed, she found herself in the midst of an angry mob. Her captor yanked her to her feet and shoved her through the murderous crowd. Switches struck at her and stones were hurled.

Terrified, Breyandra tried to protect her face, which was covered with bleeding stripes. The crowd continued to vent their rage upon her.

Breyandra realized she was near the outskirts of the village, too far from the castle to be seen or for her cries to be heard above the noisy din. She saw Moira MacPherson among the throng, the woman's eyes gleaming evilly in the glow of the burning torches held aloft by several of the mob.

"Bern the blick-heirtad deil," Moira screamed. "We'l be frae o' her eval woys fae ay."

"Aye, bern th' witch," became the outcry.

Breyandra was grabbed roughly and trussed to a post. Horrified, she watched as some of the villagers began to pile fagots of sticks around

227

her feet. *Dear God, they're going to burn me alive!* She began to sob.

"Why are you doing this to me?" she cried out in desperation. "I've done nothing to you people. In the name of God, I beg you to stop."

"Dinna ken har whids," Moira shouted. "The bluidy witch is kin to the Deil himsel'. She kil'd me guidmon, me Danold, she ded."

The crazed woman grabbed a torch from a nearby crofter. "An' ye can tal' th' Deil whe' ye ge' to heil tha' the las' ane to see ye aleave wae Moira MacPherson." Breyandra screamed as the woman thrust the burning tow into the fagots of wood. The dry kindling ignited at once.

Suddenly, from out of the dark, Wolf leaped at Moira, knocking her into the burning wood. The animal's huge jaws clamped down on the woman's throat. The crowd shouted and scattered as the soldiers from Strehlow's garrison rode among them, shoving them aside to reach the fire.

Breyandra coughed and choked from the black smoke swirling around her. Several of the mounted men leapt from their horses and brushed aside the burning sticks. With his bare hands, one soldier smothered the fire that had begun to burn the hem of Breyandra's robe. She collapsed in a heap when she was cut free.

Dazed, Breyandra gazed at Moira MacPherson, who was lying with lifeless eyes in a pool of her own blood. One thought prevailed in Breyandra's mind—escape. Scrambling to her feet, she darted into the woods with Wolf beside her as the soldiers struggled to force the villagers back to their cottages.

With enough moonlight to follow the road, Breyandra was driven to get as far away from Strehlow as possible. Nearing hysteria, she gave no thought to the terrors that might lie ahead. Nothing could compare to the horror she had just escaped.

Near dawn, Breyandra and Wolf were exhausted. She found a thicket of bushes and curled down among the leafy cover, with Wolf cuddled beside her. Within minutes, the two were asleep.

Wolf awoke her the following morning licking her face. Sunlight filtered through the leafy roof over her head. She had no idea how long she had slept. Breyandra rinsed off her face in the cold water of a nearby rill.

Finding the bushes covered with berries, she ate a handful, stuffing more in the pocket of her cloak.

The sound of approaching riders drove her back into the brush. She watched as two of the Gordon garrison rode past, obviously in search of her.

Throughout the day, Breyandra was forced to duck for cover as patrols continued searching for her. But she managed to evade them all. One goal remained foremost in her mind—to get back to Saltoun.

She spent another night curled up under bushes, drawing warmth from the faithful animal beside her. This time her sleep was restless as she tried to keep an eye and ear open throughout the night.

Wolf left her side only long enough to seek food. The small creatures of the woods were easy prey for him, a natural hunter. Breyandra was not as fortunate. She could not waste time setting a snare, so she had to be satisfied with berries and nuts.

By the end of the third day they reached the Fraser boundary. That night Breyandra settled down to sleep among the apple trees knowing that Saltoun was only another day's walk.

As she looked up at the bright stars overhead, she could not help but remember her encounter with David the last time she had been among these very trees. When she fell asleep, the vision of him obliterated the horror that had haunted her dreams for the past two nights.

Daily for the past two weeks Simon Fraser had walked the battlements, ever gazing wistfully toward Strehlow. Two weeks had passed since Elysia had left him. Two weeks of long hours fretting about her welfare.

He had known a slight respite from his worry when word had arrived that Duncan Gordon was dead. At least the threat to his beloved was gone, but why hadn't there been further word? He surmised the young Gordon was delaying Breyandra's return, but what was detaining Elysia?

As his troubled gaze swept the countryside, his attention was drawn to a distant figure of a woman walking on the road. There was a familiarity about the woman's walk that caused a surge of hope in him. Simon stared transfixed. As the dog trotting beside her came into view, hope became a reality. Simon broke into a wide grin and bolted down the stairway.

Within minutes, he was galloping down the road.

Simon leapt from his horse when he reached Breyandra. He stared aghast at the condition of his daughter.

"Father," Breyandra cried and ran sobbing into his arms.

Simon hugged her to him and Breyandra buried her head against his chest. "Sweetling," he sighed, his arms closing protectively about her.

At the feel of her father's arms around her, the strength that had sustained Breyandra throughout her ordeal drained from her body. She passed out in his arms.

When Breyandra regained consciousness, she was lying in her own bed. Her father's handsome face was leaning over her, etched with concern.

Incensed with a father's protective outrage, Simon had been anxiously studying the cuts and bruises that marred her face. A myriad theories had flashed through his head as to who might have inflicted these wounds on his daughter.

He grasped her hand and pressed a kiss to it. "What happened to you, Sweetling?"

Breyandra began to relate the harrowing tale from the time David had taken her prisoner. In the course of the narration, she often wavered on the brink of tears, but Simon listened in silence, allowing the words to flow uninterrupted. He could see her need to tell the full story.

His hands curled into balled fists and his jaw hardened grimly as she related her near burning at the stake. When Breyandra finished with a quivering sob, his heart was heavy as he took her into his arms. "You're safe now, Sweetling."

Simon was relieved when the cook tapped on the chamber door and entered with a tray of food. The interruption gave him time to brush away the moisture misting his eyes. He quelled the rage that had consumed him while listening to his daughter's narrow brush with death. His precious child almost burned at the stake! *Good God, is there no soul in that murdering Gordon rabble?*

What was he to do? As the Laird of Strehlow, David Gordon stood accountable. But how could Simon seek his revenge upon the man his daughter loved and the son of the woman he loved? The tangled web bound his hands.

Simon took the tray from the woman and brought it to Breyandra's bedside. "I want you to eat this soup and then get a good night's sleep."

"Tis guid to hae ye hame agie, m'lady," the cook said kindly as she turned to leave.

"Thank you, Corliss. It's good to be home again," Breyandra replied.

She welcomed the hot bree and began to eat the thick dumplings floating in the chicken broth. Simon watched with pleasure until she finished the bowl. When she lay back, he smiled lovingly. "Now sleep, Sweetling. I won't let anything happen to you."

Breyandra lay back with a contented sigh. "Elysia is fine, Father."

At Simon's look of surprise, two dimples dotted her cheeks. "I know you are anxious for word of her but are too much of a dear to ask in fear I would think your concern for me is any less. I love you, Father." She closed her eyes and was asleep before he could respond.

David prodded his mount to a faster gait when the walls of Strehlow came into view. He had been away from Breyandra much too long, and was desperate for the touch and taste of her, senselessly kept waiting for two weeks while the Marquis recovered from an attack of gout.

But the wait had been worthwhile, for not only had Huntley sanctioned his request to marry Breyandra, but the Marquis also had encouraged David to approach Simon Fraser to end the petty feud. If Fraser agreed, and his Mother had led David to believe there would be no doubt, the Gordons and Frasers would make their peace with one another, and David and Breyandra would be free to wed.

David sensed that something was amiss as he rode through the clachan. None of the villagers waved or even raised their heads when he passed them. They all appeared to be hanging their heads in guilt.

Elysia awaited him in the Great Hall.

David stood at the fireplace, his back taut with

tension as his mother related to him the events of the nefarious night of Breyandra's disappearance. "Were it not for Wolf waking me . . ." Elysia shuddered in horror. "We didn't know what had become of her until she sent a message to tell me she was safe at Saltoun."

David's face was reserved, but his eyes were as cold as steel when he turned around. "Thank you, Mother."

He walked outside and ordered the Captain of the Guard to assemble the garrison. When the contingent stood at attention, David addressed them.

"The Lady Breyandra was my guest and, as such, under the protection of my honor. I want to know who among you betrayed that honor."

His impassive, fixed gaze swept the assembled men. When all but two met his stare unflinchingly, David knew he had found the culprits. He called them forward.

David looked at the Captain of the Guard, whom he trusted implicitly. "Captain, were any other men involved?"

The officer shook his head. "No, my laird. They alone were responsible."

"Normally I would only whip and banish a man for betraying my honor, because I can't expect a man who does not comprehend the principle of honor to act with honor."

David drew his sword from the scabbard, his eyes flashing with the rage he had been concealing. "But you two bastards turned my future wife over to a murdering mob and will pay the full penalty for that deed."

234

The two soldiers' brows were dotted with perspiration. "But, my lord, we had no idea they intended to burn her," one pleaded.

"Draw your weapons, you cowards," David declared coldly.

"We're no match for you, my lord," the other pleaded piteously. "The fight is unfair."

"Unfair? Two against one?" David scoffed. "Perhaps you prefer to duel with the Lady Breyandra? Would that be a more suitable match to measure your manhood?"

His eyes gleamed with contempt. "You may die with a drawn sword or without one, but die you will," David declared.

The hapless men drew their weapons, and within minutes David had disposed of the cowardly pair. He sheathed his sword and turned to the others. "Any man in the garrison of Strehlow who pledges his loyalty to me must pledge the same to the Lady Breyandra. If not, he may leave now, unmolested."

All of the men placed balled fists over their hearts. "My Laird," they declared to a man. David returned the salute, then entered the castle.

Two days later a contingent of cavalry under the Gordon banner appeared at the gate of Saltoun. Despite his anger at David Gordon, Simon Fraser could not disguise his joy when the woman he loved entered the Great Hall on the arm of her son. Were it not for the presence of David, Simon would have swept Elysia into his arms and carried her to his chamber.

Instead, the patient man was obliged to follow the rules of protocol and invite David and Elysia to be seated. David told Simon of Huntley's desire to end the feud.

Elysia's eyes glowed with love when Simon agreed. "It will give me the greatest pleasure, my Lord Gordon." Her smile dissipated quickly when Simon added, "However, were it not for the sake of the two women I love, I would run my sword through your dastardly heart for the ignoble treatment my daughter suffered at the hands of Gordons."

The unexpected attack surprised David. "No one regrets that abhorrent incident more than I, my Lord Lovet. I had nothing to do with it. On the contrary, I would lay down my life to save her. I am in love with your daughter, and have come here seeking her hand in marriage. Surely Breyandra has told you how much we love one another. I beg you to have her join us, so she can tell you herself."

"My daughter is not at Saltoun at this time, Lord Gordon," Simon replied bitterly. "Breyandra knew you would come here and has gone away deliberately."

David could not believe what he was hearing. "Gone? Gone where? Why would she leave? I love her, and she loves me. I know now that I never should have left her alone at Strehlow, but surely she doesn't blame me for the actions of superstitious peasants?"

"Those 'superstitious peasants' almost killed her, my Lord Gordon," Simon declared, trying to restrain his anger. "She has asked that I tell you not to follow her."

Simon faced the wretched man bitterly. The near loss of his daughter was too fresh in his mind to feel compassion for the man. "Breyandra has told me to tell you that she never wants to see you again."

PART THREE

The Court

Chapter Sixteen

Spring 1662

Breyandra glanced out of the window to the courtyard below. She smiled with affection at the sight of the King playing with at least a dozen dogs. The frolicking scene reminded her of how much she missed Wolf, left behind in Scotland. Watching Charles romp among them as though he were a young boy, Breyandra found it hard to believe the man was England's monarch.

Her smile dissipated when a dark-haired woman walked over and placed a possessive hand on the arm of the King. Breyandra did not like Barbara Palmer, the King's mistress. The woman was a crafty manipulator, greedy for power. Despite the imminent arrival of his future wife, Charles had no intention of abandoning Barbara, a lascivious beauty, and he had established an official residence for her and their newborn daughter at the castle.

Breyandra felt sympathy for the future Queen of England, who would have to cope with the scheming courtesan living under the same roof.

With a compassionate sigh, she turned away, returned to her mirror, and finished lacing the front of her blue moire bodice. Then, grabbing a plumed bonnet to shade her eyes, Breyandra hurried from the room.

When she arrived below, she found her cousin watching the tennis match that had just begun between the King and one of his favorite cronies, the Duke of Buckingham. With a graceful turn of her wrist, the Lady Jean Fleming splayed the silken folds of a jewel-encrusted fan and raised it to her mouth.

"Brey, he's staring at me again," the young girl whispered behind the concealment of the elegant accessory.

Breyandra started to turn her head toward the object of her cousin's attention. "Don't look," Jean exclaimed frantically, "He'll know we're talking about him."

Breyandra ignored her young cousin's warning and stared at the man nearby who was leaning against a brick wall. Jean had been attracted to him ever since the young man's arrival the previous day.

"He must be a Scot," Breyandra reasoned, observing the man's appearance.

Since the Restoration, an outburst of color and luxury in clothes and materials had replaced the Puritan austerity of Cromwell. However, unlike most of the Royalists assembled at court, the young man was wigless, his own red hair hanging to his shoulders. Nor was he wearing a beribboned, knee-length gown over his dark trousers, the style presently fashionable with the dandies at court. A narrow band of lace at the collar and cuffs of a white cambric shirt was his only adornment. Even the well-made doublet spanning his broad shoulders and fashioned with crescent wings was plain. An exquisitely woven silk baldric slung diagonally across his shoulders and chest held a sword at his hip. His manner and stance were clear evidence of nobility. "But definitely a Scot. No Scot would strut around in the peacock plumage of a fop," Breyandra concluded with pride.

As if reaching a conclusion himself, the young man straightened up and began to approach them. "He's coming over here," Breyandra remarked.

The sixteen-year-old girl became visibly flustered. "Oh, no! What shall I do now, Brey?"

"Why don't you swoon in his arms?" Breyandra murmured cynically behind her upraised fan.

Still heartbroken over her relationship with David Gordon, Breyandra was no longer naive enough to believe that nothing could come between two people in love. However, she realized her cousin was too young to believe anything to the contrary and would have to learn that lesson for herself. Nevertheless, Breyandra regretted her bitter response to the young girl.

Jean Fleming had been a port of salvation in a sea of despair when Breyandra fled to Paris the year before to escape from the clutches of David Gordon. Breyandra's vivacious and often capricious cousin had become like a sister to her.

During Charles's exile, Lord Fleming had opened his French chalet and coffers to the impoverished prince. Not one to forget past favors, Charles had invited the family to London to attend his wedding. When the royal nuptials were delayed, urgent family matters necessitated Lord Fleming's return to his ancestral home in Scotland. Jean and Breyandra, at the King's insistence, remained in London at Whitehall. Breyandra had been relieved, for a return to Scotland would have brought her closer to David Gordon—a temptation she feared would be too great to resist.

The man stopped before Jean and bowed politely. "Lord Claibourne, James Douglas, Viscount of Gant, at your service, my lady. Forgive my boldness, but I've been admiring you from afar and could no longer resist the temptation to join you."

Jean's youthful dark loveliness was enhanced by a becoming blush, and her blue eyes sparkled with pleasure. She extended her hand to the stranger. "You flatter me, Lord Claibourne. I am Lady Jean Fleming and this is my cousin, the Lady Breyandra Fraser."

Douglas kissed Jean's hand and followed suit with Breyandra. "Now I beg of you not to break my heart by telling me you are betrothed, or even worse, wed?" he inquired with a charming grin.

To Breyandra's horror, Jean responded with a

nervous giggle. "No, neither Lady Breyandra nor myself are betrothed or wed."

Breyandra groaned inwardly. Why must her name be drawn into the conversation? Douglas was obviously not interested in her personal status, and if he had been, Breyandra would have told him she was not betrothed or wed, and furthermore she had no intention of ever becoming either.

In her cynical frame of mind, the smitten expression of the young man was more than Breyandra could bear. She was relieved when the tennis match came to an end, and she welcomed the approach of the King with the viperous Barbara Palmer clinging to his arm.

Charles was a handsome man, both in face and figure. He stood two inches above six feet and possessed a lean, muscular body. Large, luminous eyes, a long nose, and a wide sensual mouth were set pleasingly in a swarthy face. At the moment, a black, full-bottomed wig with rows of tiny curls covered his own dark curly hair.

Amicable and affectionate by nature, Charles enjoyed people, hated cruelty of word or action, and was essentially without malice. His only animosity was toward the men responsible for the regicide of his father.

A born diplomat, his patience and gentleness of speech, coupled with a frivolous and pleasure-loving life-style, tended to disguise his shrewd judge of character. But those close to him knew that Charles kept his own counsel and followed his own judgments.

Smiling broadly, he stopped before them. "Ah, Claibourne, what a clever young rogue you are." He gave James Douglas an affectionate pat on the shoulder. "I see you've captured the attention of these two lovely sprigs of Scottish heather."

James eyed the young women with a smitten gaze. "They are indeed that, Your Majesty."

Barbara Palmer forced a smile to her alluring features. "My dear Breyandra and Jean, I have suggested to His Majesty that the future queen will be in need of two ladies-in-waiting. Who would be a better choice than you two 'sprigs of Scottish heather,'" she simpered.

"Now, now, Barbary." Detecting a twinge of jealousy, Charles chided her lightly. "Whatever could these two charming ladies have done to warrant your displeasure?"

Just being born a female is enough to gain the dislike of Her Royal Queen Barbary, Breyandra thought, but dared not voice her answer aloud. Barbara Palmer would be a powerful enemy if crossed.

The woman's face puckered into a girlish pout. "I am riddled with displeasure, Your Majesty, knowing that soon you will be sharing your bed with that . . . with that . . . *Portuguese infanta,*" she flared. She stormed away, leaving the King with an amused look on his face.

"Ah, women, Jamie. How dull life would be without them."

Charles offered an arm to both Breyandra and Jean, and they began a casual stroll back to the palace, followed by James Douglas. "Despite

Lady Castlemaine's unpleasant outburst, I find her suggestion most valid. I would be pleased if the two of you would serve in waiting to my future Queen."

Astounded, the two women looked at one another. The request was an honor that Breyandra and Jean were thrilled to accept. "We would be delighted, Your Majesty," Breyandra replied.

James Douglas grinned broadly. "You've made a judicious choice, Your Majesty. I am in debt to you, for you've done me a great service. Now I will have the pleasure of accompanying these ladies as part of the retinue which will be escorting Her Royal Highness back to London."

Jean Fleming dipped her head, enthralled at the prospect of having the company of James Douglas on the trip to greet Catherine of Braganza when the Portuguese princess arrived in Portsmouth.

"I am afraid my debt to you for your service to me on the continent far exceeds any favor I have granted you, Jamie. I do not regard my obligation lightly," Charles said solemnly. "Someday I will find a fitting way to reward your loyalty."

The King halted, bowing politely. "Now, if you two charming young ladies will excuse me, I must console my fiery paramour. Her nature is so tempestuous." He nudged Douglas and whispered in the young man's ear, "I am sure you have discovered already, Jamie, that a spicy seasoning is a vital ingredient to the sauce." With a devilish wink he hurried away.

Later in her room, before dressing for the evening's banquet, Breyandra lay on her bed with thoughts of Saltoun swirling about in her head.

She was homesick. Her beloved Highlands would now be adorned by spring. In her mind Breyandra could see the glorious colors of the verdant hills, and she recalled the smell of the apple blossoms.

A sob caught in her throat. The apple blossoms. David. Must the memory of him forever flower and permeate her senses as did the sweet fragrance of the apple blossoms? When would the memory wither?

Restive, Breyandra rose to her feet. Almost a year had passed since she had last seen him. Almost a year since she had fled Saltoun.

Breyandra's mouth curved into a derisive smile. *But you can't flee from your memories. They accompany you wherever you try to escape.*

The long months in France at her uncle's château had indeed not obliterated her memories. The young men who had tried to court her had not diminished them. Whether in France or England, awake or sleeping, visions of David pierced her heart like the point of a lance, but there was no shield to ward off the painful thrusts. There was no man's nearness which did not oppress her, no man's lips which did not repulse her, and no man's touch from which she did not recoil. Her heart and mind, continually at odds, dueled with memories both tender and bitter.

A light tap on the door announced the arrival

of a maid, but when Breyandra rejected the offer to assist her in dressing, the young girl departed. There were many other ladies of the court who required her services.

With a resolute sigh, Breyandra approached the mirror. She made up her mind to put aside the tormenting thoughts of David Gordon and enjoy herself for a change. She would flirt outrageously, even knowing that the frivolous demeanor would necessitate warding off the advances of the King's hard-drinking companions. Nevertheless, she would not spend one more evening as a languishing wallflower.

With her newly acquired resolve, Breyandra picked up a comb and parted her hair in the center. She wove some of the hair through a wire hair piece, then stepped back to survey the results. Several curls were suspended on each side of her face. Breyandra burst into giggles. *Good Lord! There isn't one thing attractive about this style,* she thought, amused. *Why did women feel compelled to resort to such wiles? Oh, well, when in Rome, do as the Romans do,* she philosophized. Then with an impish grin, she added, *or in the court of the Merry Monarch, follow the dictates of fashion. At least we women can be thankful we don't have to wear those ridiculous wigs like the men do.* Breyandra pulled a long love curl down to her shoulder, then, satisfied with the results, reached for her gown.

The dress was the latest fashion from Paris. Her bosom swelled enticingly above a daring low bodice of pale green satin, cut to a deep point in front and back, emphasizing her tiny waist. For the sake of modesty, a rose-colored chemise peeked out in a provocative ruffle at the cleavage of her breasts and formed tiny dropped sleeves on her bare shoulders.

The skirt of the gown was of rose satin embroidered with green and white petals. Open at the front, the skirt was pulled back into luxurious drapes at her sides to expose the swirling folds of a green satin underskirt.

Breyandra refrained from wearing jewelry, electing a pair of elbow-length white gloves. After a final inspection, she spun around on the white heels of rose satin slippers, embroidered in the same pattern as the skirt, and left the room.

Chapter Seventeen

A royal ball was in progress when Breyandra entered the hall. To the people of a country which had been torn apart by civil war, followed by Puritan domination, the approaching royal wedding was a welcome sign of the return of the past grandeur of England. For weeks revelers had been arriving to attend the forthcoming nuptials of their monarch and Catherine of Braganza, the daughter of the King of Portugal.

Breyandra spied Jean talking to James Douglas and moved directly to them. Within seconds, Breyandra was surrounded by a brightly colored, bewigged swarm of suitors, who fluttered around her like moths around a flame.

A wide swath opened for Charles's approach, and he gallantly complimented both women on their beauty. With warm and lively eyes, the

King turned to Breyandra with a courtly bow. "My lady, may I have the pleasure of this dance?"

Breyandra would have preferred to refuse the invitation. During the last several weeks, in an attempt to make them feel welcome at court, the King had been paying a great deal of attention to the two young women from Scotland. As a result, both Breyandra and Jean had felt the sting of the jealous temper of Lady Castlemaine. Breyandra had no desire to further arouse the ire of the vindictive woman, but she knew that to refuse the King's request would be improper. Smiling graciously, she placed her hand on his arm, and Charles led her to the dance floor.

As he glided Breyandra through the steps of a lively allemande, the King's love of dancing became evident in the skill and grace of his movements. His charm and witty repartee soon had her relaxed and enjoying the dance.

Nearby, Barbara Palmer stood amidst a group of spectators. Her wary gaze never wavered from the dancing couple. Malevolence gleamed in the courtesan's eyes each time Charles's droll observations whispered in Breyandra's ear produced gay laughter or a captivating smile from his attractive partner.

By the time the dance ended, the crowd around Jean Fleming had thinned except for the King's brother, the Duke of York, and a new arrival who was talking earnestly with James Douglas. The man's back was turned to her, but Breyandra's footsteps slowed at the sight of the familiar span of broad shoulders.

Her heart began to beat rapidly, and she felt the heat from the flush that swept her from head to toe. Breyandra's breath caught in her throat. Her first inclination was to dash from the room before David Gordon turned his head and discovered her.

In his delight at seeing the Highlander, Charles did not notice Breyandra's reaction. He pounced on David at once, greeting him warmly with repeated slaps to the back. Absorbed in the reunion with the King he had not seen for a year, David was unaware of the woman who was lagging behind Charles, out of his vision.

Breyandra moved stiffly, her face frozen as a statue, when Charles, remembering his manners, reached for her arm and pulled her to his side. "Lord Gordon, have you had the pleasure of meeting this Highland flower?" Had Charles not been distracted at the moment by the arrival of Barbara Palmer, he would have observed the shocked look on David's face when he spun around and saw Breyandra.

In panic, Breyandra grabbed the arm of the man nearest her. "Lord Claibourne, this is our dance."

Breyandra's brash move was as surprising to Jean Fleming as it was to James Douglas. Jean stood stunned as the gallant young man led Breyandra away. Charles, oblivious to the turmoil of the situation, watched their departure with pleasure. "My, they make a handsome couple," he said with an approving smile.

Jean Fleming felt betrayed. On the verge of tears, the sixteen-year-old did not understand why her beloved Brey, who could have any man of her choice, including the King himself, would single out the *one* man Jean had set her heart upon. Heartsick, she accepted the invitation of the Duke of York, and they joined the other dancers.

Once on the dance floor, safely out of David's sight, Breyandra excused herself and left the perplexed young man alone. She was determined to return to her room where she could sit down and rationally decide what her next move should be. As long as David Gordon was present, she could not remain in London.

Weaving her way through the crowd, she was dismayed to see David and the King standing in the entrance of the hall. There was no way to get past the pair without being seen, so she headed for one of the doors opening into the garden.

David Gordon tried to appear interested as Charles continued to ramble amicably at his side. "I regretted to hear of the death of your father, David. He fought valiantly for my father's cause. You have fought valiantly for mine. The loyal service of yourself and Lord Claibourne has earned my eternal gratitude."

"I do not believe many at the court share your sentiment toward Jamie and me, Your Majesty. We Scots are not too popular," David scoffed.

Charles frowned somberly. "Don't trouble yourself with such thoughts, David. Some here are not willing to forget the role a few Scots played in my father's death. The present must not be wasted by the mistakes of the past. A previous day's grievances should end with the dawning of each new day."

David would have liked to remind the benevolent monarch that among the frailties of human nature was the unwillingness to forgive and forget. But before he could express the thought, James Douglas returned—without Breyandra. David's eyes immediately began to scan the room. Spying Breyandra slipping through a garden door, he quickly excused himself.

Breyandra had covered not more than half the garden path when David caught up with her and seized her from behind. He spun her around with a firm grasp on each shoulder, and she found herself confronted by his dark eyes, blazing with anger. "My God, woman, I'd like to throttle you."

Breyandra's own ire was an easy match for his. "Release me at once or I shall shout for help," she retorted. "I have no intention of suffering any further abuse at the hands of a Gordon."

David eased his hold on her, but did not release her. "Do you have any idea the hell you've put me through this past year? How much I've suffered?"

"Suffered?" Her brow lifted scornfully. "Spare me the woeful tale of your suffering, Lord Gordon. I don't think I could bear it. But if you want to hear of suffering, I will describe how your clansmen tried to burn me alive. Would you like me to relate the horror I endured when my clothes ignited and the flames

255

and smoke rose up around my head? Believe me, Lord Gordon, the moment is vivid in my memory."

David's grasp tightened on her shoulders. "Do you think I haven't envisioned that scene again and again in my mind?"

Her eyes flashed in derision. "Well, it's much more than an image in my mind, my lord. The smell of the smoke still stings my nostrils."

She started to turn away, but he pulled her back. "How can you blame me for the insanity of a witch hunt when I wasn't even there, Breyandra? After all we shared, didn't our love mean anything to you? Did you have to run without even a goodbye?"

"A goodbye would have accomplished nothing. I told you from the beginning that our love is hopeless, David. You refused to listen to me, refused to face the reality." She raised her head in determination. "Well, I *do* face reality. I have put the nightmare of mingling with the Gordon clan behind me. I have begun to build a new life. A life far removed from the memory of Strehlow."

His jaw hardened more grimly. "Is this your new life? Look at you. Parading around half-naked like the rest of the court whores." Breyandra cried out in pain as he yanked the wire out of her hair. "And what in the name of Mary have you done to your hair? You look like some made-up harlot."

Infuriated, Breyandra lashed out and slapped his face. "Damn you, David Gordon! Keep your hands off me. What I do to my hair or anything else is no longer your concern. I'm happy with my life, so leave me alone." Tears of anger began to streak her cheeks.

At the sight of her tears, David's anger dissolved and his face softened in tenderness. The shock of seeing her unexpectedly had caused him to lose his control and mindlessly lash out at her with the pent-up pain. She had been hurt too much already. He regretted his outburst, realizing he should have begged her for forgiveness. Instead, he had attacked her, venting his anger on her, without any thought to the deep suffering she had incurred as well. It was no wonder she hated him now.

In the pale light cast by the moon, Breyandra saw the shift of moods on his expressive face and found herself trembling—but no longer with anger. She now was struggling with the reality of her undeniable love for David Gordon. Her eyes misted as she scrutinized his face, savoring each facet of the beloved features.

For a breathless moment David gazed down at her upturned face, fighting the desire to take her in his arms, to kiss away each teardrop. He reached out and gently traced the delicate line of her chin with his finger. "I've missed you, Twit."

She forced a tremulous smile to her lips. "And I you, Sir Knave." Turning away, she left him.

David remained motionless as he watched her disappear into the darkness. Now that the shock and anger had passed, all his emotion focused on his love for her. A year of torment—of cursing her name—was forgotten as soon as he gazed down into her exquisite face.

Whether she still loved him or not, Breyandra apparently wanted to forget him. She had proven her determination by disappearing the past year.

But one tangible hope now existed for him— he had found her again.

Breyandra wasn't sure she had the strength to continue walking away from David. Leaving the man she loved intensely seemed insane. *Oh, to be in his arms again. To have him make love to me.* Concentrating on each step, one foot and then the other, she resisted the overpowering temptation to run back to him, silently reiterating, *I dare not remain. I must leave London.*

Upon entering the castle, Breyandra mounted the stairway and hurried down the gallery to her chamber. Her movements had been detected by her overwrought cousin, who hastily followed down the hallway after her.

The young girl was practically in tears. "How could you do it, Brey?"

Preoccupied with her heartache over David, Breyandra was unprepared for the question. She had never discussed David Gordon with Jean and did not understand how the girl could possibly know about him, unless she had overheard them in the garden. "I assume you saw us in the garden," Breyandra sighed. Desolately she entered her chamber. After the scene with David, Breyandra did not feel up to another with Jean. "I'm in no mood to discuss this any further tonight, Jean. If you'll excuse me, I would like to retire."

Tears streamed down the young girl's cheeks. "You mean you even went into the garden with him? Oh, Brey, how could you do this to me?" Sobbing, the girl turned and ran down the hall to her own chamber.

Breyandra was totally confused. She could not understand why Jean would react so emotionally to a situation that did not affect her. Concerned, she followed the distraught girl.

When she entered her cousin's room, Jean was lying on the bed, weeping into a pillow. "Jean dear, I do not understand why you are allowing yourself to become so upset over an issue that does not concern you."

Jean raised her head accusingly. "Doesn't concern me? You, of all people, know how I feel about him. I never believed you would betray me so."

Betray. Stunned, Breyandra began to feel numb with shock. "Jean, I didn't realize you even knew David Gordon."

"David Gordon?" the young girl sniffled. "What does David Gordon have to do with anything?"

Jean was simply not making any sense. Baffled, Breyandra sat on the edge of the bed. "Aren't we discussing the conversation you overheard in the garden between me and David Gordon?"

Jean's face pursed into misery and her tears began to flow again. "I didn't hear any conversation you had with David Gordon. I'm talking about how you threw yourself into the arms of Lord Claibourne." Sobbing, she reburied her head in the pillow, adding additional stains to a beautiful satin casing.

Breyandra had reached the end of her patience with her cousin. "Jean Fleming, I don't know what you are talking about. I have absolutely no interest in James Douglas and I can't believe you think I do."

The sobbing abated and Jean lifted her head. "Is that why you threw yourself into his arms to dance with him?"

Breyandra had forgotten that James Douglas had been the man she had asked to dance in her effort to escape from David. "Good heavens, Jean! I just grabbed the man nearest me. I had to get away from David Gordon."

Jean sat up. Her curiosity was now piqued as she eyed Breyandra with suspicion. "Lord Gordon? But why? You just met the man!"

Breyandra closed her eyes in despair. She couldn't divulge the whole truth of her relationship with David. All she could do was tell Jean enough of the truth to convince her cousin that she was not the least bit interested in Lord Claibourne. With a sigh of resignation, she picked up the young girl's hand. "Jean dear, I fled Scotland to get away from David Gordon. You see, we were . . . we were . . ."

"Lovers?" Jean asked breathlessly, her blue eyes wide.

"Yes, David and I were lovers, but our clans have long been feuding, so our situation is hopeless. I left Scotland a year ago never expecting to see David Gordon again. And now . . . tonight . . . in my shock, I reached out to the nearest man, just to get away. David found me in the garden and we quarreled."

Relieved to hear that Breyandra had no designs on the man she loved, Jean's heart swelled with sympathy for her beloved cousin and she hugged her tightly. "Oh, Brey, forgive me for doubting you."

When she drew away, Jean's eyes were warm with compassion. "What are you going to do now?"

"I haven't had time to decide. I can't remain at court with David here. He's too headstrong. He'll break down all my resolutions and this past year will have been for naught."

Jean nodded in understanding. "He's such a handsome man."

"And a persuasive one," Breyandra lamented.

Deep in reflection, Jean suddenly broke into a smile. "I have a thought. Any day we are due to leave for Portsmouth. Once there, you could feign illness and not return to London."

A spark of renewed hope diminished the sadness that had clouded Breyandra's eyes. Smiling, she rose to her feet. "Your idea is brilliant, Jean. I will avoid Lord Gordon until I can return to Saltoun. As long as I remain at court, he cannot force me into anything against my will."

Relieved, she bent down and kissed Jean's cheek. "Now repair the damage to those beautiful eyes of yours and return to the ball. Tell the

King I have become indisposed."

Convinced that her temporary crisis had been resolved, Breyandra returned to her chamber. But, once behind the closed door, her thoughts strayed to the dangerous temptation she knew was waiting below.

Chapter Eighteen

Breyandra slept late into the morning. Thoughts
of David had plagued her until past dawn, when
she finally fell asleep. Most of the King's personal entourage had assembled around Charles by
the time Breyandra joined the group. The King
was holding his year-old infant daughter, Anne
Fitzroy. Beaming with love and pride, Charles
was snuggling the child in his arms as Barbara
Palmer, the infant's mother, stood beside him
smiling possessively.

Fortunately, the previous night Jean Fleming
had done a thorough job of convincing everyone
that Breyandra was indisposed. When Breyandra appeared, all were concerned about her
health and hoped she had not passed an unpleasant night.

Charles especially was distressed over her state. Handing the baby to the nanny, he hugged Breyandra warmly. Breyandra was relieved that she could tell him with a clear conscience that she had not fallen asleep until dawn.

When David took her hand and kissed it, his eyes gleamed with mockery. "I'm sorry to hear of your infirmity, my lady."

"Not an infirmity, Lord Gordon, just a minor ailment. I trust your night was well spent."

Their glances locked in understanding. "Not as I would have preferred, my lady. Perhaps, we both suffered with the same . . . minor ailment." His smile was a subtle taunting.

"Well, I certainly hope you will not pass the mysterious malady on to me," Barbara Palmer exclaimed.

David had no liking for the ambitious woman. He smiled in response. "I can assure you, Lady Castlemaine, you have nothing to fear from me."

Charles was solicitous as his tall figure bent over Breyandra. "Are you feeling well enough to accompany us to Cambridge, my dear? Today will be Old Rowley's final race at Newmarket."

"I would not want to miss such a momentous event, Your Majesty," Breyandra replied.

Gratified, Charles hugged her. "Your interest pleases me so much, my dear lady."

"Your Majesty, I thought you enjoyed horse racing," Jean Fleming interjected innocently.

"I certainly do, dear girl, which is in fact the reason I have addressed the matter to Parliament. As Monarch of England and Scotland, I have officially proclaimed horse racing to be the Sport of Kings."

The declaration merely added to Jean's confusion. "But, Your Majesty, you just said that today would be your last race."

"No, dear, I said today would be Old Rowley's last race."

Breyandra guessed the train of Jean's thoughts too late to stop her from blundering. "But . . . I thought . . . I mean, I've heard . . . Your Majesty referred to as 'Old Rowley.'"

Charles's eyes sparkled with mirth, but his two cronies, Buckingham and Rochester, broke out into vociferous laughter. Even Barbara Palmer had to bury her face behind her fan to hide her amusement.

To avoid any further comment, Breyandra quickly grabbed Jean's hand. "Jean dear, I am in need of a scarf; perhaps you will lend me one of yours." She hurried the girl out of the room. David and James exchanged discerning glances and followed.

In the privacy of the marble hallway, the three huddled protectively around the young girl. "What is wrong?" Jean asked, on the verge of tears.

James Douglas was the first to attempt an explanation. "Lady Jean, the King is often called 'Old Rowley' after his favorite horse."

The young girl's eyes opened wide in astonishment. "After a horse? How would anyone dare to call the King by the name of a horse?"

In a plea for assistance, James cast an anguished look at Breyandra and David. Both lowered their heads, trying to restrain smiles of amusement. James's bright hair seemed to dull to orange against the red blush that painted his face. "Well, Old Rowley is a prolific stud, and the King is a notorious womanizer who has . . . has fathered several . . ."

As she realized the full significance of the nickname, Jean's eyes rounded in comprehension. "You mean . . . Oh my, I think the comparison is unforgivable! His Majesty is such a kind man. He should not be maligned behind his back."

"It's not meant in malice, my lady," David interjected. "The name is used affectionately. Charles has a great sense of humor and is not insulted. As a matter of fact, he's quite flattered by the . . . sobriquet. He likes the name better than 'Chanticleer,' which he has also been dubbed by many."

Jean was still not appeased. "Many indeed! I am sure Buckingham and Rochester are the culprits. Well, I for one shall never think of him as 'Old Rowley.'"

James Douglas winked at David. "I hope you will never have reason to, my lady."

Jean sighed woefully. "I suppose I have made a fool of myself in front of everyone." Before James could reply, David took Breyandra's arm and forcefully drew her through the entrance.

Once outside, Breyandra slapped aside his hand. "What is the meaning of this move, David?"

He put his hands on her shoulders and turned Breyandra around so she could see the couple inside. James had just taken Jean into his arms to console her. "Haven't you got enough sense to know when two people should be alone?"

"Yes, I do, and I also have enough sense to know two people who *shouldn't* be alone. So, if you'll excuse me, I'll join the others." She moved off in a huff, but David was beside her instantly.

His face relaxed into an amused grin as they walked side by side. "Where are you going? The others are in the palace."

"I can hardly return the same way I came without embarrassing Jean and Lord Claibourne." She stopped in her tracks and, with arms akimbo, glared up at him. "May I ask why you are following me? I thought I made myself quite clear last night."

David grinned crookedly. "As you yourself said, it would be indelicate to intrude on the young lovers. And I might add, under the reign of Charles one is free to do as he will as long as his actions remain within the law. As yet, I know of no law prohibiting a leisurely stroll."

"You are incorrigible." Thwarted, she increased her pace.

"But you love me just the same." David chuckled warmly.

Breyandra gritted her teeth and turned toward the stable, trying to ignore the man who stayed in step with her.

Several horses in the royal mews were being prepared for the move to Newmarket. Breyandra halted at the stall of the King's favorite stallion.

"So this is Old Rowley," she remarked in admiration. Despite her frustration with David, Breyandra could not help bursting into laughter. "Poor Jean. Will she ever live down her embarrassment?"

"Oh, Jamie will console her," David replied lightly. He began to pat the horse. "Old Rowley's a beautiful animal."

For several seconds Breyandra watched contentedly as David petted the horse. "How did Whirlwind fare this past year?"

"Without you, he was as miserable as his master." He grinned down at her. "Why don't you ask him yourself?"

"Whirlwind is here?" Her face broke into a wide smile and she swung around seeking him. She spied the black stallion in a nearby stall and hurried over to the horse. Whirlwind nickered in greeting.

"Charles has asked me to race Whirlwind against his stallion," David said, moving to her side. "He said he wanted Old Rowley to go out against the finest."

"At Newmarket?" Breyandra was surprised. The match appeared to be unfair. "Will you be riding Whirlwind?" At his nod, she added, "But your stallion is not a race horse, nor are you an experienced jacky."

"I know, I'm much bigger and heavier than the King's jack, but Whirlwind won't allow anyone else to ride him, so I will have to do the honors. Fear not, he's a stout steed with a lot of heart."

"Well, good luck, old boy," Breyandra said,

affectionately nuzzling the horse.

"Aren't you going to kiss the jacky for luck?" David asked, reaching for her.

Breyandra brushed aside his hands and stepped out of his reach. "You, Lord Gordon, make your own luck. Don't break your neck." She turned and walked away.

Smiling pensively, David leaned back against the stall and watched until she disappeared from sight. With what sounded like a derisive snicker, Whirlwind prodded him with his snout, throwing David off balance.

"I know, boy," David said softly. "You think I'm a fool for not going after her. But you should know, as well as any, that sometimes you must pace yourself slowly in order to win the race."

By the time Breyandra returned from the stable, the driveway of Whitehall had become a beehive of activity. Carriages piled high with trunks lined the wide path. Each coach was drawn by a team of four horses with two coachmen in front and two sitting on a high seat in the rear. A mounted cavalry mulled about with the Captain of the Guard shouting to be heard above the cacophony of snorting horses, creaking saddles, and the laughter and raised voices of the passengers climbing into the conveyances.

Spying Breyandra, Charles leaned out the window of a carriage. "Lady Breyandra, have a pleasant journey." As the coach began to roll, he waved a white, lace-trimmed handkerchief.

The head of Barbara Palmer appeared beside the King at the window. "Yes, dear, do have a pleasant journey," she trilled sweetly, just before the mounted guard closed around the carriage.

Liveried servants scurried back and forth carrying trunks as members of the royal entourage continued to depart. When Breyandra entered the hallway, Jean Fleming was descending the stairway followed by several men carrying her baggage.

"Brey, where have you been? Hurry or we'll be left behind."

"Oh, twiddle, cousin! I shan't be more than five minutes," Breyandra chided lightly as she skipped up the stairway.

She quickly selected a yellow gown with a contrasting brown underskirt. As she changed into the garment, a maid efficiently finished packing and dispatching the trunks. Breyandra grabbed a cloak and hurried down the stairway.

The previous confusion in the driveway had been reduced to a single carriage. James Douglas stood at the open door of the rig, chatting with Jean who was seated inside.

"I told you we would be left behind," Jean censured as Douglas assisted Breyandra into the carriage.

"At least we don't have to walk," Breyandra teased, settling in the seat opposite Jean. James Douglas entered the coach and sat down beside Jean.

Before James could close the door, David Gordon appeared at the entrance and climbed in, plopping his tall frame on the seat next to Breyandra.

She disguised her surprise with a glare of

displeasure. "May I ask what you are doing in this coach, Lord Gordon?"

"Anticipating an enjoyable ride to Cambridge with the most pleasant of company." He nodded amicably to the two people seated opposite him. Jean tittered in response and James grinned.

"Why do you insist upon pressing the issue, David? I've made my position clear."

David appeared to be a paradigm of innocence. "I'm uncertain what you mean by 'pressing the issue,' my lady. My intention is simply to journey to Cambridge. I see no reason why you should object to that."

Disgusted, Breyandra shifted in the seat to avoid any contact with the muscular thigh that had settled against her own. "I care nothing about your intentions, Lord Gordon. My objection is to your presence in this carriage."

"Why not this carriage, my lady? Lord Claibourne is my closest friend, at court or away. Our friendship is an old and treasured one. We were classmates at St. Andrew's. Were we not, Jamie?" he asked with a comradely wink. The gesture did not go unheeded by Breyandra and added to her irritation.

Jamie was unsuccessful at suppressing a grin. "He is telling you the truth, my lady. We have been stout friends for many years. If you are distressed, I will be happy to change seats with you."

"Oh, what's the use!"

Breyandra had no heart to continue. Feigning displeasure with the man she loved was a difficult task. And her determination to remain detached, when the desire to be in his arms was the foremost thought in her mind, began to weaken. Breyandra knew her only salvation would be to avoid him completely. But David Gordon was too cunning to allow that. Damn the man, he was not going to make this easy for her.

Thoroughly frustrated, Breyandra turned her head to stare out of the window. She did not utter another word as her three traveling companions laughed and bantered gaily among themselves. Their voices became a drone in the background as the steady rocking of the carriage combined with the previous night's sleepless hours lulled her into drowsiness. Soon Breyandra slipped away into slumber.

Her body was filled with sensual longing. Her nipples were hard. Each nerve was sensitized. She gasped beneath the pressure of warm lips and sighed as her tongue met the thrust of his. The sudden chill as her gown slipped from her shoulders caused a shiver which instantly turned into a heated tremor when a moist mouth closed around one taut nipple.

With a strangled sob Breyandra opened her eyes.

The sensual rapture had not been a dream; she found herself actually lying in the arms of David Gordon! His head was buried in her breasts, his hand groping to raise the voluminous folds of her gown.

Breyandra sat up, shoving him away. The move caught David unexpectedly, lost in the throes of his own arousal. He stared disoriented as she pulled up the bodice of her gown.

In her indignation Breyandra lashed out. "You rapist! Is there no end to your perversity?"

Breyandra cringed with fear when she saw his bewilderment change to fury. David grasped her shoulders, his fingers biting into the bare flesh. He was about to shake her, then gained his control and pushed her away.

"You merciless bitch!" he snarled, climbing out of the coach.

Breyandra's hands were trembling as she smoothed her hair and arranged her clothing. When she garnered enough composure to look out of the window, she found that the carriage had been pulled into the shade of some trees to rest the horses.

Jean and Jamie had sought the privacy of a nearby copse. Deep in conversation, they sat and held hands with their heads lowered toward one another. The four coachmen had moved down to the river bank and were lolling around on the grass chatting quietly among themselves.

David had untied Whirlwind, tethered to the rear of the coach for the journey, and had just finished saddling him. Adroitly David swung himself up into the saddle. Without even a sideward glance in her direction, he prodded Whirlwind and galloped away.

Chapter Nineteen

The remainder of the trip to Cambridge was an unpleasant experience for all the occupants of the coach. Breyandra sat sniffling, with tears trickling down her cheeks, as she wordlessly dwelled on her plight.

Other than an occasional pat on the hand, the sympathetic couple on the opposite seat could offer no words of solace to the heartbroken woman.

To further add to her misery, in her haste to dress Breyandra had forgotten a handkerchief. Finally Jamie Douglas, no longer able to witness her struggles with tears and sniffles, gallantly offered his own. Gratefully Breyandra snatched the proffered square of linen, dried her eyes, and blew her nose. Then she vowed she would not shed another tear on the matter.

Breyandra's suffering contained a large dose of guilt. David was no more responsible for the transgressions inflicted at Strehlow than she. Strehlow—a duty that demanded the sacrifice of their love.

She could not blame his anger. Why must she continue to hurt him? Her accusation was vicious and unjust. David was loving and affectionate. He would never force himself on her. Most likely he had intended a light kiss to awaken her. How often in the past had they wakened each other in such a manner? But his physical need for her was as great as her desire for him, and when she responded, though unconsciously, she had given him the encouragement to venture farther.

Breyandra leaned back her head and stared wistfully out of the window, remembering those sublime moments as she had teetered on the brink of wakefulness.

Oh, David! Why did I open my eyes?

It had not taken long for the King's courtiers to reassemble at Cambridge. By the time the carriage bearing Breyandra and Jean rumbled up the driveway of the royal residence, the merrymakers had resumed their revelry.

In the hope that David was among them, Breyandra changed quickly into a fresh gown and hurried to the ballroom. She was determined to apologize to him for her hurtful remark.

To her disappointment, she saw no sign of David in the crowd. Jean and James appeared self-absorbed, so Breyandra returned to her room. She spent another restless night with fretful thoughts of David Gordon filling her mind.

The chimes of a cathedral tolled the hour of six when Breyandra arose from bed the following morning. Despite the early hour, Charles was below in the courtyard, beginning his early-morning three-mile walk, a ritual he practiced daily. The King's long stride forced a vigorous pace on the few who were stout enough to join him.

Breyandra's heart leapt to her throat when she saw David Gordon join the King. From her vantage point, her eyes lovingly followed his tall figure until the small group disappeared into St. James's Park. Sighing desolately, she turned away.

Later that day, the royal colors of Charles Stuart fluttered majestically above the many banners flapping over the windswept gallery at Newmarket. Breyandra waged a losing battle to keep her chapeau at a fashionable angle. The wind caught the wide brim and lifted the hat off her head. Laughing gaily, Breyandra scampered in pursuit of the rolling bonnet. The wind toyed with her curls, and with a mighty gust swooped up her hair so that the silken strands flowed behind her head in long black streamers.

The hat tumbled across the ground, finally coming to rest against a pair of black boots firmly planted in its path. A hand reached down to retrieve the plumed finery just as Breyandra's fingers closed around it. Startled, she looked up into the dark eyes of David Gordon.

David stared transfixed. This was how he remembered his beloved, how he wanted her to remain: a laughing sprite on a windswept hill with her hair swirling around her face in glorious disarray, a wood nymph—seductive in her innocence, a daughter of Scotia, with no place among the posturing and jaded chicanery of the court. He fought the urge to swoop her into his arms and ride away with her as he once had done, never stopping until they reached the Highlands.

The unexpected encounter caught Breyandra off guard. Unabashed, she stared wordlessly at him. He looked magnificent. He was dressed in simple tartan breeks, a white shirt laced loosely at the neck, and a red Highland tam set firmly on his dark head.

"Thank you," she managed to mutter awkwardly. The look in his unrelenting dark eyes discouraged any further conversation. Nervously she brushed aside strands of hair straggling across her cheeks.

"Here, perhaps this will help." David removed his tam. Breyandra stood on the brink of trembling as he swept back her hair and set the tam on her head. Pleased with the result, he smiled. The simple tam was the perfect crown for the Celtic beauty of his Highland lass.

Breyandra could not force her gaze away from his beloved face. "I fear the hat is not a fitting complement for my dress, Lord Gordon."

Once again his jaw shifted rigidly. "Then perhaps the dress is wrong, not the tam, my lady."

"Nevertheless, the dress is what I have chosen to wear." Breyandra reached up and pulled the tam off her head. She could feel tears threatening to surface and pressed the cap into his hand. Then turning swiftly, she hurried back to the entourage assembled for the race.

Breyandra used the excuse that she had something in her eye in order to hurry past the group. When she felt confident her emotions were fully in check, she returned to the royal pavilion.

David had joined the gathering and was standing in front of the box deep in conversation with the King and the Duke of Buckingham. Whirlwind waited obediently a short distance behind his master.

"Last night I noticed you did not limp, Lord Gordon. Have you recovered from your wound?" Charles asked, as Breyandra entered the box.

"Fully, Your Majesty," David replied. His attention was drawn to Breyandra, who had taken the chair beside Jean.

However, Charles was not about to be put off so readily. "No adverse side effects? You know what I mean, old chap?" Charles inquired with a nudge to David's shoulder.

"I can assure Your Majesty, everything is functioning normally. Now, if you will excuse me, I must get ready for the race."

"Good luck, dear friend, and may the best horse win. You will give Old Rowley a good run?'' Charles asked with a hardy slap to David's back.

"You may be sure of that, my liege. Whirlwind does not like chewing anyone's dust.''

David went to his horse, swung up lithely into the saddle, and prodded Whirlwind over to where Jean was sitting. "A favor, my lady? Something I can carry for luck.''

Jean blushed with a guilty sideward glance at Breyandra. "I have nothing, Lord Gordon.''

David leaned across the head of Whirlwind and plucked a pink plume from Jean's hat. "This will be fine, my lady.'' He stuck the bright feather into the band of the horse's reins.

Breyandra felt a stab of pain at the open slight and lowered her head. She said nothing when Jamie and Jean wished him luck, and she did not raise her head until he galloped away.

Charles, who had witnessed the knightly gesture, smiled with broad approval. "Well, Lady Jean, it appears our young Lord Gordon is quite smitten with you.''

Jean giggled nervously and turned to Breyandra. She was about to voice a denial, but Jamie Douglas put a hand on her arm to caution Jean to silence. He could see that Breyandra had been shaken by the deed. Any further discussion would only add to her distress.

David had long since caught the eye of the King's mistress, and she was curious about the handsome Highlander. "Charles, what kind of wound did Lord Gordon suffer?'' Barbara Palmer inquired when Charles and Buckingham returned to their seats.

The King shook his head. "It was a sad sight to behold. Happened at Dunkirk while we were fighting that accursed Cromwell. The last time I saw Gordon he was bleeding like a stuck pig from a lance wound which ran the whole length of his thigh. A few inches higher . . ." The King threw his hands in the air in horror, rolling his eyes to make his point. "My conscience would haunt me for life. I appreciate his loyalty, but *that* sacrifice would be too much to ask of any man."

"And what a waste it would have been," Barbara Palmer reflected softly. Her eyes lasciviously followed David's broad back.

The story was just as intriguing to the Duke of Buckingham. He sat pensively weighing the King's words.

David's intent, from the time the King had asked him to race Whirlwind, had been to let Old Rowley be the victor, as a sentimental gesture of respect to a superb animal running his final race. But once the race began, David realized that Whirlwind sensed he was challenging the finest, and to restrain the steed would break the spirit of the horse. David gave Whirlwind free rein.

The long experience and skill of Old Rowley's jacky was of no consequence; the outcome of the race would be decided by the two horses alone.

Old Rowley was bred from the blood of champions, as royal as his master.

Whirlwind was a creature of the wild Scottish

Highlands, as spirited and stouthearted as the Highlander who rode him.

Each horse ran to win.

Not a spectator remained in his seat. All were on their feet cheering the resolute efforts of two magnificent stallions running neck to neck in the four-mile race.

Nostrils flared. Eyes distended. Manes flew. Stride for stride they matched one another, their thundering hooves muffled by the roar of the crowd as they raced toward the finish flag.

The roll of drums and blare of trumpets signaled the finish of the race as a tumultuous shout of approval rocked the rafters when the two horses crossed the finish line as one.

The spectators, the King among them, broke from their seats and dashed onto the track. Jamie Douglas was the first to reach David when he dismounted. The young Scotsman was ecstatic as he shook David's hand and pounded his back.

Both riders were surrounded by well-wishers. Breyandra was so proud of Whirlwind her heart was aching. She stood apart from the crowd, holding Whirlwind's reins, patting and kissing the horse as tears of happiness streaked her face.

After paying homage to his own stallion and jack, Charles and his mistress moved to the crowd surrounding David. The King hugged David as he wiped a royal tear from his eye. "Davie, old friend, that was the greatest race I have ever seen. I shall not forget it to my dying day. My debt of gratitude to you increases."

When the King moved to Whirlwind, Barbara

Palmer stepped up to David and smiled seductively. "Indeed, my Lord Gordon, I was thrilled." She put her arms around his neck and drew his head down to hers. Breyandra felt a stab of jealousy as the courtesan's mouth closed over David's in a lingering kiss. When Barbara stepped back her eyes gleamed salaciously. "Perhaps I can find a better way of thanking you for the pleasure you've brought me this day. Shall we say midnight in the rose arbor?" she whispered, then turned away with a backward smile.

Charles, engrossed with Whirlwind, had not witnessed her bold action. "Name your price for this magnificent animal, Lord Gordon. I must have him. I'll meet whatever you ask for him."

Breyandra gasped aloud and held her breath expectantly. Her glance swung anxiously to David. How could he refuse a request from the King? She knew how much he loved Whirlwind. Would David give away the animal that had been so devoted to him through the years?

"If I were to part with Whirlwind, I would be betraying a friend's loyalty and trust, Your Majesty." At the sight of David's crooked grin, Breyandra felt a tug at her heartstrings. "But I am sure he would not object to my sharing that devotion with your mares whenever you desire."

Charles laughed heartily and slapped him on the shoulders. "A bargain met, old friend."

Taking Barbara's arm, the King moved away and the crowd began to disperse. Unaware that David had moved directly behind her,

Breyandra dropped Whirlwind's reins and started to turn away just as he reached around her to remove the pink plume still tucked in the horse's band. She found herself in the circle of his arms. The close proximity was a shock to both of them, and the temptation to surrender to the moment was evident in the eyes of both. Then the desire in David's eyes was gone and his jaw shifted into a grim line. "My apologies, my lady." His head bobbed in a polite bow and he stepped away.

Breyandra followed the others back to the royal pavilion.

Charles had planned a lavish ball for the evening, and Breyandra was swept up in the excitement. Whatever else occurred that evening, this was the night she was determined to make her long-overdue apology to David.

Just thinking about it made her feel good, as if a burden were being lifted off her shoulders. David's grins and warm chuckles had been absent too long. If she bore the fault of losing them, her responsibility was to see them return.

Then, once his anger vanished, she could calmly explain to him why she would never return to Strehlow. No matter how much she loved him.

Breyandra took careful preparation with her appearance. First she luxuriated in a hot bath until she was certain not a tense muscle remained in her body. She shampooed her hair with a creamy Parisian lather, then brushed the strands until they glistened. She chose the most conservative gown in her wardrobe, a simple one-piece dress of black velvet that she had brought from Scotland. Her arms and shoulders were primly covered, and the round, scooped neckline showed only a minimal amount of cleavage.

When Breyandra surveyed herself in the mirror, her spirits plummeted and she sighed in despair. *I look like I'm going to a funeral.* Looking about in desperation, she spied one of her lavish bonnets and saw the opportunity to kill two birds with one stone. With impish delight, Breyandra ripped a pink plume from the bonnet and attached the feather to her head with a pearl-encrusted pin.

So, David Gordon, you won't be able to say I look like a court harlot tonight. Compared to all of the other women in their bright satin gowns, I'll look as if I'm in mourning. Will that satisfy you?

Smiling with satisfaction, she dabbed perfume behind each ear and grabbed a fan before hurrying from the room.

Chapter Twenty

David's eyes devoured Breyandra when she entered the ballroom. Before they could exchange a word, Charles caught the attention of those near him by rapping several times on the floor with his tall cane. Soon others in the room, using similar walking sticks, joined him in the signal.

"My dear friends," Charles proclaimed in his sonorous voice when the laughter and talk were hushed, "you are aware that one of my first official acts as your monarch was to create a royal society dedicated to furthering the pursuit of science."

"Here! Here!" voices called out and the room echoed with applause.

Charles humbly acknowledged the accolade and raised his hand for silence. "However, my esteemed comrades Buckingham and Rochester feel the society should be broadened to accept literary and poetic endeavors as well. Indeed, our dear friend Buckingham has created a work which he feels is commendable of such consideration." With a regal flourish, Charles moved aside, and George Villiers, the Second Duke of Buckingham, stepped forward.

Villiers wore a black curly periwig that hung to his shoulders. Scarlet ribbons dangled from elbow-length sleeves on the waist of a blue satin doublet. His white shirt, of the finest cambric, blossomed in voluminous folds at the lower arms and waist. A blue satin skirt falling to just above his knees was worn over matching pantaloons gathered at each knee by bright bows of scarlet ribbons. Consistent with the stylish ensemble, a wide border of gold thread wound its way up the sides of white silk hose, and bright red heels adorned the square-toed shoes of black leather.

This fashionable, effeminate image belied the true character of the man. Two years older than Charles, Buckingham was a member of the close-knit group of hard-drinking, hard-swearing cronies who surrounded the King. A cousin of Barbara Palmer, Villiers had a biting, ribald wit, often concealing the deep affection he held for Charles.

Now the center of attention, the Duke of Buckingham leaned on his walking cane, elaborately decorated with dangling ribbons, and postured theatrically. His eyes slowly swept the crowded room until his glance came to rest on

David Gordon. "I have entitled my offering 'Invocation.'" He paused dramatically, then with histrionic gestures began to recite his poem.

"Upon a wintry Sunday on a frozen
　　Dunkirk crag,
There fell a cocky Highlander in
　　Old Rowley's third brigade.
When the Roundhead raised his lance,
　　the Gordon was heard to beg,
'I can make do without my right or left,
　　but spare my middle leg.'"

Laughter erupted from those who were aware of the nature of David's wound. The story passed from lip to lip until the room was engulfed with snorts and giggles.

Jean Fleming failed to appreciate the Duke's humor. "The despicable man," she fumed. "How can he make mockery of Lord Gordon's injury?"

In the face of the poor girl's distress, James Douglas tried to appear as serious as possible. "He can joke, Jeanie, because David's injury has healed without any serious effects."

"And were it Buckingham himself who sustained the wound, would he be so quick to deride?" Jean challenged.

To her surprise, Jamie nodded. "I am sure he would, my lady. 'Tis the nature of men."

Breyandra stood silent throughout the exchange, her eyes luminous as she recalled the sight of the ragged scar. Charles and Buckingham had moved to David's side and the three men laughed good-naturedly with each other. Like Jean, Breyandra saw little amusement in what might have happened to David. For a moment her tormented glance locked with David's, before she turned and fled from the room.

When David saw the anguish Breyandra was suffering, his good humor dissipated immediately. He was not disturbed by Buckingham's gibes. Being the only Scots in the close circle of the King made Jamie and himself a favorite target of the Duke of Buckingham's wit. But since even Charles was often the brunt of the Duke's humor, and all knew the depth of Buckingham's devotion to the King, no one ever took offense to the jesting.

Breyandra's distress only confirmed David's belief of the need to get her away from the sophistication of the court. When the opportunity presented itself, he slipped away to seek her out. He found her alone in the King's privy garden.

"I cannot bear to see you so distraught," he said softly from a short distance.

Startled, Breyandra glanced up. In the moonlight, her eyes glistened mistily with unshed tears. "David!" slipped through her lips.

He stepped out of the shadows. "I'm sorry if I frightened you, my lady."

Breyandra offered a lame smile and her hand fluttered in nervousness to her breast. "Lately I find myself in a constant state of agitation, my lord."

He moved closer, his light chuckle an added warmth in the lovely garden. "I wager I'm the cause of much of your unrest."

"You alone are not at fault. I find nothing amusing in the humor of the Duke of Buckingham."

"He meant no harm by the jest, my lady."

His words pierced her. She closed her eyes to mask the sting. "David, I saw some of the pain you suffered with that wound. It should not be taken lightly."

His reply was so soft as to be a whisper. "Yet, you have not hesitated to inflict a much deeper pain."

Her remorse was evident as she looked up into his dark eyes, and when their gazes locked, Breyandra felt their very souls reaching out to one another. "I never meant to hurt you, David. I never wanted to. I wish I could convince you how much I regret having lashed out at you in the carriage. I know you never meant . . . would never touch me . . ."

". . . in any manner except in love," he finished for her. David reached out and cupped her cheeks in his hands. His touch was warm. Tender. As loving as the dark gaze that caressed her. "Lord, I love you, Twit. I've told myself I would not force the matter. I would wait until you came to me. Yet, the sight of you causes me to lose any resolve, and my mind becomes possessed with the need to hold you—to love you."

Her brown eyes shimmered with tears. "I, too, have told myself the wisdom of forgetting you. But how am I to forget the feel of your arms around me, or the thrill of your kiss? Everything pales in comparison." She turned her cheek and kissed the palm of his hand. "I love you, David. I can't keep trying to deny it."

He pulled her into his arms and held her. She burrowed her cheek against the comforting wall of his chest. David rested his cheek against her head, breathing in the sweet scent of her perfumed hair. "Then why, Twit? Why did you run away from me?"

She raised her head, but before she could answer he rained a dozen kisses on her lips, her eyes, her cheeks. Then on her neck, on her throat. He returned to cover her lips, lightly in the beginning, soon crushing in demand. Their tongues searched and toyed as passion spiraled.

Her body trembled as every nerve responded to his touch. Her heaving breasts swelled and her breathing began to come in ragged gasps.

He moved his mouth to her neck and she threw back her head to give him freer access to the slender column. David drew a moist trail to her breasts as his hands slid the heavy velvet gown off her shoulders.

His tongue played with each hardened peak until his lips closed moistly around one, drawing the taut nipple into his mouth. Her body, too long denied, responded feverishly.

David raised his head and gazed down at her face. Her lips were parted in invitation and her eyelids heavy with passion. The ache in his groin was becoming unbearable. "Tell me what I want to hear," he whispered. "I want to hear you say it."

"Yes, Yes," she sobbed in near delirium. "I want you, David. Make love to me. Now. Now."

"No more games. No more denials," he rasped. His tongue traced a circle around her parted lips. "You'll become my Mistress?"

"Yes. Yes. Whatever you say." She squirmed erotically in his arms and opened her eyes in supplication. Her fingers groped to release his trousers. "Take me now, David." The blood in his temples pounded at his skull and his throbbing groin was near eruption. With a guttural growl, his mouth crushed down on hers.

"My, my, what a stimulating scene. May I join you?"

Barbara Palmer stepped out of the shadows. The salacious gleam in her eyes revealed the length of time she had been watching them. Her tongue snaked out and moistened her lips. "Perhaps a *ménage à trois* would heighten the pleasure?"

David's hands slipped from Breyandra's shoulders. Mortified, Breyandra felt a hot flush. Her legs could barely support her. She leaned back against the brick wall.

"I think not, Lady Castlemaine. Your ill-timed interruption is as unwelcome as your presence," David said icily.

"Then may I suggest later . . . in the King's chambers? Charles might enjoy the sport."

"Don't ever make such a suggestion again or I'll wring your whoring neck." David's eyes blazed with loathing as he shoved the woman away.

Breyandra flinched, gripped by a shudder of revulsion. She felt defiled and humiliated. With a strangled sob of anger, Breyandra pulled up the sleeves of her gown and fled the garden.

David glared down in loathing at Barbara Palmer. Then he spun on his heel and stormed away.

The woman's eyes glistened with hatred as she watched him disappear. The face of Barbara Palmer curved into a cunning smile as she began to formulate her revenge.

Breyandra had reached the top of the stairway by the time David entered the hall. He was about to follow her when one of the servants approached to inform him the King had summoned David to the royal chambers.

Damnit, what now? he cursed silently as he followed the man.

Charles and the Lord Chancellor, Edward Hyde, were awaiting him. Hyde jumped to his feet when David entered the room.

"You are a difficult man to locate, Lord Gordon," Charles announced with a wink. "Poor Clarendon here has been beside himself with concern."

"Lord Clarendon," David acknowledged with a brief nod. "How may I be of service, Your Majesty?"

"I think Clarendon can best explain the problem," Charles replied.

The Earl of Clarendon was a paradox at the

court of the Merry Monarch. The older man had no taste for the frivolities of the court. Dour and intelligent, Hyde was the King's closest adviser. Loyal to the Stuart cause, he had been with Charles throughout the exile of the young prince. His loyalty had been rewarded; as Lord Chancellor of England, Edward Hyde was the most politically powerful man in the country.

However, one other person wielded as much influence over the King as Hyde—Charles Stuart's mistress, Lady Castlemaine. The politically ambitious Barbara Palmer vied for supremacy with England's Lord Chancellor.

Edward Hyde, obviously nervous, withdrew a white handkerchief from his pocket and mopped his brow. Though of the finest linen, like himself the square cloth was without frills.

"This night I have returned from the court of Portugal where the final arrangements have been made for the King's future nuptials. However, health prevented the princess from accompanying me on the return trip."

David was surprised to hear of still another delay in the royal wedding; one reason or another had postponed the nuptials for almost a year.

Hyde frowned grimly. "A source has informed me that the French will try to prevent the safe arrival of Princess Catherine and make it appear that Spain is behind the plot."

"What would France gain by such a ploy?" David asked, confused.

"France and Spain have long been enemies. If Spain was suspected of harming the royal princess, Portugal and England would align together against Spain. From a military standpoint, France could only profit."

"A simple solution would be to have the future Queen sail secretly," David suggested.

Hyde snorted disparagingly. "Over a hundred people are accompanying the Portuguese Infanta. It would be difficult to keep such a departure secret."

Charles rose to his feet. "To assure the comfort of my queen, I have dispatched the finest ship in the fleet, *The Royal Charles* itself," he said with pride, "with the Earl of Sandwich as captain. He sailed a week ago, together with a naval escort. But I fear that if the rumor has merit, the French will try to harm my precious Catherine when the ship arrives in Portsmouth."

Charles clamped a firm hand on David's shoulder. "You are one of the few men I trust with the life of my future queen. I want you to sail to France, David. We have an agent there named Emile Roget. He is attempting to learn the name of the assassin and will pass on the information to you. I am depending upon you to foil the scheme and assure the safe arrival of the Princess Catherine."

"I pledge my sword, Your Majesty."

Grateful for his loyalty, Charles embraced David. "Then I will have nothing to fear. Nor will my sweet Catherine. Tomorrow I shall go to Whitehall to await your return."

Edward Hyde still appeared disturbed. "You must leave at once, my lord." The man's dour expression deepened. "A grave responsibility rides on your shoulders, Lord Gordon."

"Ride with the wind, dear friend. Until we have the gentle innocent safe in Whitehall, I shall not spend a restful night."

When David departed the chamber, Barbara Palmer stood outside the door, her face drawn into a smile of satisfaction. "A shame our future queen has been delayed, Lord Gordon."

David was disgruntled that he had been chosen for the mission. The voyage to France and back could take a week. He had just found Breyandra, and now he had to leave her. The sight of Barbara Palmer only added to his annoyance. "I am sure you find the news distressing, Lady Castlemaine."

Barbara's eyes narrowed slyly. "And what a pity you are forced to leave your precious love. Be assured, we will take special care of her." Her lips parted seductively and she drew a moist circle with her tongue.

The subtle implication caused a knot in his stomach. He wanted to grab the woman and shake her senseless. "Madam, I am certain I made my position plain in the garden. I won't hesitate to carry out my threat."

Barbara Palmer's smile was confident and sinister. "It is unwise to make an enemy of me, Lord Gordon. No one threatens the mistress of the King."

David's eyes glared with loathing. "My enemies have learned the same about me, Lady Castlemaine."

He walked away.

David knew he must warn Breyandra of potential danger. He was certain that Charles would not be a party to Lady Castlemaine's lascivious machinations, but there were many at court who would not hesitate to join in.

Breyandra opened the door to his urgent knock. Her eyes were puffy from crying, and she rushed into his arms. "Oh, David, I never felt so humiliated. I never knew anyone as perverted as Lady Castlemaine. How can the King abide such wickedness?"

He smiled tenderly, marveling at her innocence. "No doubt, her . . . sophistication . . . pleasures him like that of no other woman he has known." Her eyes widened in shock. "While I, on the other hand, prefer a woman who has been schooled to please just me alone." Breyandra blushed profusely and dropped her eyes. Grinning, he tucked a finger under her chin and forced her to meet his gaze. "A most proficient learner."

She smiled up appealingly. "And willing student."

David kissed the tip of her nose. "Who has been grossly negligent in her studies lately."

Breyandra slipped her arms around his neck, molding herself to the solid length of him. "Then perhaps the instructor has been remiss for not reviewing the lessons."

"Lord knows he tried hard enough, my love," he whispered lightly, before he kissed her.

The moment their lips met, Breyandra felt her body ignite. A surge of excitement consumed her like a roaring fire, heating the blood that flooded her head, her breasts, the core of her femininity. In the past year their traitorous minds had often played this moment in tortured fantasy. Their long-denied bodies were waiting —were ready.

David stripped her of her clothing and lifted her into his arms. The silken sheets felt icy against her heated body when he laid her on the bed. She stretched out, sinking onto the feathery downiness of the mattress and pillows. Her face was flushed, her nipples rigid peaks as she writhed in the throes of passion. Inflamed, he tore away his clothing.

Breyandra opened her eyes, her vision a fevered blur. Uninhibited, she groaned and raised her arms to him. David lowered himself, and her arms closed around him, drawing him against her. She arched her spine, and her body pressed into the hard, muscular wall of his stomach and chest. Her fingers ravaged the length of his back, feeling the corded brawn jerking in response beneath her fingertips.

Heated blood rushed to his head and began pulsating at his temples. The sinews of his arms were taut as he gripped her and drove into her. He began to vibrate, the cords of his neck extended with strain, and she grasped his shoulders, her knuckles turning white as her fingers bit into the drawn flesh when her body and mind erupted.

The exquisite spasms continued interminably.

When Breyandra finally opened her eyes, David's head was slumped against her shoulder. They were both breathing in ragged gasps.

Her fingers lightly grazed the length of his

spine to gentle the muscled column now coated with a fine sheen of perspiration.

David raised his head and for a breathless moment gazed down in adoration before he dipped his head to press a tender kiss on her parted lips.

Breyandra felt the spark ignite and begin its fiery spread throughout her body. But her passion was quickly quelled by the sting of his words. "I must leave, my love." With a final light kiss, he rose to his feet and began to dress.

She sat up in disbelief. "You must leave?"

With a contrite glance David sat down on the edge of the bed to put on his boots. "At once. The King has ordered me to France." He saw no reason for telling her of Hyde's suspicions.

"How long will you be gone?"

"A week, I venture."

Breyandra drew a long, shuddering breath to restore air to her deflating lungs. "This is just deserts for my foolish actions. Oh, David, the time we have wasted!"

"We will make it up, my love. But until then, I want you to beware. Keep your chamber door locked and do not answer any summons. Tomorrow the King is returning to London. Stay close to Jamie Douglas. He'll see to your safety."

"But why, David? I have nothing to fear from the King."

He rose to his feet with a grim frown. "You need not be wary of the King. It is Lady Castlemaine. I have made an enemy of her, and I fear she will not hesitate to harm you in order to strike back at me. When I return, we will wed."

Bewildered, Breyandra rose from the bed, pulling the sheet around her? "Wed? I said naught of wedding."

David felt the telltale stirring begin to knot his stomach. "In the garden you promised to become my Mistress."

"And I shall be, David. Whenever you want, I will come to you. London . . . Paris . . . Edinburgh."

He was struck with the full realization of her words. "You mean as my whore?" He grasped her shoulders and stared down at her in disbelief. "When did I give you reason to believe that I wanted you as anything other than my wife? My Mistress of Strehlow?"

Breyandra felt as if he had dealt her a blow. She stepped back, her eyes rounded with an emerging feeling of dread. "No. No." The denial came out as a horrified sob. "Not Strehlow. I can't go back there, David. I could never go back there."

With a feeling of hopelessness, he let his arms drop from her shoulders. "Breyandra, I am Master of Strehlow. Strehlow is my home."

Turning, he left the room.

Chapter Twenty-one

The light tapping on her chamber door awoke Breyandra from a troubled sleep. Heeding David's advice, she had kept her door bolted since he left. Groggily she rose from the bed and crossed to the door.

A maid entered carrying a tray. Welcoming the opportunity of not having to dress and join the others, Breyandra settled back in bed to enjoy her breakfast. As always, her thoughts strayed to David.

Her lovely face grimaced in despair as she recalled his formidable and unrelenting manner the night he departed for France. A week had passed, and each day she missed him more. So much was unresolved between them. How was their love to survive with the never-ending question of Strehlow hovering over them?

When she spied a small envelope on the tray, Breyandra's spirits soared at the familiar sight of her father's script. She had last seen him over a year ago. Hastily she tore open the letter and scanned the page, present woes momentarily shoved to the back of her mind. Then squealing with delight, Breyandra put aside the tray and bounced out of bed.

She rang the bell cord, summoning the maid to assist her in dressing. Within the hour, Breyandra climbed into the carriage that would take her to the residence her father had taken in London.

Simon Fraser joyously greeted his daughter the moment the carriage stopped before the small manse near the outskirts of the city. After several hugs and kisses, they entered the house, hand in hand.

Breyandra's step was light as her father led her to a small solar bright with sunshine. She paused at the entrance, staring in amazement at Elysia Gordon. Always a beautiful woman, Elysia glowed with radiance and was lovelier than ever. Her condition became obvious when the diminutive woman rose to her feet, her arms open in welcome.

"Why . . . you're . . . you're . . ."

"With child," Elysia finished as the two women embraced. Her light laughter floated on the air like the tinkle of a wind chime. Unable to resist the lyrical sound, Simon put his arm around her shoulders, drawing his love to his side.

Astonished, Breyandra stammered, "But . . .

I thought . . . that you couldn't . . . that you were . . . barren."

"I believed that to be true." Elysia smiled up at Simon, her eyes shining with devotion. "But love finds a way to triumph over infirmity."

Simon squeezed her hand in affection, grinning broadly. "A romantic sentiment, my love."

Elysia's quick blush heightened the loveliness of her face. "Yes, my beloved. I am convinced our child is a bairn begot by love."

The older woman's happiness was infectious. Smiling with pleasure, Breyandra hugged Elysia again. "I'm so happy for you. I hope it's a girl. I've always wanted a sister."

Elysia giggled like a young lass. "And David always yearned for a brother." Too late to retract them, the words slipped from Elysia before she remembered the sensitive situation between her son and Breyandra. The embarrassed woman cast a stricken look toward Simon, seeking his help in easing the moment.

Breyandra smiled in understanding. "I know David will be delighted to hear the news, and just as surprised as I am. I can't wait to tell him."

Two pairs of eyes fixed on Breyandra in surprise. Simon voiced the question on both of their minds. "You've seen David?"

Breyandra nodded. "At court. He came to London for the royal wedding."

The stricken look on Elysia's face altered to one of joy. "David is here in London?"

"I'm afraid not at the moment. He departed a

305

week ago for France on a mission for the King."

Elysia could not disguise her disappointment. "Then I've missed him." Crushed, she sank down in a chair.

"He is expected to return any day. You're remaining in England for the wedding, aren't you?" she asked, trying to bolster the poor woman's spirits.

Simon shook his head. "We've already tarried too long on the Continent. Elysia's delicate condition is nearing her time of waiting. I'll not delay our return to Scotland any longer."

He moved to Elysia and put a hand on the back of her chair. "I won't risk the health of Elysia or our child. David can come to Saltoun when the wedding is over."

"Yes, that is the wisest thing to do," Elysia sighed softly. "But, oh, to have missed him! I yearn to see him so much."

Breyandra could easily sympathize with the sentiment. She sat down to relate whatever details she could recall about Elysia's wayward son.

Later that afternoon while Elysia napped, Simon and Breyandra strolled through a garden abloom with spring flowers. As she stood admiring a budding rose, Breyandra's thoughts strayed to her tragic memory of the rose garden at Strehlow. Deep in reflection, she was unaware that her father was studying her intently.

"Are you still in love with him, Sweetling?"

Breyandra glanced at him in dismay. "Am I so transparent?"

"To one who loves you as I do." He opened his arms and Breyandra hastened into his embrace. She pressed her head against his chest and closed her eyes with contentment when his arms closed around her. "Father, what am I to do? I love David so much. For the past year I've run away from everything and everyone I love. But I can't keep running."

"Does David love you?" Simon asked, kissing the top of her head.

Breyandra looked up at him, her young face wrought with misery. "Yes, as much as I do him."

He smiled sagely. "Then why keep running, Sweetling? Why are you fighting what is in your heart?"

"I can't go back to Strehlow, Father. I turn rigid with fright every time I think of that hideous place. I can't put the horror out of my mind."

Simon felt her begin to tremble and grasped her hand. Breyandra's fingers were icy to the touch. Sighing sorrowfully, she burrowed her head against his chest. "What am I to do, Father?"

Simon embraced her protectively as he commiserated with her suffering. But he knew only she could wage the struggle within her. Smiling tenderly, he lifted her chin to force his daughter to meet his gaze. "Sweetling, I know you have the intelligence and the courage needed to reach the solution you seek." With a rueful smile, he added, "Like Elysia, I want to believe that love can overcome any obstacle."

Unconvinced, Breyandra looked up at him. "Father, how am I to convince David that I love him enough to face whatever the future holds, when I'm unable to erase the past?"

Simon's eyes were troubled as he stared down sadly at her. "I can't answer that for you, Sweetling. You're the only one who can weigh the price you must pay for love."

Later after Elysia rejoined them, they kept the conversation light and amusing. Neither Simon nor Breyandra wanted to alarm Elysia with the knowledge that Breyandra's problems with David were still not resolved.

Breyandra had just finished her meal when a servant informed her that the carriage had arrived from Whitehall. Breyandra hugged and kissed Elysia goodbye with a promise that she would return to Saltoun when the time neared for the delivery of the baby.

Simon walked with his daughter out to the coach and the two embraced. "I wish you were returning with us tomorrow, Sweetling."

"I promise I'll return as soon as the royal wedding is over," Breyandra assured him.

They lingered, neither wanting to say goodbye. The coachman cleared his throat. "We'd best be underway."

Disgusted with the man's impudence, Simon glared at the driver. He barely had time to close the carriage door before the man whipped the horses to motion.

Breyandra leaned out of the carriage window and waved. "Goodbye, Father. Take care of Elysia. I love you."

Simon watched the coach rumble away. He didn't want her to leave. For some inexplicable reason, he felt an unusual sense of loss at this parting. He raised his hands to his mouth to call back the carriage, then thought better of it and dropped his arms to his sides, turned, and entered the house.

David Gordon prodded his mount to a faster gait. The closer he got to Whitehall, the greater was his desire to see Breyandra. Lord, how he loved her.

He could not sustain his anger with Breyandra. The exasperation he felt at their previous conflicts was outweighed by the need to hold her in his arms.

He knew he must somehow resolve the problem of Strehlow and convince her to return. Until then, he would not press her to marry him. He would enjoy each day they could have together.

When he reached Whitehall, a groomsman took his horse, and David hurried into the palace. He wanted to seek Breyandra at once, but knew the King would be awaiting his return.

Charles and Barbara Palmer were engaged in a game of cribbage when David joined them. At the sight of David, Charles threw down his cards and jumped up from his chair. "Lord Gordon! I've been most anxious for your return."

David bowed in greeting. "Your Majesty." Negligently acknowledging the woman's presence, he added, "Lady Castlemaine." He turned his back to avoid accepting her proffered hand.

"Dear Barbary, you will excuse us," Charles requested.

Barbara Palmer was already seething at David's affront; the abrupt dismissal by the King only fueled her fury. Pegs and cards flew in all directions when she slammed down the cribbage board. She swept from the room without uttering a word.

Eager to hear David's report, Charles paid no heed to the petty tantrum of his mistress. "I'll summon Lord Clarendon at once," Charles said. He rang for a servant, and within minutes Edward Hyde scurried into the chamber.

Once they were all seated around the table, Charles turned to his young emissary. "Now, David, feel safe to speak freely."

"Your Majesty, I met with Emile Roget. He relentlessly pursued the rumor with all his contacts at court and the underground. Roget and his colleagues are convinced that there is no plot by the French court to harm Catherine of Braganza. The rumor was traced to a bistro in Marseille. Two Portuguese seamen raped and killed a young French girl. In a drunken rage, the girl's brother vowed revenge and threatened to harm the Portuguese Infanta. The man was later killed in a barroom brawl."

Charles leaned back in his chair and smiled with relief. "Then my Queen is safe."

Edward Hyde was equally relieved to know that the marriage of the King would not be impeded any further. The Lord Chancellor was uneasy about the delays of the royal nuptials. Despite Charles's personal popularity with his subjects, Hyde knew that these were still troubled times. England was a Protestant country. The Anglican Church did not look favorably upon Charles's brother and heir, the Duke of York—an avowed Catholic. The sooner Charles wed and produced an heir, the sooner England —and Edward Hyde—would rest easy.

David tried not to appear impatient when Charles insisted the two men join him for a glass of wine. Several of the King's dogs trotted into the room, and David was obliged to pass another quarter hour watching Charles greet and pet each animal. During the whole delay, David was thinking about Breyandra, who was somewhere within the very walls of the palace.

When Charles raced playfully from the room, pursued by a dozen tail-wagging spaniels yapping at his heels, David and Edward Hyde exchanged tolerant glances and departed.

David mounted the stairs two at a time and went directly to Breyandra's chamber. A maid who was cleaning the room spun around in surprise when he entered unannounced.

"The Lady Breyandra?" David asked, chagrined not to find his beloved.

The woman curtsied politely. "Gone, m'lord, since morning."

"Do you know where?" His disappointment was immense. Yet another delay before he could hold Breyandra in his arms!

"Yes, m'lord. Lady Breyandra received a letter from her father here in London and has gone to visit him."

The news was a pleasant surprise. If Simon

Fraser was in London, David knew his mother would be as well. "Do you know where Lord Lovet is residing?" he asked.

The woman shook her head. "No, m'lord, but Ned the coachman will know. 'Twas he who drove her."

"Thank you. Thank you," David said enthusiastically. He fled from the room and rushed to the carriage house.

David had no problem locating Ned, who told him of the location of Simon Fraser's house. "It won't be necessary for you to go back for the Lady Breyandra. I'll see to her return," David informed the man.

"Thank you, m'lord, but it won't be necessary. A carriage departed to transport m'lady back here not more than a quarter of an hour ago. The driver said his orders were to fetch her." Ned's brow furrowed in a frown. "Surprised me, it did, m'lord, since I'm Lady Breyandra's driver."

Struck by a premonition, David felt the hair bristle on the nape of his neck. "Who was the driver?"

His misgivings intensified when the coachman answered, "I don't know, Lord Gordon."

David grasped the man's arm in alarm. "You mean he wasn't one of the regular coachmen?"

The frightened driver did not understand David's cause for concern. "No, m'lord. His name and face were new to me. He asked me the house, same as you, then left."

By this time David's spine was taut with

tension. "Did he take one of the royal carriages?"

Nearly cowering before David's mounting distress, Ned shook his head. "I don't know, m'lord. I paid him no mind."

David called the coachmen together and, to his dread, none of the men were aware of a new driver. Furthermore, all the carriages were accounted for.

His suspicions confirmed, David dashed to the mews and saddled Whirlwind. Within seconds he galloped away.

From a vantage point of a window in her chamber, Barbara Palmer watched his hasty departure. She threw back her head and laughed.

Chapter Twenty-two

Sighing deeply, Breyandra sat back in the carriage for the return ride to Whitehall. After a short distance, the driver reined the carriage to a stop. Breyandra leaned out the window to see what had caused the delay. She saw a man step out of the shadows. Before she realized his intent, he had opened the door and jumped into the carriage.

Breyandra tried to scream, but the man clamped a hand over her mouth. As she struggled to free herself, he overpowered her, shoving a dirty scarf into her mouth. Breyandra struck out at him while he tied a torn strip around her mouth to hold the gag in place. Her nails drew a bloody streak down her assailant's cheek.

"You bitch!" he snarled, and he lashed out

with a backhand across her face. The force of
the blow knocked her down on the seat.
Breyandra writhed in pain when he jammed his
knee into the center of her back, pressing her
face into the seat, while he yanked her arms
behind her back and tied her wrists together. He
then grasped her legs and bound her ankles.

The blackguard threw her to the floor of the
carriage, then settled down in the seat with a
cruel sneer.

Breyandra was in near panic as she struggled
to free herself, but the fetters held securely. All
the horrors of that frightful night at Strehlow
closed in on her. She gasped for air, but the gag
in her mouth kept her from drawing deep
breaths into her lungs. The harder she tried to
breathe, the more her panic escalated, until she
finally blacked out. She lay unconscious as the
carriage continued down the lane.

Galloping along the road, David encountered
several coaches but saw no sign of Breyandra
when he glanced through the carriage windows.
Most of the coaches appeared to be occupied by
couples on their way to the opera.

He had no difficulty locating the house Ned
had described. Reining up Whirlwind, David
leapt from the saddle before the stallion had
come to a complete stop. The servant who
opened the door to David's steady pounding
peered warily at the agitated man.

"I'm Lord Gordon. I've come seeking the
Lady Breyandra," David snapped anxiously.

Attracted by the loud rapping, Simon Fraser

entered the foyer. "Who is it, George?"

Simon drew up in surprise when David shoved past the servant and entered the hallway. "Lord Gordon!"

David was too distraught for formalities. "Is Breyandra here?"

Simon sensed the gravity behind David's curtness. "She's been gone these past ten minutes. What is the cause for alarm?"

"Damnation!" David cursed, recalling the last coach he had passed. The carriage bore a gold crest painted on the door and seemed to have a lone male occupant.

When David moved to depart, Simon grabbed his arm. "Is Breyandra in danger?"

David looked the man squarely in the eyes and nodded grimly. "I think she's been abducted. The coachman who fetched her is not from Whitehall."

Simon did not wait for further explanation. "Saddle my horse at once." The servant rushed away to obey the command. "I'll get my sword."

David was already out the door. "There is no time for delay. I am certain I passed the carriage on the road." He swung himself up into the saddle.

By the time Simon strapped on his sword, his mount was saddled. Whirlwind's dust had not even settled to the ground, when Simon thundered down the path in pursuit.

Clouds moved across the face of the moon, casting the road in darkness. After a short time of hard riding, David spied the lantern of the carriage in the distance. Breyandra's abductors had not anticipated being pursued and were not exercising any caution to avoid being seen.

A wide gap separated him from the carriage, and as he neared a congested area of the city, David was forced to reduce Whirlwind's gait. However, he was still able to keep the coach in sight.

In the meantime, Simon had caught up with David. Silent and grim, the two men rode along side by side. The coach turned a corner and swung off in the direction of the wharf. By the time the two pursuers reached the spot, darkness had swallowed up the carriage.

A few lanterns dotted the lonely wharf. Hearing the clang of bells from buoys bobbing in the harbor, eerily muffled by a misty fog rolling in from the ocean, David and Simon peered through the darkness. They were able to discern the tall, skeletal shadows of the few ships anchored in the harbor.

"I venture one of those ships is either Moorish or Chinese." The ominous thought quickly fueled Simon's greatest fear. "The villains intend my daughter's fate to be a Barbary Coast harem or a Chinese crib!" Simon's dark eyes gleamed with deadly fury. "Who could be behind this foul scheme?"

David had reached the same conclusion and he struggled to keep his own anger in check. "I'm uncertain, but I suspect Lady Castlemaine."

His answer shocked Simon. He raised his

head, asking incredulously, "The King's mistress?"

David nodded. "The woman is a vindictive bitch."

"But why would the King's . . ." Simon's eyes narrowed with suspicion and indignation. "Damn you, Gordon! Don't tell me you've cozened the King's mistress, too?"

David regarded the older man with affront. "Good Lord, no! Barbara Palmer frightened . . . indeed, terrorized Breyandra. I warned the malicious bitch to leave Breyandra alone." David wanted to believe that even Barbara Palmer was incapable of such cruelty. "Breyandra's abduction so soon on the heels of Barbara's malevolence may just be a coincidence."

"I suggest we find my daughter and save your theorizing for later," Simon declared curtly. "Whoever abducted her couldn't have gone too far with her."

The two men dismounted and began to move cautiously through the shadows. The sound of laughter erupted from nearby and drifted down to the deserted pier. Wordlessly they advanced toward the source of the laughter.

Amber light filtered through the broken shutters of a waterfront inn. A sign bearing the name Cat's Paw dangled askew on a rusty chain. When a wide shaft of light appeared, they stepped back into the shadows. A man emerged from the inn and walked to a carriage standing near the dingy building. The man climbed up on the driver's seat and pulled out a bottle.

David and Simon moved stealthily to the carriage. David smiled in relief when he spied the golden crest on the door. "She must be here," he whispered to Simon.

The coachman had just taken a long draught of ale when David yanked him from the seat. The liquid dribbled from his mouth as he was flung to the ground. He found himself flat on his back with David's heavy boot planted on his chest and the tip of a sword pressed to his throat.

"Where is she?" David demanded. The cold, unrelenting glare in the dark eyes staring down at the startled man made no further question necessary. "Trussed up . . . in the room above."

The sword's tip moved away, but the boot remained. "You'd better be telling me the truth," David snarled. "Bind him."

Simon checked the coach for a rope. When his search proved futile, he cut off a length of the rein. They quickly bound and gagged the blackguard, then tossed him into the carriage.

David drew his pistol and cocked the hammer. "Do you have a firearm?"

Simon shook his head. "Only my sword."

The response produced a grimace from David. "I hope you get close enough to wield it before one of them shoots you," he remarked drolly.

"Don't fret about me, laddie. Watch your own back," Simon retorted. "I was fending off rougher men than this before you were born. Gordons among them," he added.

David ignored the jibe. His mind was busy

formulating a plan of rescue. "You secure the stairway, and I'll take care of the men in the tavern."

"No matter the number?" Simon asked. He found the young man's cockiness irritating.

"There can't be more than a dozen of them," David replied with a negligent shrug. His glance was stern when he turned to Simon. "Don't let anyone get to Breyandra."

Simon nodded and drew his sword. David opened the door and the two men sprang into the room.

The pungent odor of stale smoke and ale swirled above the heads of the dozen or more men seated about the room. The appearance of the two Royalists standing in the doorway transformed the noisy din into a quiet hush.

Behind the bar, a slovenly man regarded David and Simon with hostility through the round, piglike eyes in his mottled face. A long, greasy queue hung down to the center of his back. "What be yer business 'ere?" he growled in a gravelly voice.

"The girl," David demanded. "Where is she?"

"Thar be no gal 'ere," the bartender snarled. "Yer best be on yer way."

The men seated nearest the entrance shoved back chairs as they jumped to their feet. Malevolence gleamed in their eyes.

"Uh-uh, I wouldn't do that," David cautioned when several men reached for their cutlasses. He waved the gun to motion the men to the other side of the room. Amidst glowers and grumbles, the sailors obeyed.

"We'll be gone as soon as we get the girl we came for," David announced calmly. "If no one tries anything foolish, nobody will get hurt."

Simon left David's side and moved toward the stairway. Chairs crashed to the floor as the men in his path scrambled aside to avoid the sweeping arc of his sword.

The bartender grabbed a pistol from beneath the bar. He raised the weapon and took aim. David turned in time to see the man's intent and fired at the same time. The scoundrel's shot went astray, but David's bullet found its mark. The bartender slumped across the bar with lifeless eyes.

The shots goaded the others into action. Cutlasses and knives appeared in the hands of the scurvy lot. Simon's sword quickly disposed of two who advanced on him, then he turned to fend off an attack by two more.

David's sword flashed as he moved adroitly around the room, preventing any of the villains from getting behind him. Those reckless enough to rush him immediately felt the sting of his sword.

Meanwhile Simon held his position at the stairway, preventing the blackguards from getting past him to reach Breyandra.

With out-thrust swords, two men lunged at David from opposite sides. He leapt on top of a table to avoid them, and the two men's swords plunged into each other's chest. They fell to the floor dead.

"These are the clumsiest oafs I've ever encountered," David bantered. "If I didn't know better, I'd swear they were Frasers."

"Be glad they aren't, laddie, or you'd be tasting your own blood by now," Simon retorted. He hopped up to the second step of the stairway when one of the rogues, closely followed by two cronies, lunged at him. With a powerful kick, Simon shoved his boot into the assailant's stomach. The man crashed into the two behind him, and all three landed in a heap on the floor. The sight of the tip of Simon's sword hovering above them caused the trio to throw up their hands in surrender.

"Get out of here," Simon ordered, and the defeated men scrambled out the door. Two more, seeing the others fleeing, followed behind.

"From their eagerness to yield I'm tempted to label them Gordons," Simon drawled. He lowered his weapon and leaned back to watch David fend off three of the remaining men.

"Don't offer me any assistance," David grunted sarcastically. He parried an opponent's thrust, then drove his blade into the man's side.

Simon stuck out a booted foot and tripped one of the rogues who was sneaking up behind David's back. The man and his weapon sprawled on the floor. "You ordered me to secure the stairway, Lord Gordon. It appears I have done that." He shook a warning finger at the fallen man crawling across the floor to retrieve his weapon. The man wisely heeded the admonition and continued on his hands and knees through the door of the inn.

Amusement danced in Simon's dark eyes as he addressed David. "If you need any help, just ask."

"It will be a cold day in hell when I ask for the help of a Fraser," David grumbled, breathless. With a strong slice, he knocked the sword from the hand of an attacker. Weaponless, the frightened man bolted for the door.

One sailor remained. David's eyes blackened with fury at the sight of the bloody streaks on the man's cheek. "I venture those scratches are from a recent struggle. Perhaps with a woman trying to protect herself?"

"And she paid the price for it," the sailor snarled boastfully.

"You bastard!" With a simple swipe, David knocked the cutlass from the man's hand. Then he cast aside his own sword, choosing to fight the sailor at his own level.

Simon guessed his intent. "Don't be a fool, Gordon."

Ignoring the warning, David's eyes remained fixed on the sailor. "You made a fatal mistake, swine. You picked on the wrong woman." He reached down and drew a dirk out of his boot.

The surprised seaman found himself snatched from the sure jaws of death. His skill with a sword was scant compared to the stranger's, but a knife . . . The man's face twisted into a leer . . . a knife was his weapon. He pulled a long, double-edged blade from his belt.

In a low crouch, the two men circled one another. The sailor slashed out, but David parried, delivering a grazing cut to the man's cheek. "Tell me who paid you to do it and I might let you live." David continued to circle his adversary, the force of his hatred for the vile scum directed into a deadly calm.

Still confident, the sailor wiped the blood off his face. "When the crew has their way with 'er yer fine lady's gonna wish she was as dead as yer gonna be."

He sprang at David like a coiled snake.

David stepped back to avoid the strike, and stumbled over the foot of a fallen man. The distraction was enough for the sailor to inflict a cut to David's shoulder.

Seeing his opponent's shirt stained with blood, the cocky sailor inched closer for another jab. It was the move David was hoping for. He sank his dirk into the man's stomach.

Shocked, the sailor's mouth gaped open. His knife slipped through his fingers and clanked to the floor. Then his eyeballs rolled to the top of the sockets and he pitched forward.

The battle was over. David retrieved his sword and slipped the blade into its scabbard. Simon and David surveyed the room with curiosity. Eight men lay dead or wounded. Tables and chairs were upturned, and tankards and bottles were strewn among the ruins.

Neither man felt sympathy for the fallen. The filthy lot had been willing to sell an innocent girl into slavery. Wordlessly the two men mounted the stairway, seeking the woman they loved. David opened the door of the room at the top of the stairway.

Unsuspecting, he stepped into the darkened room, and fell to the floor when a pitcher crashed down on his head.

Chapter Twenty-three

While Breyandra twisted and maneuvered on the bed, struggling to get free of her bonds, she was consumed by frustration and anger. Her heart beat rapidly. The more she fought the ropes that bound her wrists and ankles, the greater became her determination to free herself and somehow escape these scoundrels. Finally exhausted, she relaxed to catch her breath and ease the strain on her wrists.

Who has abducted me and for what reason? David, my sweet David, will I ever see you again?

Thoughts of her beloved flooded her mind, his last words to her a haunting echo. *Breyandra, I am master of Strehlow. Strehlow is my home.* The simple truth rang with a chilling finality.

Since David had departed one long week before, a pervasive feeling of self-doubt, tentative at first but dominating as the days passed, had troubled her. Now, in her present peril, the realization that she had been unreasonable about Strehlow reemerged.

Gradually, as she stared at the ceiling of her garret prison, her thoughts centered on a paradox; the decision to wage battle against her captors stood in marked contrast to the cowardice she had shown after her ordeal at Strehlow. *Running from Strehlow forever. Oh, David, how could I have forsaken you?*

Suddenly her anger at her captors changed to a fury of self-reproach. Why had she allowed the screaming mob on a witch hunt to destroy her spirit and cause her to behave as timidly as a deer, bolting at the first sign of danger?

Fear. Fear had paralyzed her reasoning, transforming Strehlow into the manifestation of all evil.

But Strehlow itself was not evil; the mob was evil.

Once again she began to grapple with the rope that tied her hands behind her back, while an inner voice muttered mocking words of self-contempt. *I was always blaming Strehlow. As long as I stayed away from Strehlow, I would be safe. Ha! Whatever I suffered there, I survived, didn't I?*

She had survived only to encounter yet another evil; the nefarious band of blackguards who held her captive. *Avoiding Strehlow has not kept me out of harm's way. What a foolish "twit" I have been.*

How could she have docilely accepted defeat

at the hands of witch hunters or any other Godforsaken lot of heathens? The Almighty himself would determine her destiny.

If I am strong enough to wage a battle against these scoundrels, then I can return to Strehlow and fight for David.

Fear of Strehlow had been an overpowering obstacle for her. David had been so patient.

Oh, David, my dearest. If you can forgive me, I will not leave your side ever again.

With renewed strength, Breyandra intensified her efforts to free herself. Finally she succeeded in untying one knot of the rope. Within minutes, she felt the next loop begin to loosen.

Breyandra's thoughts were interrupted at the sound of two gunshots. Wide-eyed, she listened to the clamor of crashing furniture and the clash of steel from below. "Those animals must be killing one another." Listening intently and puzzling over the cause of the melee, she feverishly resumed the task. The noise grew louder from the room beneath as the fighting continued.

Finally the knot slipped. Breyandra expelled a deep sigh of relief. After freeing her hands, she unbound her ankles. The bed creaked loudly as she slid to the floor, and fretfully Breyandra paused when she heard the tread of footsteps on the stairway.

She scanned the room in desperation, seeking a weapon. Her glance fell on a chipped ewer in a basin. Breyandra snatched the pitcher and moved to the doorway, pressing her ear against the door.

The footsteps stopped outside the room. As

the handle turned, Breyandra stepped aside and watched, transfixed. The door creaked open.

Her heart pounding, she raised the pitcher and brought it crashing down on the head of the man who stepped into the room. When he fell to the floor, Breyandra darted through the door, the only avenue of escape from the windowless room.

The man on the floor reached out and grabbed the skirt of her gown. Breyandra screamed and tumbled to the floor. She found herself staring up the length of a sword pointed at her throat.

"Good Lord! Breyandra!"

Her brown eyes rounded in shock when they met the startled eyes of her father. "Father! Is it really you?"

Simon Fraser sheathed his sword, leaned down, and drew his daughter into his arms. "Oh, Sweetling, what a scare you've given us."

Torn between tears and laughter, Breyandra basked in the security of his arms. "How did you know where to find me?"

A muffled groan interrupted the reunion. David Gordon sat up and raised a hand to his throbbing head. With contrition, Breyandra turned to the poor man.

"David!" she exclaimed at the sight of her beloved. She dropped to her knees and embraced him. "Oh, my love, I'm so sorry. I didn't know it was you." She began to smother him with kisses.

David Gordon may have been groggy but he

was not senseless. He leaned back, savoring the demonstration.

When the kisses began to deepen and David's arms tightened around his daughter, Simon Fraser tactfully cleared his throat. "Ah . . . I think we should consider departing before any of those scoundrels return."

Reluctantly the lovers separated. For the first time, Breyandra saw the stain on David's shirt. "You're bleeding!"

"It's just a nick," he said negligently and started to rise.

She pushed him back down to examine the wound, and her face constricted into a grim frown. "Just a nick? Must every drop of blood drain from your body before you'll admit to a serious injury?"

Breyandra ripped off a piece of her slip and padded the wound. "Your body is nothing but one long scar from head to toe," she scolded.

"Twit, your father," David whispered as his eyes shifted pointedly to the figure standing in the doorway. Remembering too late the presence of her father, Breyandra turned as red as the stain on David's shirt.

Simon Fraser also was embarrassed at hearing the revealing disclosure of intimacy between Breyandra and David. He made a hasty departure. "I'm going to make certain Breyandra marries that accursed Gordon whether she wants to or not," he grumbled aloud to himself as he stomped down the stairs.

When they descended the stairway, David

wrapped his arm protectively around Breyandra and hugged her to his side. She paled as she viewed the dead and wounded. A few of the men who were tending to their wounds cast them cursory glances, but none attempted to stop the three people from leaving.

There was no sign of the carriage outside. David emitted a loud whistle. Seconds later, Whirlwind trotted out of the fog followed by Simon's stallion.

David mounted Whirlwind, then Simon lifted Breyandra up into the young man's arms. After settling his love snugly against him, David prodded the horse to motion. Simon swung up into his saddle and followed behind the pair.

The two horses vanished into the misty haze, leaving only the sound of hoofbeats behind.

Elysia was ashen by the time her loved ones returned that evening. Were her pallor not enough, David's concern for his mother's condition increased when she informed him she was carrying a child.

Once assured that Breyandra was unmolested, Simon unscathed, and David's wound trifling, Elysia bowed to Simon's insistent demands and agreed to retire for the evening.

She stopped at the door of the library for a lingering word with David, who was being tended to by Breyandra. "You will be here in the morning?" she asked, hopefully.

David's endearing grin warmed his mother's heart. "Of course, Mother. We'll talk then. Now you get some rest."

"Breyandra dear, will you see that David gets whatever he needs to pass a comfortable night?" Elysia's worried frown reflected her motherly concern for her son.

Simon's own disapproving frown reflected his fatherly concern for his daughter. "I'm sure she will," he grumbled. "Now come along, my love." He placed a firm hand on Elysia's arm and led her out of the room.

"Well . . . will you?" David asked, chuckling warmly. He was sitting on the edge of a long tester table, with Breyandra standing between his legs cleansing his shoulder.

She didn't look up but continued at the task. "Will I what?"

He drew her into the circle of his arms. "See that I get what I need to pass a comfortable night?"

Breyandra arched a brow and met the mischievous gleam sparking his dark eyes. "And what, Sir Knave, will aid your comfort during the night? An added quilt? A downy pillow?"

He nuzzled her neck with a slow slide of his mouth to the pulse at her throat. "You can begin by showing me again how sorry you are for hitting me on the head."

She wove her fingers through the thick pelt of his hair. "My mind is muddled on that matter, my lord." David raised his head and regarded her quizzically. "I'm relieved your crown is so thick I did it no harm, Sir Knave, but alas, too often in the past I've had to butt heads with that same thick skull."

His arms slid down and lightly looped around

her waist. "But there have been pleasant moments, too, Twit."

Breyandra was drawn into the depth of his adoring gaze. She cupped her hands around the sculpted lines of his high, Celtic cheekbones. His nearness and masculine scent had already begun to affect her. She dipped her head, and her finger toyed with the cleft in his chin. "Aye, Sir Knave, there have been pleasant times as well."

Instinctively he tightened his arms around her, covering her mouth with a deep, penetrating kiss. Their desire for one another escalated until breathlessness forced them apart. David laced his fingers through the silken lustrousness of her hair. "Lord, I cherish you, Twit."

Breyandra traced his full sensual lips with her fingertips. "And I you, Sir Knave."

When he rose to his feet and lifted her into his arms, she placed a restraining hand on his chest. "David, we shouldn't . . . my father is upstairs."

"Yes, he's upstairs . . . with my mother. And need I remind you of her condition?" The bitterness in his voice was a painful reminder to Breyandra that Strehlow was not the only unresolved issue between them.

David lowered her feet to the floor and turned away. Her stricken gaze followed his broad back when he moved to the fireplace. The irritated young man stared moodily into the flickering flames, the scope of his frustration evident in the taut set of his shoulders.

"Your father's aversion to my clan does not carry to my mother. Is she less Gordon than I?"

Breyandra moved to his side and put her hand on his arm. "Does loving me make your aversion to my clan any less? So why do you expect more from him than you are willing to concede?"

David swung around, grabbing her shoulders in a firm grasp. His fingers pressed into the soft flesh. "Your father's concessions be damned. They matter not to me. Your feelings are my concern."

"How can you doubt my love, David?"

His laugh was bitter. "You ask me that, when you run from me at every opportunity?"

"I shall attempt to overcome my reservations, David."

In his anger he didn't even hear her compromise. "I wish *you* were with child, not my mother. Then there would be no question of our marrying."

"The feud between our clans has no bearing on my love for you, David. In truth, the feud is the greatest proof of my feelings."

His brow raised with skepticism. "The greatest proof?"

"Yes, because I love you *despite* the feud." Against her intent, Breyandra's eyes welled with tears.

The sight was too much for him to bear. His anger drained. "Lord, Twit, don't look at me like that," he whispered in a husky plea. His eyes worshiped her. "Why must we always spar like enemies? Are we to be restrained forever by the shackles of the past?" With a muffled groan David swept Breyandra into his arms and carried her up the stairway.

Once in the privacy of their chamber, he slowly undressed the woman he loved, then lowered her to a furry pelt on the floor. His eyes devoured her hungrily as he divested himself of his clothing.

Under the force of his lustful gaze, her body was gripped by an erotic shudder. She stretched her arms above her head. The flame in the fireplace cast the silken sheen of her body into shimmering opalescence. David sucked in his breath. "My God, you look like a fire opal." He covered her with the long length of his heated body.

Whorls of passion spiraled through her. She arched against him when he slid his warm palms in an erogenous path up the length of her outstretched arms. He laced his fingers through hers, then slid lower and dipped his head.

His tongue laved the sensitive tips of her breast, until he drew one of the taut peaks into his mouth. Breyandra's breath became gasps and, swept by spasms, she began to writhe beneath him.

He shifted lower, swinging their arms outward, their fingers still entwined. David paused to allow his tongue to toy with the provocative depression of her navel.

Breyandra's chest heaved from the pounding of her heart. He parted her legs with his knee, and lowered his mouth to the throbbing focus of her sensuality.

No moan or cry escaped her. For a few mindless, interminable seconds, she drowned in a sea of sensation, gasping frantically for breath as her body convulsed under wave upon wave of ecstatic tremors.

When her shuddering ceased, she was finally able to draw air into her tortured lungs, and she opened her eyes.

David was waiting. At the sight of the intense gleam in his eyes, she guessed his intent. "No more. I can't bear it," she murmured with a breathless sob.

He rose up and entered her. As she began to respond to the escalating tempo of his lovemaking, Breyandra discovered how mistaken she had been.

The following morning while dressing, Breyandra viewed her torn slip in the mirror. "Our lovemaking has been damaging to my garments, my Lord Gordon. I've ruined another underskirt."

David, who had been shaving, wiped the remaining lather off his face and walked up behind her. The pleasant fragrance of laurel teased her nostrils when he slipped his arms around her waist and drew her against him. "I have observed, my lady, that you are inclined to rip off your garments in my presence."

"You coof!" she scolded while trying to escape from his arms. But David's grasp held firm and he began to nuzzle her neck, pressing light kisses to the slim column. "And just what is the reason for the ripped garments, my lord? To bind up the wounds you keep getting," Breyandra railed in her own defense.

She turned in his arms to check on his latest

injury. "It appears this scratch will not leave a scar. You are fortunate the wound was not deeper."

David chuckled at her concern. "I told you as much at the time. And may I remind you, my lady, our lovemaking is harder on my hide then on your underskirts. Championing your causes has exacted a bloody toll on my battered and scarred body."

Breyandra hung her head sheepishly, solemnly tracing his wounds. "I fear you are right, my lord."

He lifted her chin with his fingers and smiled down lovingly into the beauty of her upturned face. "I willingly cry 'yield,' sweet enemy, and beg you to be merciful," he said in a husky whisper before his lips closed over hers in a tender kiss.

Breyandra slipped her arms around his waist and nestled her cheek against the firm wall of his bare chest. "I love you, David," she sighed contentedly.

His arms tightened around her. "And I you, my beloved."

She stepped back and smiled up at him. "Now go and visit with Elysia. I'm sure Father and she are waiting. I will join you when I complete my grooming."

An escort had arrived to accompany Simon and Elysia to Saltoun. Watching their men close rank around the carriage, Breyandra smiled with longing.

As the coach rumbled away, a lone horseman

galloped up the driveway. Jamie Douglas glanced back with interest at the departing carriage, then dismounted in front of David and Breyandra.

"Thank God!" he exclaimed. "What in the name of Mary happened to the two of you?" The relieved young man grinned charmingly. "The rumor at Whitehall is that Lady Breyandra has been abducted by pirates, and that you, dear fellow, have been murdered. The King is about to raise an army, and poor Jeanie is hysterical behind the locked door of her chamber."

"And in what manner is Lady Castlemaine bearing the tumult?" David inquired sarcastically.

"Walking around looking like the proverbial cat that swallowed the canary," Jamie drolled.

David lifted Breyandra onto Whirlwind, then swung up behind her. "Dare we hope she chokes on the feathers?"

Chapter Twenty-four

When the trio arrived at Whitehall, Charles himself, along with a dozen yipping, tail-wagging spaniels, rushed out of the palace doors to greet them. He embraced Breyandra and David. The King's genuine elation moved the young woman deeply, forcing her to brush the tears out of her eyes.

Then, with David and Breyandra on either side of him, Charles linked arms with them and led the young couple into the palace.

Breyandra made a hasty exit, leaving the telling of the previous night's adventures to David. Playing down his own role in the rescue, he praised the exploits of Simon Fraser.

"I do wish that Lord Lovet had returned to Whitehall with you, so I could have thanked him personally," Charles bemoaned when David finished relating the harrowing tale.

"Well, once Lord Lovet executed the rescue of his daughter, his concern was to return to Saltoun." David saw no reason to inform the court gossips of his mother's impending accouchement, which had necessitated the return to the Highlands.

Barbara Palmer had listened silently throughout the narrative, hiding her thoughts behind slanted, heavy-lidded eyes. When David had finished, the courtesan rose to her feet and slipped from the room.

"I shall dispatch a missive of gratitude to Lord Lovet at once," Charles announced. With that, the King and the spaniels dashed away.

Anxious to be free of the crowd, David wanted to confront Barbara Palmer with his allegation before she had time to fabricate a rebuttal. Before he could depart, however, a flagon of ale was thrust into his hand, and David found himself compelled to relate the whole incident again.

"It's a sad state of affairs indeed when the streets of London are no longer safe for a lady of quality," the Duke of Buckingham said indignantly. "I think we should summon a troop at once and rid ourselves of all the waterfront scum."

"Don't be hasty," David cautioned, challenging the duke's impetuosity. "The waterfront houses many decent and honest sailors. The abduction was not an accident. The scoundrels who made off with Lady Breyandra were privy to her whereabouts and deliberately sought her out."

Buckingham slammed down his tankard. "Surely you aren't suggesting that someone at court is behind the plot?"

David realized that the blustering fool would recklessly draw his weapon to champion the court of Charles.

"My Lord Buckingham, I am not accusing anyone. The culprits could have been enemies of Lord Lovet's who abducted Breyandra as a means of revenge. I am relieved that the Lady Breyandra and her father emerged unscathed from the incident." David turned away from the man, hoping to end the discussion.

But the arrogant duke, secure in his position at court and never quick to silence his tongue, eyed David with rancor. "Is not a *Gordon* the sworn enemy of Lord Lovet?"

Buckingham's insinuation that a Gordon had masterminded the abduction was a challenge no man of honor could ignore. The few observers waited with apprehension. Feigning composure he did not feel, David lowered the tankard he had just raised to his mouth. He placed the vessel on the table before him and turned slowly to face the belligerent man.

"My Lord Buckingham, in the past I have accepted your taunts to my dignity with the spirit in which they were meant, but under no stance will I countenance a slur to my clan." David slid his hand down to rest on the hilt of the sword hanging at his hip. "Unless you are prepared to die for that dastardly insult, I advise you to use your glib tongue to offer an apology at once."

George Villiers was a practical man, more interested in debauchery than adherence to the principles of honor and decency. And, foremost, this second Duke of Buckingham was a survivor. He had no wish to duel with a skilled warrior like David Gordon.

Quick to dispense with his own honor, Buckingham gushed his repentance. "My apologies, Lord Gordon. No offense intended. For if I am destined to die at the point of a man's sword, may the thrust be bestowed by a cuckolded husband."

David nodded in acceptance, and lowered the hand poised on his weapon. A few of the assembled laughed nervously, then moved away, relieved that the explosive situation between the two men had passed.

David withdrew to his own room, intending a change of clothing. Weary, he lay down on his bed and, before he realized it, fell fast asleep.

Upon her return, Breyandra called for a bath and change of linen. She had just finished her toilette when Jean Fleming rapped on the door and rushed into the room.

"Oh, Brey, I have been so worried about you." Jean's anxiety reflected on her face and tears began to streak the young girl's cheeks. "I thought I would never see you again."

Breyandra hugged the weeping girl in an effort to console her. Jean's distress was so severe that Breyandra momentarily forgot that she had been the one in jeopardy and not her stricken cousin.

When Jean's tears finally subsided, the young girl's misery turned to anger upon hearing the details of the terrifying tale. "Who would conceive of such a foul deed?" she fumed.

"David suspects Lady Castlemaine."

Jean's eyes were round with shock. "But you have done nothing to earn her wrath."

Breyandra returned to the dressing table to add the finishing touches to her toilette. "Lady Castlemaine's hatred is toward David. She knows that we love one another, and by threatening me, she is striking out at him."

The young girl's face twisted into an angry pout. With arms akimbo, Jean began to pace the floor. "I wish the whore would go back to her husband where she belongs. Lady Buckingham told me yesterday that 'tis rumored Lord Castlemaine is considering dissolving the marriage. Barbara hoodwinked him into accepting her first child, but since she is now carrying a second child by Charles, Roger Palmer declared he will not acknowledge another of the King's bastards."

Breyandra dabbed rice powder on her flushed cheeks. "She'll never leave the King until he tires of her, and at the moment he adores her. I pray David does not pursue his suspicions. It would only raise the King's ire to accuse his mistress without evidence. The wisest course is to let the whole matter drop."

"Well, there has to be some way to get even

with the witch," Jean fumed. Her dark curls bounced perkily as she flounced out of the room.

When Breyandra came downstairs, she found the King and his entourage gathered at the tennis court. The sport of tennis, a favorite recreation of Charles, had inspired one of his early renovations to Whitehall, the installation of a lavish indoor court with quilted nets and wooden floor.

Because he preferred to play between six and seven o'clock in the morning, Charles now reclined on one of the daybeds provided for comfort, watching a match between his brother and the Earl of Rochester.

When Breyandra failed to see any sign of David, or even Jean Fleming, she turned to depart.

James Douglas spied Breyandra and hurried over to greet her. "I am relieved to see, dear lady, that you look none the less beautiful despite your recent tribulations."

"A splendid compliment, Claibourne! Splendid!" Charles extolled, jumping to his feet. "Not a mark remains to flaw the perfection of that face." Breyandra was crushed against the robust man when the demonstrative and playful King snatched her into his arms in a bear hug.

Charles released her and grinned with Stuart charm at James Douglas. "You take care of this precious child, Jamie."

"Indeed I will, Your Majesty," Jamie replied. Turning to Breyandra, he extended his arm, which she reached for gratefully. The King returned to watch the tennis match, and the couple strolled away.

When she was certain they were out of earshot from the others, Breyandra asked worriedly, "Have you seen David?"

"Not since our return to Whitehall," Jamie responded.

"I hope he isn't off doing something foolish," Breyandra sighed. She glanced fretfully toward Barbara Palmer, who had just arrived carrying a small platter of her favorite sweetmeats. Holding the miniature silver salver to her generous bosom, the courtesan sat down and greedily began to pop the delicacies into her mouth. Breyandra watched in disgust until Jean sauntered up. Then she left the two lovers alone and returned to her search for David.

She decided to try his room first. After tapping lightly on the chamber door and receiving no response, Breyandra opened the portal slightly and peeked into the room. To her relief, David was asleep on the bed. Breyandra stepped into the room and closed the door behind her.

She crossed the room to the bed. Her gaze fell tenderly on her sleeping lover, his manly face softened by the tranquillity of slumber. Her heart swelled with love for him. Gone was the formidable warrior; in his stead lay a soldier at peace.

And however fleeting their time together, she would willingly choose that sweet moment above the promise of eternity with any other.

David opened his eyes and smiled up at her. "Hello, Twit," he said lovingly. To Breyandra the simple words were a greater expression of love than any ever penned by bards and troubadours.

Breyandra smiled down at him, and David reached out a hand. Their fingers intertwined, and he pulled her down to sit on the edge of the bed. "I missed you," she said softly.

His grin was sheepish. "I must have dozed off. I came up here to change my garments and lay down on the bed." He released her hand and sat up, placing a light kiss on her lips.

David draped his legs over the side of the bed and proceeded to remove his boots, then rose to his feet and discarded his shirt. He padded barefoot across the room and began to rummage through the armoire for clean clothing.

Breyandra's heartbeat quickened as she watched the ripple of muscles play across the broad slope of his shoulders. Her steady gaze never left him, excited by the beauty of his partially clad body. David returned to the bed and sat down beside her to pull on his hose.

"Allow me to assist you to dress, my lord." Breyandra took the white stockings from him and knelt down at his feet.

"I'd prefer that you assist me to *undress*, my lady," he teased lightly.

He raised his foot to allow her to slide on the stocking. When Breyandra finished the task, her eyes remained riveted on the long, well-made leg. Her hands continued to trace the length of his leg until they came to rest on the firm brawn of his thigh.

She felt as if her body were aflame. He watched the rise and fall of her chest above the low decolletage of her gown. Helpless, she glanced up at him. "David," she whispered through lips that suddenly felt parched.

His dark eyes were laden with desire. The plea added fuel, igniting the flame sparked by her touch. His moan became muffled in the thickness of her hair as he lifted her into his arms.

The palace buzzed with excitement when David and Breyandra joined the others later. Homing pigeons brought messages of the sighting of *The Royal Charles* off the coast of France. The ship was expected to dock within forty-eight hours. Charles intended to leave for Portsmouth in the morning to greet the future Queen of England, Scotland, and Ireland.

After dining that evening, the guests at the palace assembled to watch the performance of The King's Players, a theatrical group commissioned by the King.

A velvet curtain had been hung and a double row of lamps provided for the stage on which the actors would perform. Charles derived great pleasure from the theater, especially comedies. His enthusiasm that evening was heightened by the anticipation of the long-delayed arrival of his future wife.

David had no interest in watching the performance, but took a seat in order to be near Breyandra. Jean and Jamie joined them as well.

Shortly after the play began, Barbara Palmer hurried from the room. Breyandra turned to her cousin in surprise when Jean Fleming raised her fan and giggled. "I laced her sweetmeats with calomel," Jean confessed *sotto voce* to Breyandra.

"But calomel is a purgative," Breyandra exclaimed. "Why would you give Barbara Palmer . . . ?" Her eyes brightened as the purpose of the young girl's prank became clear. "Where in heaven's name did you get the powder?" Breyandra whispered, stifling her amusement.

"My mother always insists I carry some, in the event I become ill. Dear Mama believes that the purging of the body cures all maladies."

Breyandra was concerned at the young girl's daring. "If Lady Castlemaine finds out what you've done, she'll have the King order you out of the court."

"How will she know?" Jean laughed confidently. "I made certain no one saw me when I put the powder into the candy. It will not harm her. I used only enough to make this evening unpleasant for dear Queen Barbary. Small payment for what she did to you."

Breyandra was still aghast that her cousin would take such a risk. "But, Jean, we aren't certain Lady Castlemaine was behind that deed."

"I'm certain!" Jean said firmly. "The woman is without conscience."

The two women exchanged amused glances when Barbara Palmer returned to her seat, only to flee from the room again a few moments later. The third time she fled, Jean and Breyandra could no longer contain their mirth. They buried their faces behind fluted fans and erupted into laughter. Fortunately, the comic actor John Lacy was performing at the time, and their outburst could be attributed to the man's accomplishments. The girls' laughter became as contagious as a yawn, and the whole room followed suit until the sound of hilarity carried to the rooms above.

The play had just ended when Lady Castlemaine returned after her last hasty exit. Jean Fleming was the paragon of innocence when she approached Barbara Palmer. "Dear Barbara, I noticed you departed several times during the play. Did the performance meet with your displeasure?"

Barbara Palmer, too shrewd not to suspect something, eyed Jean curiously. "No, not at all. Just a slight indisposition. I intend to retire at once."

Jean shook her head sympathetically. "And what a shame, dear Barbara. Especially since this is the King's last night before he returns with his Queen."

The sultry siren smiled with confidence. "The rumors I've heard regarding the Portuguese Infanta leave me with little fear that the timid sparrow will displace me. I wager Charles will summon me to his bed the very night of his return." Her smug look quickly disappeared when she sped away, hastily mounting the stairway.

"I hope our future Queen is more resourceful than rumors would have us believe," Jean grumbled.

Chapter Twenty-five

In addition to beautiful women, horse racing, tennis, and his beloved dogs, the King avidly pursued another passion, inspired by his life-long love for the sea. A superb sailor, Charles was as comfortable at the helm of a ship as he was on the throne. To no one's surprise, when the *Royal Anne* sailed for Portsmouth the following morning, Charles manned the helm.

The Duke of York and Edward Hyde, looking grave as usual, stood on the deck engrossed in conversation with the Portuguese ambassador. Designated ladies-in-waiting to the future queen, Breyandra and Jean enjoyed the privilege of accompanying the expedition. Barbara Palmer had been left behind at Whitehall to scheme and sulk.

While David and James were occupied with

the royal guard, Charles entertained the two women, patiently giving instructions in the technique of steering a proper course. Then, to their delight, he allowed them to take the wheel of the yacht.

Later in the day, Breyandra and Charles shared a quiet chat as they sat relaxing on deck. Away from the frivolity and pomp of the court, Charles seemed a different man entirely. He had shed his dandified garb for unadorned trousers and a shirt, and Breyandra could understand why women were easily attracted to the charismatic monarch. He was a man who took genuine delight in people and life.

The impending royal nuptials were foremost in her thoughts. "I've heard many tales of nervous bridegrooms, Your Majesty, but you appear to be quite calm, despite the fact that you are marrying a princess you have never met."

"Not true, my lady. Her Highness and I have met often." At the sight of Breyandra's perplexity, Charles smiled and the warmth lit his lively dark eyes. "In correspondence, my lady. I feel as if I know the sweet woman very well. She has a good and modest nature. Prudent, but always kind. I am certain my queen will bring a dignity to the court which has long been absent."

"Then you are eager for the marriage, Your Majesty?"

"Eager? Indeed yes, Lady Breyandra." Charles sighed pensively and reached for her hand. "I fear that I am more man than monarch. I've always sought affection. Oh, to know the real love of a woman." His sigh was full of longing, "The real pleasures of life can only be known by two people in love."

"But surely, Your Majesty, you've known the love of a woman," Breyandra said sadly.

"I've known many mistresses, but love . . ." Charles shook his head. "But love . . . I fear not."

Since Charles was already thirty-two years old, the revelation astounded her. Breyandra was at a loss for words.

Shaking off his morose humor, he smiled and squeezed her hand. "Ah, but I am glad to see you do not suffer from such a malady. The young Scot is most attentive to you."

Absorbed in her thoughts, Breyandra was unaware that his remark was accompanied by a glance at James Douglas and not David.

"Ah yes, love . . . the capricious sprite has eluded me so far. And in confidence, my lady, I envy those who know such a state. Their lives are secure."

Breyandra's dimpled smile carried to the depth of her brown eyes. "Shame, my liege. For a moment you led me to believe you were romantically seeking true love, when in truth you are but seeking a secure and settled life."

"Which I fear will be a worthless endeavor, dear lady. For I look upon all women with deep affection, and I'm too set in my wicked, wicked ways." He leaned over with an engaging grin. "But seek I shall, because I believe a happily married life is the one human condition which imparts a sense of permanence to an impermanent state. As undeserving as I am, I know my

Catherine will bring me peace."

Listening to the disclosure, Breyandra realized how much Charles was prepared not only to marry but to love his bride. Whatever his dalliance with the likes of Barbara Palmer, Catherine of Braganza would have an inviolable place in the heart of this enigmatic man.

The romantic sentiment brought a glow of contentment to Breyandra. After Charles kissed her hand and departed, she sat back and smiled. A deeper appreciation of David's love for her flooded her being.

David had watched the intimate scene with keen interest. Goaded by a spark of jealousy, he walked over to Breyandra. "You appear to have succumbed to the charms of England's greatest womanizer."

She glanced up at him with a sage smile. "No, my Lord Gordon. Charles is not a womanizer; our King is simply a man who loves women."

Breyandra walked to the companionway and, before going below, turned back with a lingering smile. David had not moved. He watched her with a contemplative frown, regretting his spiteful remark, and his mind dwelled on her words.

The weather, which had been threatening all day, took a turn for the worse and all were forced below. Even Charles abandoned the helm for the refuge of his cabin.

In response to a light tap, Breyandra opened the door of her cabin. David filled the small opening. Her eyes flashed merrily, "Oh, I thought perhaps you were the King."

David stepped into the room and closed the

door behind him. Laughing, his hands spanned
her waist and he lifted her off the floor, spinning
around in a circle as they smiled into each
other's eyes. "You minx! You beautiful . . .
provocative . . . incredible minx! And I'm such
a foolish, jealous pawn in your game."

When he stopped and began to lower her,
Breyandra looped her arms around his neck. He
held her, her body suspended, pressed against
him as their lips met.

His kiss drugged her. A shiver rippled along
her spine. She smiled, grateful he held her up
because her legs felt as if they had turned to
jelly.

"Oh, David, I love you," she uttered breathlessly when his mouth slid down to her neck.

"I love you . . . I love you . . . I love you," she
continued to murmur as he carried her to the
bunk.

After a long and stormy sea voyage, the future
Queen of England, Scotland, and Ireland arrived at Portsmouth quite ill. She retired directly to the privacy of the chamber provided for
her. Six ladies-in-waiting accompanied Catherine, so Breyandra and Jean were not needed to
attend her.

Edward Hyde had not exaggerated the size of
the entourage the princess had brought from
Portugal. Over one hundred people of various
occupations, including a deaf duenna and a
barber, disembarked from *The Royal Charles*.

When Charles joined the anxious English fac-
tion after a visit with his future bride, he seemed

quite pleased, and, being Charles, he was charitable. The young girl had lived up to his expectations, and although Catherine's beauty did not compare to that of her rival at Whitehall, the King had nothing but praise for his future queen.

The city of Portsmouth began to swell with people arriving to attend the nuptials. By week's end, the seaport swarmed with English and foreign dignitaries.

Finally, after a week's delay, Catherine was well enough to arise from her sick bed to wed. Following the Lord Chancellor's sage advice, Charles honored his future wife's religious piousness and submitted to a brief and private Catholic ceremony in Catherine's chambers.

Later, for the auspicious public occasion, Breyandra chose a sky blue satin gown with a blue and white patterned underskirt. The gown had a long pointed bodice, laced in front, and the sleeves were set well below the shoulders, falling just below her elbows. Her hair, drawn to one side over her ear, hung to her shoulders in long locks.

Jean Fleming was just as lovely in a green gown with a pale yellow underskirt. The natural glow of the excited young girl rivaled the most painstaking cosmetic application of the other women.

One man stood out in sharp contrast to the others assembled. That man was David Gordon, the Highland Laird, the ruler of a clan older than many of the countries whose dignities were in attendance. If his stance and bearing were not enough to proclaim him Laird, the gold medallion on a chain around his neck bore further evidence.

He was dressed in the kilts of his clan, with a fitted black velvet jacket showing off the breadth of his shoulders. He wore a shirt of the finest cambric, gathered at his wrists into a lace-trimmed ruffle that fell over each hand.

Knee-high stockings sheathed David's long legs, and an elegant baldric was draped diagonally across his chest. The red tam on his dark head was adorned with a cockade in honor of the formal occasion.

James Douglas wore the formal dress of his clan as well. The imposing mien of the two Highlanders presented an image of strength among the dandified assemblage, and provoked a frisson of unrest among many of the foreigners present whose countrymen had felt the might of Highland warriors in the past. They stole fearful grudging glances at this reminder of the force that belonged to Charles for the beckoning.

The guests pressed forward for their first glimpse of Catherine of Braganza when she entered the room on the arm of Charles. The young queen wore a rose gown covered with blue love knots. In respect to her husband, her lace veil was embroidered with Tudor roses and English emblems.

Due to the size of the crowd, the wedding took place in the Great Chamber of the Governor's palace, rather than the smaller chapel. The bridal couple made their way to two specially fashioned thrones set behind a rail, so placed to

ward off the shoving swarm witnessing the
event. David and James formed a protective
shield for Breyandra and Jean against the press
of the crowd, so that the two women could
witness the couple taking their vows.

A collective sigh swept the assemblage when
the bishop proclaimed the royal pair husband
and wife. Once again, Britannica had a Queen.

The tiny Queen looked doll-like beside her
tall, strapping King as they walked among the
guests. Despite Catherine's royal upbringing,
Breyandra could see that the shy, convent-bred
young woman was overwhelmed by the crowd.
Only her royal station kept the people from
physically reaching out for the new Queen.

When Charles presented Breyandra to his
Queen, Catherine read the compassion in
Breyandra's eyes. Unhesitatingly, the woman
snipped off a love knot from her gown and
offered the piece of ribbon to the Scottish girl.

Breyandra was moved by the gesture. She
curtsied and bowed her head. The sensitive
woman sensed an immediate friend in the
young Scottish girl. Gratefully she slipped her
hand into Breyandra's, and the two women
exchanged understanding smiles. Charles took
Catherine's arm and led her away before any
word could pass between the two women.

This was not a court that would offer kindness
to anyone other than their own. Already, *sotto
voce*, some of the women had remarked that the
Queen's nose appeared too long, her teeth pro-
truded slightly, or she was too dark.

Just as Catherine caused a stir among the

women, her Portuguese ladies-in-waiting had the same effect on the dandies looking them over. Unlike Catherine, who chose an English style of dress, the other women wore the wide-hipped farthingales so popular with the Spanish and Portuguese.

"Have you ever seen such frights?" one count commented unkindly to a group of men who stood observing the young women.

"How does one ever get near the women?" the Earl of Rochester remarked.

Buckingham's satirical wit was much in evidence. "The style of dress must be Portugal's version of a chastity belt," he derided in a droll tone. "I would guess a man's passion could wane considerably in the course of unstringing all that wire."

David remained detached. He had his Breyandra and cared nothing about the newly arrived women from Portugal. "The ladies probably heard about the reputation of the court and adopted the style for their own protection," he offered in mild sarcasm.

"Well, their efforts were not in vain," Buckingham quipped. "Send them back to King Louis, I say. No ship needed—they can all float home on their gowns."

Already bored with the conversation, David moved away when he spied Breyandra leaving the Queen's parlor. "The Queen is still ailing and has retired for the evening," Breyandra whispered.

"Without her King?" David chuckled, amused.

Charles's wedding-night dilemma was of no significance to David. As he watched his beloved move gaily among the crowd, his own plans for the night were already formulated.

The following morning, the King announced he would be spending his honeymoon at Hampton Court. As designated ladies-in-waiting to the Queen, Breyandra and Jean were to accompany the royal couple.

David did not take the news gracefully. Frustrated at the prospect of another separation, he implored Breyandra to accompany him to Strehlow. "I promise no one will harm you, Twit."

"You know I can't go with you at this time. I shall ask the King to release me from my obligation to the Queen soon. But for now I must accompany them to Hampton Court."

"The Queen has half a dozen ladies-in-waiting. She won't miss you." David was not easily appeased.

"David, I can't defy the King."

As if to confirm the statement, Charles approached her. "Dear Lady Breyandra, I'm relying on you to make Her Majesty feel comfortable. Everything is so strange to the dear woman."

"I shall do my best, Your Majesty." Breyandra turned back to David when Charles moved on to say his farewells to the departing guests. David's face was dark with anger and he turned away to control his emotions.

Later that morning as the ship sailed out of

Portsmouth, Breyandra stood on the deck and waved goodbye to David seated astride Whirlwind on a wind-swept bluff overlooking the harbor.

A white silk handkerchief fluttered in Breyandra's hand. The lacy square was snatched by a gust of wind and for a few seconds soared toward shore, only to drop into the sea and sink. Her gaze remained fixed on the tall figure sitting motionless on the huge black stallion. David didn't return her wave, and a sense of sadness enveloped her. She didn't want the separation any more than he did, but she doubted that he believed her.

David's parting declaration echoed in her mind. "I will return as soon as I am certain all is well at Strehlow."

Breyandra smiled, wistfully. "I'll be waiting, my love," she murmured softly, hoping the wind would carry the words to the ears of her beloved.

Chapter Twenty-six

The days at Hampton Court were idyllic for the honeymooners. Charles adored his wife, and the gentle woman clearly reciprocated the feeling. She tried eagerly to please her handsome husband.

Since all knew that Charles was on his honeymoon, visitors became a rarity. The palace of Hampton Court was fifteen miles away from London, but those fifteen miles were not enough to discourage one caller—Barbara Palmer.

Catherine was resting in her chamber the day Barbara stormed in on the King. With her arms crossed and her sensuous mouth curled in a pout, the King's mistress made no attempt to be discreet.

Pregnant with another of Charles's bastards, she informed him that her husband, Roger Palmer, had decided to have their marriage dissolved. She insisted upon remaining at Hampton Court.

"But, Barbary, this is my honeymoon," Charles reminded her. "It would be most indelicate to have you here at this time."

The sullen woman flew into a raging tantrum that left the King holding his ears to shut out the sound.

Appalled, Breyandra turned away in disgust when Charles could no longer bear the outburst and acceded to the screeching woman's demands.

One person, however, dared to challenge the unwise decision. "Your Majesty, you must consider the Queen," Edward Hyde protested. His loathing for Barbara Palmer was undisguised.

The Lord Chancellor knew that when Charles wed, the King had not intended to abandon his desirable mistress. Still, Hyde had hoped that Charles would accept the role of husband and lover to his Queen and begin to change his philandering ways. But Hyde's optimism was rapidly dwindling.

"Clarendon, I am responsible for Lady Castlemaine's plight. I have tarnished her reputation, she is carrying my child, and now her husband is severing the marriage."

And for good cause, Breyandra thought contemptuously. Usually, Breyandra would have felt a twinge of sympathy for a woman in Barbara's straits—pregnant with an illegitimate child, the mother of another bastard, and facing the public embarrassment of her husband dissolving their marriage. But Barbara Palmer had caused the trouble she faced and, despite her circumstances, had nothing to fear. She knew that Charles did not abandon his bastards. Even the Duke of Monmouth, the son of a former mistress, lived at Whitehall.

Edward Hyde reminded the King of his generosity. "Your Majesty has provided Lady Castlemaine with her own quarters at Whitehall, including a nursery for her daughter." He cast a disdainful glance at the rounded evidence of another child who soon would be sharing those rooms.

Once again Charles found himself in a tug of war between the two powerful court rivals. But the guilt and responsibility he felt for his mistress prevailed.

"The child you refer to is *my* daughter as well, Clarendon." Charles was becoming piqued. Although uncomfortable with the arrangement, he could not tolerate further ranting from Barbara or lectures from Clarendon. "The matter is closed."

Upon the King's pronouncement, Barbara Palmer's tearful visage twisted into a vicious smirk of victory. Frustrated, Edward Hyde stomped from the room.

Breyandra too left the room. Her heart ached for Catherine. The new Queen had struggled hard, adjusting to a new country and customs. The task had been made easier by one factor. The new bride had fallen deeply in love with the man she'd married. Barbara Palmer's presence not only would be an embarrassment to Catherine, but his mistress posed a distraction to Charles that would break the heart of the Queen who loved him.

Breyandra realized that David had been right from the beginning: she, Breyandra, did not belong at this court of intrigues. She would ask the King this very evening to release her from any obligation to remain.

Breyandra spoke of her intent to Jean. The girl responded with heartfelt joy since she too anxiously wished to leave the court and return home. James Douglas had confided that once Jean returned to Scotland, he would press his suit for her hand in marriage.

Breyandra waited the remainder of the day to speak to the King. Since his mistress's arrival, Charles and Barbara had spent the afternoon in his chamber. When they finally appeared that evening in the antechamber, Catherine entered the room before Breyandra had the opportunity to approach him.

The Queen had never seen Barbara Palmer, but the courtesan's name was notorious. The Portuguese ambassador had thoroughly schooled Catherine in the facts of the woman's relationship with the King of England.

Charles introduced Barbara to his bride. At the mention of his mistress's name, the shy smile disappeared from the face of the Queen and her eyes filled with tears. The stunned woman fell to the floor.

At once her entourage swarmed around the

fallen woman, unaware of the reason for her prostration. The distraught Queen, still in tears, was carried away to her chamber. Charles followed solicitously.

Barbara Palmer appeared to be the epitome of innocence in the midst of the turmoil. In a fury of youthful indignation, Jean Fleming stormed over to the woman calmly sipping ale from a silver chalice. "You scheming bitch!" the young girl cried out before running from the room.

Barbara's thoughts remained disguised behind a sly smile, but those present knew that Jean would pay dearly for her outburst.

The following day, Hampton Court was in an uproar. Catherine declared she would neither leave her chamber nor talk to Charles until Barbara Palmer had been removed from the premises.

The King bellowed in a foul temper. Having succumbed to Barbara's manipulations out of a sense of guilt, his pride would not allow him to bow to the will of another hysterical woman. And yet, he suffered deep feelings of guilt over his treatment of Catherine.

But having given his word, he stood firm on the promise to his mistress. "Furthermore, I want that whole entourage to return to Portugal. I cannot afford to keep them. Her Majesty may select a few to remain, but the others must leave."

Shocked by the declaration, Edward Hyde immediately protested. "But, Your Majesty, such drastic action is not fair to the Queen."

Charles could abide no more interference in

his decisions. Already pushed to the breaking point, he vented his frustration in an outburst alien to his good nature and diplomacy. "Fair to the Queen? Am I not King here? I will determine who leaves and who remains. Which sovereign do you serve, Clarendon?"

"You, my liege," the austere man said humbly.

"Then do as I say. I am tired of your censure. Since my Queen has expressed an aversion to my presence, you may convey my decision to her." He dismissed the faithful servant with a wave of his hand.

Clarendon, aware of Catherine's fondness for Breyandra, cast an imploring glance at the Scottish girl. Breyandra knew he expected her to accompany him. How could the Queen accept the devastating news that not only was Lady Castlemaine remaining at the palace, but the King was sending the Queen's entourage back to Portugal? Sadly, Breyandra rose to her feet and followed the unfortunate man.

When they told Catherine of Charles's latest announcement, the distraught woman burst into tears. She reached out in need to Breyandra.

Breyandra soon became the inseparable companion of the forlorn Queen. Consequently, several more weeks passed without Breyandra approaching the King with her request to return to the Highlands.

In the end, Catherine's gentle nature prevailed and she accepted her husband's wishes. By the time the royal couple returned to London, a semblance of peace existed in the domestic life of the King. Charles, being a natural charmer, managed to divide his attention between both women; he spent as many nights with his dutiful wife as he did with his seductive mistress.

Breyandra's joy was unrestrained when, after an absence of six weeks, David appeared at Whitehall. That night their lovemaking was fervent and intense.

Later, as she savored the feel of his arms around her, Breyandra knew she could not bear to be parted from him again. As much as she hated to hurt Catherine, she belonged with David. Too much time had been wasted in lengthy separations.

Her fingertips tingled from the exciting contact of his body as her hand traversed its length. "I seek evidence of new wounds," she teased in answer to his responsive groans of pleasure.

"You'll find none, other than the wound that pierced my heart from missing you," he offered.

Breyandra sat up and gazed down at him, love shining in the depth of her eyes. The globes of her breasts gleamed like white silk against the black curtain of dark hair that hung to her waist.

David pressed her nearer, and his mouth closed around one tempting peak. A wave of heat surged through her. She closed her eyes, shutting out all sights and sounds, allowing her senses to dwell on the erotic sensation consuming her.

"I must be depraved," she uttered in a breathless moan.

David raised his head and grinned. "Depraved?"

Breyandra shuddered and laced her fingers through his thick pelt of hair. "Truly 'tis sinful to glean such enjoyment from the pleasures of the flesh."

David sat up and Breyandra trailed her fingers down to the firm wall of his chest. He smiled down at her, framing her delicate face in the palms of his hands. His thumbs began to toy with the sensuous curve of her lips as he gazed, enraptured.

"What I feel when we make love goes far beyond carnal pleasure, my love. I feel . . . oh . . . I feel secure and sublimely content, as if I had at last come home from a long and restless journey."

He lay back, drawing her down to him. "Without such a feeling, we would not know this." His mouth closed over hers in an arousing kiss, igniting a new blaze within her.

That evening, Barbara Palmer's cunning mind devised a plan not only to vent her revenge on Jean Fleming, but to satisfy her old grievance with David Gordon.

"Charles, I've often heard you speak of your debt to the two young Scots. What better way to repay their loyalty than to betroth them to the women they love? Lord Gordon appears quite smitten with the Fleming girl, and Lord Claibourne is utterly besotted with Lady Breyandra."

Charles swung his glance to the foursome

engaged in a game of cribbage across the room. He nodded reflectively. "I've noticed Lord Claibourne's fascination with our lovely Breyandra, but other than at Newmarket, I've seen no evidence of Lord Gordon's affection for Jean."

His brow deepened in a frown. "Frankly, the young girl appears quite naive, for a man of Gordon's sophistication."

Barbara raised her fan and leaned over, allowing him a generous view of her ample bosom to distract his reasoning. "I saw the two in the garden last night," she whispered. "The scene was quite stimulating." She fluttered the fan rapidly and giggled wickedly. "*Quite* stimulating." Barbara rolled her eyes to embellish her point.

Charles laughed in delight. "Ah, Barbary, how you captivate me."

"I heard Jean refuse Lord Gordon's plea to wed. Something to do with her parents' preference that she wed a Frenchman."

Charles leaned back in his chair and eyed the young girl intently. "I would hate to displease her father. Lord Boscomb is an old friend of my father's."

"Is not Lord Gordon a closer friend to you?" Barbara asked slyly. "Besides, dear Charles, it is an honor to have the King betroth a couple. The young girl's father would be flattered by such distinction. And once you publicly betroth them, no one could challenge a decree by Your Majesty. Even the young couples dare not disobey the wishes of their king," she added. Charles did not see the craftiness gleaming in her eyes.

"I shall do it, Barbary. At once," Charles exclaimed with enthusiasm. He jumped to his feet and clapped his hands for attention. "Dear friends, I have an announcement to make. At this time I ask my loyal subjects Lord Gordon and Lord Claibourne, as well as Lady Breyandra and Lady Jean, to come forward."

"What now?" David grumbled to Breyandra as he pushed back his chair.

Charles watched with a broad smile when the four young people approached him. "Surely you all are aware how much the court is indebted to Lord Gordon and Lord Claibourne. In gratitude for their loyal service to me, I, Charles II, Sovereign of England, Scotland, and Ireland, betroth David Gordon, Lord of Strehlow, to the Lady Jean Fleming; and I further betroth Lord Claibourne, Viscount of Rubly, to the Lady Breyandra Fraser."

Murmurs of surprise and only a spattering of applause accompanied the announcement, since most assembled were aware of David's attachment to Breyandra. Charles, oblivious of the relationship, continued. "It will bring me further pleasure if these two loving couples have their nuptials performed in London at Westminster Abbey."

Stunned, Breyandra glanced swiftly at David, who was staring, appalled, at the King. Although her body had gone numb, Breyandra's head felt as if it were swelling to a gargantuan size. The sounds around her became a muffled drone, and the last thing she remembered before she blacked out and collapsed to the floor was the shocked look on David's face.

When Breyandra opened her eyes, David was leaning over her. Dazed and helpless, she stared up at him, her brown eyes round and luminous like a wounded deer.

"Da . . . David." Breyandra could barely force the word past her throat.

A servant appeared with a flagon containing ale. David raised her head and held the liquid to her mouth. Breyandra took a few sips. Slowly she sat up. Without any further word, David swooped her up into his arms and carried her out of the room, impervious to the astonished glances that followed them.

Once in the privacy of her chamber, David held Breyandra until she stopped trembling. Finally she drew back and glanced up at him. "David, what are we going to do?"

"I will speak to the King. I am certain that once he becomes aware of the facts, he'll withdraw his decree."

Still stunned, her mind groped to understand the whole muddled affair. "But why . . . why did he do such a thing?" she asked. "I thought he cared for us."

A light tap prevented any further conjecture. David opened the door and James Douglas entered the room. He exchanged a troubled glance with David. "What a bloody mess! I took Jean to her chamber. She's in tears and has retired for the night."

He cast a solicitous look at Breyandra. "How are you feeling now, Brey?" She shrugged helplessly and shook her head.

James looked contrite. "I'm afraid I may be the bearer of further bad news. I have a message from your father. The rider said it was urgent."

For the first time Breyandra noticed the square of paper in his hand. When Jamie handed it to her, Breyandra hurriedly broke the seal and read the cryptic message.

"I need you, Sweetling. Please come home at once."

Chapter Twenty-seven

The sun had long set when the weary travelers reached the gates of Saltoun. Breyandra was surprised to discover the Great Hall ablaze with light at such a late hour. "Is Lord Lovet ill?" she asked, casting a worried glance toward the stairway.

"Nae the Laird, m'lady. 'Tis the Lady Elysia. She be 'n birthin'," a servant informed her. The woman shook her head sadly. "These pas' twa days."

"My mother?" David asked, alarmed. "Where is she?"

"Cum wi' me, m'lord."

Hastily David shed his cloak and baldric. They followed the maid up the stairway. Breyandra was not surprised when the woman led them to the Grand Chamber.

Long tapers flickered in pewter candelabra and several sconces burned on the wall. Elysia lay in the bed, and Simon sat in a chair at the bedside. A doctor hovered nervously in the corner of the room.

David approached the bed apprehensively. He gasped in shock at the sight of his mother. Elysia lay between the sheets, her eyes closed as an abigail sponged the perspiration from her face and head. The only color in Elysia's face was the purple circles under her eyes, giving her a ghostly appearance. Her usually luxuriant hair was plastered to her head and some stray strands lay dankly against the pillow.

On seeing Breyandra, Simon rose to his feet and embraced his daughter. Breyandra couldn't believe the change in her father as well; he seemed a broken man. His smile of welcome quickly changed to somberness when she asked about Elysia's condition. Simon shook his head, sat down, and buried his dark head in his hands.

Breyandra glanced frantically at David to discover he was staring dazed at Elysia. He had grasped the full severity of the situation. His mother was dying.

A contraction woke the tortured woman from her brief sleep. She opened her eyes and saw her son.

Despite her condition, joy obliterated the evidence of pain that had contorted her delicate features. "David," she murmured weakly, reaching up to him. David grasped her limp hand.

Breyandra drew Simon out of the room to

allow the mother and son this moment together. The prudent doctor and nurse followed.

A few moments later, David was grim-faced when he left the chamber. Simon and the doctor hurried past him to return to their vigil.

"David, I'm so sorry," Breyandra said softly. She slipped her arms around his waist and David embraced her. "Oh, God, Twit, I can't believe we're losing her." He clung to her, drawing comfort from her nearness. "And she's in so much pain. Hasn't she borne enough in the past?"

Breyandra framed his face in her hands and smiled tenderly into his tormented eyes. "We must never give up hope, David. I want to believe your mother has the will and strength to endure this." She slipped out of his arms. "You're exhausted, my love. I've ordered you some hot grog." Taking him by the hand, she led him to a nearby chamber. A fire was burning on the hearth and Breyandra sat David down before the warming blaze. Numb with shock, he gave no resistance.

Breyandra pulled off his boots and then poured cups of the heated drink for David and herself. She sat down on the floor at his feet and laid her cheek against his thigh. Deep in their own memories of Elysia, the two sat silently, sipping the hot brew.

Breyandra awoke to discover that David had mercifully fallen asleep. She rose to her feet and tiptoed out of the room to return to the Grand Chamber. Elysia was asleep. Her father had dozed off in a chair beside the bed. Light snores emanated from the doctor in a far corner; there was no sign of the abigail.

Simon opened his eyes when Breyandra approached the bed. Fatigue sat heavily upon his face. "Father, why don't you go and rest? I'll sit with Elysia and call you the moment there's a change in her condition," Breyandra gently whispered.

Simon shook his head. "I don't want to leave her."

"What can you do for her, Father? The doctor is here when the time comes."

The look in Simon's eyes was resolute. "I want her to know she is not alone."

Breyandra knew that further argument would be useless. She drew up a chair and sat down beside him. "Where is Lord Gordon?" he asked.

"David is sleeping, finally. He rode relentlessly to get here and never closed an eye from the time we left London."

Simon nodded numbly, forcing words for the sake of conversation. "I'm glad he came. Seeing her son has lightened Elysia's heart."

The abigail entered the room with a tray holding tea and scones. She opened the drapes to let in the morning sun and then departed. Breyandra rose and poured her father a cup of the hot brew, but he sat muddled, not even sipping the liquid.

Elysia's body was suddenly wracked with a spasm, and her eyes opened, glazed with pain. A weak moan escaped her as her head rolled from side to side on the pillow.

Simon picked up her hand and brought it to his lips, tasting the blood where Elysia's nails had cut into her palm. "Beloved, it's Sim," he murmured softly. Gingerly, he seated himself on the bed.

Elysia turned to him, trying to focus on the sound of his voice. She tried to smile. "Sim." She was barely able to form the word.

"Don't try to talk, love," he cautioned as he bent over to brush her lips with his own.

Another spasm gripped her body. In pain, Elysia clutched his hands. When the contraction ended, she smiled up at him. "I love you, Sim."

Simon brought her hand to his mouth and kissed the palm. "And I you, my love."

Her eyes welled with tears. "I wanted so dearly to give you a child. Now I fear neither the baby nor I—"

"Hush, love, don't waste your energy. You must save all your strength," he pleaded.

Elysia's hand balled into a fist as her body contracted in pain. "I don't think I have any strength left. I'm so sorry, Sim. I'm just so tired." Her voice trailed off weakly, and she closed her eyes.

Her body was seized by another contraction, and her glazed eyes swung to him. Simon sucked in his breath at the sight of her blank, lifeless expression. She was losing her will to live. His beloved was slipping away and he was helpless to stop her.

He clutched her hand to his chest. "I beg of you, don't leave me, my love." Simon's eyes misted and a tear slid down his cheek. "I need you. You're my life, Elysia, my precious love. Try to draw from my strength."

Elysia closed her eyes, and Simon reached out to caress her, brushing aside the tears that lay upon her pale cheeks. At his touch, a soft smile of contentment crossed her face.

In desperation, Simon turned to the doctor. "Surely there must be something you can do?" he accused.

The frantic plea had been made several times. But again the doctor shook his head sadly. "My lady is too small to deliver the bairn, Lord Lovet. 'Tis an insurmountable complication."

"My God, I can't bear to watch her suffer any longer. Take the child. Don't just let her suffer like this."

"We are talking about a human life, Lord Lovet."

"You're goddamned right!" Simon exploded. His patience had long been obliterated by anxiety. "A human life, the woman I love, lies there. I order you to take the child out any way you can, but don't let my lady die. What purpose is accomplished by letting both her and the bairn perish?" he shouted.

Elysia groaned in pain as her body arched convulsively. The doctor glanced nervously at Simon. "I am certain it won't be much longer, my lord. Her contractions are constant now," he added in an attempt to appease the distraught man.

"How much more do you think she can bear?" Simon desperately beseeched. "Good

Lord, can't you see she is not going to make it if you don't do something right away?"

Breyandra, who had stood by silently, placed a restraining hand on her father's arm. "Elysia's wish is to save the child, Father. You must honor her request."

Simon turned to his daughter as if she had betrayed him. Before he could speak, Elysia screamed in pain. Both men rushed to her side, and the doctor leaned over her worriedly. "I think it would be wiser if you left the chamber, Lord Lovet."

Simon Fraser, a Highland laird, was a man used to issuing orders and having them obeyed. His rank was never more evident than in his obdurate response. "I shall remain here."

The doctor nodded grimly. "Lady Breyandra, if you will be so kind as to call the abigail." Breyandra nodded and hastened from the room.

At the sound of the closing door, Elysia cried out in panic. "Sim, where are you?"

"I am right here, love," he said soothingly as he turned back to her.

Elysia opened her eyes and smiled up at him. "For a moment, I was so frightened, Sim. Don't leave me?" she pleaded.

"I promise," he said tenderly. "But you must give me the same pledge, my love." Her hands groped for his, and her nails dug into him as she screamed in excruciating pain.

In a short time, the only sensation that penetrated Elysia's pain-wracked body and mind was the strength surging from the hands grasping her own.

The son of Simon and Elysia entered the world mucky and mottled, crying lustily in anger at the long delay.

After the delivery, Elysia looked paler than ever as she lay deathly still on the bed. The lengthy labor, and loss of blood that followed, had weakened her further. Her eyes were closed, and the rise and fall of her chest was slow and faint.

Simon would not relinquish his grasp on her hand, but sat for hours leaning forward on his arms, holding the almost lifeless hand between his own.

Wanting these moments alone with his beloved, he sent all from the room. Simon Fraser had not practiced his religion, but he was a God-loving man with charity of heart and soul. From the time he became Laird, his clansmen had the freedom to follow the dictates of their personal religious beliefs as long as they respected the right of their neighbors to do the same.

He now prayed, thanking God for the gift of a son. He prayed to express his gratitude for the blessing of the daughter bestowed upon him. And he prayed pleading to the benevolent Almighty to take his life and spare this woman whose only sin was love.

Elysia opened her eyes and lay silently watching Simon. His head was bowed in prayer. Her heart swelled with love for him. Weakly, she squeezed his hand, and he lifted his head to find her watching him.

At once his eyes filled with tenderness. "We have a son, beloved."

Tears of joy began to streak Elysia's cheeks, and Simon's eyes misted at her happiness. "May I see him?" The question was a bare whisper.

"Of course, love." Simon walked over to the cradle and gently lifted the baby. He carried their son to the bed and laid the tiny bundle in his mother's arms. The baby yawned, stretched his little arms, and settled back into sleep.

Elysia's eyes glistened with tears as she smiled down at the pink-cheeked face. Dark hair covered the tiny head. "Oh, Sim, he's so beautiful," she said reverently. Her chin quivered as she forced back her sobs. "One day he'll be as handsome as his father."

Simon lifted the sleeping child out of her arms and returned the baby to the cradle. He knew what Elysia was thinking. She wouldn't be there to see her prediction come to pass. His knuckles turned white as he clenched the side of the cradle, fighting for composure before turning back to her.

Elysia's lids were lowered when he returned to the bed. He sat down, once again picking up her hand. Simon lowered his head in anguish. He fought to restrain his tears. How could he bear to say goodbye to her?

"Regrets, my lord?"

Simon lifted his head and found her gentle eyes on him. Elysia was smiling through the tears that slid down her cheeks.

He raised her hand to his cheek, turning his head to kiss the palm. "None, my lady. And you?" he whispered tenderly.

"None, my lord. You've brought me more happiness than I've ever known. I've cherished every moment we've had together, Sim."

"We'll have many more, my love. You and I, and our son."

She smiled wistfully. "Will we, Sim?" She closed her eyes, slipping back into slumber.

Simon lowered his head, his body wracked with sobs, unaware of the tall figure standing silently in the doorway.

David had not meant to eavesdrop on the conversation between his mother and Simon Fraser, but he could not force himself to interrupt the poignant moment between them. For the first time since his mother had become Fraser's mistress, David recognized the depth of their love for one another. How could he have doubted it? Condemned it? Maligned it?

His love for Breyandra made him aware of how easily one person can entwine the heart of another. Why had he believed that only he and Breyandra were entitled to real and lasting love?

David was overwhelmed with shame. Ashamed of his own shallow thinking. His self-righteousness.

And now it was too late to beg his mother's forgiveness. Nevertheless, he knew he would make his peace with the heartbroken man who loved her—the man he was bound to by the child in the cradle.

David entered the room and walked over to

the bed. He reached out and placed a comforting hand on the shoulder of the grief-stricken man.

Simon Fraser looked up, and for a moment the older man's eyes locked in understanding with those of the younger man. Neither spoke. Words were not necessary.

Elysia opened her eyes to witness the moment of comradeship between the two men. Her heart quickened and she felt the resurgence of strength to her body. As she drifted back into slumber, her lips curved into a smile of contentment.

Chapter Twenty-eight

The pall of woe continued to shroud Saltoun throughout the following day. Neither the clang of the blacksmith's hammer nor the hollow clatter of hoofbeats reverberated in the courtyard. Servants with bowed heads and downcast eyes passed one another with nary a word or glance. In the scullery, the clamor of pots and pans was silenced as the cooks pursued daily rituals without the usual grousing and glowering at interlopers who dared step foot within their domain.

The gentle manner of Elysia Gordon had won the hearts of the people. Now, all mourned her condition, fearful the gracious lady would meet the same fate as the Laird's beloved first Mistress of Saltoun. Many a prayer was murmured and candle lit in Elysia's behalf.

The wail of the wee bairn brought an occasional smile to those within earshot of the Grand Chamber, but their faces would quickly sober in concern for the mother who lay hovering on the brink of death.

Elysia asked that the baby remain with her. As much as Simon would have preferred to shield his beloved from disturbance, the tender-hearted man could not deny her request. One of the maids who had given birth was found as a wet nurse for the infant.

On the second day after the birth, a steady rain added to the gloom. By evening, the weather took a further turn for the worse. Thunder rumbled across the glen. Lightning set the sky ablaze with fireworks and crashed around the walls and battlements of Saltoun, hurling spears of flame.

The superstitious servants, convinced the turbulence was an omen, huddled in prayer at the chapel of the castle.

"Aye, this nicht someone wil' dee," the terrified mumbled. "The angel o' death is hoverin' o'er Saltoun. 'Twil wrap a budy in a windy sheet befar the nicht be gane."

Breyandra nervously paced the floor of the Grand Chamber, unnerved by the loud crashes of thunder that threatened to split the earth. She had succeeded in convincing her father to retire to another room. Exhausted, Simon had relented after securing his daughter's promise to awaken him in two hours.

Since neither man could do anything for

Elysia except to be there on the rare times she awoke, Breyandra had convinced David to follow suit.

With both men finally dispatched, Breyandra sat down and picked up a piece of needlepoint. Unaffected by the turmoil outside the walls, Wolf stretched out on the floor at her feet for an evening's snooze.

An hour of her vigil had passed when Breyandra looked up from her stitching to discover Elysia, awake. The older woman offered a weak smile as their glances met. Breyandra put aside her stitching and rose to her feet. "Would you like some water, or perhaps, a cup of tea?" she asked solicitously.

"No. Nothing," Elysia murmured. "I've been lying here watching you. You're so beautiful, my dear."

Breyandra's eyes misted. The thought was so like Elysia. Even in her dire condition, the sensitive woman still had a kind word for another. "I wish you would try some broth," Breyandra ventured softly, brushing aside her tears.

Elysia reached out to her. Breyandra took her hand and sat down on the edge of the bed. "You'll never regain your strength until you do."

Elysia managed another feeble smile. "Later. I'll try some broth later." An awkward silence developed between them until Elysia spoke. "Please tell me, my dear . . . how is it . . . between you and David?"

Breyandra dared not tell her of the latest

setback, created by the King. Elysia's crisis had shoved the unbelievable situation to the back of her mind.

"Will you return to Strehlow with him?" Elysia pursued when Breyandra failed to answer her question.

"I hope to." Breyandra felt her answer was honest, if incomplete, and that therefore she had not deceived the woman.

"Oh . . ." Elysia sighed with a bit of joy. However, she knew that Breyandra's dread of David's home had kept the two young people apart, and she continued to probe, anxious for a response that would bode well for the loving pair. "But what of your past fears of Strehlow?"

"I shall do whatever is within my power to attain the happiness I seek with David." If Breyandra's answer was evasive, Elysia did not notice. She closed her eyes.

"I wish I could see you wed, but I fear . . ." A tear began to trickle down Elysia's cheek.

"I'll not listen to any sickbed lamentations," Breyandra chided gently. She tenderly caressed the woman's cheeks, brushing aside a few tears. "You must get well, dear Elysia. The baby, Father, David . . . we all need you. Is not our love tonic enough to strengthen you?"

Elysia opened her eyes and gazed sadly at Breyandra. "If I had the say of it. But I do have peace of mind in knowing that none of you will be left alone. Sim will have our son; you and David will have each other."

Now barely a whisper, Elysia's voice cracked. "I have sinned against Our Lord, and leaving all of you is the atonement I must suffer for my grievous sin."

The tears of the two women blended together as Breyandra leaned down and laid her cheek on Elysia's. "No, dear Mother, the punishment would be inflicted on those you left behind."

Breyandra raised her head at the sound of a faint fluttering from the nearby cradle. "The little one stirs. It must soon be time for his feeding," she deemed.

Elysia's glance turned to the cradle. "I wish I were well enough to suckle my son."

"And how do you expect to be well until you begin taking nourishment?" Breyandra chided lightly.

The admonishment had a positive effect on the ailing woman. Elysia sighed deeply. "'Tis a wise argument. I will try some hot broth now, please."

Elated, Breyandra rose to her feet and opened the chamber door. The long corridor, lit only by a few flickering sconces, was deserted. "I'll be back momentarily," Breyandra declared. Yawning, Wolf rose to his feet, stretched his long body, and followed his mistress.

Breyandra made short work of ladling a bowl of broth from the cauldron that steamed on the hearth. She set a pot of steeping tea on the tray as well. Wolf discovered the bone he had abandoned earlier and remained behind to chew on the forgotten delicacy.

When Breyandra reached the chamber, she drew up in shock at the sight of the ghostly specter standing above the bed. Lucretia Fraser,

her long black hair hanging to her waist in wild
abandon, stood staring malevolently at the helpless Elysia. The madwoman clutched a silver
candlestick in her hand. Breyandra cried out
when she saw the end of the heavy holder coated
with blood.

At the sound, the woman spun around and in
rage threw the candlestick at the girl in the
doorway. The heavy object struck Breyandra on
the head, and the tray she carried crashed to the
floor.

The baby awoke with a loud wail, and Elysia's
eyes opened wide with alarm. For a brief moment, she thought delirium had created the
fiendish apparition her eyes beheld.

Lucretia rushed to the cradle and snatched
the infant into her arms. She dashed past
Breyandra and raced toward the stairway leading to the battlements. The crazed woman appeared to fly up the stairs as the folds of her
white gown billowed behind her like wings.

"My baby!" Elysia screamed, trying to rise
from the bed.

Still dazed from the blow and with blood
dripping from a gash on her forehead,
Breyandra gave chase.

Lucretia's flight was slowed when she reached
the top of the narrow stairway. She threw the
weight of her body against the jammed door and
the portal burst open. Laughing maniacally, she
ran out into the storm and raised the crying
child above her head, bent on hurling the infant
over the battlements.

Breyandra reached her side and grabbed

Lucretia's arm, pulling her back. The fury of the storm raged about them as the two women wrestled over possession of the child. Breyandra finally succeeded in wrenching the squalling baby out of the deranged woman's arms.

Lucretia shoved her away with a powerful blow, and Breyandra fell back against the wall of the corbel battlements, shielding the infant in the cradle of her arm. Breyandra screamed as she toppled over the battlements, frantically grasping the stone ledge. She dangled helplessly by one arm, clutching the baby to her breast with the other.

Lucretia's shrill laughter, as demonic as the gleam in her eyes, resounded hysterically. Her fingers curled into talons, ready to pry loose Breyandra's tenuous grip, but she halted abruptly at a spine-chilling growl that emanated from the stairway. Lucretia swung around to see Wolf bolt through the door.

The dog's eyes glimmered yellow and feral in the darkness. Wolf's lip curled back, exposing pointed fangs that gleamed like a row of sharpened spikes in the glow from the relentless lightning.

Her eyes rounded with terror, Lucretia backed away, and in panic haste she lost her footing on the slippery stone. She fell back, landing precariously against the ledge of the battlements, and for several seconds the terrified woman tottered on the edge. Then, with a blood-curdling shriek, she toppled backward, plunging into the courtyard below.

David, bare-chested and grasping a drawn

sword, reached the battlements first. At the sight of Breyandra dangling by one hand, he cast aside the weapon and pulled her to safety.

Trembling and crying, she sank to her knees, still clutching the infant in her arms. David swooped up the two of them and carried them inside. He sat down with her on the top stair and hugged her tightly.

The sounds of the commotion had wakened Simon as well. He rushed to the Grand Chamber to discover Elysia in hysterics. "The baby!" she cried out.

By the time Simon bolted up the stairway toward the battlements, others in the castle followed close behind. When Simon reached the top of the stairway, he found Breyandra sitting securely in the protective shield of David's arms.

"Lucretia . . . tried to . . . kill the baby," Breyandra sobbed. The wet nurse shoved past Simon and tried to take the screaming child from her arms.

Breyandra drew back defensively, clutching the baby tighter in her embrace. "Give her the baby, Twit," David said gently. "She'll see that no harm comes to him."

Dazed, Breyandra stared down at the tiny bundle in her arms. The infant suddenly stopped crying and lay quietly, staring blankly at her with round blue eyes.

Breyandra gently kissed the soft little cheek, then placed her infant brother in the out-stretched arms of the wet nurse. Shivering, she turned to David and burrowed her head against his chest. David's arms tightened around her.

He sat rocking her in his arms as he would a child while she spent her tears.

Simon stepped outside on the battlements and leaned over the wall. Below in the courtyard, he saw several men carrying the broken, twisted body of Lucretia to the chapel. Sadly, the Laird of Saltoun shook his head and turned away. His step trod heavily as he slowly descended the stairway.

The safe return of her baby in the arms of the wet nurse calmed Elysia's hysteria. Strangely, the chain of events had a salubrious effect on the weakened woman; rather than drain her remaining strength, the danger to her baby seemed to rally her vitality. A flush of color enlivened her pallor, and a renewed verve sparked the eyes that had been coated in dullness for the past several days.

In the chamber above, Breyandra's tears subsided after several moments. Cupping her face in his hands, David gazed down at her. Rain had flattened her lustrous hair to sodden strands. The dripping water, mingled with the blood on her forehead, ran down her cheeks. He brushed aside some strands of hair that clung to her face and wiped away the streaks of blood. The near loss of the woman who had become his purpose for living left him shaken and silent.

Breyandra read the depth of emotion in his dark eyes.

She, too, struggled with a new reality. In the past, whatever her fears had been, be they Strehlow or the force of nature on a rampage, Saltoun had always remained sacrosanct, an inviolable haven in any storm, where she could seek safety and shelter.

However, in the dark moments as she dangled just a fingertip from death, her belief that Saltoun was an invincible refuge had been shattered. Her true and lasting sanctuary existed only in the arms enfolding her now.

Smiling, Breyandra raised her face to the man she loved.

By the time they tended Breyandra's wounds and donned dry clothing, the storm had passed. David and Breyandra returned to the Grand Chamber just as Simon was departing in search of Juanita, Lucretia's duenna. Curious, the couple followed him to the isolated suite in the tower.

The old woman lay on the floor, her gray hair matted with blood from several seeping gashes inflicted upon her by Lucretia. Beyond medical help, the dying woman called for a priest.

"I forgive *mi pequeña*. Mistress not mean to harm me. She and Carlo love me." The old woman's voice trailed off weakly.

Simon leaned closer to hear her. "Carlo? Who is Carlo?"

"Mistress' twin brother. *Mis niños*. My two babies."

Simon's startled glance locked with Breyandra's as they leaned over the prostrate woman. "What are you saying, old woman?" Simon was aghast. "Lucretia had a twin brother?"

"*Si*. Carlo. Never should come here."

"Here? You mean to Saltoun?" Simon prodded.

"These past years. When you in France."

Astounded, Simon became indignant. "Why wasn't I told of such a visitor?"

"Carlo and his men hide in woods. At night steal into castle through rear passageway. Visit *mi belleza.*"

The revelation added further to Simon's shock. He thought the abandoned passageway had not been used for decades. "But why did he remain concealed? He could have identified himself, and the gates of Saltoun would have been opened to him."

The old woman coughed, and a stream of blood trickled from the side of her mouth. "Carlo sick. From baby, like my mistress. He flee Spain. When he find how you treat his *pequeña hermana*, Carlo vow revenge—my two babies keep feud alive. Kill Frasers. Kill Gordons . . . keep feud."

David had been listening silently. At the mention of his clan, he leaned down to the old woman. "Carlo was responsible for the killings and mutilations on the moor?"

"You kill him," she snarled venomously.

Breyandra recalled the eyes of the leader of the cutthroats who had attacked them the day Duncan Gordon was killed. "Of course, that's why the dead man looked so familiar to me! He was Lucretia's twin brother."

Appalled, Simon could not believe what he was hearing. "Why . . . why would anyone carry out such carnage?"

The woman's mouth curled into a narrow slit. "You ask such question when you cause my sweet mistress to sorrow? You brought whore into castle. Lucretia life end."

Simon stared, aghast. The old woman had no remorse for the death of the innocent crofters who had been murdered in the ghoulish scheme. Only a twisted conscience could condone the meaningless debauchery. "My God, woman! You're as insane as they were!" He rose to his feet and stood shaking his head, unable to comprehend such malevolent evil. "All of you . . . insane, under this very roof."

"A priest. I want priest," Juanita pleaded. "Do not deny me last rites."

Breyandra shivered as a chill swept her spine. She moved to Simon's side and took his arm. "The scourge lingers in this room, Father. Let us leave. Tomorrow we shall burn everything within these walls." She led the bewildered man out of the room.

For several moments, David stared down in contempt at Juanita. He felt no sympathy for the dying woman. She could have prevented the deaths of the innocent victims, Gordons as well as Frasers, who had fallen under the knife of the madman.

Juanita saw the scorn in David's eyes. With her final breath, she reared up and spat on his boot. Then the old woman fell back and, like the mistress she served, died without the absolution she sought.

Chapter Twenty-nine

The dawn of a new day brought a slight easing of tension at Saltoun. Simon had taken the attitude that every new day would make Elysia stronger and increase her chances of surviving.

In a quiet ceremony, Lucretia Fraser and her devoted duenna were buried in a small plot outside the gate. With his daughter at his side, the grim-faced Laird of Saltoun stood at the gravesite. David Gordon had remained at the bedside of his mother. A few of the servants attended the rites, out of curiosity rather than respect, for none present mourned the passing of Lucretia Fraser.

After the Mistress of Saltoun had been lowered into her final place of rest, everything in the tower suite was put to the torch: tapestries, paintings, clothing, jewelry, furniture. Simon

Fraser wanted nothing preserved as a reminder of the evil woman.

Breyandra's heart caught in her throat when she later entered the Grand Chamber and saw David awkwardly jostling the infant in his arms. Elysia lay watching him, her face curved with a poignant smile, pride gleaming in her eyes.

Simon crossed to the bedridden woman and took her hand, raising the palm to his lips. As he gazed adoringly at Elysia, his renewed optimism was evident in his attitude and bearing. When David and Breyandra moved to depart, Simon raised a hand to detain them.

"Breyandra. Lord Gordon. I wish you to remain. I have summoned a minister of the kirk from the village to wed Elysia and myself."

Elysia's shocked gasp turned into a sob. Simon got down on his knees and clutched her hand to his cheek. "Forgive me, my precious love, for not first speaking of this with you. I want us to be one, joined as husband and wife, not only in the eyes of God, who has already made us so, but in the ledgers of the church and court as well. Our son shall not be called a bastard, and from this day on will become the next Laird of Saltoun."

Unable to restrain her joy, Elysia sobbed openly. "Then don't you believe, Lord Lovet, with such a fine title as 'the next Laird of Saltoun,' our son should have a proper name as well?"

Simon began to chuckle at the reminder that in the distress of Elysia's condition, the baby had not been properly christened. "Good Lord! We've not named the wee bairn, have we?" His loving grin at her was engaging. "What is your preference, love?"

"*Simon,* after his father," Elysia said instantly.

"And what is yours?"

Simon stroked his chin reflectively. "I've never had a fondness for my name. I'd hate to burden the tyke with it. What say you of *James,* after my father?"

He turned to Breyandra and David. The young couple were thoroughly pleased, though flabbergasted, with Simon's swift strategy. Indeed, in light of Elysia's illness, the marriage had best take place as soon as possible to legitimize their son. Thereafter, no usurper could claim title to Saltoun.

"Why don't you call him *David*?" Breyandra exclaimed.

"Have you forgotten I already have a son with that name?" Elysia reminded her, casting a proud look at David. "I advise you to preserve that name for your own son," she added slyly.

The innuendo brought a bright blush to Breyandra's cheeks. David chuckled warmly, grabbed her hand and squeezed it. "I think you should name him after our sovereign, *Charles,* the 'Merry Monarch.'"

"That was my father's name as well," Elysia reflected.

"The 'Merry Monarch'! To think I always addressed him as *Grandfather.* He seemed so staid to me," David joshed.

Elysia cast a suffering glance at her eldest son

but covered her mouth in a giggle. At the sound of the pleasant ring, all heads swung in surprise to look at her. With heightened color and a sparkle in her eyes, Elysia looked far from the woman who lay at death's door less than a day before.

By the time the minister arrived, Simon and Elysia had decided upon a name for their son.

Then, with Breyandra dabbing at the tears on her cheeks, David grinning like the father of the bride, the servants of Saltoun gathered in hushed reverence, Simon Fraser stood solemnly holding the hand of Elysia Gordon as the minister pronounced them husband and wife.

Shortly after the echo of applause had stilled, James Charles Fraser, Viscount of Saltoun, was christened in the name of the Almighty.

When all had offered their congratulations and returned to their duties, Simon sat at the bedside of his bride, clasping her hand in his. The excitement had exhausted Elysia, but just before the weakened woman slipped into slumber, her face curved with a smile. "I'm so happy, Sim. I've never known such a blessed day. Our Precious Lord has been so merciful to this unworthy servant."

The Laird of Saltoun gazed down with adoration at the serene loveliness of the sleeping woman, her face still graced with a smile. Simon raised her hand to his lips and pressed a kiss to the palm. "He cherishes you, as I do, my love."

David whispered into Breyandra's ear, "Let's leave them alone, Twit." Breyandra nodded, and hand in hand they tiptoed out of the room.

As a diversion from the dreary confinement of the past days, Breyandra and David decided to take a short ride. They rode into the bright afternoon sunshine with Wolf trotting beside them.

The previous day's rain had left the air smelling fresh and the earth revitalized. After a short gallop, they halted their mounts in a shady copse of birch and rowan trees beside a stream running heavily with the rain from the previous day.

David lifted Breyandra out of the saddle and swung her to the ground. She sat down and leaned back against the trunk of a leafy birch. Wolf took a long drink after his hard run and stretched out in the shade of a nearby tree for a much needed snooze.

After watering the horses, David plopped down and laid his head in Breyandra's lap. He looked up at her as she sat smiling contentedly. Unable to resist the lovely vision, he sat up and framed her face in his hands. "I love you, Twit."

David dipped his head to claim her lips. Breyandra closed her eyes and gave herself up to the persuasive sensation. He shifted and pulled her down so she lay stretched out beside him. Leaning over her, he began to press slow, sensuous kisses on her face and eyes. No spot remained untouched.

His tongue circled the outline of her lips, until, sighing, she parted them and he slipped it into the honeyed chamber of her mouth.

For endless moments of erotic pleasure, David played with her, brushing the roof of her mouth with teasing strokes, curling his tongue around hers, licking her lips, her eyes, her teeth. When he raised his head, she opened her eyes and met his dark gaze. "You're wicked, David Gordon," she murmured in a breathless whisper that sent a tremor down his spine. "You use your tongue for purposes the Lord did not intend."

He chuckled warmly and slipped her gown off her shoulders. "One of the Lord's purposes for the tongue is a tool for tasting, my lady."

He dipped his head and lightly stroked his tongue down the column of her neck to the cleavage of her breast.

She groaned aloud when he began to brush the turgid peaks, suckling and stroking, suckling and stroking, until she writhed beneath him.

David pushed the gown off her hips, shoving her underclothing along with it, until she lay naked. He used his tongue to toy with the provocative dip of her tiny navel.

"Stop. You must stop," she pleaded, convinced she could not bear another moment of the exquisite sensation.

He continued his downward slide past her dark mound. Breyandra moaned helplessly when he parted her legs. She could feel the core of her being coiling tighter and tighter, ready to spring at the first touch.

When his tongue reached the throbbing source of her passion, a wave that felt like flame rushed to her head, threatening to rob her of consciousness. She rode on the crest of the sensation, hovering between sanity and madness as her body erupted with tremors.

David raised his head, gazing down at her while he quickly shed his clothing. With her slim white body stretched out before him, she became a seductive temptress. Her lips parted, and her passion-laden lids were almost closed. The round, firm mounds of her breasts rose and fell in her struggle to control her breathing.

She opened her arms to him. The fever of lust raged through him. David lowered himself and crushed her mouth in a hard, bruising kiss. His tongue drove into her mouth and dueled with hers.

"Lord, I love you, Twit," he groaned hoarsely as their breath mingled.

Breyandra tightened her arms around his neck. His muscles jerked beneath her fingertips as she lightly grazed a teasing trail across the flat plane of his stomach to his groin, around to his buttocks, then traced a single nail up the taut column of his spine.

Her lips were warm and moist at his ear. "And 'tis time, my Lord Gordon, I show you that the Lord's design for the hands goes beyond wielding a broadsword."

Later, the loving pair frolicked in the stream, splashing and laughing like children. Wolf joined them in the romp, barking and jumping with the energy of a young pup, until shivering, David and Breyandra scrambled out of the water and pulled on their clothes.

"It's good to be home, isn't it, David?" Breyandra said as she dried the strands of dripping hair with her undergown. "I never again want to go back to the court." The mention of the word reminded Breyandra of the unsolved problem that loomed before them. "What are we going to do about the King's decree?"

"Let's get married, Twit. Now."

Her eyes rounded with shock. "We can't defy the King."

He laughed harshly. "I am not going to marry Jean Fleming just to please Charles Stuart. And you will never wed James Douglas. I shall see to it." He sat up and wrapped a coil of her hair around one of his fingers. "Day by day, my mother regains her strength. Once her health is restored, I shall go to Whitehall and inform the King how we feel about each other. I am sure Charles will rescind his decree when he hears the truth."

"But what if he doesn't?" Breyandra challenged. "To defy the King is surely to provoke his wrath. He could strip you of your titles and banish you. Or put your clan to the horn if you resist him."

David grabbed her shoulders in a strong grasp and stared down at her with determination. "Damn the King. I care not a whit what he thinks or decrees," he said angrily. Then his eyes softened, and his voice gently pleaded his innermost concern. "I only care that you not allow your fear of Strehlow to keep you from marrying me."

Breyandra smiled with assurance. "I have put that fear behind me. And last night I learned that

Strehlow isn't the only place harboring skeletons in the closet. Yes, David, I will marry you and go home to Strehlow."

Moved by her acceptance, David swallowed hard. Then he grinned broadly and laughed for joy. His hands spanned her waist as he raised her up and spun around in circles. "Then come, we'll wed now, before anyone tries to stop us."

David put Breyandra on her horse and swung himself up on Whirlwind.

"You want to do what? When?" Simon Fraser snorted, jumping to his feet.

Breyandra cast a nervous glance at her intended groom. "David and I intend to wed today."

"Should I be flattered you seek my consent?" Simon shouted. "What of the banns?"

David would not allow Breyandra to bear the man's fury, but responded in good humor. "We were so inspired by your example, dear Father, we sought to omit the archaic custom. As for your permission, I failed to hear you seek consent from the Laird of Strehlow when you sought to wed my mother."

David's snide reply only raised Simon's ire to a greater degree. He leaned across the table on his hands, and glared at his soon-to-be-acquired son-in-law. "You make tolerating you a difficult task, Lord Gordon. Though I should be thankful that you intend to make an honest woman of my daughter."

"As you finally did my mother," David taunted.

Near exasperation at these two men rattling swords at one another, Breyandra intervened. "Oh, please, Father. I love the two of you more than any others. My heart aches to hear you spar like this."

David slipped his arm around Breyandra's shoulders and drew her to his side. "I love your daughter, Lord Lovet. I pledge my heart to keeping her content and my right arm to keeping her safe."

Simon straightened up and studied the woeful look in his daughter's eyes. His disapproving glance then swung to David, who stood resolute and inflexible. And, as always, when Breyandra's interests were at stake, Simon followed his heart.

He offered a bone of peace. "On several recent occasions I *have* had cause to witness the effectiveness of your right arm, Lord Gordon. But I mean to warn you now, keep it strong in defense of my daughter, for if you fail . . ." Simon shook his balled fist at David. However, he was unable to suppress his smile.

And so it happened—the venerable Fraser opened his hand to the stalwart Gordon.

Breyandra emitted a very unfeminine yelp of joy, which caused a similar response from the dog at her feet. Simon opened his arms and she ran into them. For several seconds her father held her tightly. His eyes glimmered with tears when he stepped back and smiled down into her upraised face. "It seems just yesterday you told me you would never love any man but me."

Breyandra returned his smile through her

tears. "And you said you hoped I was mistaken. Now I know the wisdom of that message, Father."

"May you always know happiness, Sweetling." No further words were necessary. The moment was too poignant for either of them to express the feelings in their hearts.

"Now come. Let us tell Elysia. I know the news will add to her recovery. She is so sentimental," Simon said as he wiped his eyes to suppress a sniffle.

As her husband predicted, Elysia was ecstatic, but quickly reduced to tears. After an exchange of kisses, Breyandra and David left Simon to calm his joyous wife.

The Very Reverend Angus Fraser, a second cousin to the Laird of Saltoun, had just sat down to high tea when summoned to the keep for the second time that day. Fearing that the new Mistress of Saltoun had taken a turn for the worse, Angus grabbed his Bible and hurried to the castle.

The startled minister shook his head in disbelief when confronted by yet another bridal couple in the Grand Chamber. Only that morning he had performed the nuptial ceremony for the Laird of Saltoun, with these very two in audience. Now the Laird's daughter wished to wed. In the Grand Chamber as well! With all the holy rites staged there of late, the disgruntled clergyman did not understand why the Laird just didn't stain the window of the room and move in an altar and font. *I ken th' Laird's Spanish wife wasna th' only ane tetched 'n th' haid*, he mused in silence.

Never in his forty years of ministry had he known of a man and his daughter wed on the same day, both dismissing the customary banns. Granted, the perplexed man reasoned, the Laird had sought a hasty wedding because of the failing health of Elysia. *Bu' why hae th' twa young anes saught to do th' same?* he pondered as he opened his Bible.

Over the top of his holy book, Angus Fraser glanced at the ravishing beauty who stood before him. Her hand was held in a firm grasp by the handsome man at her side.

Breyandra had changed into a rustling gown of yellow silk with a white stomacher and undergown. A sheer headrail of white batiste covered her long black hair, now brushed to a satin sheen and flowing past her shoulders.

Aye, th' lass shur dinna liik ailin, he resolved with a grimace.

Angus finally conjectured that the only reason the young couple would wed so hastily must be that Breyandra carried a baby. The minister cast a sly glance at the Gordon who stood beside her. *Aye, th' lass be carrin' a wee bairn*. After a longer look at the braw young man, he summarized perceptively, *An' it willna be th' last ayn, aithar*.

Later that evening the young couple joined their parents in the Grand Chamber to share a combined wedding feast. Elysia Fraser was able to sit up in bed for a short time and join in a wedding toast to one another.

Within the week Elysia had progressed to the stage where the doctor declared her out of danger, and, though bedridden, she could sit up to take her meals. Wee James was moved to a nursery during the night, and a bed was brought to the Grand Chamber for Simon to spend his nights near the woman he loved.

David and Breyandra decided to leave Saltoun and return to Whitehall; facing the wrath of the King had best be done before more time passed. With a saddened heart Breyandra kissed Elysia and her father goodbye.

Wolf rose to follow her, and Breyandra knelt down on her knees and hugged him. "I have a protector now, lad," she cooed in his ear. "The little bairn has a greater need of you."

Wolf cocked his head and looked at her with his round, alert eyes. "Guard him faithfully, as you did me." Her eyes misted when she hugged the big dog once again and kissed his furry head.

As though understanding her every word, Wolf obediently trotted over to the cradle where James lay sleeping and stretched out his long body, resting his head on his paws. But his sad gaze followed Breyandra as she departed through the door.

Chapter Thirty

Charles greeted David and Breyandra with his usual elation when they returned to Whitehall. After learning of the dire circumstances that had summoned them to Saltoun, Charles beamed joyously to hear of Elysia's recovery and her subsequent marriage to Simon Fraser.

As David continued to inform the King of all the details, Breyandra's glance swept over the people in the Great Hall in search of Jean Fleming. She spied the girl sitting alone in a far corner with her hands folded in her lap, looking like a child who had just been reprimanded.

The poor girl had languished heartbroken during Breyandra's absence, spending most of the time in her room sobbing into her pillow. Her beloved James Douglas had not spoken more than a dozen words to her since the night

the King had betrothed her to David Gordon.
Jean reasoned she had apparently just been
someone for him to trifle with while at court,
and now the young lord had found more fasci-
nating game with the prospect of wedding her
beautiful cousin.

Breyandra's gaze traversed the room again,
seeking James Douglas. She glimpsed his red
hair among a group standing against a far wall.
He appeared to be as crestfallen as Jean. Jean's
avoidance of him since David's departure had
crushed his spirit. He had once felt certain that
the enchanting sprite was in love with him,
when in reality she had her eye on his best
friend.

Breyandra wondered why both Jean and
Jamie had avoided greeting her. Dismayed, she
surmised that the two had not broached the
King with their displeasure and his decree stood
unchallenged. It seemed that Jean and Jamie
had left the protest for David and herself to voice
upon their return to Whitehall. Breyandra was
disgusted with both of them for their cowardice.
On the other hand, fear of countermanding the
King *was* understandable.

"The marriage of your mother to Lord Lovet
now officially links you and Lady Breyandra,"
Charles announced with pleasure. As King of
Scotland as well as England, Charles was comforted to know that all Gordons and Frasers, the
two great feuding Highland clans, were united
by the bond of marriage.

David, not one for dilly-dally, addressed the
matter on his mind forthwith. "The wedding of

our parents is not the sole bridge to the unity of our clans, Your Majesty. While at Saltoun, the Lady Breyandra and I were also wed."

Charles's smile disappeared as quickly as it had emerged. "You jest, Lord Gordon."

"I do not make banter concerning my love for Lady Breyandra, Your Majesty."

A momentary gleam of displeasure flared in Charles's eyes before he composed his bearing and to assert his authority, adopted a sovereign tone. "A noble sentiment, my young lord, but ill-grounded. Perhaps even contrary to fact. On good authority, information has come to our attention that you led the Lady Fleming to believe your intentions were sincere."

"You have been misinformed, my liege. Your informant has *no* authority. I have never expressed any feeling for my wife's relative other than a cousinly regard." David clasped Breyandra's cold fingers. "My love for Lady Breyandra has always been foremost in my heart."

"We have seen no evidence previously of the love between you, Lord Gordon." Charles struck a regal pose. "And what of the two people you have willfully wronged? Lord Claibourne and Lady Jean have been desolate since your departure."

At the mention of his name, James Douglas stepped forward to intervene. However, David responded quickly. "Their unhappiness is not due to our absence, Your Majesty, but to the terms of your dictate."

Charles took offense at David's remark. He

turned to Jamie. "Is this true, Lord Claibourne?"

Remembering Jean's actions of the past days, Jamie responded, "I can only speak for myself, Your Majesty. I am not in love with Lady Breyandra. Lord Gordon's feelings for her are well known to all the court."

"Not to all, Lord Claibourne." Charles prided himself on his perceptiveness. The King was now embarrassed to discover how easily he had been duped by his mistress. And pride caused him to vent his humiliation on the victims of Lady Castlemaine's connivance rather than on the perpetrator. He regarded the two Highlanders with displeasure. "You try our patience, my lord Claibourne. If Lord Gordon and Lady Breyandra had such feelings of the heart, why haven't you said as much to us?"

Why indeed! David thought grimly to himself, as displeased with Jamie as Charles now appeared to be.

"And your actions, Lord Gordon, are worse. You have deliberately acted in disobedience to your sovereign, and your ignoble deed has publicly disgraced the Lady Jean Fleming."

Charles threw up his hands in hopelessness. "No other option remains open." He fixed an inflexible stare on David. "Despite our aversion to dueling, for *honoris causa* we must insist that honor be served."

Once it was declared, there was no retracting the mandate. Shocked, David stared at the King, unable to believe that Charles would force a duel of honor now the truth had been exposed.

Charles could not meet David's gaze forthright. He glanced with disgust at his mistress. The scheming courtesan's face was curved in a smirk. Witnessing the exchange, in an instant David realized who the instigator of the villainous deed was. Once again the perfidy of Barbara Palmer had prevailed.

James Douglas recognized the need to prevent David from fighting an opponent appointed by Charles, which would surely lead to bloodshed. He acted swiftly, confident that his friend would do him no serious harm. "Permit me to act in defense of the honor of Lady Fleming, whom I have admired from afar."

Since no other man present was foolish enough to raise his sword against the Highlander, Charles accepted Jamie's offer.

"We will allow Lord Claibourne this request. Gentlemen, you will meet at dawn tomorrow in the Great Hall of Whitehall. Weapons will be rapiers, not broadswords," he added pointedly for David's sake.

"Since the honor of the Crown must be served as well, We will not allow either of you to choose a second. So be it," he declared with a regal wave of dismissal.

David Gordon's prowess with a sword was common knowledge to all. Upon hearing the King's announcement, Jean Fleming cried out and slumped to the floor in a faint. When James Douglas rushed to the fallen girl, Barbara Palmer's face curved with a malicious smile, while others in the room remained too stunned to speak or move, except for the Queen. Catherine rose to her feet and hurried over to comfort the stricken girl.

David turned to Breyandra. Her knees trembled so, she feared they would not support her. He clasped her shoulders in his hands and she looked up fearfully. "God forgive us, David. What disaster have we wrought?"

Once they were alone, Barbara Palmer's triumph was shortlived when Charles began to admonish his mistress. "You deceived me to achieve your own end. Whatever your reason, Lady Castlemaine, I consider malice one of the greatest human weaknesses."

The sonorous voice sounded even more resonant because of the fury that lay below the surface. "Falsehood and cruelty are as much an abomination in our eyes as they are to those of God. Why a beautiful woman feels compelled to perform such reprehensible deeds is beyond the comprehension of this mere monarch . . . but *not* beyond his displeasure."

Charles drew himself up to his full height, and his eyes pierced her with a cold stare. "I have observed, dear Barbary, that one who overplays his hand will often find himself alone at the gaming table." Then, with the majestic dignity so ingrained in the Stuarts, the King walked away, leaving the conniving woman to reflect on his words.

David Gordon was just as agitated. He paced the floor of his chamber like a caged animal. Breyandra stood silently staring out of the window. "Fight a duel with Jamie Douglas! Good Lord, whose honor has been impugned?" David snorted. "Jean Fleming doesn't care for me. Why didn't she declare so?"

In his frustration, he kicked at the corners of the lavish rug at his feet. "The King is angry because his trusted whore Barbary made a fool of him, not because I disobeyed his decree. If he insisted upon salving his vanity, why didn't he just put me in the Tower for a month?"

Having listened to David's ranting for the last hour, wearily Breyandra turned her head to him. "What are you going to do now, David?"

"I won't raise a weapon. I'll let Jamie draw first blood, and the damned duel will be over."

Breyandra gasped in shock. "But if you don't intend to protect yourself, Jamie could injure you . . . or worse . . ." She caught her lower lip between her teeth as tears glimmered in her eyes.

Breyandra knew that Jamie would never intentionally harm David, but accidents were known to happen in duels. For the last hour she had wrestled with the fear that the man she loved would be lost to her forever because of a misstep or slip of the hand.

David saw her distress and drew her into his arms. He tipped up her chin to force her to meet his loving gaze. "What's one more scar, Twit?"

Her tears blended with their kiss, and she buried her head against his chest. "When I think of how our time has been wasted, David, and now dueling with Jamie . . ."

A delicate clock on the mantel chimed twelve.

"And we're wasting this night as well," he chided lightly. He began to unbutton her gown. "Tomorrow we'll return to the Highlands where we belong."

A tap interrupted his intent. With irritation, David walked to the door and flung it open. A page waited outside. "Lord Gordon, the King requests your presence in the Great Hall."

"Tell him I'll be there at once." David closed the door and turned back to Breyandra, who had been listening. "I must see what he wants," he said with a shrug of his broad shoulders.

Breyandra nodded and stepped into his arms. She closed the buttons of his shirt. "Please return as soon as you can."

David grinned and kissed the tip of her nose. "You can be certain."

When the King left Barbara, he was suffering an emotion rare to his easygoing nature. Charles Stuart was angry; angry with his mistress for manipulating him, and angry with himself for failing to discern the truth before serious damage had been done.

Good Lord! Charles thought with self-derision. *Was I the only one blind to the truth? My betrothals are at fault in the scenario—not the players.*

Now he feared it was too late. The wheels had been set in motion. One of the Scots could be maimed, or even killed. Two young men who had been so loyal. This was their reward for devotion to the Crown.

Distraught, Charles sought the privacy of the garden. Even the spaniels sensed his need to meditate. They trotted behind him, sniffing out an occasional insect among the flowers, careful not to distract the master from his reflection.

Charles meditated, and soon one fact became clear; he had created the predicament, and therefore he had the responsibility to resolve it. Honor must still be served. But how?

He ceased ambling and sat down on a stone bench, propped his elbows on his knees, and rested his chin on his hand. The spaniels gathered about his feet and lay looking up with luminous, trusting eyes at their beloved master.

After a long concentration Charles raised his head. "I've got it!" He jumped to his feet, as did the twelve dogs, and moved with a quick pace into the palace, accompanied by the devoted retinue.

Charles hurried to the Master of the Guard.

"But, Your Majesty, all our swords are razor sharp," the dumbfounded man exclaimed upon hearing the unusual request of the King.

"Then see that two are dulled and bring them to me by sunrise tomorrow," Charles demanded. He left before the man could reply.

"Dull them?" the bewildered man mumbled. "How am I to dull them?" He glanced out of the window and saw one of the dogs lift its leg against a tree. The man's face curved into a smile. "George! Willie!" he called out at the top of his voice. "Come at once and each of you bring a sword."

Having set his scheme into motion, Charles waited for the arrival of the two pawns in his game. David Gordon entered the room first.

"Your Majesty," David acknowledged and sat down at the King's invitation.

Immediately Charles offered the Highlander a flagon of ale. "I trust your return journey to Whitehall passed comfortably, Lord Gordon."

"Very, Your Majesty. The journey was spent in pleasant company." Even though Charles's remark appeared solicitous and innocent from any guile, David suspected that the King had something up his satin sleeve. When James Douglas arrived on the scene, David knew for certain that his suspicions were correct.

After James was seated with a tall flagon in his hand, David continued sipping his ale, waiting for a sign that would give him a clue to the King's intentions. Charles had obligated them to fight the duel within a few hours; it made little sense to David for the King to sit drinking ale with the same men he had condemned to such lunacy.

However, Charles appeared not to have a problem with the ludicrous concept, as evidenced by his friendly smile. "Now drink up, my friends, this may be our last opportunity to do so together."

The message gratified neither of the men. When Charles refilled their empty tankards, they took deep swigs of ale and once again extended their tankards to be filled. Beaming broadly, the King obliged.

Now light-headed, David and Jamie did not notice that Charles had covertly emptied his own flagon into a bowl at his feet, as he had been doing all along. Several eager spaniels awaiting the treat eagerly lapped up the ale.

After several hours Charles was the only sober body in the room, dogs included. David Gordon leaned across the table and regarded his sovereign suspiciously through a pair of very blurred eyes. "Don't shink . . . hic . . . I'm not . . . hic . . . wise ta . . . hic . . . wha' yoush . . . hic . . . doin . . . hic, . . . Yer Magy . . . hic . . . Magisshe." David eyed him with a narrow frown. "Yoush have . . . hic . . . shumthin . . . hic . . . up yur . . . shleeve."

A loud belch emanated from Jamie Douglas. "Oh, shorry." He grinned sheepishly and covered his mouth.

A similar rumble echoed from one of the spaniels. The dog stretched out and promptly fell asleep. Shakily, Jamie rose to his feet and staggered the short distance to the animal. He eyed the spaniel dubiously. "Thish dog has a definite problem. Poor poosh." He leaned over to pat its head, but instead toppled over head first. The spaniel slept on undisturbed.

Charles forced back his laughter and jumped up to assist the drunken man to his feet. Through the fuzzy recesses of his besotted mind, David realized he had drunk too much and must sober up if he were to have a clear head for the duel. With that thought foremost in his mind, he took another deep draught of ale.

When Edward Hyde and the Duke of York, both privy to Charles's scheme, arrived on the scene at dawn to witness the contest, Jamie and a dozen belching and snoring dogs were stretched out on the floor around the room.

They found David asleep in a chair, while Charles sat sleepily resting his head on his arm.

Frantic, Breyandra rushed into the room. She had spent a sleepless night and her panicked gaze searched for her husband. As David and Jamie were awakened by the contest's officials, the Master of the Guard brought the two swords for the event.

The captain's night had also been sleepless; he had spent it attempting to saw through a tree with the rapiers. It had taken him almost till dawn to achieve the desired dullness, and the tip of each sword was broken.

"A task well done, captain," Charles said approvingly as he ran his finger along the edge of one of the rapiers.

The Queen and Jean Fleming joined the spectators while the besotted duelists were properly positioned. Noticing the stricken expressions of the three women, Charles moved over to them, leaned down and whispered conspiratorially, "Trust me, my ladies." Breyandra's startled glance swung up to meet the mischievous gleam in his dark eyes.

Weaving like two reeds in a windstorm, David and Jamie went through the formality of addressing one another with their foils. "Remember, first blood," Charles announced.

James Douglas blinked several times, trying to focus on his opponent while peering through fuzz-marred vision. Even in his thoroughly inebriated state, David's muddled mind clung to the intention of allowing Jamie to draw first blood. He lowered his weapon, stepped back, and stumbled over one of the sleeping spaniels. Struggling to maintain balance, he twisted about and in his clumsy drunken state fell face-forward to the floor.

Groggily he raised a battered head, exposing a face streaked with the crimson of blood flowing from a broken nose.

"First blood!" Charles yelled, jumping to his feet and halting the duel. "First blood," he repeated with regal finality.

Then he turned to Breyandra and, with an audacious grin, the Merry Monarch winked.

Having remained awake throughout the night, Charles decided to forsake his usual morning walk and retire to his chamber. The King was pleased with himself; the scheme had been executed with the fine precision of a Swiss clock.

Before departing, the King announced he would hold court later that afternoon. All the principals were ordered to attend. Remembering that David had defied him once, Charles stopped at the chair where Breyandra held a linen to her husband's injured nose. "I will expect to see you there, Lord Gordon," he cautioned the understandably bewildered Highlander.

The setting glowed with crystal chandeliers, the walls were adorned with lavish tapestries, and the mood abounded with tension as the players assembled to enact the final scene of the exciting melodrama.

Breyandra, elegant in a gown of rose brocade,

entered the hall on the arm of her handsome, if somewhat beleaguered, husband.

The bloom of youth had returned to the cheeks of Jean Fleming, proudly escorted forth by James Douglas.

Now well rested and refreshed, Charles and Catherine regally sat side by side on thrones of radiant splendor, casting loving glances at one another in unspoken intimacy.

Edward Hyde's customarily austere mien appeared to be somewhat relaxed. The Duke of York, Buckingham, the Earl of Rochester, and the throng of court dandies stood about in their usual circles, as raucous as ever.

Noticeably missing from the setting was the Lady Castlemaine, who had elected to entertain her daughter in the garden.

On the dais at the royal couple's feet, lounged the resident company of spaniels.

The room hushed when Charles slowly raised his scepter. "Lord Claibourne, in deep appreciation and gratitude for your noble championship of this court, I hereby betroth you to the Lady Jean Fleming."

On bended knee James Douglas bowed his head. "Your most obedient servant, my liege. I pledge to honor your request." The hall rang with a joyous cheer as Jamie rose and reached for the arm of his betrothed.

When the clamor diminished, Charles's face sobered. "Lord Gordon, the union of the two great clans of Gordon and Fraser brings great joy to the heart of this court. May your marriage be harmonious and prolific. Return to the Highlands to resume your duties and responsibilities as Laird of Strehlow. Go in peace, Lord Gordon."

Recognizing their cue, the assembly shouted in boisterous approval.

David bowed on bended knee. "Your most obedient servant, my liege."

He rose and began to reach for Breyandra, but Charles raised his scepter to stop him. "My obedient servant? We all know you are not *that*, my Lord Gordon. Therefore, as penance for defying the court, the Lady Breyandra shall be obliged to remain with the Holy Sisters for ninety days."

David started to balk at the startling development, but Charles majestically arched a brow. "Perhaps in the course of your separation, Lord Gordon, you will of necessity reflect on the error of disobeying the wishes of your sovereign."

David eyed him with rancor. "I can hardly storm the walls of a nunnery, Your Majesty."

Charles smiled in accord. "I suspected as much, my Lord Gordon."

Breyandra put a restraining hand on David's shoulder. "'Tis a small price to pay." She smiled into his eyes. "We've suffered other separations. I will pray this will be the last."

David hesitated, then grimaced and lowered his head. "Your obedient servant."

"You are excused to say your farewells." The King's eyes smiled into David's glare. "'Tis a mild punishment, my friend. The Holy Sisters will take good care of her."

Charles waited as the young couple departed from the room, then, lowering his scepter, dismissed the court.

"Charles, surely you aren't going to separate that dear couple?" Catherine implored.

"Not if it displeases you, my love," he said graciously.

A smile of gratitude transformed her face into loveliness. "Thank you, dear Charles, I shall always be grateful."

His eyes sparked with a wicked gleam. "As will Lord Gordon. But let's not tell the rogue as yet. Let his loins dwell on the thought for a while. Then, as that clever bard so aptly penned, all's well that ends well."

Basking in his own romanticism, Charles turned to the Lord Chancellor with a smile of satisfaction. "Ah, Clarendon, I hope someday history will record all I have done for love."

Edward Hyde glanced through the window at several of Charles's bastards frolicking on the lawn below. His dour face pursed into reproach. "Indeed it will, Your Majesty, if the historians do not lose track of their count."

Always one to appreciate a joke, even at his own expense, Charles laughed aloud. "Why, Clarendon, I am shocked."

He extended his arm to his queen; his dark eyes gleamed with mischief and a rakish brow arched roguishly. "Will you join me in my chambers, Your Majesty?"

Blushing profusely, Catherine demurely

dropped her eyes. "Your most obedient servant, Your Majesty."

To the Lord Chancellor's further consternation, the Merry Monarch threw back his head in laughter, clutched the hand of his Queen, and hand in hand the royal couple made a hasty exit—followed by a dozen spaniels.

Chapter Thirty-one

Nearing the clachan of Streyside, the large procession of men and horses on the road created a fervor among the villagers. At the sight of the approaching Stuart colors, crofters left their tasks and ran to see the excitement.

James Stuart, the Duke of York, rode majestically at the head of the column. All were anxious to see the handsome duke, brother of the King, and, if Charles failed to produce a legitimate heir, the man who would succeed to the throne of England, Scotland, and Ireland.

Behind James rode Simon Fraser, followed in an open carriage by Elysia Gordon Fraser holding her precious baby son securely in her arms. Wolf, the faithful sentinel, ever mindful of his responsibility, trotted alongside.

Strung out behind them, a military contingent of English and Fraser soldiers completed the cortege.

Word had carried to the castle, and the gates of Strehlow had been opened wide. David was not pleased to see the Stuart banner, for the colorful flutter reminded him of the frivolous court that amused itself by usurping wives and creating duels of whimsy. Nevertheless, the Laird of Strehlow rode out to greet the new arrivals when the Duke of York raised his hand and halted the procession outside the gates.

With awe and fascination, the villagers gathered around the royal prince. Under the watchful glower of Wolf, James took the baby from Elysia and held the infant in his arms. "We have come here today so the villagers of Streyside may celebrate the christening of the child who represents the merging of the blood of the Gordons and Frasers."

A grimace of distaste appeared on the faces of a few, but James ignored the disgruntled and continued. "Let this tiny babe be the symbol of unity between two great clans. I am here as a representative of the child's godfather, Charles, King of England, Scotland, and Ireland. The King wishes all of your clansmen to join in commemorating this proud and auspicious occasion, and desires that you will accept the responsibility of assuring the health and welfare of his godson. Furthermore, he will be greatly distressed if you do not."

Simon tried to restrain a smile as he whispered to Elysia, "Good God, the man is virtually threatening them!"

"Och, Yer Hee'nass, we'll luv th' wee bairn lik' ayr awn," one of the villagers called out. The others nodded in accord, mumbling their agreement to one another.

As he returned the infant to his mother's arms, James Stuart tried to keep a solemn mien in the face of such eager capitulation. "We all have further cause for jubilation, the marriage of the Laird of Strehlow to the Lady Breyandra Fraser."

At first the crowd reacted with stunned silence; the very mention of Breyandra's name revived the guilt that had wracked the conscience of Streyside since the night she had fled for her life from the stake of fire. And now that same woman was the Laird's wife! The rapidly enfolding events were simply too much for the villagers to comprehend.

They looked to their Laird and saw an unhappy face, stern and dejected. David turned his sorrowful gaze to his mother. Elysia smiled at him through her tears. Even Simon Fraser looked as proud as any father on his daughter's wedding day. Then the villagers, unaware of the reason for the despondency of the groom, began to mumble and whisper among themselves as they tried to guess the reason for his unnatural gloom.

Only a noble few knew of the basis for David's unhappiness. James Stuart, observing the long-faced Highlander, could not remember when he himself had been so amused. He raised his hands to regain the attention of the villagers. "Our beloved Monarch has put a great burden of responsibility on the citizens of Streyside. He has requested that you pledge yourselves to the protection and care of the new Mistress of Strehlow." Tongue in cheek, James added, "The King has confidence you will not disappoint him." Needless to say, the purpose for the presence of the King's brother at Strehlow was to make *certain* the people would not disappoint him.

The air rang with cries of "Long live the King," mixed with shouts of "God bless the Laird an' his Lady."

All eyes had been fixed on the royal prince; nobody saw the slight figure slip away from the rear of the column.

When she reached the gate, Breyandra looked about covertly. Satisfied she had not been observed, she pressed the stone that opened the door and slipped into the passage.

She groped for a candle and, after lighting the taper, hurried down the long passageway. Since everyone had gone outside the walls to greet the Duke of York, Breyandra did not encounter a soul when she entered the Great Hall and hurried up the wide stairway of the castle.

Without thinking, she entered David's former room, then remembered that, as Laird of Strehlow, he now occupied the Grand Chamber. Her heart pounded with excitement as she sped down the corridor to his stately room.

Once safely inside, Breyandra leaned back

against the door, stunned for a moment by the splendor of the mammoth chamber. She walked over to a chair and picked up David's plaid. She clutched the folded tartan to her breast, and a wave of love and pride chilled her flesh. Then, as she neatly replaced the honored cloth, a seed of inspiration began to germinate in her mind. Suddenly her eyes lit up with deviltry as a mischievous plan danced through her thoughts.

She moved to the armoire and lovingly ran her fingers over a brush that lay on top of the chest. Breyandra opened the doors of the huge oak cabinet. A red tam on the shelf caught her attention. She picked up the cap and pressed the treasured beret against her cheek, recalling the day at Newmarket when David had placed the hat on her head. With an impish grin, Breyandra began to shed her clothing.

Hoes and shovels had been pitched aside, pikes and swords discarded. After the private rite at Saltoun, peerage and crofter, Fraser and Gordon, Scot and Englishman, all were gathered with bowed heads for the public christening of James Charles Fraser, the 7th Viscount of Saltoun and future Laird of the formidable clan that had only recently been dreaded by many of the participants. Past feuds, grievances, and suspicions were forgotten as the assemblage witnessed the solemn rite of an infant's covenant with the Almighty.

When the ceremony had been completed, the festivities began. Casks of wine and ale were rolled out from the castle. Hares, chickens, and hunks of venison were spitted and put to roast. Breads, cakes, and tarts appeared from huts and cottages. Fruits, nuts, haggis, and fish had been accumulated to be spread out in a mammoth feast.

By nightfall torches blazed and the merry-makers danced jigs to the music of makeshift musicians.

Elysia sat beside her husband proudly holding her son. During the course of the evening, singularly or in pairs, the villagers braved the circumspect scrutiny of Wolf to approach and admire the lad.

The benign and joyous mood of the happy people sounded the death knell for the heavy conscience which had plagued the community ever since the night of the witch hunt and the demise of Moira MacPherson. On this evening the burden lifted, and once again these simple folk could hold up their heads, and with pride look one another in the eye.

All but David Gordon enjoyed the festivities. For him, revelry was not possible without Breyandra there to share the moment with him. Disgruntled, he sat beside the Duke of York and watched the merry throng with resentment. A groom whose bride was cloistered in a convent! Why wasn't she here with him to witness the outpouring of joy and love? Damn the King! Snow would freeze in hell before he would ever again raise his sword in defense of the Stuart throne.

And despite the many sincere wishes for his good health and happiness, not one person expressed surprise or sorrow that his bride was not at his side. Was he the only one concerned over her absence? Even her own father gave no heed to his errant daughter.

David watched negligently as old Gwendys ambled over to view the sleeping infant in the cradle beside his mother. The old woman's eyes shone brightly as she nodded approvingly. Then she turned and whispered into the ear of a young lass dressed in the plaid and tam of a Highlander. The girl drew back in surprise as the old woman scurried away, cackling like a hen.

There was something about the girl's stance that drew David's instant attention. She hovered in the shadows, and he could not see her clearly. David watched intently when she bent down and said a few words to Elysia, then turned and walked away.

Spurred by a nagging curiosity, David bolted to his feet, intent on following her. But by the time he worked his way through the crowd of well-wishers, the girl had disappeared.

He approached his mother and saw Simon holding Elysia's hand like a love-struck swain. The sight furthered David's irritation with the whole evening. "Mother, who was the young girl you spoke to a few moments ago?"

Elysia looked perplexed. "Which young girl, David? There have been so many."

"The one dressed in Gordon plaid."

"I really can't say, dear." She glanced at Simon. "Do you know who he means, Sim?"

Simon shrugged. "Most of these people are

strangers to me. And certainly, someone wearing Gordon plaid.''

"For a moment I thought . . . I hoped . . .'' Dejected, David turned and walked away.

Elysia's heart swelled with compassion as she watched her son's broad shoulders, sloped in depression, disappear into the crowd. "Oh, Sim,'' she said contritely.

"Now, now, love,'' he soothed, patting her hand. "All's well that ends well.'' Grinning, he drew Elysia to her feet. "And shall we end this night as well?'' he added with a pun that surely would have brought a smile to the face of the Merry Monarch.

"What do you have in mind, Lord Lovet?'' she asked shyly.

Simon's eyes flashed wickedly. He motioned to the baby's abigail. "I think our son has passed a long enough day.'' Relieved that she could finally retire for the night, the woman picked up the cradle. Wolf trailed the weary abigail as she plodded on her way.

Upon leaving his mother, David Gordon had witnessed enough of the night's merriment, and he returned to the castle. As he entered the Great Hall, his step echoed slowly, and without conscious thought he took the path that led to the rose garden. Deep in gloom, he sat down on the stone bench.

At a loss without Breyandra, his thoughts rambled. Life was a void without her presence. Ninety days bereft of the woman he loved would seem like an eternity. Charles Stuart was an inhuman deviant, unworthy to wear the crown.

Ninety days! He groaned in anguish at the thought.

Steeped in despair, he buried his head in his hands.

He finally rose to his feet and happened to glance above at the ramparts. To his amazement, he saw the lass in the Gordon plaid framed in a glow of moonlight. His heart leaped to his throat, for there was no mistaking the face now clearly illuminated. Breyandra smiled and waved. He laughed with joy and bolted from the garden.

After racing up the wide stairway, David quickly ascended the narrow stone steps that led to the battlements. When he reached the top and burst through the door, Breyandra was waiting. For a brief moment he drank in the sight of his beloved draped in the plaid of his clan, her long black hair hanging from beneath a bright red tam.

Were he to live to antiquity, he would never behold a more beautiful sight.

David swooped her into his arms and kissed her passionately, hungrily. When sheer breathlessness forced them apart, he rained dozens of kisses on her face, her eyes, her lips, and voiced words of both love and admonishment over the distress she had caused him.

Finally he just held her, savoring the feel of her in his arms. He had never known such a moment of happiness.

When his trembling ceased and a modicum of composure was restored, David gazed down into her upturned face. "You minx. You incredible minx. I would wring your neck if I could bear to live without you. You came—"

"With the Duke's party." Breyandra's eyes glistened with unshed tears.

"Then my mother and Simon knew . . . and the whole party . . ."

She nodded. "I begged them not to tell you. I wanted to surprise you."

David shook his head, unable to believe the incredible ruse. "Even my own mother . . . a party to your wicked ways." He frowned in frustration. "I vow, I'm going to chain you to the wall to keep you from disappearing again."

Breyandra raised her hand and caressed his cheek. "I only sought a few moments alone. Then, when I went to your room, I found your tam and plaid. I knew I had to wear them. The *Gordon* plaid, David. Don't you see? I needed to feel accepted by your people. I wanted to walk among them alone."

"And how did you fare?"

"I met simple crofters who appeared to be as kind and as God-fearing as my own clansmen. Your people greeted me with the utmost courtesy and respect."

Her eyes glowed earnestly as she gazed up at him. "One of the men who had tied me to the stake that night got down on his knees and begged my forgiveness. He held out his arm toward me and pleaded with me to sever the offensive hand."

David's probing stare studied her inquisitively. "And what did you do?"

"I kissed his hand," she said solemnly. "And

then we both wept." His arms tightened around her. "No, my love, chains will not be necessary. I'll not stray from you again."

"And what, pray tell, made you avoid the one Gordon who loves and respects you most of all?" David's face sobered in mock disdain.

"Nay, I avoided not, my Lord Gordon. I wanted to watch my beloved from afar."

"And whatever did you observe 'from afar'?" Mimicking her words, he raised his brows in humorous pose.

"I saw a crushed and desolate man. Totally wretched without the woman he loves."

Unable to resist her, David drew her into his arms. "You are right about that, Twit. I do love you." He kissed her again, with a long, tender kiss that affirmed the intensity of his words. "How could I have celebrated a wedding without my bride beside me?"

"You could not, beloved. But now we *are* together, and may every night be our wedding night, my Lord Gordon."

Breyandra sighed contentedly and pressed her cheek against his chest, reveling in the fulfillment of being in his arms. Neither Strehlow nor clan feud, indeed nothing, would stand between them again.

Struck by a sudden thought, Breyandra popped her head up excitedly." I realized something else tonight, David. Gwendys' prophecy has come true." Her eyes glowed as she looked up at him. "The feud is over, so the past no longer lies between us. Your home is my home now, and I shall grow to love Strehlow because you are Laird and I am your devoted Mistress."

Her brow curved fretfully. "But something about the prediction still puzzles me. Gwendys said 'The one who wears the crown will make it come to be.' I know now, the prophecy referred to the Stuart crown. But in truth, David, 'twas the Duke of York who today resolved the past. Yet, it is Charles who wears the crown."

"Good Lord, Twit. Why do you take every word the old crone says so seriously?"

Breyandra stepped out of his arms and looked up at him, her face earnest with concentration. "I've been giving the matter serious thought. If her words are true, then the prophecy tells us that one day James will wear the crown."

"Which could only happen if Charles died without a legal heir," David scoffed. "Not likely now that he has a wife."

Her eyes sparked with excitement. "But suppose, just suppose, Sir Knave, that Catherine is barren. Then James would succeed to the throne at the death of Charles." She clutched his arm excitedly. "Just think, David, we are privy to the course that history might well be taking. Isn't it exciting?"

David stared down at her in disbelief. "After all we've gone through, I can't believe we are wasting time discussing the mad ravings of a demented old woman!"

Breyandra's eyes rounded with innocence. "Then you don't care to hear the prophecy Gwendys made to me tonight when she saw Baby Jamie?"

David heaved a suffering sigh. "Very well,

what did the old harridan say to you?"

Two dimples came into play in Breyandra's cheeks.

> "Brother an' sister,
> Each hae he one.
> An' the wee bairn's brother
> Is th' father o' yer son."

Breyandra waited with an expectant smile for David to absorb the meaning of the prophecy.

Impatient, David frowned. "What is the mystery? We know you are the sister and I am the brother of the bairn." His face altered in shock when the implication of the prophecy finally penetrated. He grasped her arms, staring down at her with astonishment. "You mean . . . are you saying that I'm . . . that you're . . ."

She giggled. "I'm not saying so. Gwendys is. But I must be, if her prediction is true."

David's warm chuckle brought a shiver to her spine. "Well, perhaps there's some merit to the old crone's twaddle after all." He grinned broadly. "A son, huh!"

Breyandra smiled at him with adoration. "Oh, I love you, Sir Knave."

He framed her face in his hands and gazed into the rich warmth of her brown eyes. "And I love you, Twit. You are my life."

She turned in the circle of his arms, and they stood contentedly watching the activity below.

Most of the revelers were beginning to return to their cottages or barracks. The Duke of York snored as he slouched in a chair, surrounded by a protective contingent stretched out on the ground around him.

Captain Trevor, Simon's Captain of the Guard, strolled away hand in hand with a dark-eyed widow who had caught his eye when he had visited Strehlow incognito.

David spied Simon Fraser and his mother as they stopped below. Simon took Elysia in his arms and kissed her, then they continued into the castle.

The faint glow in the sky heralded the dawn of a new day; a day that would bring rays of peace to Strehlow and a contentment long absent from her majestic walls.

David smiled and tightened his hold on Breyandra. He had waited patiently for this day. And the woman in his arms was now a part of his life's new dawning.

His beloved Twit. His Mistress of Strehlow.

His sweet, sweet enemy.

AUTHOR'S NOTE

As the wise old Gwendys predicted, after a reign of twenty-four years, Charles II died in 1685 without leaving a legal heir.

His brother, James II of England, succeeded to the throne in a stormy reign that lasted only three years. His son James, "the Old Pretender," and grandson Charles, "Bonnie Prince Charlie," both tried, unsuccessfully, to regain the throne.

Barbara Palmer, who Charles later made the Duchess of Cleveland, was his mistress until 1674. She bore him five children (Fitzroys) before he no longer was able to tolerate her vicious tongue and manipulative actions.

Edward Hyde, the Earl of Clarendon, always unpopular with the English court cabal, was dismissed from his duties in 1667 and lived in exile in France until his death in 1674. His granddaughter Mary, married to William of Orange, became Queen of England in 1689, and another granddaughter, Anne, became Queen of England in 1702.